HASINA

——My great escape——

Elizabeth Johnson

Dedication

I dedicate this book to God Almighty for the inspiration, love, and the confidence He gave me to pursue my heart's desires. Thank you, my Father, for your unfailing love. Without you, none of this will be possible.

To my family, who encourage me every day to follow my passion.

I thank you all for your endless support.

Prologue

Dear Mother

If you have found this letter, it means that I am long gone. It breaks my heart to break yours this way, but you and father have left me no choice. I must make my own way in life and I want you to know that you have raised me to be sensible and practical in my choices in life. I have decided to put these qualities into practice. You are probably wondering why I have chosen to do this, it's simply because the man you have chosen for me to marry, I cannot be with him and I will not be his wife. It will not be practical for me to pretend to love him when I do not even know him.

I know that to you this would seem as utter dishonour, and my running away be considered as an unforgivable act, but to gamble my life away in the manner you have chosen for me, I am likening it to a prison sentence or perhaps a game of Russian roulette.

Sorry Mother, I cannot choose that life, I will find my own way and I hope one day you will be proud of my choices.

I'm truly sorry to have disappointed you. I want you to know that wherever I find myself, I will be fine, and when you look up at the sky at night, just know that I am doing the same and thinking of you, too. Please do not hate me for this, I wouldn't be able to bear it if you do, but I will try to understand as I have broken your heart and shamed our family. However, I am hopeful that one day, you will see the world the way that I do, that I have only gone in search of my own happiness. That's what truly matters in life, isn't it? Please tell father that I am deeply sad to have left this way; perhaps I am a coward for doing this or perhaps you and father will later see this as an act of bravery. Only the future can tell, but, whatever happens, at least I will know that I did it my way. Goodbye mother, with all the love in the world.

Your-daughter,
Hasina Suri.

Chapter 1

"Father..." I called, interrupting him. I waited for him to shut me down, but he was quiet, so I continued. "I am sorry for the pain I caused you and mother... I am sorry that I did this and made it necessary for you to have to kidnap me. I wish I did not have to put you through that, but I wanted a different life for myself than the one you and mother planned for me. I wanted to make my own choices, to do the things ... that mattered to me, I wasn't happy at home; I knew if I told you I wanted to live on my own you wouldn't have approved of it. So, I hid things from you, like who I really was and how I felt inside. If I knew you would understand, I would have come to you, I would never have thought about running. You wanted to marry me off to a man I hardly knew, I felt like a prisoner. Besides, you are meant to love me, which means my happiness should matter to you, but I don't think it did. But now, I'm happy, I found someone that loves me and I love him..."

"Enough of this nonsense, you think this is a good life that you are living? Selling yourself cheaply? Living with a man that is not your husband? You have shamed me; I can barely look at you." He got up and walked towards the door. I did not want him to go, I just had to let him understand that I was still the same as when I left home. I had no intentions of bringing him shame. Perhaps, if he understood that, he will see that Robert is a good person and his intentions are good.

"Father, I am happy here… I am not going back with you; I love Robert and he loves me so. Oh, father, if you would just let me explain it to you, you would understand. He is a good man and he wants to marry me and that's all the happiness I want," I pleaded with him. He turned around stoned faced.

"Who told you, that you have a say in this, you ungrateful child. I cannot bear to think about the things you've been up to. We raised you up a good Muslim and you decide to ruin yourself. Did you lose your senses? Did we not teach you right from wrong? You call yourself my daughter and you sleep and uncover yourself in the sight of a man that is not your husband? You have shamed us greatly. What do you really think this man of yours was after? Men are just after one thing, or in your case two things, your body and money. Or are you too stupid to realize that? Do not worry, he shall be dealt with appropriately. And for your own sake, I hope you have not lost your innocence. You will not bring that shame to my house; from now on, you are no longer my problem, but another man's. Ashraf is here with me... he never gave up; he went through hell when you decided to go missing. I do not know what it is but he loves you, he never gave up, he still wants you after all of this, despite all the shame you caused. And you will make this right. You will marry him; you will show him gratitude for taking you back. I am done with you, but you will remain with him as his wife, a little ceremony would be conducted at the request of Ashraf to make it official, but there would be no celebration as you have made it clear you do not want one. Goodbye, Hasina." "No!" I screamed as he headed for the door.

Father abandoned me, I had lost my voice from crying so much, my heart sank in deep wretchedness. I had to try to convince father to let me lead my own life. But I guess I was always right about him and mother, which was why I ran away in the first place. I know now, I would never see Robert again. However, what is that saying again? It is better to have loved and lost than to never have experienced love.

If anyone is reading this now, you would be wondering how all of this happened. How I became the daughter that shamed her family. Who are Robert and Ashraf? You may wonder, and how did they come to play in my life? But in order to answer all of that, I will have to start at the very beginning and tell you how I planned my great escape and along the way met the great love of my life.

Hasina suri FayeD
January 24, 2010

My heart was pounding against my chest as I approached the check in counter. I tried to steady my hands but my palms were sweating profusely. I looked guilty and if I don't get
it together now, it won't take long for anyone to know that something wasn't right.   There was a woman with her two children on the queue ahead of me; I would be next. I tried to steady my heartbeat, but it was impossible. I wiped my palms over my jeans.

"*Calm down*," I said quietly to myself. If only saying it out would help. I took a deep breath and exhaled slowly, but it did nothing to my nerves. I knew nothing would help until I was safely away. I heard an announcement and fear gripped me again. I looked behind me; no one else was on the queue. A security man was coming through, he was on the radio, he looked in my direction and my body seized. I tried to look away, but it was as if I was no longer in control of my body. I didn't know what to expect, I felt sweat gathering on the top of my head. I heard the woman say something, but it felt like she was only mouthing from a good distance away. I tried to turn as the security man was still talking, but he walked closer to where I stood. I shut my eyes in fear, my stomach twisted in me. Then, he stopped a few feet away from me and he looked at me blankly. My heart exploded in me as I thought about what to say if I got caught. He then looked down and then straight at me again. His eyes looked like they were about to question me and the frustrating thing for me was that I couldn't think of anything to lie my way out of whatever he was about to ask. Then, as though by some miracle, he looked from me to his right and then as if instructed by the person on the other end on his radio, he walked away hurriedly. I took a deep breath in relief and let out the air at once. It was not over yet, but I knew that if I could keep hold of my nerves, I would succeed. It was easier said than done.

"Excuse me," I heard someone faintly at first and then I heard it again.

I turned as I heard the woman with the two kids say to me as she tried to manoeuvre her hand luggage and her two children towards the exit. I nodded and swallowed hard as I forced my body into motion. As I moved out of her way, the woman behind the counter said,

"Next please." I managed a smile and she responded with a more natural smile. I handed the document I had just procured from the locker to her. I steadied my hands and held my breath as she went through it. She typed something into her computer and looked at me. I told myself to remain calm.

"It would soon be over," I repeated inwardly in my head. I wiped the sweat dripping down my neck when she was not looking; the last thing I wanted was to be delayed for any reason. Another announcement came through and it startled me, but I tried not to let her see the fear that consumed me inside.

"Everything looks fine," she said smiling. I smiled in return.

"Do you have any luggage you want checking in?" she asked. I shook my head. But she looked on as though she wanted me to vocalize my response. "No," I said. "I don't have any."

"Okay," she said, continuing with the typing. After that, she asked, "Would you like an aisle seat, or do you prefer a window seat?" I did not have time to choose, none of that mattered now. The only thing I want more than anything is to be on that plane as soon as possible.

"I don't mind, any would do." I said.

The woman smiled. "Hmm! People always have a preference, but since you don't mind, I have booked you a window seat," she said. She handed me my passport and boarding pass. "Hurry, the plane would soon start boarding."

"Thank you," I replied. It was a good thing she told me to hurry, like she knew I needed an excuse. I tried walking fast, but I soon broke into a run. No matter what happened today, that plane would not leave without me. What I was doing felt wrong, but I could not stop myself from doing it though. The alternative was unbearable for me to accept.

"I am giving myself a chance. If I don't, I will regret it," I whispered to myself. It gave me more strength and conviction to stay on the course. I pushed the guilt away, but I couldn't run from it. It was eating me up. As I ran, my mind raced through the events that have led me to take matters into my own hands.

I never gave much thought to how my wedding was going to go because I had other pressing matters; I had to play along so no one was any wiser to what I had planned.

I turned twenty-two only a week ago and my father went all out to show the world and his friends all that his money could buy as he pretended, he was throwing me a birthday party. I had to play along. They, my mother and him already had my life mapped out in front of them, but I was not going to roll over and play dead. I was old enough to be responsible for my own life and I was unwilling to allow anyone else apart from myself control my path in life. I had been told what to do and how to do it for too long, but it ends now.

My mother, who I adore very much, seemed overjoyed with all the plans and preparations she had been putting in place. She had not stopped smiling since they announced to their entire guests the date of my marriage to Ashraf: the monster I had to be joined with during the speech my father gave at my party. It came as a shock to me because I was not warned that they had decided on a date, neither was I told it was going to be made into public knowledge on my birthday. I had given my consent to marry him after I lost the battle of wills between my parents and me. However, little did they know that although I may have lost that battle, I had other things planned to help me win the war. For the longest part of my life, as far back as I could remember, I always wanted to be like my mother. The grace with which she carried herself, her poise and the beauty that radiated within her when she smiled. To say she was beautiful was an understatement; she was truly the epitome of beauty. The confidence with which she walked into every room, knowing all eyes were on her, but effortlessly she graced about making everyone warm and comfortable. Those talents, I had come to envy about her and I wished that she had passed on those qualities to me through my genes. Although she's my mother and I was her only child, I do not think some things are inherited. They must be learnt and she had mastered those acts so easily.

She knew how to handle my father, although he saw himself as a disciplinarian and a very strict Muslim. However, he could not resist her charms. I saw the way he looked at her with pride, almost every time. I had never seen him look at me like that, as if I mean to him, the entire world. The way he looked at her, as if he had just fallen in love with her. After so many years together, to still love her like that, and be mesmerized by her, by her very presence, amazed me. He loved her more than he loved me, but I had no right to feel this way about this because I was his daughter and she his wife. Sometimes when he lost his cool, she only needed to look at him or touch him gently before he calmed down. If anyone knew my father, they would understand that getting him to calm down when he got angry or when he felt wronged wasn't easy. However, mother knew what to do to make him human again. Although she had this power over him, she rarely exercised it. Only when she deemed it necessary does she bring him back to earth. Well I guess if he did not love her the way he did, then she would have no power over him, but he did and she held his heart and he hers.

As I grew up, I loved the way they loved each other even though that meant I came second all the time, but now I am grown and I see that their love for each other have made them selfish about my life and my needs. I had been told that I was the image of my mother and most times, I stared at myself in the mirror wondering if the reflection looking back at me was as beautiful as my mother. I wanted what she had, I wanted a man that would love me and put me above everything as my father did to her. What I did not want was to be told who to love, what to do and what not to do. I hated being controlled, it made me want to rebel, which is why I am here now and now find myself running like a fugitive away from the life I have known all my life.

My mother was half Saudi Arabian and half Indian. Her mother was the Indian and what a great beauty she had been too. I was told that she died during childbirth. She gave birth to my mother, after which she bled to death. My grandfather was inconsolable; he dedicated his life to raising my mother. He never remarried no matter how pressured he was by his family to take another woman.

My grandfather's family never supported his marriage to my grandmother because she had been Hindu. Their only reason and condition were that she had to be converted to Islam, but he had had no intentions of forcing her to change her religion. They turned their backs on him, but that did nothing to stop him. For grandfather, love came first and he couldn't see pass that. Although, he had tried so hard to fight it, but the more he did was the harder he fell for her. To be together they had to move away from prying eyes. Yes, he never stopped being a Muslim, yet he let her practise her religion until her death. Some of his relatives rumoured amongst themselves that her death had been a punishment, that it had been Allah's way of chastising him for what he did. When I was young, my grandfather used to tell me stories about her, it brought smiles to his face and I loved that look on him when he spoke of her. As I grew, he became older and weaker and I would try to get him to tell me more about their love; he would only smile and say, "Hasina, I see her when I close my eyes, she is waiting for me. I will do anything to hold her in my arms again." I did not understand what he said then, but it dawned on me when he passed on. I was only thirteen when he had died and I still miss him a lot. He told me never to allow anyone rule and decide how to pursue my dreams. I like to think I am more like him, although I haven't loved anyone like he did his wife or as my father loved my mother, but I hope to someday find love like how they did. And when I do, no one would take it away from me.

My grandfather did everything to raise my mother the Islamic way so the Muslim community would not cast her off. Most people forgot with time about her Hindu roots and accepted her as one of them. It was not hard to accept her. After all, she was and is still a good Muslim and her and warm personality outclassed anything else. When she came of age and would be married, there were too many suitors desiring her hand in marriage. That made my grandfather happy. She allowed her father to decide about who she married. My grandfather had chosen my father for her because once he met my father, he said that he knew my mum would be happy with him. And he was not wrong. She could not have made a better choice herself. She told me that they only met once before they got married. The thought of that scared me; it was risky of her to stake her life on someone she had only met once, she could have been miserable all her life. When I asked why she agreed to marry my father, she said that she knew her father would not have chosen my father for her if he were not sure. Sure? How could anyone be that sure of anything in life? I thought, talk less of letting another decide for them whom to marry. She was his only child just as I am hers and he wanted the best for her just as they claimed they wanted for me. Nevertheless, I am too head-strong and too strong-willed to allow anyone to make such an important decision for me. However, as much as I am against arranged marriage, I must say theirs is one union I am not opposed to, for one it brought me here.

My eyes. Those were the only things my father gave me. Mother always teased that our eyes could pierce through a man's soul. Some argue that my eyes made me more beautiful than my mother, which I find very funny because I did not think Allah could make anyone more beautiful than her.

I was so deep in my thoughts that I did not realize my mother was speaking to me.

"Hasina! Hasina!"

After the announcements were made about my marriage to Ashraf, I knew now was the time to put my plans to action. I had been given no choice. I tried to get out of it for two years. We had argued about this marriage and it had taken almost as long as it took me to plan my great escape.

"Hasina," she called again. It took me a while to focus my attention on her; I was waiting for her in my room to hear my father's verdict on my plea to travel to New York in America with mother in preparation for the said wedding to Ashraf. My father didn't want me to leave home before the wedding took place, he feared the very thing I was planning, but I was not going to have a no for an answer.

Therefore, I persuaded my mother to talk to him and make him see sense. To do that, I had to convince mother that I was finally happy about the prospect of my union to Ashraf. She did not buy it at first, but I knew how to have her wrapped around my fingers, and soon enough, she believed or wanted to believe I was on board. She was jubilant that I had finally shown a little excitement about the prospect of being Ashraf's wife. I was strategic in my showmanship; show too much excitement and she would see through me, give her glimpses of acceptance of their decision and she falls for every act and words that drops from my mouth. It was my fault they have been so hard and head-strong about not allowing me to leave the house in the past. I protested too much… I was foolish enough to think they would ever listen to me or allow me to make my own choices. However, I had learned and grown, and I was no longer that little girl they can push around to do whatever they thought was befitting for my life.

They had been planning this wedding for more than a year now, even though they only just made the announcement officially. My parents and Ashraf and his parents have been planning this for a while now.

This wedding was meant to be the wedding of the century; my parents planned to spend money like it was going out of fashion. Each time I heard my mother mention a ridiculous amount of money she was spending or had spent on things like flowers, jewelleries or tableware, my heart sank Not because they couldn't afford it, the money was not the issue. It was the time and effort she spent on making sure everything would be perfect that I was sorry about. But it was their fault, hence, I was not completely sorry. If she had someone that could foresee the future for her then she would know that all her efforts would be futile because there would be no bride walking or to be carried down the aisle.

"Hasina, your father has accepted!" I could hear the joy in her voice as she cupped my chin in her hands. I was not expecting this news at all; I was so sure father would not agree to let me travel because of my stubbornness in the past.

"What's the matter?" she asked me, her joy now replaced with confusion. "Nothing Mother," I said, smiling, "I was not sure he was going to agree to let me go with you to New York. I was worried that we were never going to get a chance like this again, you and me together before I get married. That's all." I lied.

"Don't worry about him darling, you know by now how he gets, but he knows how important this trip is for us," she said, trying to read my face.

"Your father is glad you're coming around to the idea, he is very happy with you, but he just needs to trust you more, you can't blame him. You know how adamant you were in the past and then finally you gave your consent to marrying Ashraf. He is glad you've come around; he is just a little wary. You know he only wants what is best for you as do I." I nodded in response and feigned a happy smile.

"I know mother, it's my fault. I gave him grounds to doubt me, but as you know, I have been thinking about this for a while now and I know the two of you only want the best for me. Moreover, I do not want to fight anymore, I just want us to have some fun together. It has been a while," I said, hoping that she bought the lie.

I knew that if I could get away with fooling her that I was happy to be getting married to this stranger, I would be a step closer to getting what I really wanted. Consenting to this marriage was the hardest decision I had ever made. Especially because I had never met nor seen the monster, they wanted me to marry.

This was no fault of theirs. I refused to see him or know anything about him in the past. I had thought they would give in to me and let me choose who I wanted, but they would not hear of it. It was always about "Ashraf this" and "Ashraf that", then I knew I had to escape. So, I began to hatch out a plan, which required that I give in to their constant badgering about the so-called groom that was supposed to be the salt of the earth and every woman's dream. An arrangement had been put in place to finally meet with him as much as I wanted before the ceremony took place. However, if everything goes as planned, hopefully I shall be saved from such agony.

My life's dream is to dance. I want to dance professionally. My father must not hear of it. I tried telling my mother a few years ago and she had a fit. I knew it didn't seem good to them, but it gave me joy. Mother almost fainted when I insisted that was all I wanted to do; she forbade me from discussing it and from wishing such an unrefined profession upon myself after lecturing me on whose daughter I was. "You are not going to pursue a dance career," she said, "And you know your father must not know that I allowed you to take dance classes; you will stop this rubbish at once, it's never going to happen. Think carefully, Hasina, what do you think your father will do if he finds out? What will people say? Please Hasina, don't shame me, you must forget about all that nonsense, you are forbidden to ever raise that subject".

"But mother…" I was going to protest

But she would cut me off. "Hasina, it is not going to happen, please do not mention this insanity again. No daughter of mine would dance for a profession. I thought you were bored, so I allowed you a little freedom and this is how you are going to repay me? I told you then, it was just something for you to do to kill time, get this foolishness out of your mind now. You are going to be married soon, you must prepare yourself for that."

There and then I started to resent her and father, they only saw what they wanted. So, I was prepared to see them hurt as I was already on the inside.

***

The boarding gate was still far. I still had to get through security. I bumped into many people as I ran; the finish line was so near now,

Elizabeth Johnson

I could almost smell victory and freedom, but I was not out of the woods yet, I had been gone for far too long and I was tired, but the fear in me pumped more adrenalin and I found the strength to keep running. I took no notice of the people around me, everyone looked at me suspiciously, or so I thought. It could be me suspecting everyone to be after me. I was paranoid from dread, I must not be caught, I kept thinking. As I almost got to security, I bumped into a man; I did not have time to properly apologize.

"Sorry!" I yelled as I continued my race to freedom.

***

I had always wondered what my life would have been if I was not born into my family. Having all the wealth in the world, but still feeling like a prisoner. All father wanted was a nod and smile at every suggestion. To him, that spelled what a good daughter was, one that would eventually make a good wife.

I have often wondered if they would have treated me the same way had I been a boy, perhaps I would have had more liberty, less chaperones and my life's choices respected.

I loved being a girl, but it seemed that where I come from that it came with a steep price—my freedom: my right to choose; to have a say; to freely love and be loved; to be happy; to dance; to be me. My very freedom.

"You don't look okay," My mother said, very concerned.

"Oh mother, I was day-dreaming about all the fun we are about to have," I said wide-eyed.

Her expression changed, she smiled. "You know darling, you worried me a little, be happy my love, that is all I want for you in life," mother said to me. She didn't seem to be buying what I said, so I tried to convince her again just so she doesn't just decide we no longer needed to travel.

"It's nothing, you worry too much about me. I was just thinking about all the shops we would visit, you know how exciting it'd be," I said, trying to sound very convincing; she looked at me through a serene, reassuring eye, as if to say everything was going to be all right from now on.

"Hasina, you are a woman about to be Ashraf's wife, this means you will be moving into your husband's house and away from me. So trust me darling, I intend to make this trip a very fun experience for both of us, you do not have to worry. I always take care of everything, don't I?" she asked peering observantly. I quickly nodded in response.

"Besides, I can assure you that when the time comes and you move to Ashraf's house, you would not lack a thing. That boy is as excited as we are that you are going to be his wife. I am truly happy you agreed to this union. Though you are as stubborn as your father is, but I knew you would come around eventually. You kept us high on our toes and, Ashraf, he was over the moon when your father told his family you had finally agreed to marrying him. He adores you; his eyes light up each time we mention your name. You will lack for nothing, and when you are finally married to him, you will have even more wealth at your disposal. So, don't worry, love, everything will be fine just as it is meant to be," she smiled at me and kissed me on the forehead.

"I know mother, I respect yours and father's decision and I am very sorry I gave you such a tough time about this marriage. I don't know why I protested so much. Thinking of it now, I admit, I was fearful of living away from home and being with a stranger but from all you've told me of Ashraf, I don't think there is anything to worry about and I trust you both have my best interest at heart." I said persuasively.

She grinned genuinely at me. "My child, you've grown so much and I truly will miss these little talks we always have. I always knew that eventually, if given some time you will come around and finally see that everything, we do is for you to have a beautiful and happy life."

I sighed; I tried not to show how resentful I was feeling. It was a way of life now, hiding my true feelings and lying through my teeth. I was tired of being locked in my room and being chaperoned everywhere, as she spoke all I saw through her eyes was the freedom I will gain when all my plans turn out my way. I almost wanted to breathe out in relief as the excitement of being free washed through me, but I held it together.

My mother had a hard life growing up, so it was important for her to be accepted. She pleased her father immensely, and never complained about any decision he made on her behalf. This behaviour pleased my father as well. Not that he forced her into doing anything she didn't want like he was, butter in her hands, but still his confidence that she would do anything he said to her made him love her more. I looked at my mother and wished for a second that I was built like her, obedient and not defiant, then I would truly be excited to be Ashraf's wife.

"We leave first thing tomorrow morning, Hasina. I will get someone to prepare your luggage for you. All you need to do is get your beauty sleep, I will see you in the morning." she said and smiled in satisfaction.

"Okay, mother." I replied.

"Okay, love. Goodnight." She said as she walked out of my room.

I waited until I could no longer hear her footsteps before allowing myself a quiet scream and rolled on my bed in jubilation. Going to New York was indeed a victory and would make today my last night of imprisonment.

The ball had been set in motion, everything was going as planned, my ticket, "escape money" and a new passport were all waiting for me at JFK airport, thanks to my friend, Louise. And all I needed to do now was disappear for good.

Chapter 2

Louise, my saving grace

Louise and I met at a dance class my mother had enrolled me. At first, I saw her two to three times a week, but then mother cut down my classes to once a week. Louise is the only friend I have. All my life, I had been told who to be friends with, who to keep as acquaintances and who to keep at arm's length. Nothing ever had been my own decision. That was why my friendship with Louise meant so much to me, as the choice to befriend her was entirely mine. Plus, we had been friends since I was twelve. She understood my predicaments, every one of them, although we only met once every week for an hour and fifteen minutes during dance classes. We always found time to catch up and fill each other in on what went on in our lives when we had not been together. We had no secrets, and nothing was out of bound. Louise is a good listener, she never complained when I nagged her constantly about my life. She had thought that being a rich man's daughter, I had it all, but in reality, it was I who envied her life. She could visit the mall anytime she wanted, go to a public school and be trusted to choose whomever her heart desires as a husband. My life and hers were stark contrast. I always looked forward to meeting with her, because whenever we were together was when the best version of me surfaces.

Louise loves to braid, so I always let her practice her braiding on me. She even taught me how to plait, so I could fix her hair in return, though I never had her skill sets. I always loved the different ways she would style my hair. It was such a shame that I could never show it to anyone, not even my beloved mother. If she had even the slightest hint about my rapport with Louise, she was sure to find a way to get between us. I had always wondered why we had to cover our hair as Muslims. Why would God give us such beautiful hair only for him to want it covered? Has it not been said that a woman's hair was her crowning glory? Why must it be seen by her husband alone?

When Louise and I were together, I did not have to cover up. Louise brought me western clothes and I dressed up, let my hair down, had a breather, and stared at myself in the mirror. I always wondered what it would feel like to live my life as the girl in the mirror. She looked like the better version that Louise had helped bring out of me.

Louise and I had been planning my escape for two years now, ever since I had that conversation with my mother about wanting to join a dance group to improve on my talent and she had told me to never bring the subject up. At first, Louise had been very sceptical about the whole idea, she wouldn't as much discuss it. She even labelled my plan as stupid and crazy. Her disposition, however, had changed right after she saw how unhappy I had been—especially when I told her I was to be married-off— she came on board then and had been my partner in crime ever since.

Louise understood perfectly what was at stake, so, even though she wasn't a big fan of me running away, she supported and stood by me. After all, that's what best friends are for, right? It was her who coached me into giving a false consent and to stop fighting just so I could have enough breathing space to put the plans into play. She told me she knew someone who could help with the papers and passports and aid my escape. I saved every bit of money I came across since we started to plot my escape. She helped me in keeping custody of them alongside a few jewels I was gifted by my parents. This was how we raised enough cash to pay for the documents and leave me some more to spend. When my mother and I will be in New York, Louise and her parents will be holidaying at the same time in New York. Thus, our plan so far had been plain sailing.

She already sent me an email with information about my tickets and hotel reservation in London, United Kingdom. So, once I landed in New York all I needed to do was get away from mother without raising any suspicions.

***

Sleeping was out of the question, I was restless, fearful and excited at the prospect of another life, I tossed and turned all night pushing the thoughts of how broken this decision would leave my family away from my mind.

Eventually sleep caught up with me and I woke up feeling more tired. And more anxious. I had not slept enough, my brain was being overworked, plus, we had a plane to catch in the next three hours. Everything I needed to get ready was laid out for me and as I contemplated about going to have my bath, my mother rushed into my room all excited.

"Hasina, you need to get ready now! We haven't got time to waste and we don't want to be late for our flight." She sounded very eager to get to New York, so was I. Mother loved to shop and so did I, but little did she know that this trip was not going to be like the previous ones we had had together.

"Good morning, mother. You look almost ready," I said, looking away from her as I made my way to the bathroom. I didn't want any hint given away. I didn't want her getting a glimpse of anything that could end my plans. With the excitement on her face, one could even reason she was the one being carted away for marriage.

Nevertheless, it seemed that I had underestimated her attention for details, especially when it came to her most passionate project, me.

"You don't sound excited," she said and held my hand to stop me from going any further, turning me around so she could take a proper look at me. I took a deep breath, looked at her in the eye and remembered that I was getting away today, and then I smiled before speaking, killing two birds with a stone.

"I'm fine mother, I am just tired. That's all, stop scrutinizing everything," she looked me over; I could tell she was starting to feel uncertain with my new positive outlook to the world, especially when it comes to this wedding. I had to stop her from doubting her new misgiving before she says the words that would destroy my life. "Mother seriously, I am fine. I didn't get enough sleep. That's all,"

"Wait, you look worried!" Mum said.

"No not worried, I was just thinking, you know. I want to have what you and father have when I marry Ashraf. I want to please him like you please father. I'm excited about it, mother, even though I'm a little fearful, but I'm sure it will all work out in the end just as you said. So, stop worrying about me so much! Everything will work out the way it's meant to be. We all get to be happy in the end."

Her face relaxed. "What can I say? I've raised you well, darling. Okay run along now and get ready! We can't miss our plane."

"That was what I was up to before you started profiling me! You look stunning, by the way; I mean you always look stunning mother," I said as I walked towards the en-suite bathroom, raining compliments on her in order to distract her as best as I could. She smiled and turned her attention to the clothes that was picked out for me. She looked relaxed now. Though, still in her dressing gown, but her makeup was already in place. I didn't think she needed any, however.

"And you are even more beautiful, Hasina. Get on with it, we need to go!" She replied looking through the pile of clothes picked out for me. I listened for her pacing footsteps away from my room; I allowed myself a little guilt, but took comfort in the know that the end justified the means in my case.

The journey to the airport was long and quiet; I was nervous, so I decided to bury my mood with some sleep. Mother did not think anything of it, she tried to rest my head on her shoulders, and I let her, knowing if all went as planned, these moments were the last we would share up-close until such a time when I can come back home having found my purpose in life. I knew I would never be forgiven for what I was about to do, just as I could not forgive the way they had led my life for me.

Soon we were at King Fahd International airport. It took us about 45 minutes to get there from where we live in Dammam.

When we were aboard the plane, mother brought out magazines with pictures of bridal dresses. She brainstormed ideas with me, I also got into it by telling her the styles I preferred and accessories we both thought would go with it. If only the circumstances had been different, I thought to myself that this could really have been us together having a true mother and daughter moment, but I pushed the guilt away and filled my mind with unfamiliar dreams of an uncertain future. My heart began beating so fast that I was sure she could hear every single drum against my ribs. Taking a deep breath to steady myself, I pulled away, I noticed my palms were beginning to sweat. I tried closing my eyes and yawned to show tiredness, then rubbed my sweaty hands on my dress. Even with my eyes closed, mother would not stop talking about the places she planned to visit once we landed at JFK. She talked about everything and anything, gave clues to a special wedding present that she heard Ashraf plan to surprise me with … blah, blah, blah, I did not care. I knew people would judge me for this but I had lived the life of a prisoner far too long and my sights were now set onto one thing only—freedom.

With my eyes closed, I began to think of ways with which I could escape without her being any wiser. The time window I had between arrival and departure of my flight was just a little over an hour. And there was still the case of retrieving my documents and money—five thousand pounds—from the locker Louise had put them in at the airport. All I had to do was buy myself fifteen to twenty minutes of space away from mother and then make a run for it.

The thought of hurting her made me sad; it made me panic inside, this could be the worst mistake of my life. I thought, but the will to be free was stronger than the guilt ravaging my mind. I wondered if I could survive on my own, after being sheltered all my life. Yes, I had a little money with which to start my new life, but it was peanuts compared to what I was accustomed to. I had never worked a day in my life, I was useless at doing any type of house work. The heck, who was I kidding? the fear of failing gripped me. I could hardly breathe. At the same time, I fought hard to keep mother off the loop of what was going on in my mind. If I do this, what if the world consumes me whole and spits me out again as one devoid of a parent's guidance. I felt stupid, all of my plans made sense earlier, but now, in the moment of opportunity, I wasn't so sure. An announcement was made, I heard nothing. My mind went blank. All of Louise's warnings came to the surface. "Anna." She warned, as she fondly calls me. "This is not going to be as easy as you think."

"I'll be fine" I'd always assured her.

"I'm just scared that something may happen to you and it will be my fault because I gave you this idea and I'm helping you get away from the life you know." She worried.

"Don't worry Lou, I will survive, If I don't at least try, of what use is my life?"

"What about your mother? This will kill her, you know?"

"I know, but if I marry that man, it will kill me." I had argued.

"I'm just afraid for you should you get caught, given what you've told me about your dad. Listen Anna, maybe marrying Ashraf, isn't as bad as we think. We've painted him out to be this monster, but you know I have heard different about him. He is young and educated, he might see things differently than your parents. I hear he is very crazy about you. Everyone talks about how he is so besotted with you. You never know, you could marry him and still have it all." Lou tried to talk me out, but my mind was set. I had already started hoping and dreaming of a life different from what I knew. Tears rolled down my cheek as I saw my hopes draining away at every of Lou's word. If she does not help me, I will be stuck, and I rather be dead, I thought.

"Stop it Lou, I can't live my life on a bunch of what ifs, everyone keeps telling me he is besotted with me, but how could he, to begin with, when I don't even know him? Who falls for a person they don't know? If I stay and marry him, I may never love him, that's what matters to me. I will never dance; I will never be happy. We have to do this, if I go and pursue my dreams, I may come back or I may not but at least it's my choice."

"Okay, then! It's fine! But, if we do this, you can't fail. Because no one knows what will happen to you when you get caught."

"I won't fail, don't worry I won't. I will survive and nothing will happen to me." I promised her.

"Okay, then, I'll help you escape."

"Thank you, Lou, we may not be connected by blood, but you are like a sister." I said as relief washed through me and we hugged.

***

Then I heard mother's voice saying something. It pulled me back into reality. But I couldn't make out what she was saying yet. As my eyes fell on her lips, all I could see her say was the name, Ashraf. That was enough to shock me back to my senses and I somehow regained all the strength I needed to pull this off.

"You are stronger than you think." I mouthed to myself.

I turned away from mother and allowed sleep to consume me for the rest of the flight.

When I opened my eyes, we were landing and I became anxious again about what I was about to do.

As soon as my passport was stamped, I tried to collect it, but mother took it and placed it in her purse. I looked at her, she smiled and said,

"It's only for safe keeping, Hasina," she smiled, I was thankful that I did not need that passport. However, that indicated to me that she too was being careful with me. But it did nothing but make me even more adamant to follow through with my plans.

As we made our way to the baggage pick up, I pretended like I had an upset tummy. "I need to use the ladies, my stomach hurts." I said.

"Okay, baby, I'll come with you." She said. But I wouldn't have that. It won't favour the plan, so I had to convince her to let me go alone.

"Seriously, mother, you can't follow me everywhere, I am a grown woman now. I am getting married, I won't be living under your roof in a few weeks, so I'm sure you can trust that I can use the restroom on my own."

She looked me over and said, "You keep reminding me lately that you are no longer a child, but you know that you will always be my baby. Hasina, you are the apple of my eyes. I love you so much. But you are right; I can't keep treating you like a child. Are you sure you won't need me?" She insisted.

"I'll be fine mother stop smothering me." I insisted.

But she persisted, "Why don't you leave your bag here with me?" It seemed like she knew my plans.

I swallowed hard. Everything I needed to disguise my look was in my hand luggage, there was no way I was handling the bag over to her. My mother was beginning to dig and I couldn't let her catch on, she is a bit like a dog with a bone when she senses something is not quite right. I only had this one chance to get away from all the oppressing and life-pungent choices that they had made for me, so I was not going to let this opportunity slip out of my hands.

"Mother, we just discussed you letting me be a woman of my own. I can't believe we are talking about me using the ladies' alone. Where am I going to run to, anyway? You have my passport remember, and I thought this trip was meant to be fun for the two of us. If you insist on coming along, then come watch me use the loo, or you could let me go now before I have an accident here."

"You're right; you are no longer my little girl. Okay, I will go get the bags. Just follow the signs to the baggage area and I will be waiting for you there, hurry up now! And don't be long!" she smiled and gave me a hug. I realised with that hug the moment had finally come when I will be disappearing from her life. But there was no turning back from here, it was now or never.

"Hurry back, darling," she said as she walked off.

I couldn't move for a moment, but then I found my tongue and I called her. "Mother!" I yelled, she turned back. "I love you," I said. She laughed and blew me a kiss and resumed her walk to get the bags. I was relieved, but I was trembling inside still. The guilt consumed me suddenly, it ate at me constantly. My heart raced within me again so much so I felt it would jump out of my chest. My eyes clouded with tears, I blinked back the watery dread before they could force their way through as I hurried towards the rest room.

My flight to England was in an hour. I changed to a pair of light blue jeans and a dusty brown sweater, packed my hair into a ponytail and then covered my face with a baseball hat. I rummaged through my bag for the key to the locker that Louise sent to me a few days ago. Locker thirty-two was where I would find everything, I needed to start my life afresh. I snuck out of the rest room and rushed out of arrivals, and on my way out, I saw mother standing with our bags and looking worried, but she did not see me and neither would she recognize me if she did see me in my new guise.

Finding the locker was easy; I opened it with the key and got my documents out. framed onto my anxious mind was my mother's worried face, but I constantly pushed it away. I stashed the money in my bag, picked up the tickets and my new passport and placed it inside too. Everything was in place now; I had to have a new identity for this to work. Louise had paid someone to get my name changed. She had met him through a friend's boyfriend, as she put it. I did not mind, I wanted anything and everything done that would make it difficult for my parents to find me. As I approached the check in desk, I looked at the name on the ticket. I was now Anna Fey. I was panicking. I could hardly get it together and time was running out, I had less than an hour to board the plane. The word "Hurry up…" Rang continuously in my head. After checking in, I made a run for the boarding gate, my body bumping into strangers as I did. I stopped for a moment to look at the information on the board so I knew where I was going exactly. I got confused, I could not find my flight, then I stopped a lady in uniform. I figured she worked at the airport and could direct me. She pointed in the right direction. I thanked her and resumed my race. As I ran, I heard another announcement, I almost jumped out of my skin because I knew my mother would raise hell when she realized that I had escaped from her watch. Every announcement that was coming in sent my heart racing. I was almost at the departure gate when I bumped into a man. I yelled sorry as I made my way to the security checks. It was not over yet; I still had yet to pass through the checks and then board the plane. The queue was long there was about ten or more people in front of me; this was not looking good to me. I looked at my watch, I had been gone for about forty minutes now and I knew mother would have started raising hell. It seemed like the security people were deliberately slow. I was annoyed at the excruciating, painstaking time that they took with each check. "Take off your shoes and belt," I heard them say to a man as he was emptying the contents of his pockets and another security man frisked off a man that had just went through the security barrier. My heart kept pumping with fear with each passing second, knowing that every second spent here was a second too close to getting caught. Mother would be ballistic now with worry and definitely mobilizing a search at the moment. And by now, father would have already received word of my disappearance and he would be yelling at her for having convinced him to let us travel in the first place. All the scenarios I figured would be going on right this moment were the reasons my plan must not implode.

Chapter 3

I tapped at my legs impatiently as I waited in the queue. I tried not to look anxious; boarding a plane and looking this jumpy, coupled with my ethnicity was no good combination. Another security of officer walked closer and then passed by me. I very nearly fainted. Every now and again, the announcements kept me on the edge, and I felt as if any moment now, I would hear my name or see my face on the screen.

"*Hurry up!*" I said, inwardly. I sucked in air slowly to slow my heart rate down, but my palms won't stop sweating. I rubbed them down my jeans again, least I was mistaken for a terrorist. There were nine people in front of me, so I bent down and started taking my shoes off for the check. While I was pulling my shoes off my feet, someone tapped me on the shoulder and I nearly passed out.

I looked up slowly, it was a man dressed in black. He looked the business.

"Excuse me, miss," he said, looking from my face to a paper in his hand. It was obvious to me what was happening, I almost made it and now I had to go back home and bear the consequences for

29

what I had done. He looked like he was trying to match my face to whatever he was holding in his hands. Mother must have handed them my picture, I thought. They found me; I took in a deep breath. I thought of what I would say to mother, but my mind was blank. I knew that what I was doing was risky, but I had not prepared to get caught. What will I tell her? How would I explain any of these to her? My face went white, as blood and life drained out of me.

"Ye... y...yes." I stammered in a whisper, unable to speak. He looked at me cautiously.

"Are you, all right? You look like you have just seen a ghost," he said and I just stared at him, slowly realizing that he wasn't a security officer. He smiled at me. I felt so relieved at the realization that he was just a passenger, and then this warm feeling came over me as life slowly returned to my body. Maybe because I was grateful, he wasn't who I thought he was. While he smiled, I stared, it felt like he had just triggered something strange inside me.

"You dropped this!" he said as he squatted beside me. For the first time, I heard his accent, he sounded British or so. I have never been this close to a man who wasn't a bodyguard. My heart began to beat even faster, not out of fear of being caught by my mother any longer, but by his presence, I was mesmerised and I did not know why.

"Thank . . . you," I said.

He handed me the paper, our hands touched slightly and my heart vibrated. My eyes were locked onto his, and his on mine and it felt like the whole world had stopped for a moment. The way he looked at me, like he could see right through me and like I meant the world to him. I was fascinated at this man, this stranger that I had only just met.

I broke my gaze from his, embarrassed by how shamefully I lusted at him. I tried to get up and he helped me up holding my hands as he did and our bodies touched again. I trembled all over. It felt so good to be touched by him; I took in his manly scents and closed my eyes as I briefly taught my memory cells to remember it.

I was not nervous about my mother any longer, I was nervous about being this close to this stranger. I did not know how he felt, but he must have sensed something from me. I turned away quickly, but from the corner of my eye, I thought I saw him smile.

"Do you want to sit down for a moment? You look shaken!" he said, truth be told, he was right I was shaken from fear of being caught and from fear that I had not even escaped and my heart was lusting after this stranger. This was a strange way to feel, was it not? I couldn't make sense of it but I knew my mind wasn't right, not at this moment.

I looked in front of me, it was a slow day, still about eight people ahead of us. I nodded at him and allowed him hold me up. He placed his hand gently on my shoulders as he led me to a seat by the walls. We were the last two on the queue.

"Do you want something to drink?" he asked after I was seated and placed my hand in his as though he could sense I wasn't alright. The feeling of his touch shook me and rendered me speechless. I shook my head; although I was patched, but I still couldn't find my voice. I realised just then that his hands patted mine as though to calm me and I liked it. A security man passed by us cautiously looking us over and he got up to speak with him, letting go of my hands.

I waited a while, I didn't know what they were speaking about, but when I looked up it was my turn to go through the security. I stood up, not wanting to leave his sight, but I knew I had to go through the checks now. I passed through the checks, glanced back and caught his eyes on me, he looked worried that I had gone. I turned back around and walked towards the gate to the plane. His face was etched on my mind. As I approached the plane, I glanced back again to see if he was still behind me, but I did not see him again. Disappointed, I boarded the plane, found my seat and sat down in relief.

"I made it!" I said to myself happily. I knew I would face the consequences later, but now was not a time to worry about that.

Fifteen minutes later, we were in the air. I closed my eyes as I allowed all the adrenaline that had built up in me to die down and then, his face clouded my mind. My mind replayed how our hands touched and the feelings that shot through me at that moment. I thought of his eyes and how they caressed mine and made me feel safe. I recalled his scents, the curl of his lips as he spoke and I wanted to bath in it. His smile had a certain charm about it, and my heart leaped helplessly at the thought of this strange British man. I wanted to see him again, so I could understand why I felt the way I did. Surely, this wasn't love, but it was something very strong. My thoughts crossed over to my mother, and I pushed her out of my mind, I felt no remorse for what I had done just regret that I never asked the stranger for his name.

Chapter 4

Robert Philip Parkman

I was on the beach, absentmindedly throwing stones into the sea, remembering the times my dad and I spent there together when I was a child. He was my hero; I admired him, his style, his love for life and his love for his family. I always loved the time I spent with him and dad always made sure he gave his time. He was a builder, a developer, tearing down and building incredible houses was his niche. Business blossomed, contracts came in from left, right and centre, but no business was ever more important than his children or his wife. He shared his time equally between his three children, Alex, Jane and I. There was no favouritism, although I sometimes felt like I had a slight edge over the others for some reason. Maybe because I was the first child. There were days he went away on business; he would return with gifts and apologise for anything he had missed while he was away. He was my superman; incapable of being wrong in my eye. Mum, was his significant other—the disciplinarian. She brought structure to the house and made sure we did well in school. There were no idle times spent lazing around, as she made sure we kept busy always. So, it was always nice when dad was home, he made her relax the rules a little. My only wish was that he didn't work so much; but dad always said he worked hard so we didn't have to when we grew and then he will ruffle my hair and say, "You need to grow up quickly, Rob! You need to take over the business so your mother and I can go and lie down on the beach somewhere." I would laugh and he would wink at me, but I never thought he was serious; it was all a joke to me. I did not know what I wanted to be, but I did not think building houses was anything like it.

Coming to this beach had become a ritual; every year at the anniversary of his death, I came here, closed my eyes and tried to relive my memories of him—of the little boy chasing after his dad. They say time heals, but I am not sure it does, at least my case has proved to be an exception. It's been ten years since he died and the pain and the hole that was left since he was brutally taken from us would not heal.

I had heard that forgiveness is the key to healing, but I do not know if I could forgive those who took him away in his prime. Even though they themselves are dead, I still feel bitter that he had to die. To forgive felt like I was letting him go. I could not forgive my part in all of this mess, how my stubbornness and disobedience had cost him his life.

The vibration from my mobile brought me back to reality. I reached for it in my pocket, it was a text from Jane and she wanted to know if I could pick her up from her Uni. I was not conscious of time, it seemed that I had only just got here; I looked at my watch and I could not believe how much time had passed while I stared into space.

I got up and half-jogged back to my black Range Rover. I rarely took time off work, only on dad's anniversary, so Jane knew I would be available today. Mum was making a special dinner just for the three of us in memory of Dad. A tradition we had been observing every year since his death, but Alex would not be attending this year. He had moved to New York a few years ago. So, he always flew down to London for Dad's anniversary. It was always nice when he was around, because it helped to have a family member who was not always on my back telling me to stop working too much, to settle down, blah blah blah.

It was always the same conversation with Mum and Jane; no matter what the topic of discussion was, they always managed to stir it right back to me. I should have been dreading this dinner, but for some strange reason, I was looking forward to seeing them both today. It had been a while since I last visited, I always travelled for business, I made no time for family or leisure, I did not remember the last time I went on a holiday, but all that was about to change. I needed to start doing things differently, business was on the top. I had made more than I knew how to spend since I took over Dad's business when he passed because he wanted me to.

Initially, I had thought I would run it to the ground, but it turned out that I had a passion for making money. The company was worth hundreds of millions of pounds and I was still under thirty. I worked tirelessly to make my family proud, to prove a point to myself and to make my dad proud, until I found it hard to press the pause button. I couldn't stop and my family worried for me. Nothing kept me going but the drive to make a success of the business, but inside, late at night, I felt empty. I felt vacant inside, so to fill the hole, I worked harder. I tried to make time for relationships, but they never worked. Each relationship I had ended badly, I had no time for them, I bought expensive presents and flowers to make up for my continuous absence, but it was not enough I had no genuine feelings towards anyone.

I still felt vacant. I had ended each relationship because they did not fulfil the purpose, I engaged in them for. I realized I wanted more from life but I didn't know what it would take to satisfy me. But that I was in need of a break from work, that much I knew.

After dinner with mum and Jane, I will travel to New York to visit Alex. A change of scenery for a few weeks might do me some good, I thought. Jane reckoned that she could fix me by matching me up with strangers. I should tell her to stop; there was no dating site that she had not created a profile for me. I knew that I did not need a relationship to fix what was wrong with me. My many failed attempts at being a boyfriend was testament enough: I got bored easily or realized I was not as attracted to them as I had originally thought. With Jane badgering me to go on dates, I just get to repeat the process all over again. Except for the occasional meaningless sex.

The longest relationship that I ever had ran a course of two years

It was when I was in my teens before Dad died.

Her name was Katherine. She was fun to be with and I was very fond of her. She was quite pretty and she loved me. I knew this because she said it all the time, but for some reason, I never got around to saying it back. I did not want to say something except I meant it. She complained and nagged me because I never used the L-word.

At first, I didn't say it because I genuinely was not consumed by the feeling, but then as time went on and the nagging continued, I realized that I was not capable of loving her. I did not know if it was because she complained about every little thing I did or just because in a way, somewhere deep down, I was fed up and I wanted out. We had only been seeing each other for six months and I wanted to end things. Each time I summoned the courage to tell her, she came around and did something special and I could never bring myself to breaking her heart on such occasions. I was not sure if she was reading a sign that told her that I was about to bow out of the relationship.

Like the time she raised money for some cancer patients by running in a marathon. I had planned to tell her a week after the event, but then she fainted during the race and was hospitalized for a week. I could not bring myself to break up with her, I had to be the good boyfriend and when she was okay again, I just let things return to the way it was. She was close to my family, in fact,

36

she became like another sibling and everyone loved her except me, not that I did not love her as a person: she was fantastic, but for some reason, I could not fall for her.

My parents couldn't sing her praise enough, it was always Katherine this, Katherine that, so I let things be and the relationship carried on for so long, while I absentmindedly participated in the rituals of what made us seem like a couple. She must have known I was not fully given to her. I wanted her to end it with me, because I couldn't bring myself to do it. Instead, she tolerated every shitty behaviour I threw at her. To help speed things along, she invited me to her parents' wedding anniversary, I told her then that I'd rather spend the weekend with my boys. I could tell, that was going to be the final straw that breaks the camel and it worked. I almost wanted to shout a Hallelujah and burst out into songs, but I couldn't do that, she was hurting deeply. I could not celebrate in her sadness. But I felt free! And that felt good. She cried and lamented hysterically, and pointed out all my bad behaviours. She was right, there were no redeeming qualities in me when it came to being a good boyfriend. Although in my defence, I never once cheated on her. I wondered why she stayed even though I paid her no attention, no one was worth such hard work, not even me. If anyone was to blame, it was I. So, I took all that she had to say in silence. Although I think that a part of me must have cared enough about her to let what we had stay for so long, but I knew that whatever it was that I felt, it sure wasn't the belly dropping love that I was meant to feel.

It was uncomfortable for me to watch her cry so much. It felt like she was waiting for me to beg her to stay. What we had was unhealthy and she deserved better but I had to comfort her too.

"Katherine, I'm sorry I caused you so much trouble..." I apologized. She looked at me, as though she wanted to say something, but then decided against it. So, I continued. "Listen, I have been unfair to you, I stringed you along. I thought that with time my feelings were going to change, but it didn't and you must have known this, why did you put up with me? Why didn't you walk away? I don't deserve you; you know that." I explained.

"I don't know. Perhaps, in my foolishness I thought you would change. I thought you will see how much I loved you and one day you will feel the same too. It is hard and it hurts when you think you've found the one and they don't see you as you do them, it kills you inside. You and I, we could be perfect, but I've been afraid that you will leave me for so long. You don't know how that feels. I love you… I love you so much and I cannot help it, I can't stop. I love your family, they are like my family, but I can't do this to myself anymore." Tears rolled down her cheeks uncontrollably.

"Loving you is a punishment." She continued. "You don't touch me; you don't kiss me. If I get as much as a smile from you, my heart leaps. It's like waiting for crumbs. You hug me in public only when I make you do that, but when we are together, you just go into yourself. And to top it all, you have never said that you love me. It kills me inside knowing you will never love me, that is why this charade has to stop, I should have walked away a long time ago. I held on to you too tightly even when I knew you were not mine to have," Katherine agonized.

"I'm sorry I put you through so much. I have no words. You deserve the world; you are a better person than I am." I said. Katherine chuckled amidst her tears.

"You got that one right," she said as she tried to force back another stream of tears flowing freely down her cheeks. I took out my handkerchief and held it to her; she took it from me and gently wiped her face with it.

"Life is so cruel," she remarked.

"I know," I said,

"I could have had my pick of boys, but it had to be you that I fell for? Promise me we can still be friends."

"Yes! Friends! I was going to suggest the same to you. There is no reason not to be friends." She smiled and we hugged, then she held my face gently.

"One day you will meet the girl of your dreams, and she will be everything I'm not. You will be hopelessly in love with her. Your heart and hers will beat as one, only then can you understand how much I love you. Goodbye Robert." Katherine left my house and even though we agreed to be friends, that was the last I saw of her for a very long time.

***

I pulled into the parking space as Jane waved me down and jumped in the car beside me: she looked excited to see me.

"Hello, big brother, you took your time," she smiled. It felt good to see her and she looked more lady-like than since I last saw her.

"What happened to you? You've grown while I was away," I teased.

"Really? That just shows how much we don't see you. I wasn't even sure you were going to turn up today: you cancelled on us so much that seeing you has become a festive present," She explained. I felt bad, I knew I should have seen them more, but I worked and travelled so much that I barely had time for anything else. "Mum has been counting days since you said you would come, it's the most ludicrous situation ever, Rob. One would think you are visiting from Australia, erm…? we live in the same country, Rob, and you don't have time for us. It now feels like if it's not Christmas or Dad's Memorial Day you don't remember you have a family.

I felt bad, but in my defence, I worked so they didn't lack for anything.

"Is it really that bad, huh? But wait a minute; I thought I came a week before mum's birthday dinner?" I asked, unimpressed at the amount of time I give to my family.

"No, you didn't: you were on your way and then you cancelled and you said that you had an emergency. Robert, it is so bad, you sent presents and flowers by mail and since then, I have not seen you until now. Anyway, I am glad you came; at least you never miss Dad's memorial dinner. It is funny how you care for the dead more than the living. I am happy though, and I know mum will be so ecstatic to see you," she essayed.

I looked from her to the road as I pulled out of the parking space and began the journey to our family house. I always knew that I should visit more, but since our father passed, my continued challenging work had ensured that mum was able to maintain the family house, the holiday house and enjoy the extravagant holidays that she had become accustomed to through my father. Jane's university tuition was paid and Alex was able to live like a king in New York. I was not looking for appreciation, I had always felt it was my role to provide, but I wished that they cut me a little slack when I didn't show up. because my hard work ensures they never lack. I was drowned in my own thoughts when Jane started again.

"So, I met this girl at lunch today, she was absolutely..." I knew where this was going so I cut her off before she finished.

"Not again, Jane! We are not doing this again!"

"But you haven't even heard me out," she said pleadingly.

"And its better you don't say anything; I don't want you arranging dates for me. I will sort myself out when I am ready. But thanks for always looking out for me. Believe me, I know your heart is in the right place, but seriously, you have to stop. I have told you so many times, I don't have time to put into any relationship."

"Robert, you say this all the time, but I only do this because I care and I feel that if you have someone in your life, maybe you wouldn't work so hard. Maybe you will take a break every now and then and we can all see you more. Why do you need to work all the time, you are rich?! You are so rich that you have your own private plane. We want for nothing and still, you cannot stop. It's time you let someone in; we accept we can't help, but come on, a few dates to let your head down surely won't hurt you," She explained.

I chuckled: what she said made sense, but since Katherine, I had been afraid of getting into another relationship for fear that it would spin out of control and I wouldn't be able to bring myself to stop it. "Don't worry about me Jane, I am okay," I said, pulling her cheek with my left hand. She rolled her eyes and sighed. I knew she still had more to say.

"How many times have you said that, I mean, don't you get lonely, living in that huge house all by yourself? Seriously, Rob, how long is this going to carry on for?"

"I just told you I don't want to have this conversation with you," I said, concentrating on the road.

"Here we go again. No one is asking you to marry, we just want you in a sort of relationship with someone, so we know that each time we lay our heads on our pillow to sleep, you are not alone. That you have allowed someone into your heart and that that person cares for you. Wow! Now I am beginning to feel like mum," she said, throwing her hands in the air, I could not help laughing.

"Jane, why does it bug you so much?" I couldn't help inquiring.

"Because I want you to be happy: you pretend to be, but you're not happy and I can tell," Jane replied.

"So, what, you think dating one of your friends will do the job?" I asked.

"I am not saying that exactly, but you haven't even tried."

"Did too," I said

"No, you did not," she said, gritting her teeth.

"I went on all the dates you set me on, didn't I?"

"And you honestly did not fancy anyone of them?"

"Nope" I retorted, shaking my head in disagreement. She worried about me, but I knew what my problem was—I see a girl once or twice and if I did not feel any sparks, I did not pursue it any further.

I felt Jane's gaze on me, her eyes narrowed into slits. She had a look about her as if she just had an epiphany.

"Oh," she said, her jaw wide opened.

"Oh what?" I asked, wanting to know what she had come up with now. She was quiet, but I wanted to know what it was she had in mind now.

"What are you thinking in that head of yours now? Come out with it, girl" I said again. She looked away quickly, covering her mouth with her hands and then she looked at me.

"Robert, you are..." she did not finish, she looked away again. Now her eyes were on the road, as if she was waiting for me to fill in the gap or confess to a crime. I did not understand. What was she on about now? I wanted to know.

"Jane?" I said, looking at her, "What's on your mind now?"

"I should have known, I can't believe it took me this long to figure it out and it's been staring at me in the eye all along," she pulled her eyebrow together.

"Figure what out?" I asked, not knowing where she was going with this.

"It's always the good-looking ones,"

I looked at her, genuinely confused now. "Really, you might want to bring me up to speed, what are you on about?" I asked again.

"Rob, it doesn't matter to me anyway, you're my brother and I love you regardless of who you are, I just want you to be happy. I cannot believe I did not see this. Oh gosh, what must it have been like for you... me setting you up with all those girls and all the time not realizing you didn't fancy anyone of them because you are..." she spoke so fast that I could hardly pick up what she was saying, I looked at her, extremely-puzzled.

"Slow down, little one. Because I am what?" I asked. I wish I knew what she was getting at. She ignored my question and blabbed on, and then she stopped and looked at me.

"Seriously, Rob, it does not matter to me at all about who you love. Do you have someone in your life now, and have you been hiding your relationship from us, which will really explain why we don't get to see you? You can tell me, you know. All that matters is that you are happy and I am sure that mum will feel the same way too. Really, your happiness is all we care about. How could I have been so blind?" I was turning into the drive now and I was glad because I needed to understand her better. She had definitely reached a conclusion of some kind and I was still not sure what she was rambling about.

As soon as I parked the car, and turned off the engine, I turned towards her.

"Okay, spit it out. What is this craziness you are insinuating?"

She sighed, "Isn't it obvious... I mean that if that is who you are, I know that you cannot help it, but you do not have to keep it a secret anymore." I tried to think through what she said to make sense out of it, but I really was not getting her. I shook my head disapprovingly.

And then, she said, "Don't worry, Rob, I have a friend. He says that he is bisexual, if you don't have anyone now, I can set you up…"

"What?" I busted out with laughter; I could not get angry at her, even if I wanted to. "So, how does not having the time to date translate into me being gay?" I found myself still laughing, the more I thought of her reaction the funnier it seemed.

"It's not funny," she said.

"Yeah-right, -it's-not"-I-responded.

"So why are you laughing?"

"What else would you have me do, get mad at you for calling me…gay?" I said and shook my head. "So, I don't fancy your friends, now you think I must be gay!"

She stared at me and then she said, "That's the only thing that fits, you can tell me, you know. It's not like it's the end of the world…I mean what else could it be?"

I chuckled. "Jane, you are unbelievable and impossible. Okay listen, I am not dating because I have not met that person that makes me want to stop. If I do, you will be the first to know. Now little one, you have to stop worrying about me, I should worry about you, come to think of it, you should be dating yourself. Do you even have a boyfriend, you are twenty-one years old, you should be having the time of your life. Leave the worrying to me. I am your big brother, and I promise you, I am not gay. I do not fancy men. Look, I will not be alone forever, I see it bothers you, but I am going to take some time off work and relax. Maybe I will meet someone I like, maybe not, but one thing I know is that you can't force these things, okay?" I said.

"Okay," she smiled as I pinched her nose. "Ouch, that's not nice!" I ignored her, got out the car to meet mum standing in the doorway with a big smile plastered on her face.

****

I had not seen my brother, Alex in over a year. The last time he visited was two Christmases ago. Alex flies to London almost every year, but last year he met a girl. April. They met while on holiday, he called me every now and then to fill me in on his life and to get more money from me. I did not mind giving him all the money he needed, but I wished he showed a little interest in helping to run the business. At least he had a girl he was serious about that's more than I could say for myself.

Dad knew us all better, he knew I wasn't one to settle for anything that wasn't right. So, he had begged me to join the family business, since I wasn't out playing in the field. But I had turned him down repeatedly only to pick up the trade out of guilt right after he died. Not long after I started to run things, I found out that I was not only good at it, I got a high out of making millions. Alex is the fun brother and no matter how depressing life became; you could always count on him to liven things up. For some reason, he didn't get any pressure from Dad to join the family business. I wasn't sure then if Dad had put the pressure on me simply because I am the first child or if he didn't think Alex had what it took.

I announced to my mum that I was taking time off work and going on a much-deserved holiday, she and Jane came up with the idea that I go visit Alex instead. There was no arguing with them, having not seen them in such a long time. I wanted to please them, plus it would be good to see Alex after such a long time. So, I took their advice and decided to visit with him and unwind my mind for a few weeks. Instead of staying at the hotel, Alex, Jane and Mum had insisted I stay with Alex and his girlfriend in his three bedroomed penthouse in New York.

If I had a choice, I would not be going to New York, it only reminds me of Dad's death, but everyone seemed to think it's time I got over it and I reckoned it's time that I buried the pain as well. I had used work as a shield to not think about the pain that he must have gone through as he died; I couldn't help blaming myself for his death. We were so close until he started barging me about joining the family business and my stubbornness led to his death. So, I was going to go to New York and possibly come to some kind of peace in my heart.

Alex hinted on the phone that he wanted to propose to April during my visit. This was fantastic news for them both. I was happy that he was making a life for himself; I only wished that he worked as hard as he lived his life. This was one of the reasons, I did not think that I could stop working so much, they were all so used to the standard of living that my hard work affords them. Still, they did not all get it. They love to complain about my availability but forget I cannot say NO to them when it comes to things they need. As happy as I was for Alex, I did not understand why he had suddenly chosen to propose and marry a girl that he had only known for six months and he was only twenty- seven years old. Too young to tie himself down if you ask me, but unlike them, I always kept my opinion to myself. However, I did not begrudge him, if he feels that he had truly found love, at least he gets to live the life I someday hoped to have.

Chapter 5

The flight to New York was long and I had wished I had taken my own jet instead because of space and waiting times at the airport.

However, I was glad when it was over, sitting down for long hours, that I wasn't used to at all. Alex and April met with me at my arrival. I walked over, gave April a hug and patted Alex on the back, but he was not having any of it. He threw his arms around me and squeezed me tight.

"You finally did it, it's good to see you, bro," he said, almost laughing.

"Yeah, me too, it's been too long," I said as I wrapped my arms around my brother. We let go of one another and looked each other over as if we had not met in the past decade.

"You actually came, I didn't think you would," he said, bewildered. I winked at him, I was not sure what it was that surprised him the most: the fact that I left work for a while, or that I came to New York?

Ignoring him, my eyes fell on April. I placed my arms around her shoulder, pulling her closer to me, and we walked towards the car.

"And you must be April, the woman who's stolen our Alex's heart? I am glad that we finally met," she smiled nervously.

"Me too, I tell you, I just feel like I know you already, Alex speaks about you all the time, his big hero brother, what he didn't say or didn't prepare me for is that you are ridiculously beautiful, and I can't believe I actually just said that out to you," she smiled sheepishly. I smiled back: already, I had a feeling that I would enjoy this break much more than I had anticipated. I already knew that with Alex I would be fine, but I had been a little apprehensive about April, because I did not know at first how she and I would get along. But now I felt confident that the three of us were going to have an amazing time together.

"Ah, you are too kind. Don't believe any nonsense Alex's been feeding you about me. I'm sure you will soon find out I'm not all that…"

"We'll see." She cut me in. "How was your flight?" she asked.

"Very long and tiring, but I am glad that I made it here in one piece. Enough about me, you both must promise me, you won't make this time together about me in any way,"

I looked over my shoulder at Alex, struggling to keep up as he pulled my bag along. I paused so we could all walk together. Alex caught up and I took my bag from him. "Give me that, Alex. I was just saying to April how that I don't want you two to stop doing the things you do just because I am here. Just carry on like you normally do, I'm not here to be in the way." I said as I pulled my luggage towards me.

"What are you talking about? You can never be in the way, we are family, right April?" Alex said looking at April for confirmation.

"Off course, we are. You are not getting out to being treated like a king, if that's what your aim is here." April joked. I chuckled. There was no point arguing with her, I could tell she was fire, just what Alex needed.

"Okay then, I guess I will have to bear and grin then." I joked in return. "Well in honesty, Alex, I got a bone to pick with you." Alex looked up at me questionably.

"Really? What have I done now?" He laughed nervously.

"First of all, you never said April was this good looking. You must have begged, stolen and borrowed to be worthy and deserving of the heart of this pretty woman?" I asked jokingly while squeezing April's shoulders a little tighter. She blushed with embarrassment. Alex moved to the other side of April and gently and jokingly pulled her away from me.

"Oi! Your hand off, this one is all mine!"

"Maybe while you are here, you might be lucky enough to find someone as special as April is to me," Alex added.

And April laughed and turned towards me, "Robert, to tell you the truth, I don't believe for one second that you will have any sort of difficulty finding the woman of your dreams here. We are in New York, it's the land where dreams become reality. I mean… come on, look at you. I have only just met you and already I am falling for your charms not to talk of your beauty, work ethics, money… you have a lot going for you, Robert, I wouldn't worry too much. Am I allowed to say that to him, Honey?" She glanced at Alex for approval, Alex shifted his head in doubt and said.

"Hmm, well just this once, and only cause he is my brother and I love him."

I felt awkward, hearing her gush about me, I wish I was that perfect, but I wasn't, and I knew it. I didn't want to let her down and have her pity me just as Mum and Jane do.

April began speaking again, "Don't worry, you won't be going back to England single, you are going to be snatched up before you know it. I have got many gorgeous good-hearted friends, tell him Alex. How about Vicky? She is a good girl, you will agree, and she has a good heart, wouldn't you say?"

"No, not Vicky." Alex pushed back.

"Why not Vicky? She is a nice girl." April pressed.

"Yes, you will say that, but she's not Rob's type." Alex argued.

I was tired, I had not even gotten in the car and already the subject matter was about me and girls to hook up with. It felt like April would not stop speaking, and I liked her already, but I was too tired to join in the conversation.

"Don't mind Alex. Wait until you meet her, Robert, you will just love her, and if not Vicky, there is Erika, another nice and beautiful girl." April explained. I smiled, I wanted to burst into laughs; I could not believe that I had only just left my mother and Jane behind just to come and spend time with another match-maker. And by the looks of things, I didn't think I could get away from it. I looked at Alex, he shrugged, knowing that I hated being set up.

"Darling, leave him alone for now. Look at him, he's tired. We'll talk about this later." He suggested, and I was thankful. Although truth be told, I wasn't looking forward to revisiting the topic. But there was nothing he could really do.

"I know, I'm sorry. I was just putting it out there that I have friends that will snatch him up."

"April, stop already, he only just got here. I told you that he doesn't like being set up," Alex whispered to April. By now, we were by the car. The chauffeur got out and opened the door to Alex's Bentley; he took the luggage from my hands. Alex and April got in the car and I went in last.

As soon as we were in the car and the chauffeur started the car, April asked,

"What sort of girl is your type, Robert, if you don't mind me asking?"

Alex smiled nervously, "April baby, can't you see he is tired, let him be, honey. Look at him; he looks really out of it." I smiled, I appreciated Alex looking out for me, but I did not want them to get in a fight over me because April cared about me.

"It's alright, Alex. I am tired, that much is true, but I am not too tired to talk to April," I said. April gave Alex the look that said, 'I told you so'. "April, to answer your question, I don't think I have a type. I will like to think I am very open, but I do not like to waste my time. I would only commit if I think that there is something there. And, to be honest, I have not found that woman yet. You know, that one person that makes me want to drop everything," I tried to explain myself as truthful as I could. April nodded, but she was staring at me, I wondered if I had said something that she did not like. Alex nudged her; she smiled and rested her head on his shoulder. I could still feel her eyes on me, but I was tired: I did not want to initiate any more conversation. I wanted to shut down and just rest, it seemed that staying out of work was making my body experience a strange weariness.

I heard Alex say something to her, but I was too drained to make out what it was. I could not wait to get in the shower and lay on a bed.

When we got to his penthouse, I was shown to my room; they were both excited as they opened the curtains to show me the views. I politely obliged, but as soon as they were out of the room, I took of my clothes, hit the showers and then lay on the bed right after my lights went out. For three days in a row, I was no good company; I just woke to eat, sat around April and Alex for roughly half an hour and then found my bed again. The bed was quickly becoming my new best friend, I could not help it, plus, my body needed the rest.

It felt good to not have to worry about work, but a little weird, though. It felt like how I used to feel when my father took care of the family and I did not have anything to worry about but myself. There was nothing to do but hang around and watch loads of crap on the television, which then turned to a chore itself. Alex told me that he found a job with a stockbroking firm; I was happy for him as I did not know he worked and it was good to see him getting up in the morning to go somewhere productive. Moreover, April worked some shifts in a fashion shop of some kind. I was happy that they both had things to do, if they didn't, it would have worried me a bit, but then this left me alone with my thoughts and I wasn't prepared for this type of silence. I started taking long walks to avoid dealing with my own company; it only reminded me of how empty my life was. This was supposed to be the holiday that would make me feel better, I thought, but nothing has changed apart from the scenery.

Thankfully, Alex had us fully booked this weekend. First, we were all going to see a basketball game and then on the next day, we would be going to a gig to listen to some new band called, 'Cords of Rock'. The weekend turned out to be enjoyable much more than I expected. Alex kept making me laugh, it was like back in time when I didn't have the weight of the world on my shoulders. I even bought a CD of the band to remind me of this weekend. I spent the remaining weekends going on double dates with Alex and April and April's three lovely friends. First, there was Vicky: she was lovely, but I did not think I had anything in common with her; she just wanted to be a homemaker and had no dreams of her own. As much as I respected her views, I always thought a woman should have their own dreams as well. She seemed the type that would support the man that she marries with everything and while all that was good, she wasn't the type to allow herself a little bit of a dream of her own and I didn't like that. I was not in search of a woman that I would constantly feel like I was walking all over. Then there was Erika and Erika... I dare say was a handful and very fun. I liked that about her, but she was too wild and I was not attracted to her. The last of the lot was Lauren. At first, I thought we were onto something because she seemed intelligent, but I later realized that she just agreed with everything I said. That was just a desperate attempt to make me think that we were alike and we thought the same way, but I could see through it.

Before I knew it, four weeks had passed and I was glad it was over. Alex and April seemed like the perfect couple; Alex proposed to April on my last weekend with them at a basketball game. It was beautiful and they both deserved all the happiness in the world, but I had to say that I got tired of seeing my brother and his girl kissing each other every now and then, declaring their love for each other at every passing minute. Night times were even worse; as I could hear them doing their shenanigans. It felt awkward afterwards in the day time when I had to sit with them and make conversations, pretending like I didn't hear them each night. I was happy to see them so loved up, but it only reminded me that I had never felt like that with any woman, which was possibly the reason I always felt vacant inside. I had to get away from them before I started to pity myself.

Alex and April drove me to the airport; although I was relieved to be going back, I was going to miss those two. April kept hugging me, she did not want me to go. I can't tell why that is. I was not that entertaining. April insisted I come visit again just for one weekend and I promised her that I would when I had the chance.

At first, when Alex informed me that he was going to marry April—then when I had not met her—I thought he was a little crazy. I also thought things were moving too fast, but I was glad that I never voiced my initial opinion on how I felt, because I have never met such a lovely person as April. My mother and Jane would love her too when they eventually meet up as I am sure they will all get on. Before leaving, I pulled Alex to the corner.

"I must say, she is a fantastic girl. You caught a good one there, whatever you do, don't lose her." Alex smiled sheepishly.

"I know, that's why I had to give her the ring so quickly." Alex said,

We both shared a quick laugh. And then paused for a moment. Whatever the case, I had enjoyed being with my brother again and I knew I was going to miss him.

"I'll miss you and April." I said. Alex nodded and threw his arms around me and we hugged. April crossed over to join us and threw her arms around the two of us.

Alex and April were not the perfect couple from what I had experienced with them. They always argued but made up so quickly. Sometimes, I thought they fought on purpose, just so they could make up for it. Watching them was like a soap opera, they were fun to be with, and there was nothing unhealthy about their relationship. Anyone with eyes could tell they were madly in love with each other. I guess that was what being in a relationship was all about, which constantly reminds me of what I lack in my life and for once, I envied my brother's happiness.

They both insisted that they would stay with me until I had checked in at the airport against my will. I did not think it was necessary, but April was not having it my way.

After checking in, we hugged and said our goodbyes. I had to put my foot down; I did not think it was necessary that they wasted the day on me, when they could be out, enjoying time together. I waited until they had left before I started making my way to the boarding gate. It was a long walk to the gate; I was almost there when I noticed a girl run past me. I looked back to see if anyone was after her, but there was no one. *Strange*, I thought to myself. She got on the queue and I was right behind her. I could not make out her face because she had her back to me and she had a cap on. Nevertheless, I could tell something was wrong. I assumed that everyone around sensed the same thing: she was jumpy, kept looking about her as if she was afraid of something. She tapped her feet nervously and I noticed the tension and jerks she had on her each time an announcement was made. *What could be wrong with her?* I thought, *who or what made her so scared?* Her strange behaviour made it impossible for me to take my eyes off of her, even though all I had was her back to me. I couldn't explain it, I just somewhat got this pull towards her and suddenly I had this urge building in me, I wanted to see her face. I wanted to know what this girl, who had stolen my attention, looked like. It was like a need. Then she bent down, as she did a paper dropped from her. This was my opportunity to see her better. I picked up the document and noticed it was her boarding pass, she was boarding the same flight as mine. I moved closer to her. She smelled nice, I found myself half kneeling just in front of her to get a better view of her face. She looked up at me, and something about her eyes, as worried as they were, they caught hold of my heart. They carried me away with her. "Excuse me, miss," I said as I waited with anticipation. It felt odd to me, but for some reason, I wanted to look at her face, the smell of her perfume got me ravished, and I took another deep breath just to smell her. It was as if time had stood still. I noticed her dark hair as it swayed on her back, bonded into a ponytail underneath her cap. I suddenly felt a need to reach out and touch her hair. This was madness. *What am I doing or even thinking?* I told myself, restraining my hands from touching her; I waited as she slowly looked up with the most bizarre expression on her face.

I heard her say, "Yes?". It was more like a whisper. She stared at me as if she was expecting me to do something or say something more to her. I noticed her skin suddenly went pale, but that was not what I was looking at. Even with the pale skin, I had never seen anyone so beautiful in my life. It was her eyes, there was something about those eyes as they stared at me and it was as if she could see all the way to my soul.

I felt naked but full before her a moment passed before us, I forgot what I was about to say. Somehow, I noticed that she was not just staring at me, she looked disturbed.

"Are you alright? You look like you've seen a ghost," I asked, smiling. She looked puzzled and just stared at me, but I did not mind so much because it somewhat felt good.

"You dropped this," I said, giving her back her boarding pass. My hands brushed hers slightly as she took the pass from me and in that instant, I saw her blush and I felt all warm inside, satisfied that I had such an effect on her. I knew right then that I wanted to know her more.

I started to think of what to say so that I could strike up a conversation with her, I was happy for once in my life. *Could this change be an effect caused by Alex's and April's love?* I was suddenly interested in someone that I knew I would go with to the end of the world, if it required that to keep feeling this way. I could not take my eyes off her, I offered her my hands as she tried to get up. As our hand touched, I felt a current like I had never felt before pass through me.

I didn't want to let go of her. She still looked shaken, "Would you like to sit down for a moment?" I asked.

She nodded. Not speaking, I led her to a nearby bench.

I wished I had a bottle of water near me, she looked like she could use some. Something wasn't right, and I didn't know if it was right to ask her about it having just met her. A security man passed by, looking at us suspiciously, I felt her body tense up as I still had her hand in mine. Looking into her eyes, I told her, "I'll be back." She nodded once as I reluctantly let go of her hands and got up to speak with the security man.

The man questioned if she was okay, and I told him she was fine. I asked if he knew where I could get water for her. Just then I noticed she got up without saying a word to me. But I was in a conversation with the security, it would be rude to walk away while he was pointing me towards a water fountain. As I turned to see where she was, I saw her going through the checks. I ended my conversation with the man and hurried towards her, she turned around to look for me, which warmed my heart. Then out of nowhere I heard an announcement with my name mentioned. I had to go, and she was leaving, I had not gone through the checks yet. I wanted to ask her for her name. I felt reluctant to leave; I heard the announcements again, I looked across to see if she would look at me. She turned back again, and our eyes met for a few seconds and then she resumed walking and I had to go. When I got to the help desk, it was April and Alex. Apparently, April forgot to give me the presents she bought for Jane and my Mum and that was why I had to walk all the way back and for the first time, I wasn't too pleased to see them both because they both may had just cost me the woman of my dreams.

I mean, for the love of God, what a timing! I took the bag from April and paced back quickly, I went through the security and boarded the plane. I looked around as I boarded the plane and she was nowhere around. The good news was that I knew that she was somewhere on this plane and I was prepared to scan each aisle until I found her. The airhostess graciously took my boarding pass from me and showed me to the first-class seats.

My mind kept wondering about her, this had never happened to me before—thinking about a girl like this! All I could see was her face, her eyes, her jet-black hair, I tried to remember how she smelt and the touch and feel of her hand. I just wanted to be with her again. It was crazy. It felt like I had lost something that I had always wanted. I waited until the plane took off, an hour into the journey; I got up and began my search. It was embarrassing, going from seat to seat, looking at people's faces. I had never done a thing like this before, but I did not care as long as I was able to find her. Half way through my search, the airhostess came to me and asked me to return to my seat. I told her that I was looking for someone and I did not know where she sat. She asked me for her name, I stared at her clueless. I sighed and tried to explain the situation to her without appearing as a fool. She looked at me weird, I had to be mad or high on something to be acting this crazy.

"Please sir, without a name or any idea where she may be seated, I cannot help you. Moreover, I must ask you to return to your seat, we are about to experience some turbulence," She ordered politely. I apologized and regretfully went back to my seat. I thought about trying again later, just before the plane lands, but then the weird look I saw on people's faces earlier discouraged me. What would I have done, supposing I found her? Would she even want to talk to me? I had not really thought through it for my craziness. She may not want to have anything to do with me, she might even be married, engaged, or in love with someone else.

"Hmm," I sighed. Even if all the above are strong possibilities, I still wanted to meet her. I wanted just to look at her again and see her look at me like she did when we met briefly. Her eyes, they did something to me, they touched me as no other woman had ever done.

Chapter 6

Why her, of all the girls I had been with, why her? I decided that I had to try to forget her; this clearly was the result of living with Alex and April. They switched something on in me and now I was messed up.

After what seemed like a battle between my heart and my head, I finally decided to stay put and use the latter, I must truly be going out of my mind and she would probably think the same, suppose I even found her. After debating with myself about the right and courteous action to take about this, I concluded that I had to see her. I would wait until we landed and then I would look for her amongst the other passengers, and when I find her, I would go to her and ask if I could have a word with her.

It was as if I had gone mad. Every now and then, I took a minute to rationalize my thinking: I gave myself reasons for why what I was about to do was wrong. However, what I could not ignore was the feeling of wanting to know her coursing through me; the memory of the current that passed through me as we touched. It became a need, a necessity, and it intensified the more her thoughts took over my mind. I could not understand why I would want anything to do with her, she seemed young. I closed my eyes and tried to remind myself of her eyes, how pure and rich they were, but they were afraid. I wondered what could have been troubling her, I wished I had summoned up the courage and asked her name, or even asked her what troubled her. I may never know now; I may never meet this girl again.

It occurred to me that all this time, I never once thought about work. I smiled, this was a good thing, all this time I thought there was something wrong with me and it just took a brief meeting with a strange beautiful girl for me to know that I would drop everything in a heartbeat to be with her.

As soon as we landed in London and I had completed all the immigration rituals, I collected my bag and sat down in the arrival lobby. My eyes pinned to the arrival entrance; if we boarded the same plane, she should be out here any minute. As I was waiting, a couple approached me: they were asking a question in English, but I couldn't pick up what they were saying as they spoke in a thick accent of some kind. I wanted to help, but I also knew that they were a distraction. If I couldn't concentrate, then there was no need for me to be here waiting for her, she could pass or could have even passed by and I wouldn't know. After what seemed like a lifetime of trying to explain things to the couple, they thanked me, and they walked away. I was not too pleased because I knew the time, I spent concentrating on their needs instead of mine could have cost me the loss of the girl of my dreams. An hour later, I did not see her still. It was either she never got on the plane, or while I was helping the couple, she passed, and I never saw her nor would I see her again. There was no point hanging about; I took a resigned breath before forcing myself to walk away. Pushing myself forward, a part of me, a very dominant part of me was still hoping that that face would show up here somehow. This was nonsense, I finally concluded. It was time to stop living in fantasy land and come back to earth. Here on earth, I did not do crazy things like those that I had just done in the past twelve hours over a stranger whom I had no clue if she even remembers coming across me.

I got out into the open air, took in a deep breath to clear my head and waited for the chauffeur to deliver my car. I made conscious effort to think about work, Jane and my mum, anything, but her. I watched as other people struggled with their trolleys and luggage, in particular, a woman at the far end to my left and her toddler. She had him sitting on the trolley with her luggage as she pushed, but the child was bent on getting off the trolley. I watched her while she tried to pacify the screaming child and at the same time, push the trolley forward. She was clearly frustrated, but she was trying hard to keep a lid on it.

While I watched, the chauffeur arrived with my car. I was on my way to my car, when I heard the child scream again at the top of his lungs. I automatically glanced in their direction when suddenly, I saw her waving down a cab.

For a moment, I could not move. it was as if my heart stopped. I could not tear my eyes away from her and all my reasoning went out the window. I found myself walking towards her as if there was a magnetic pull, pulling me towards her and I could not stop myself even if I willed. I wanted her to see me, I wondered if she noticed me, but her eyes were not looking in my direction.

She was talking to someone else. Reluctantly, I tore my eyes away from her to see who she was talking to; it was a black cabman and before I knew it, she was in the cab. I ran towards the cab, waving my hands foolishly, to gain the drivers attention. The cabbie looked in my direction for a tiny second and pulled away. I dropped my hands in frustration and just watched as the cabbie drove her out of my reach and my life.

I went back home, feeling frustrated and stupid for allowing myself to get distracted by the couple. She may not be for me, supposing I met with her again, but at least I would know that I had given myself the chance to find that out. The opportunity was gone. There was no point beating up myself about it, she had occupied my thoughts for almost a day and since I knew I might never see her again, it was time I forgot about her and resume my boring life.

I tried to concentrate on other things, but it was difficult and I did not like it. This was the first time I really knew what it felt like to like someone and I loved the feeling, but I did not like the misery that came along after having that feeling.

Three weeks passed since I saw her at the airport. Something about her face that has somehow engraved itself on my mind. It irritated me that I needed someone the way my heart dictated to me. I had become impatient and snappy at work; something was eating at me and I couldn't get to the bottom of it. It felt like an unfinished business. I knew what it was, but it was infuriating because there was nothing, I could do to stop myself from feeling the way I was. I didn't like that a girl I clasped eyes with for a few minutes had created some power over me and to make matters worse, I could only relax when I allowed myself to think about her. I needed to do something quickly to fix this situation, and I knew that the answer was to allow someone else in. Perhaps, meeting her was just a reminder that I needed to be in a relationship. I could not use work as a distraction any more, I wanted someone in my life and I wished it was her, not just anyone. However, I had no idea where, or who she was or why she had this hold over me.

Three months dragged by and the mess in my head had not been fixed. It felt more like meeting with her had been a punishment for all the girls I had wronged in my life. I went and saw my family doctor and told him that I was suffering from anxiety. I also had trouble sleeping. I was sure there was more to this situation than a brief encounter with a stranger.

I found myself working more hours to get things back to normal. Visiting Alex was meant to be good for me, but it had not turned out as I thought it would. Witnessing his relationship with April made me feel very lonely, which resulted in me developing some sort of attachment syndrome for the first girl I came close to.

There must be some medical explanation for what was happening to me and I wanted it fixed immediately.

My doctor prescribed something to help me sleep better at night, which I usually took immediately when I returned from work to stop my mind from tirelessly replaying her face to me.

The pills helped, but they did not stop me from dreaming about her. Bizarre as it may seem, I always looked forward to seeing her in my dreams, it was that pathetic. It was usually the same dream with a slight difference each time. I see her on an island, waving at me or beckoning on me to come to her, but I was always far at sea on a boat, battling with the ocean to get to her. The water was always very stormy, it made it difficult to get close, the harder I tried, the more the current took me further away from her in a different direction and then, I would wake up. However, there was this one time I was so upset that I jumped out of the boat and began swimming against the current to get to her, but the waves just increased the distance between us. The more I tried was the further the current threw me and then I'd wake up. When I opened my eyes, I was usually covered in sweat from head to toe; as though I had been drenched in water. "*Phew*," I would whisper. It felt strange that each time I awoke, I was usually very happy to see that face again. I knew by now that I needed some sort of intervention or an electric jolt to my head if I wanted to be normal again.

Chapter 7

It was now almost four months and my feelings were still the same as the day I saw her. If I'm asked, I could not measure how I felt, but I would say, with her stealing my dreams as well it seems like my desire for her had increased over time. Nothing had helped, not the prescriptions, not even work could get her out of my head. I had often heard that you needed to be with another person to get over the one in your heart. Thinking about it like that made it sound stupid. How could I feel or love someone that I had not even been with and why did this happen to me. I felt that she had spelled me, this clearly couldn't be normal. This clearly cannot be called love. So, I came up with a simple plan, just can't be so sure it would work out well. I was going to move in with Jane and my mum to avoid being lonely and I was going to start dating someone to help preoccupy my thoughts.

I already called my mum on my way to work this morning to tell her I would be crashing at her place for now. She did not ask why, but her voice let on that she was over the moon. My mother, Fiona Elizabeth Parkman, loved every opportunity she got to have me home with her; to get me to come over in the past, she would ask that I come and change the light bulb—something she could have asked the gardener to do. To stop her from always calling for things like this, I got her a full-time handy man to help her with the petty things that she needed fixing, because I could not drop work to be with her. I always knew it was not about that, and that she just wanted more time with me. But at the time, I could not spare any. There was also a time when she said she was ill, she needed me to take her to the hospital. I tried to get someone to take her, but she insisted that she only wanted me, so I went, only to have her set me up with her neighbour's daughter.

Living with her and Jane will normally be my idea of a nightmare, but I was so looking forward to it, anything to stop the madness that had come over me. The thought of facing another day alone had become unbearable.

The Idea of Staying with family made me happier than I had been these past few months because I was not going back to a huge house with no companion. My housekeeper was usually out of the house by the time I got home. Who would have ever thought that I would find the idea of living with my mother so tasteful? She was still on my mind but now, somehow, I could control things in my head a little better.

Since living with my mum was helping, I decided to change a few things at work as well. I never went out to lunch at work, except when it was a business lunch. However, because I was in a better mood, I made the decision to start going to lunch.

I walked into the restaurant; it was half full already. There was a queue, so I waited in line, but the manager spotted me and showed me to a table for two. I normally had business lunches here, but today was not about business. However, they were not to know. A waiter came for my orders. For the first time in a very long time, I was aware of the people around me. I never took the time to observe things in the past. The restaurant's decor was exquisite, I watched as people talked and giggled while they ate. I wondered why I never before now took the time to notice life in its beautiful shades. It suddenly felt like a scale had been removed from my eyes and I silently promised myself that I'd find a good balance between work and a good social life. That made me think of my friends that had stopped calling to invite me on their many outings and events because they knew that I would not show. "Hmm…" I sighed. That was another issue I had to fix. I had to call them up and see if I could get back into their good graces. Finding time to socialize had suddenly become a priority and I loved the new me.

I may not know where this stranger that had created this feeling in me to do better is, I was very grateful for my very brief encounter with her.

"Hello, Robert" I heard someone say and I quickly looked up at the familiar, but more mature voice. I narrowed my eyes in disbelief, I could not believe whom it was that stood before me.

"Katherine?" I asked.

She smiled. "May I?"

"Yeah, sure," I said as I got up to pull out a seat for her. If nothing, I still considered myself a well-mannered man.

"Thank you," she said as she took her seat and I went back to mine. "Do you normally dine here?" she asked, still smiling.

I thought at that, still shocked to see her after so many years. "No, not always. Have been here a few times, though," I replied, studying her face. She would not stop smiling; she looked pleased to see me, I guess. She was still as pretty as she used to be. Nothing much had changed apart from her hair colour. She used to be a natural brunet, but now, she was a-blonde-haired woman and her hair seemed shorter than it used to be. She looked very classy and all business-like. The Katherine I knew years back was different from the one sitting across the table from me. She had truly matured; she smiled and cleared her throat as I quickly averted my

66

eyes from her face. I had been staring; she looked very beautiful with a bit of understated sexiness. And I wondered in that moment what it was about her that made me not see her then like I was seeing her now.

"Why are you looking at me like that?" She asked unexpectedly and more self-aware.

"Sorry, I didn't mean to be rude. It's just that… you look different, but in a good way. I guess it's because I haven't seen you in a while, I mean it's been years since we saw each other last and time has truly been kind to you. You look very beautiful."

"Thank you," she replied, "You took the words right out of my mouth, Robert. You complimented me, I was just about to say the same to you. I mean, you've always been good looking. But now, I mean… look at you, very sophisticated. Still unbelievably handsome and you know what went through my mind as I saw you? I was sitting with some friends when you walked in and they were all gushing, adjusting their hair, putting on their lipstick. I looked up and saw you and at first I was in shock, but then I started to enjoy seeing the way the women around adjusted themselves for your pleasure and you did not even notice anyone of them and I smiled because it reminded me of why we have not seen each other in a very long time." I smiled and looked down; I guess I was not as aware of my environment as I thought I was.

"Where are your friends now?" I asked.

"They left. I wanted to come over and say hello and I didn't want them to know I knew you."

"Why, am I that embarrassing?" I asked jokingly.

"No, it's not that. They were all… They were obsessed over you for the last half hour and I just didn't want to bring up the fact that you and I dated for two years because I know that they won't leave it alone."

I chuckled, "Fair enough," I said as she shrugged. "It's good to see you again, Katherine." She winked at me and crossed her arms. "Would you like to have lunch with me?" I asked her.

"No thanks, I already had lunch with my girlfriends, but maybe some other time."

The waiter returned with my order. I looked from her to the waiter and thanked him, placing the napkin on my lap. I looked at her. "It's a shame you are rushing off. Another time then?" I liked what I was seeing, but I was not sure that she was what I needed now and I did not want to push towards anything in particular. We had both done this before and now that I was dying for a distraction, it will be unfair for me to use her for that purpose.

"Sure, how about we do dinner tonight?" she said and quickly added, "That's if you aren't already tied down." To be honest, I was surprised. She suggested having dinner after the way things ended the last time, we were together. I wanted to say no and use work as an excuse, that would be the right thing to do, but I could see in her eyes how disappointed she would be if I declined. It was not as if she asked me to marry her, it's just dinner. I thought about it and knew that it would be better than listening to Mum and Jane nag me all night.

"Yeah, why not, let's catch up over dinner. I would really want to know what you've been up to all this time. Should I make reservations for... say seven?" I suggested.

"Yeah, seven's good, but at my place, I will be cooking," she replied in a very sexy tone, looking down at me as if I was something to eat. I was taken aback at first at the turn the conversation seemed to have taken. I wondered what she was after, I had had a few one-night stands in my days, but I could never associate her with that. Even though I was not in love with her, I felt protective of her in a weird way, but funny enough, it seemed like it may just be the doctor's recommendation for me to try to put the stranger out of my mind.

"Hmm, that's settled then; dinners at your place. How do I get to you?" She took my phone from the table and put her number on it.

"Call me after you have finished here, and I will text you my address, see you at seven," she said, leaning over to reveal her cleavage as she got up to leave. "Sure, seven it is." I nodded and smiled; she smiled back and turned on her heels towards the exit, deliberately wriggling from side to side.

Chapter 8

Hasina suri Fayed aka anna Fey

New Surroundings

It had been months since my lucky escape, although I was glad that I made it; I was also very worried about my parents. The guilt of what I had done ate at me constantly. By now, they must have figured out that I had planned for this escape a long time. I wrote so many letters to my mother to let her and father know that I was okay, but I had not found the courage to post them. As important, as it was for them to know that I was safe, writing to them would also mean that they would be able to find me. There would be no sense in doing all of this just to lead them back to me. I was sure that my father would have employed the best detectives and all the missing-people-specialists that money could afford. Anyone with any kind of authority would be out there looking for me, not to talk of his own security detail. I knew this before I left and I had to do all I could to ensure that I remained unfound.

My father must have taken it all out on my mother and even though I knew she was heartbroken, disappointed and angry about what I had done, she would be hoping and praying for my safe return. She would be praying that I come to my senses, run out of money or miserably fail at taking care of myself just so I'd shamefully need to return to her bosom.

Since my arrival, I checked into the hotel Louise booked for me. Seven days later, I started looking for an apartment to rent as I could no longer afford the luxury life style I was brought up in with the little money I had. Finding one on a budget was difficult; the rents that they were asking were too high for me to consider, if I wanted the little money, I had on me to last a little longer. I needed a job; I need it fast and I was not confident that anyone would be willing to employ me. That was another worry for me, finding work. I had never done a day's work in my life. However, no one here knew that apart from me, so as long as I could give it my best, I was hoping and praying that God will smile on me and favour me. Eventually after spending an extra three days on top of the initial one week stay at the Hotel; I was able to find a newly renovated studio flat within my budget. Somewhere around Kensington in London. Apparently, I should not be able to afford the rent on the studio flat with my little budget because of the location. I saw it advertised as I went on a walk in the evening. There was no pricing, just a number to call, so I called and I was asked to come and view it that same evening. So, I went and saw it. It was furnished with a double sofa bed, a dresser, a wardrobe, and a small reading table. It was an open planned sort of thing; the kitchen was only ten to fifteen feet from the sofa bed. There was a cooker; I had never used one in my life, a little under counter freezer and a washing machine. The floor was covered in dark-oak wood, the walls painted white. Apart from the front door, the only other door was the one that led to the bathroom. A manageable sized bathroom with a stand-alone bath and cream tiles on the walls and floor. It looked basic compared to what I was used to, but I loved it. It was clean. The flat still smelled of fresh paints, but I fell in love with it immediately. It was cute and for the first time, I could have a place of my own, choose my own outfits, be in my own world and watch and listen to whatever I wanted. I felt a sense

71

of freedom as I stood in the middle of the flat with a wide grin on my face. The landlord must have thought I was mad, I couldn't stop smiling, but I was a little scared, I still didn't know how much the rent was, or whether I could afford to pay as much as was needed to live in this studio flat that already felt like home to me.

I looked at the property owner; it was time I knew if this was just a dream or if it could become my reality.

"How much is the rent to live here?" I asked. He looked at me and said,

"Eight hundred pounds." Immediately when I heard the figure, my heart sank. I didn't need to do the math to know I could not afford to pay as much as that, knowing that I had no job and in three to four months I would run out of money and be thrown out and onto the streets. The grin and the dream of having my own space waned off my face and the landlord could see it.

"It's a lovely place, but I am sorry, I can't afford the rent, sorry I wasted your time," I said as I began to walk towards the door.

"Wait," The landlord said.

I stopped and wondered what he wanted, *surely, I did not owe him anything for coming to view*, I thought to myself.

"Listen, your face earlier, it showed that you loved the place, am I right?" He asked.

I nodded, I wasn't sure what he was getting at, I had told him I couldn't afford the rent and there was no way he could talk me into paying the money I knew I couldn't afford.

"Listen, how much can you really afford to pay?" he asked. I looked at him shocked, was he saying what I thought I was hearing,

"Sir, I don't have a lot of money; to be truthful, I was hoping it would be around five hundred, that was the most I could afford each month and I am already three hundred pounds out," I responded dejectedly.

The man sighed and took one quick look around the flat and said, "Ok listen, this flat was meant for my daughter, I renovated it for her, but for some reason, she didn't want it. She suddenly decided last minute after it was finished that she was taking a job in another country and now I had to rent it out because I couldn't let it sit here unoccupied," he looked at me again, "I saw your face when you were looking around, you loved it, which was what I was kind of looking for in my daughter. If you want it, it's yours for five hundred a month," he said, shrugging his shoulders.

I was in shock; I opened my mouth in disbelief and almost burst into tears. I reached into my bag immediately trying to get all my money out. The man waved at me to stop,

"Come back tomorrow, at noon. It's too late now, we would sort out all the details then and I will hand over the keys to you."

"I don't know how to thank you, I am very grateful and I promise you, you won't regret this," I said. He smiled and led the way out of the flat. I was over the moon; I now had a cute little place I could call home. This was indeed a cause for celebration, only I had no one to celebrate with me.

I could barely sleep; I spent the night dreaming of the start of my new life. When I woke up, I packed the little things I had, went for breakfast, checked out and made my way to the flat. I was a little early, but I didn't mind. I sat outside on the stairs that led to the flat and waited for the man to arrive.

Two hours later, he arrived in time. He asked me if he gave me the wrong time because he got a call from someone, (neighbours, I guessed) that I had been sitting here. I told him I had nowhere else to go and that was why I chose to come early. He opened the door to the flat and we both got down to business straight away. He read me a tenancy agreement, which we signed. I paid a month's deposit and a month's rent.

He handed me the keys, "There you go, Miss Fey, it's all yours. If anything should go wrong like a blocked pipe or something, anything to do with the flat, just call me and I will try and sort it out."

"Okay. Thank you," I replied, loving the sound of my new identity. I saw him to the door. He just waved and got into his car, I waited for him to drive away before shutting the door.

I was excited to say the least; I had a place to call home. I laid on the sofa as though a bed. Everything was working out fine, it felt like an angel was watching over me and putting everything in place. Now that I had a place, I needed to go out and do some shopping, buy some food, clothes, bed sheets, everything essential to make my little flat a home. I was beginning to live the life I had dreamt of for so long. I finally began to relish the feeling and meaning of true freedom.

I smiled as I recalled the fear that overtook me at the airport, that day as I stood in line for security check. Then his face appeared on my mind, the man that held my hands and stole my dreams... I remembered the way he looked at me and the way my heart jolted at his sight. I had never felt that way around any one before. How could I when I had been a prisoner in my own home.

I wished that I had met this man on a different day in a different circumstance. I rolled over to my side and wondered where on this planet he might be and what he was doing and thinking about right this moment. I wondered if he still remembered seeing me, if he spared a moment of thought for the clumsy terrified girl, he met that day.

I closed my eyes and I tried to remember the sound of his voice, the way he smelled and how I felt when his hands held mine, the way he looked at me like he was afraid I would break as he led me to that bench. My mind had replayed my memories of him a thousand times since the last time I saw him. I liked thinking about him, it gave me a strange feeling in the pit of my stomach and I liked it. I embraced it. There had been nights when I had tried not to think about him, but when the guilt of what I had done to my parents consume me, I found solace in my memories of him. I knew that I may never see him again; who knew if he even got on the same plane as me, but it did not matter so much for now as long as he stayed alive on my mind.

Is it possible to miss someone you didn't really know? Someone you didn't have the right to miss? It definitely isn't right to feel that way about a complete stranger. I was attracted to a fantasy and it was strange for me, especially because I had not been brought up to feel this way for another man except the man I marry. My mother told me nothing about love, especially because if I had married Ashraf, I would not be calling it love. To me, it was just an arrangement between his family and mine, nothing more than a business transaction whichever way they sliced it. I did not know Ashraf and had no intention to do so; I had not attempted to see him even when he came with his family to talk to my parents, I was not interested in being his wife. Whereas, I felt completely different when it came to this stranger that I barely met. There was something about him, that was unforgettable. It was not just about his looks, no doubt he was gorgeous; that alone should set any woman reeling for him, but it was more than that. It as if a part of me needed him in order for breathing to be possible, like he had been etched into me somehow and without him, I feel almost incomplete.

Chapter 9

The excitement of having my own place, the pace at which it happened, and thoughts of this stranger made it impossible for me to do anything. I soon found my eyes closing and the next time they were opened, it was evening. I didn't really have anywhere to be, I looked through my bag and picked out my toothbrush. I made my way into the bathroom, switched on the lights and turned on the tap. I splashed water on my face and proceeded to brushing my teeth. After I did that, I let down my hair; it had been in a ponytail. As I brushed, I felt the velvetiness and suppleness of my hair against my skin. I normally had someone that brushed my hair at the end of the day and it felt good to be doing something that everyone should do for themselves. Pathetic, I knew, but that was the world I was raised in. There was no time for anything else, I would have loved to have a bath, but I had no towels, nothing really. I needed to shop the next day and get all that I required to begin living and then I would start the hunt for a job.

I picked up my handbag from where I left it, I had to go out and find a restaurant as I was starving. I walked down to the end of my street and soon, I was on the high street, where there were a few shops. I almost walked the length when I saw an all-you-can-eat buffet, a Moroccan restaurant. I walked in, spoke with the man behind the counter and was

shown to a seat. There were a few families and friends enjoying dinner together. I did not want to think about being with family; my family was nothing like the ones I was witnessing anyway. I was always meant to behave a certain way, especially when my father was around. Therefore, I was not going to give myself any grief about missing them. I got up and took a selection of food from the platter of food on display, from starters to mains and then dessert. I sat down and ate to my heart's content. I could barely move when I finished eating, I settled my bill and I was on my way out when something caught my eye: it was a newspaper. I doubled back and asked the person behind the counter if I could look at the paper. He told me that I could take it if I wanted to. "It's last week's paper," he said. I was amazed, he did not see what I was looking at. I picked it up, folded it and quickly placed it in my bag as I walked out. I walked as fast as I could until I got to my new flat. I closed the door behind me and brought out the newspaper and stared at the mirror image of myself plastered on the paper with the caption "Missing Heiress" at the top. Sub-titled below was the Saudi Arabian Heiress to the Abubakar Fayed fortune feared kidnapped. My heart began to beat so fast; it felt for moments that I thought I had been found, but then I calmed myself down and read the story and realized that they had no idea where I was. Another picture at the bottom right of the same article caught my eye. It was the picture of me at the airport with a man. You could not see his face; he was facing me heads down and his back turned to the camera. In the picture, you could see the fear in my eyes; they obviously thought he had kidnapped me or had something to do with my disappearance. I did not need to see his face to recognize him; I could still remember every single detail about him. I cut out the bit where he was and taped it above my bed, where I could see it always and then I tore the rest of the paper into shreds and dumped it in the bin. Today was not about my family, it was about me celebrating my freedom and the start of a new life.

This was not going to be as easy as I hoped it would be, but if I was careful, I was hoping that I would not be found. I was also hopeful that most people will be too busy with their lives to remember the face plastered on a newspaper a week ago. Perhaps there were more papers out there with my face on them, but I did not know that and as long as I kept my head down, things should be just fine. I tried not to worry too much, I had a busy day the next day, I had to go shopping and fill the house with as many things as I could afford.

I laid down on my sofa bed, rolled around until I was comfortable enough to sleep and then dosed off. The next day, I took a bus to the closest shopping mall after getting directions from the neighbour living above me. She knocked on my door in the morning to introduce herself: she seemed nice. I told her that I was on my way out to do some shopping and she suggested the nearest shopping mall and gave me directions of the bus routes. Not that I asked, but I was glad she helped. Although I did not want to encourage any kind of invasive behaviour into my life. I had always enjoyed shopping, but when my mother and I went out shopping, it was always to the expensive stores, to buy jewelleries, clothes—just about anything too expensive for the average human to consider owning. I would not even call it shopping because we were waited on hands and foot all through. This was different—buying on a budget—but I was loving it, I bought towels, pillows, bed sheets, clothes, kettles, pots, plate sets and anything I felt was necessary to make me comfortable. I soon realized that I could not carry them all by myself after I added the purchase of a twenty-eight-inch TV. I was given a cab office number and they were quick to come after I called them.

The driver was putting everything I bought into the boot when I noticed someone staring at me. I looked away from him, avoiding eye contacts, but I could feel his eyes on my back as I turned away from him. I felt nervous; I wished the driver would hurry up already. Then I heard his footsteps as he walked up to me.

"Hello," he said. I did not answer. "Do you need help with anything?" he asked, I turned around to face him.

"No thanks. I think he's got it," I said, looking in the driver's direction.

"Sorry but…you look… familiar; don't I know you from somewhere? Have we met before?" he was persistent.

"No, I do not think we have," I replied, looking straight on, the driver had finished loading everything and he shut the boot and got in the cab. I immediately got in the cab too. Then he walked towards the passenger side where I had sat. My heart was pounding, I did not understand what he wanted from me and why he would not leave me alone.

"I remember where I've seen you from," he said, narrowing his gaze on me. By this time, my patience had worn thin and without looking at him, I asked the driver to leave. He pulled away, but I heard this person shout after us,

"Oi, you are that missing girl from the paper!"

I sincerely hoped no one took him seriously as we drove to my flat. I felt the cabbie looking at me from time to time and when he noticed I saw him, he asked,

"Are you alright miss?"

"Yeah sure. I'm fantastic."

"Sorry, it's probably none of my business, but you look a bit shaken, that's all."

Why won't people ever mind their own business, I thought. Yeah, it is none of your business, I wanted to say to him. Then I thought that he was probably a good person, he was just looking out for me, so I held my tongue. Then, I decided on something subtler.

"I am alright; I have just had a very stressful day that's all but thank you for asking." He nodded and I smiled and he put his focus on his driving. It was time for a change of plan, there was no way I would let this man drop me in front of my house, I might as well just have called the police myself to come and look in on me. The man that yelled after us had aroused his suspicion and I forgot to mention the reward money my father placed on my head. If he knew how much giving me up was going to pay, today would be the last time he drove a cab.

"Please can you just take me to the station instead?" I asked.

"Excuse me?" he asked.

"Sorry, the person I was supposed to meet up with just sent me a text, she's not at home, it's very typical of her, I am just gonna go home. So, if it's no problem, can you just drop me at the train station instead?" I asked.

"No problem, wherever you want to go, I will take you. Or you want me to drive you home instead, because of all the things you bought, I mean?" he asked politely.

"No, that will not be necessary. It's fine; I have an arrangement in place already," I responded, very casually, trying my best not to give anything away. He drove me to the station and unloaded my things. I paid him, but then he gave me this worried look for a brief second before returning to his cab and driving off. I made sure he was out of view before I got another cab to take me home. I had to be extra careful, it took me years to plan my escape and I did not want it all destroyed so easily or any sooner.

When I got back to the flat, I put all the stuff I bought where they belonged. I looked around and my little flat was beginning to look like a home. I loved it because it was mine to call home.

As I sat in the flat, flipping through the channels to my newly bought TV, I thought about things I could do to change my looks.

I wondered if I should cut my hair short and change the colour as well. However, I loved my hair too much to destroy it like that. I wondered what my mother would say if I ever did that to my hair. The baseball cap I have been wearing will do for now, and in the meantime, I probably should not go out as often as I had been doing. Nevertheless, there were still things I needed to do, like finding a job. Moreover, when I eventually do, I'd have to do my best to cope with living and working under the radar without being spotted.

Next day out, I took the tube to the West End. I still had a bit of money left, but the bulk of it was for my rent. I needed more clothes, I reminisced as I walked past the likes of Harrods, Selfridges, House of Frazier and many more designer stores that my mother and I frequented. These were places I would be going into without blinking if I was with my mother, but I didn't have that kind of money to spend now and I didn't live in that world any longer. I remembered when I was sixteen and we came to London on holiday, my father had opened a Barclay's account in my name with a very large sum of money. This was not the first account he had opened for me. But he always said I had no need of it now and he would keep putting money in the accounts until I was old enough and married. Well, I guess I was old enough, but not married and so I will never be entitled to his fortune.

I entered a store called Top Shop; they had a lot of fancy clothes, most of the prices were fair enough. They were doing a mid-season sale, lucky for me. I was able to buy very nice dresses at a reduced price. I was on a hunt for bargains and when I left Topshop, I went into another store called New Look. The prices were not as high as the formal store; I picked up a few things as well. I called by a drug store and bought a few toiletries and on my way out, I saw a sign posted outside the store. It read 'currently recruiting'. I turned back around and looked for a shop assistant. This was the type of opportunities I was looking for. I asked the person I found about the position and she pointed me in the direction of the store manager. I thanked her and walked towards him. As I approached him, he stopped what he was doing and smiled at me, watching me as I got closer.

"Do you need help with anything?" he asked.

"Yes, please. Erm…. I just want to enquire if you still need a shop assistant? I saw the posting on your window, about recruiting?"

"Oh, I see, do you have any experience working as a sales assistant?" he asked again, looking me over.

I thought about lying, but then concluded that it was better to tell the truth, well, part of the truth. "No, I am new here I recently moved to England, but I am a fast learner and I promise to work very hard if I get the job," I pleaded.

He chuckled at my attempt to beg, "What does a girl like you want with this job anyway, you don't look like you've worked a day in your life."

"I need a job. Please give me a chance and I won't let you down," I begged again; he looked at me and sighed,

"Okay, you will need to fill in the application form online or you can take a hard copy and return it by post or you can bring it here for me to consider. If you qualify, we will call you for an interview and if we think you can do the job, we will let you know."

"Okay, do you have a form here I can fill?" I smiled. He nodded and walked over to the counter and took a form, handed it to me. Then he said,

"Why don't you try your luck at modelling, you look like you will do better there." I smiled; I did not know if that was a compliment or a joke. Perhaps, he was trying to let me down gently because he felt that I couldn't do the job. The thought of becoming a model made me laugh, if only he knew what my parents will do to me if

I became a model. My father would disown me immediately, that's if he has not already done so.

"Thank you!" I responded as I made my way out. I did not know what to say, I felt a little awkward.

On the train going home, I noticed a couple looking at me, but I pretended not to be bothered. I had to remember not to do anything that will attract attention to me. I picked up the Metro paper from the seat next to mine and pretended as if I was reading its content. I contemplated getting off at the next stop; I was not sure if this couple recognized me or if I was just becoming paranoid.

I stopped at a grocery store at the end of my street and bought a bunch of foodstuffs. I had no idea what I would be doing with them, but I needed to learn how to cook one way or the other and as I couldn't afford to dine out any longer.

Chapter 10

The next few weeks crawled slowly; I had nothing to do, I was bored out of my mind. The little space I had in my flat was not big enough to dance in. Dancing was my passion; it was the main reason I left home, plus, I did not want to be married off to Ashraf. I went out occasionally to hunt for jobs; I filled so many application forms. I bought myself a tablet with internet bundles so I could find work online. Every time I went food shopping, I bought the newspaper to check if there had been anything written about me since the last one I saw. Luckily, nothing more about me had been published, that didn't mean my parents had given up, it just meant the world had moved on to other issues and that suited me fine. One day, I flicked through the TV channels for something interesting, I was feeling lonely and nothing held my attention. I switched off the TV and picked up the newspaper I had picked up at the newsagent that day. As I guessed, there was nothing in there about me but then as I flicked through the pages, an advert for a dance audition caught my eye. And my spirit lit up, I circled it and cut out the page. Not wasting any more time, I called the organizers for more information with the number attached to the ad. I was told to register online. Auditions would take place in twelve weeks. Finally, I had something to wake up to and get ready for each day.

This was good, a step in the right direction I thought.

There was only one problem—space. To really prepare, I needed a studio and my little flat wasn't it. Still, I was buzzing with happiness, I felt like a little girl in a candy store. This was the beginning I thought every other thing I had dreamed of would soon all fall in place I hoped. Like meeting the man of my dreams, sharing my first kiss, butterflies fluttering around in my tummy, going on dates just like I had seen in the movies. I knew in my heart that I was only fantasizing, but it was good to know that there was a possibility that these things could one day happen to me. I looked at the paper cut of the stranger I placed above my head and imagined sharing some kind of life with him one day. I knew it was impossible, but a girl could dream, I suppose. I also knew that this great escape of mine could blow up in my face one day if my father catches up with me or, God forbid, I ended up in the wrong place at the hands of his enemies. I shook my head; this was not the time for pessimism. Instead, I allowed my mind to wonder back to the stranger I met at the airport and I thought if I ever was in love, I would want it to be with a man that looked like him. My hands traced the picture of him on my wall, something about him that pulls me to him, but it made no sense at all.

I knew it was not normal to keep the picture of someone I barely knew, but it was the craziest thing that had ever happened to me. I had found myself looking for a little bit of him in every guy I've met since I came to London. It was beginning to feel like an obsession. if I knew where to find him, I would have gone looking for him. The worse that could happen was that he rejected me, but then I would know I did the best I could to understand what I was feeling.

I always thought falling in love was meant to be magical and not by having some crush on a stranger. I had looked forward to it so much while I was growing up and this was what I got! He might probably be at his house with a wife or a girlfriend. A man that looked that good would never be single and that made me sick to my stomach, the thought that he may belong to someone else.

"Great, this is the height of insanity," I muttered to myself.

If I had not been rebellious and I had stayed home and married Ashraf, I definitely would not be in this situation. But whatever life threw at me here was always going to be better than becoming a supressed wife or losing my freedom again.

I wished Louise was here, so I could tell her about it, she always knew what to do. I felt like I had just left one prison for another— a lesser, though; yet I still missed Louise, whom I had in the former. I was in desperate need to talk to someone, Louise and I made a pact not to communicate except it was absolutely necessary. I was not going to call her and bother her about this. All eyes and ears would be on her, mother knew how close we were, and she would not trust that Louise did not have anything to do with my escape.

****

At last, after two and a half months of applying for jobs, I got an email invite to an interview, I was so thrilled. It was a home accessories shop; I had sent my application to them about three weeks earlier for the position of sales assistant and had written a thesis on why I thought I was right for the job. I really did not know what to expect during the interview, but I was looking forward to it anyway. I was either going to get the job or not, I was hoping it was the former for me not only because I needed the money, I was eager to make new friends: I was tired of being lonely.

The interview was the next Monday at nine in the morning. I did not know what to expect, I did not know what questions would be asked, but I was not going to let anything worry me. I needed the job desperately, as my livelihood literally depended on it. I went online and did some research on what to expect in an interview.

Even though I was not expected to work, my mother ensured that I got the best education; I had a tutor that came to our home three times a week. I devoted four hours each day to learning. The English literature fascinated me the most, if I did not love dancing so much, I may have considered a career within that discipline. I picked out outfits from my new collection of dresses, placing them over my body to decide which one to wear. I wanted everything about me to be perfect. In the end, I decided on a shirtdress and a pair of tights.

At nine a.m. on Monday morning, I was taken to the staff room along with three other people, two of whom were women. Another woman came in and spoke to us briefly and welcoming us and telling us a little brief history of the business and the benefits of working for the company and then we were asked to wait until we were called one at a time to the manager's office for the interview. I looked around me, I was beginning to get nervous; I noticed that everyone else seemed relaxed and confident; I wished I had their confidence. I tried to distract myself, my palms were sweating and I wiped them on my dress. Then I got up and picked up a magazine from a pile to help defuse my nerves. A moment later, a young woman came in all smiles and called the only man amongst us to the manager's office. Fifteen minutes later, one of the two girls was called in and the next fifteen minutes, the last of the girls was called. None of them returned to the staff room, my heart was pounding. I did not even see the purpose of waiting to be interviewed because I could not control my fear of failing at this, everything depended on me getting this job. It was almost an hour since the last person was called and it rather looked like they had forgotten about me, I looked at the time and it was almost eleven. I placed the magazine on the table in front of me and then the same young woman that came to call the others appeared; she smiled at me and apologized for the long wait and off I went.

"Hello," she said, looking through what I supposed was my application form.

"Please sit down," she said, gesturing to the chair across her table. My heart was beating so fast; I was afraid she could hear it.

"Good morning," I said. She looked up at me and smiled, but then continued to go through *my* form and then she looked up and said,

"So according to what you wrote in your application form, you have no experience whatsoever in sales?"

"No, I don't," I replied.

"Did you read the requirements for this position before applying? If you had, we specifically asked that only people with at least two years' experience could apply for this role," she asked, looking at me for answers.

"Yes, I saw the specifications and it's true that I don't have any kind of experience, but I love home decor. If there is something, I am good at, it's putting accessories together to make any room beautiful. It's like an innate gift. To tell you the truth, I need a job and I figured if I could make you understand that and the fact that I would give more than it required to learn and be the best sales assistant, then I did not think it was fair that my lack of experience ruled out my chances completely. Hence, I took the risk and applied," I responded.

She kept quite as if she was still expecting me to say something more, so I continued, "I would have offered to work free, just to gain all the experience I lack if I did not need the money badly. but I do and I just hope that I catch a break. But I promise you, I will not let you down."

She sighed, "You must be wondering why you were invited for this interview." I nodded.

"Well I liked what you wrote, about why you should be employed. It might be a long shot, but we are willing to give you the training you need and the opportunity to prove to us that you are willing to work as hard as you wrote in your application form." I could not believe what I was hearing, was she saying what I thought I was hearing. I did my best to contain my joy even though I was bursting on the inside with joy. Was I hearing right, was I being offered a job? I could not believe it.

"You would be given two weeks of training, during which time we would teach you and see how fast you learn. However, you are going to be on a three months' probation," she was still speaking.

I heard what she said about being on probation, but none of that mattered. I now had a job and I was going to do everything to keep it.

"Your wages per hour is eight pounds and fifty pence; you get three pounds per day for sustenance, which will be paid every fortnight," then she began to read out the code of conducts, the dress code blah blah blah… I was just so hyped I had a job. She didn't have anything to worry about, I already knew I was going to be a model employee.

"If you still want the job, I need to know how soon you can start, because we want to start training you as soon as possible. How soon can you be available?" she asked, she did not understand that she just saved my life from boredom.

"Immediately," I blurted out, she smiled.

"Okay then, it's settled. Your training would begin tomorrow, nine a.m., we would have someone show you round and tell you all that you need to know and just teach you how things are done. Do you have any questions?" she asked.

I shook my head, "No, I don't, I just want to thank you so much for giving me this opportunity," I responded.

"The pleasure is all mine, welcome aboard, work as hard as you said you would and just enjoy being part of the team. If there's nothing else you want to know, I will see you tomorrow, be on time," the woman said.

"Thank you so very much, I am really grateful for the opportunity."

"You're welcome," she replied and I saw myself out.

I wondered what happened with the other candidates that came for the interview. Especially those two girls, they seemed like they knew it all, or maybe they offered more than one person the job. I went to bed very early; I knew I had to prove myself the next day and I wanted to be ready for it.

Chapter 11

I arrived early for work; the manager asked the lady that called us in for the interview to show me round, and also told me she would be the one in charge of my training for the next two weeks. Her name was Jane Mary Parkman. Jane did like to talk a lot, but she was one of the nicest and friendliest people that I had ever met in my life. She was very patient with me and we just hit it off. She was not bossy at all, which made me feel like I'm part of the team.

My first day was easy because Jane eased me in, and every nerve I felt before arriving disappeared quickly. I thought we got along quite easily, probably because we were somewhat close in age; I liked her dry sense of humour. She only worked part-time, but I could tell why she was given so much responsibility. She was very well organized, dependable and very effective. I was happy I had her as my mentor. Before I knew it, my two weeks training blew by, then a month passed, and I had gradually fallen into the pattern of how things were done. I worked in the back room and sometimes at the front house, replenishing stocks. As any first job went, I was enjoying what I was doing; I made sure I put in my best efforts always. I knew if I did my best, I had a greater chance at keeping my job. Jane helped a lot; she sang my praises to the bosses always.

We quickly became more than work colleagues and graduated into real friends. We lunched together at work, and during work hours, we attacked each duty we were given together. Work became fun and I was no longer lonely. Most times, Jane would drive me home after work, and sometimes, she would pick me up in the morning on her way to work.

My life was now like a well-oiled machine, every part working fine, apart from the times I regress a little for guilt of what I had done to my family. Other times, it was my crush over the stranger that made me unhappy. Else, life is beautiful.

Though, nothing I could do about the guilt of having run away, but I was no longer going to be controlled emotionally by some stranger I met for a few minutes. The first thing to do is destroy the paper cut I placed on my wall. It was time to stop fantasizing and start living in the real world.

Who knows, I could meet someone soon and start dating like Jane had hinted a few times and I knew that would help me focus on what was real before me and not my idea of what a man should be.

Two months passed since I started working and four months since I escaped to London.

While Jane and I were at lunch she suddenly said, "Sometimes, you seem very far away."

"What... what does that even mean? I don't understand." I said, bewildered.

"I mean, you are here, but your mind is elsewhere. You always have this uneasy look about you like you've slipped into another world. What's on your mind? You know a problem shared is a problem solved. Come on, spit it out," she persuaded. I half laughed.

"How do you know you can solve what's going on in my mind?"

"Well, you will never know if you don't tell me."

I rolled my eyes; the truth is I was dying to tell someone everything especially because I couldn't reach out to Louise, but I didn't want Jane to think I was insane.

"What is on your mind?" she asked again.

"Nothing, I am just enjoying life, you know I like to take it all in," I lied. I wasn't sure she bought the lie. Jane smiled and looked away from me for a moment and I was glad. Because had she kept poking, I could have spilled my gut.

"Do you have any plans this weekend?" she asked.

"What do you have in mind?" I questioned.

"Nothing really, I just felt it would be nice for us to do something together outside work, what do you think?" she asked.

I love the idea a lot, but since I started working, my weekends had become precious to me; I needed the time to practice my dance routine for the audition. She did not know that about me yet and I wondered if I should tell her. Before I had a chance to tell her, she said, "I was kind of playing with the idea of us spending the weekends in each other's houses. You come to mine and then we stay at yours the next weekend. My mum and brother would really like to meet you, I've spoken to them about you and I just want you to meet them if you don't mind."

"Jane, that sounds awesome. You know I would really love to meet your family, but I already have something planned for the weekend, can I meet them another time." I said, feeling terrible to have turned her down.

"Oh sure, another weekend then. I kinda sort of hoped you would be free to hang out, but it's fine." she said and then she eyed me and asked,

"So, what's this thing you got planned then?"

"Erm, it's um…"

"It's a guy, isn't it?" she cut in.

"A guy! I wish it was," I replied with a shy smile.

"You honestly want me to believe that there is no male involvement in you not wanting to hang out all weekend; I mean what else is more important at this time of your life. Come on look at you, you are hot and still single, why is that?" She joked.

"Jane, you are hilarious, look who's talking, I think you should ask yourself that question. I may have my reason for not dating what's your excuse? I don't see you with anyone either, so you can't really go there."

"Hmm, excuse eh, tell me what's this excuse a hot girl like you has not been snapped up?" Jane pressed.

"Nothing, there's nothing to tell. Look, there is no guy, no one has shown any interest in me. So, there you go, really Jane I wish there was, but no luck there."

She looked at me, eyebrow raised,

"Have you seen yourself in the mirror, Anna? You are gorgeous and really, maybe you aren't sending the right signal that lets hot guys know you are available for dating." She joked

We both shared a laugh.

"In all seriousness, Anna, not everyone gets to look like you do. Don't you want a boyfriend?"

"I do... but…"

"I knew there was a but somewhere there, but what?" Jane pushed.

"I feel like I just don't want to date for the sake of dating, I have to feel right with whoever I date, you know, it has to be right."

"I get what you mean, but if you never try, you know, you will never know for sure."

"Yeah I guess you are right, it's just as much as I want to dive in into this dating world, I just lack the desire to actually do it right now."

"Why? You are young and beautiful, now is the time for you to explore life and I mean men by that. There must be someone that you fancy. What about Dave? You have seen the way he looks at you, right? Well, all the boys at work seem to fancy you, anyway. Not like you've taken any notice of them."

"Really! That's news to me. Jane, I have not noticed anything like that. Right now, I'm just not attracted to anyone, I'm just going to concentrate on work and earning money. And if a guy should eventually come along, if it's to be then it will be. I am on a completely different thing at the moment."

She shook her head, "You sound like someone I know."

"Who's that, then?" I asked.

"My brother! He is also all about the work and the money and has no time for love. Well if you don't fancy anyone at work, you don't mind then that I kind of like Dave?" It was now my turn to raise brows.

"Dave. Dave Porter! I didn't know you liked him," I said in shock.

"He's alright, isn't he?" she enquired.

"Yeah, of course he is...he seems very nice, but I would never have put you together with him, you are always mean to him."

"I know, it's all a front, it's like a shield you know. I like him more than I should and I do not know if he even sees me at all. I feel like every male at work kind of see you as their ideal girl and I say that with no disrespect. But it's a little hard when you like someone and you don't know if they like you back."

"You know he is always hanging around us; seriously, Jane, is that not a clue to something? He may actually fancy you too, despite your meanness. I just can't get over your liking him, you are a brilliant actress, I really thought you hated that guy."

"Wow, have I really been that bad to him?" she asked. I nodded over my can of coke.

"So, what do you think I should do? It is frustrating not knowing if someone you like likes you back and, yes, I have noticed he comes around us a lot, but I have always thought it's because of you and I still think that. Every one of them guys fancy you, you seem to be the only one unaware of this fact, and I really think Dave Porter is one of them," she explained.

"You can't be sure that it's because of me he comes around, it could be because of you, I hardly speak to him, but he comes to you every day to ask questions that I sometimes think he surely knows the answers to, but he lets you insult him anyway. Go on, think about it, Jane, he likes you and I cannot believe I did not notice that until now."

Jane shook her head in disagreement. I sighed.

"I can't believe you are shaking your head. Jane, it's you he wants, not me and I think you should go for it, stop being mean to him and just tell him you like him." Her face lit up with excitement and nerves.

"You really think that I should tell him?"

"Mm-hmm!" I nodded.

"I will rather he tells me or at least give me a clue that he likes me." Jane opted.

"Well maybe if you stop pretending to be mean to him, he will actually come out plain with it."

"Yeah, I agree."

"And if he doesn't tell you, depending on how much you really like him, you might as well just… tell him how you feel." I suggested.

"You think so?"

"Yeah, but that depends on how much you really want him."

"Well, I don't know, I just can't control how I feel about him, I find that I think about him every time, even before I sleep. It's really crazy, but he's taking me over."

I laughed, half surprised, half amused. Jane's fix reminded me of my feelings with the stranger. Now I know I wasn't crazy to feel the way that I do.

"I know that feeling." I blurted out with an air of familiarity.

"You understand then what I'm going through."

"Totally." I said with a grin. "Nothing is stopping you. Just tell him you like him; you have nothing to lose and everything to gain." I reassured.

"Wait, what if he declines, what if he tells me he does not feel the same? Anna, I will literally die of shame?"

"Jane, you won't know until you ask, you clearly did put up this wall against him even when you knew you fancied the life out of him, so you have to make the effort now. He won't know your mind if you don't tell him. You know what, ask him out this weekend," I encouraged and suggested.

She placed her hands on her chest, as if to try to calm her beating heart. "I wouldn't know the first thing to say to him, Anna. My heart is beating so fast, I am that scared," she said.

I smiled, happy to see what it felt like for someone else to be so taken by another.

"Just go for it and be yourself, bring that wall down. You are one of the loveliest people I know and I am sure Dave sees that in all your bravado as well."

"You think so?" she asked.

To build her confidence, I said, "I know so."

"Alright then, I think I will just ask him out then and see what he says." "You better do," I encouraged.

Then she asked, "Ok, now over to you Anna, just now you said you knew how I felt. You may decide to say nothing again, but I think you have your own share of boy trouble and don't you dare deny it."

I could see where she was going with this.

"I don't need to tell you that we have become very close friends even though we met a few months ago."

"Mm-hmm, I agree."

"So why do you hide things from me?"

"I'm not... okay, it's just I didn't want to pull you into the madness in my head." I said in my defence.

"Try me and see, we just discussed my own madness. Just tell me, it's boy trouble, right?"

I swung my head from side to side and said. "It's half boy trouble and the other half has to do with family and I don't want to talk about that right now, if you don't mind."

"Okay, I will leave the family thing alone. Let's talk about the boy, who is he?"

"First of all, he is someone and no one at the same time."

I could see confusion etched on Jane's face.

"Okay, how so?"

"Erm, how can I say this?! you know when I said I was not attracted to anyone, that was not entirely true. There is someone that occupies my thought. It's almost like what you feel with Dave really, difference being you can go back to the store and ask Dave out, but I cannot because I do not know where he is, I only just met him briefly for all of five minutes and then he was gone. But the crazy thing is I think I fell for this man that I don't know, I can't stop thinking about him. I have tried, it's like a curse now. I scan every face I see for him, even you when you smile, it reminds me of when he smiled at me. So, you see it's stupid really, I told you it's madness." I said.

"Okay, that's unusual but it can happen. So at least tell me you know his name and we can google him."

I shook my head regrettably. "I don't know his name, I never thought he would leave such a lasting impression on me. I mean while we were together, I felt a strong spark; but my head space then was not clear. I wish I asked him his name but that's done now. What I need help with is forgetting him. I tell you Jane, I see his face in my dreams as well, it's that strong and I don't know if that means anything or it's just the build up from me fantasising about him that results in me seeing him in my dreams as well."

Jane stared, mouth agape.

"I told you, it is pathetic," I laughed nervously, mostly because I did not know what Jane was thinking.

"Anna, I don't know what to say, I mean the only way to forget him will be to start dating and you clearly aren't ready for that yet, but you should try if you want this to go away."

"Yeah, I thought so too but I can't force it, I'm not ready now, but hopefully soon. I think."

Jane shook her head, "I always knew it was boy trouble; but never in a million years did I think it would be this crazy yet an absolutely romantic situation. Does this really happen to people, this love at first sight thing? Who knows Anna, maybe he's in the same predicament as you?" Jane laughed.

I rolled my eyes. "I don't think so. You didn't see him: he is gorgeous, he is probably married with kids or in a very loving relationship. And we met in the US, so what chance do I have really."

"Not that it matters, the probability of you seeing him again is one in a billion at the moment."

"Thanks!"

"No, I'm a realist. Just saying, you just said he is probably married, and doesn't live here in the UK."

"I don't know for sure where he lives, we met at the airport."

"That means he could be anywhere in the world as we speak."

"Mm-hmm." I agreed

"I don't want to tell you to forget him, I love a good love story but, in this case, we don't know much about him, we can't search for him online. So, you know you must try to forget him, right?"

"I know, but I don't want to, if I'm really being honest. I don't want to get involved with someone else and then he turns up again in my life."

"I understand, but the chances of that happening is too slim. That's if any at all. My advice? You can't hold on to what you don't have. You must do your best to forget him. you are so beautiful. Make room in your heart for someone else."

I smiled. "You're right. I will try."

I got up, we had chatted about men and love all through our one-hour break. She got up as well and we began walking back to the store.

"Wow, that's something…I don't even know what to say to that," Jane responded.

"I told you, pathetic, right?" I said.

"No, not pathetic at all, I mean it is… well it is somewhat sad because you clearly are taken by this person. And I could feel your passion the way you spoke about him. Yet it's like you guys have been thrown apart. I guess if you are meant to be together, fate would always bring you two back together; but for now, live your life Anna," Jane said.

I shrugged and smiled "I can't promise anything, but I will try. Thanks for listening and not being judgemental." I smiled.

She pulled me closer and our arms interlocked as we walked back to work. We felt closer than we had ever been.

"So, what's this other thing you have planned for the weekend?"

"Oh! I have this dance audition coming up in a few weeks, I have not really prepared for it because of work. I need the money coming in from work, but I also need time as well to rehearse. But the problem I'm facing is space for me to really get into it, but you know I must manage somehow." I tried to explain.

"Wow, you never cease to surprise me. I never knew you could dance; what type of dance are you into? Don't tell me—street dance? I will just faint, Anna," she said.

I laughed. "What's wrong with street dance?" I asked.

"Nothing, I think it's fantastic and anyone that can do it is really gifted. I can't dance to save my life. That's why I'm in awe of you, I am as stiff as they come. My mother wasted her money for years thinking they could get some kind of rhythm out of me and, believe me, Anna, that was a massive disaster. Can I come watch you rehearse? Please say yes?" she requested and pleaded.

"I don't know, I haven't really come up with a proper routine yet, I am still working on it. And have you seen where I live? There is no room for me to practice let alone entertain an audience."

She was quiet, we were almost in the store now, I could tell she wasn't too happy that I didn't invite her over, hence, I quickly added, "Don't worry, when I am a bit confident with my routine and I feel a little ready, I wouldn't mind so much, if you are still interested."

"I will hold you to it, Anna," she said.

"I know you won't let it go. And by the way, it's contemporary ballet, not street dance."

"Hmm, all the more, reason for me to come get entertained. I am sure you would do well."

"Ah, thanks. I hope so too."

Jane asked if I wanted her to take me home while we were in the stock room. Dave Porter was there when she asked, and he surprised us by asking if he could get a lift too. I was shocked and happy he had the confidence to ask her. I was clearly right, he liked her too. Jane suddenly became clumsy; she dropped the stock she was holding. I almost laughed aloud with joy, but I did not want her embarrassed. It was a little awkward, because Dave was waiting for Jane to say yes and she was still in shock, he had summoned up the courage to ask her for a ride.

I quickly stepped in, because, for some reason, Jane became tongue tied,

"Yes, Dave, we'll let you know when we are ready to go," I said.

He looked at her for confirmation.

She nodded and said, "Yeah, what she said," Jane finally found the use of her tongue.

"Okay, thanks, Jane; I'll wait outside for you then," Dave said to her.

We waited for him to be out of hearing range before speaking.

"What was that? Did you put him up to this?" Jane asked.

I looked at her, surprised that she thought I had anything to do with it. "No! I am as shocked as you are, but I told you, he likes you, now you see. Listen, I am not going to let you take me home today. In fact, I am not going to join you guys, you two need the space and I am not going to be the third wheel," she was still in shock.

"No Anna, do not do this to me! You can't leave me alone with him, I wouldn't know what to say to him. Please, Anna, you have to come with us," she pleaded.

"No, I am not going to do that, this is your chance. Remember, you were going to ask him out. Listen Jane, if you feel you cannot go for it now, just so you know, don't say anything yet. And, you just be yourself. Drop that wall you have built to keep him out. He

103

is trying: he usually goes home with Faisal; so, for him to want a lift from you...? I'm just saying..." I tried to put it in perspective for her.

"My hands are shaking, I don't know what to do, or say!" Jane confessed.

"You have to help me."

"Sorry, Jane, I can't come. Now is your chance to see if you guys flow, ask him what he does when he's not at work, you know stuff like that see if you are compatible."

"Okay, I will." She smiled

"See, you are smiling already. You've got this. Just call me and tell me all about it later." I said.

We quickly finished what we were doing and logged out. Jane ran into the bathroom to freshen up. I waited until she got out. We walked outside together to an awaiting nervous, but confident looking Dave. We hugged and said our goodbyes and I left them to be together.

Chapter 12

Robert PhiliP Parkman.

I drove straight to the family house from work. I did not need to go back home for clothes, I had my work emergency travel bag at the office and I had a date with Katherine later at evening. I did not really know why she was back in my life, especially at this time, but it was clearly what the doctor recommended.

When I got to my mum's, Jane was already waiting for me. She had actually called me three different times today to confirm if I was still coming. I did not blame her, they were used to me cancelling on them, but not this time, I needed them in my life.

"Wow! Rob, you were not joking, you really came," Jane acted surprised to see me.

"I told you I would come, didn't I? You've got me for a while now, little sis," I said as I made my way from the hallway to the stairs. "Where's mum?" I asked.

"She went out. You know what she's like every time you visit. I just got back from work, I didn't meet her at home too, but she sent me a text saying she's buying some groceries, you know what that means. Don't worry she will soon be here.

"Hmm, I don't know what that means?" I said as I walked up the stairs to my old room.

"Well, it means she wants to celebrate the return of her lost son," Jane joked. I smiled while I heard her laugh as I entered into my room. I dropped my bag on the floor and looked round; it had been years since I last came up here. Each time I had come around, I never climbed up the stairs. The room was exactly how I left it ten years ago, clean, but nothing had changed.

Mum really had a hard time dealing with change; if she had her way, Dad would still be alive, and all her children would be living with her under the same roof. There was a knock and I knew who it was already.

"What do you want, Jane?" I asked. I laid on the bed and kicked off my shoes.

"I have just been to the kitchen, and I saw a platter of someone's favourite foods."

"You mean me? Ah, mum likes to stress too much. I have to go somewhere later, I am meeting an old friend, I wouldn't be able to do dinner." I knew they were both not going to like that, but if I ate, I would not have any room to eat what Katherine was preparing.

"Mum is definitely not going to like that. You know mum, she likes to fuss over you. You need to go downstairs and see for yourself. The food in there would feed an army, I am not exaggerating." We both laughed. I didn't need to see it to believe it. And as bad as I knew, she would feel if I didn't eat, I wanted to run out to Katherine's before she came back.

My mother was a good cook, but she did this each time I came around.

"Did she prepare it all herself or did the chef help her?" I asked Jane.

She shrugged. "I don't know, I told you I just got back from work. You should call her now and tell her you already have plans for dinner."

"Yeah, I don't know, I think I will stay, have a few bites and then leave.

She has gone through all that trouble because of me, I will hate to disappoint her."

Jane hopped towards me and then sat on my bed.

"So, who are you having dinner with, eh?" she probed.

"Erm… no one you know," I dared not mention that I met their beloved Katherine. They will use it as an opportunity to push their agenda.

"Okay, so what's brought this on then?" she asked.

"What's brought what on?" I asked as I got up from my bed. I felt her eyes following me. I picked up the bag I brought with me and started to unpack my clothes.

"This change in you, I mean we hardly see you, but here you are moving back home. I mean, don't get me wrong, I love having you here, even though we both know you will be gone soon, I just want to know why?" Jane probed.

I smiled, I tried not to think of why I left my own house, I could not tell her the truth, no matter what happened.

"Must there be a big reason? I just fancy a change of scenery. You worry too much, Jane; and you know if you continue to make my problems yours you will age before you can tackle your problems." I joked.

"Not funny. Fine if you don't want to tell me, but don't think mum won't ask you the same question."

"Hmm, and I will tell her what I just told you."

"You mean the lies you just fed me with?" Jane said raising her brow

"Come on now, don't be like that, I'm not lying to you. You know when I visited Alex, I just enjoyed his company and so I thought I don't see you two as much, but if you don't want me here, I could go back."

"Don't be ridiculous! Of course, I want you here, I just worry about you, that's all. If you say you are fine, then I guess I just have to believe you." "Jane, I'm your big brother, you don't need to worry about me."

"I know. But I do, I can't help it. You're my brother and I love you. I don't want you in any trouble. Are you in some kind of trouble, Rob?"

I left what I was doing and sat down next to her.

"No, Jane, I am not in any kind of trouble. I have been working too much and I have not been here for you and mum. I want to change that. I want to change the way I have been living my life and I cannot just say it without doing something about it. That's why I'm here, so, you need to stop worrying so much about me. I know you can't help it, but you need to live your life."

She smiled.

"Do you have a boyfriend?" I asked her, she looked away shyly, "Don't get all shy now; you do the same to me. Seriously, are you dating anyone?" She laughed nervously and got up from the bed.

"I don't know, maybe, I don't know, it's still early days, but there is this person I like, and he asked me out today. I am really looking forward to it. So maybe soon I may have a boyfriend."

"Yeah, good for you, you look very happy, so you must really like him then?"

"Yes, I do"

"Well, I hope it all goes well for you and I hope he knows you have big brothers that are ready to do anything for you if he ever messes you about."

"Robert, stop, you are making me blush. I am out of here." She left my room; it felt good to know what was happening in her life.

I could hear my mother downstairs announcing her arrival; I changed from my work clothes into something more casual. My dinner with Katherine was at seven and I did not want to keep her waiting. I was actually looking forward to it; I went downstairs, kissed my mother and sat by the kitchen island. She was fussing about, I wanted to let her know that I could not stay through dinner, but before I got the chance, she presented me with this full plate of delicacies. I heard Jane chuckling somewhere behind me.

Then, she said, "Mum, I thought I told you, Robert already has plans this evening and he can't eat all of that," Jane protested.

"It's alright," I said, "I will just eat a little. Mum, don't worry about it." I wanted to make my mother happy. I picked through the food, it was delicious and I had to restrain myself from filling my stomach, I had to leave room for Katherine's food.

"So, where are you going then?" Mum asked.

"I have a meeting with an old friend," I replied.

"Is this friend you are meeting for dinner a man or a woman?" mum asked again.

I looked up from my plate. "What an odd question, what's that got to do with anything?" I questioned.

"Nothing, I just want to know. Jane said something the other day, but never mind. Eat your food, Robert."

I wondered what she was getting at; I looked at Jane who acted as if she did not hear what mum just asked me. There would be time later to talk about it, I thought. I got up and mum picked up my plate before I could do so.

"Are you leaving now?" Jane asked, I nodded as I wiped my mouth with a napkin.

"I forgot to tell you, there is someone I want you to meet," Jane said.

"Seriously, Jane, leave it out. I thought I told you, we are not doing this again." I said calmly, but I tried to be clear I did not want any more set up dates from her.

"Rob, please, I know I said I wouldn't set you up again, but I think you should meet this person and if you decide she's not for you then I promise not to meddle again."

"How many times have I heard that from you... Jane? It's in your nature and you can't change. Stop making promises, you're never going to keep your word."

"Please, Robert, just give me this one chance and if, when you come back, you're not happy, then this would never happen again."

"Hmm. Okay, I know I am going to regret this, but after I do this, you must back off. You can never do this again, agreed?"

"Okay! Agreed, I am so happy, I could kiss you right now. You will not regret this one, I promise. How about Friday evening, are you free?" Jane asked.

"Yeah, do what you have to do, I have to go now. See you later, mum," I said quickly. I couldn't believe that I just agreed to another set up from Jane, was I that desperate? I got in my car and punched in Katherine's postcode. I sent her a text after lunch and she texted me her address.

The course of the evening and my date with Katherine seemed to have made an impact. I had not thought about the girl from the airport. I did not know if it was because I had not really had the time to live in my head as I usually did, but I felt normal again. Which reassured me whatever I was doing was working.

Chapter 13

At Katherine's

As I drove to Katherine's, I started to doubt my decision to have dinner with her at her home this soon. We only just met after such a long time, I was not sure what to expect and how far I was willing to go with her if things took a different turn. As much as I knew I needed to be in a relationship. I did not know if Katherine was that girl for me, we had both done this before and I ended up hurting her.

I parked in front on her house, switched off the engine and sat in the car. For some reason, I did not feel like going in anymore. That buzz I had earlier that pushed me into wanting to see her had suddenly died down and was replaced with guilt.

What I was feeling guilty for I did not know, perhaps, it was because for me I knew this was not going to go anywhere. I wanted to spin the car round and just go back home. Although, when I saw her earlier today, she made me feel like she was over what happened between us years ago, but I didn't feel comfortable anymore about returning into her life. I did not think the idea of someone else obsessing over me while I tried to fight my own secret obsession was the antidote to the problem I had, even though it looked like this was the only thing that might work. I was about to start the engine and spin the car round, when the front door opened. She stood by the doorway and beckoned to me to come in; I could not leave any longer.

She was wearing a red halter dress that clung to her body revealing her curves, with a split that ran all the way to her upper thigh and a red matching heel. She looked hot and sexy. This wasn't right; I wanted to see beyond the sex appeal, but it was difficult.

"How long are you going to sit there for?" she asked.

I sighed and took a long deep breath; I picked up the champagne and flowers I had purchased earlier before getting out of the car. As I walked closer to her, she shot out her hips revealing more of her skin. I looked up at her face instead. This wasn't the Katherine I knew before.

"Don't tell me you were getting cold feet," She said.

"Don't be silly," I replied.

"Then come on in... I don't bite." I kissed her on both cheeks and followed her into the hallway.

"These are for you," I presented her with the flower and champagne. She took it and buried her nose and half her face in the flowers.

"Thank you, Robert, these are gorgeous."

I smiled and followed her to her beautifully decorated open planned living room with a well-lit wooden fire. I could smell the aroma of food coming from the kitchen.

"Please sit anywhere you like and make yourself comfortable, I won't be a minute." She said as she went in to the kitchen to check on what she was cooking.

The TV was on with hardly any volume and there were candles lit all around the living room. The setting was a little too romantic for my taste. She returned moments later with a glass of wine and sat next to me, her dress leaving more of her thighs exposed. I tried not to look.

"The food would soon be ready, I have been slaving all day, prepare yourself to be impressed," she joked.

"Really, I can tell, the deliciousness has over-powered me," I said.

"I am hoping it lives up to its hype. No pressure really," she said.

"Don't worry about it; I am sure it will be fine, as long as it is eatable," I said to ease her, it was clear she was nervous. I did not know why, I used to be the nervous wreck before and now I had suddenly been relaxed and I wanted her to be relaxed as well. She leaned towards me, grazing me a little with her arms and revealing more of her cleavage as she picked the remote control and switched off the TV.

"There, no distractions," she said, smiling. I could smell her seductive perfume; everything seemed staged and perfectly placed. There was a sudden tension building up and it made me a little uncomfortable because I felt like she invited me to play a role. To ease the tension, I decided to engage in small talks.

"I like your décor; did you do it yourself or you used some help?" I asked.

"Yes, I did, when I bought the house, it was only half way to completion. So, I had it customized to my own liking," She explained.

"Hmm, very creative. I really like it a lot," I said as I downed the wine she gave me earlier; I felt her eyes on my wine glass.

"Yeah, me too, I love being at home. I mean what's the use of a beautiful house if you are never in it? More wine?" she asked.

"Sure, why not… so what do you do these days?" I asked, still trying to make small talks.

"I work with a law firm. You always knew I was going to law school right? My dream is to start my own firm one day and I think that should happen very soon."

"Good, I love that you are doing so well. Who knows, when you start your firm, maybe I will employ your services," I said as she smiled and poured herself more wine.

"So, I hear you took over your Dad's business. And, if my sources are good, I hear business is booming." she said.

"You have been spying on me, then," I responded.

"Quite the opposite, actually. um… my mum, she tells me everything about you and she says that your mum updates her," she tried to explain.

"Ah, I should have known," I chuckled. I was more relaxed than I was earlier. I tried not to think about the reasons I thought she might have invited me over for and started to enjoy her company.

"We can always count on our mothers to do just that," she laughed.

"I have forgotten how pretty you look when you laugh," I had said it before; yet I realized that she could mistake my compliments for a flirty advance, but I could not take it back. There was a little silence and then she spoke.

"Thanks. Let's gets something to eat, shall we?"

"Yeah, after you," I said.

"I made scallops, tomato with avocado for starter. And, if I recall, you used to love it back in the day?" she inquired, I smiled politely.

"Yeah, I still do, you have the memory of an elephant," I commented.

"I have been taking a cooking class, so in a way, I am experimenting on you. But, in a good way. I hope you like it."

"I hope I do too." I had a bite and it was surprisingly very good.

"This is very delicious, it's really good. Well done, I am actually impressed," I said, taking another mouthful.

"I was hoping to impress, thank you. I am glad you like it."

The starter was good, but I did not want to eat too much and I knew there were two more courses coming. She did not eat, she just watched as I ate, I pretended as if it did not bother me. I took a few more mouthfuls; there was only so much I could eat in one day. I ate more than I wanted at home to make my mother happy. And although this starter was lovely, I just could not get any more of it in me.

"Katherine, this is so good, but believe me, if you want me to eat any more of the delicacies that you've painstakingly made, I can't and must not eat any more than I already have," she giggled,

"It's okay, if I remember correctly, you used to have such an appetite. What's happened to you?" I did not want to tell her I had dinner at home before coming.

"Yeah, that's true, it comes and it goes, I blame everything on work these days," I said.

"Alright then, are you ready for another?" she asked.

I would have preferred not to eat anymore, but I hate to disappoint.

"I made lamb curry, this one is my specialty and you would love this one."

"I have no doubt. Not after that beautiful starter," she came back with two plates of curry, curry was one of my favourite meals and she had not forgotten.

"Thank you, you are spoiling me, Katherine. This looks and smells amazing," I said.

She smiled, "You remember, you used to take me out every Friday night for curry. It was too spicy for me, I didn't like it, but with time my taste buds adjusted and I started to enjoy it too because you loved it so much."

"I never knew you didn't like the spices, you never said. I took you with me because I thought you loved it too," I said, surprised.

"You didn't have a clue and back then, I was so in love with you. I would do just about anything to please you," she said. I stopped eating; she was looking down at her plate. I did not know what to say.

"I wish you would have told me, Katherine, I would never make you do anything you don't like; you know me."

"I know, Robert, it's in the past. I was young and back then, you were my world and I just loved being where you were, but look, it paid off. I love curry now."

"Well, I am happy I had something to do with you loving curry so much that you cook it this good."

She smiled shyly, we both ate in silence, but every now and then I felt her eyes on me and if this were any other girl apart from Katherine, I would not mind so much. However, Katherine loved me in the past and I was not completely sure she had moved on. This night made it clear to me, I didn't want to be back here again, everything was lovely, but I didn't get any sparks from her, it had been a good distraction, but that's all it was. I definitely did not have any room for desert; I put down my cutleries and wiped my mouth with a napkin.

"Katherine, this has been lovely to say the least, but I don't think I can eat anything more. I just don't have the room," I tried to explain, "Let me help you with the dishes, it's the least I can do after all the trouble you went through," I offered.

"No, I wouldn't dream of it. You are my guest. Please go back to the living room and relax, I will join you shortly."

I got up and sat back on the sofa, I knew I had to leave soon. I sensed a vibe from her and for some reason, I just did not want to fuel or encourage any kind of flirtatiousness. She came over and sat closer to me this time, I tried to relax and stop my mind from overthinking things.

We were both quiet, I did not know what was going on in her head, but I was tired. It had been such a long day.

"Are you seeing anyone at the moment?" she asked unexpectedly. I took my time before answering the question, because I knew if I said I was not seeing anyone, that may kindle her interest in me.

"No, I am not dating. My life as you've heard is all about work, but I am hoping that that would change soon," I said. That did not quite come out as I wanted.

She smiled, "You've always been picky, Robert. I hear you've not been in anything serious with anyone since we broke up?" she asked, enjoying the fact that she was my last long-term girlfriend.

"I wouldn't quite put it like that, I have been with a few girls, but I haven't had the time to commit to them. However, I think when the right person comes along, I would make the time. I used to think it would be impossible, but my mind has changed recently, I am hopeful the right person for me is out there." She laughed nervously,

"Or in here with you, I mean I am not trying to put you in an uncomfortable position, but don't you think the universe is trying to tell us something? I mean, the last time I saw you, I was eighteen, and you were nineteen. What were the odds of us meeting now when we are both mature, single, successful? Sometimes, what you are looking for is actually right under your nose."

I was not paranoid; she was up to something and she was not wasting any time either. I shifted in my seat uncomfortably; I did not want to do this again, not with her. "Katherine, we had our time, it didn't work out. I am not positive it would now. I mean, what has changed really? We are still the same people."

"I know, but we are mature now. We can make each other happy. You knew me when I had my dreams and I knew you before you took over your family business. Our families know and love each other and I adore them. If we try, I mean really, really try, we could be happy." She placed her hands on my thighs, and quickly moved on top of me. I could almost hear her heart beating, as she leaned into me and hot air from her mouth greeted my face. I didn't like this whole situation. She was moving too fast, what she said made sense and if I had not encountered that girl at the airport, I may have even considered her proposal.

She moved her hands over my thighs to arouse me and placed her lips on mine lightly at first. I did not respond, but her lips moved over mine again and then she whispered, "Tonight, does not have to mean anything serious, we are both adults, let's just have fun together." Then, she resumed kissing me, and I could not fight the urge building in me any longer and I began to kiss her back. We were all over each other within seconds and then, "I've always wanted you, Rob, I have been thinking about doing this with you for so long…" she whispered, and something clicked in me as soon as she said those words: the face of the girl from the airport popped into my head and I just did not want Katherine touching me any longer. I felt like I was cheating. I pulled away from her.

"I am sorry, Katherine, I can't do this. I don't want to do this with you, I shouldn't be here, I have to go."

"What is wrong, Rob? Please don't stop!" she whispered. She moved her hands to the back of my neck and tried to pull me closer, but there was nothing she could do to get me to reciprocate her affection.

"Katherine, please stop. I told you we can't, I can't do this with you, it's never going to work, believe me, I know," I tried to explain the best I could.

"Rob, please don't do this. Just relax and let me make you happy," she pleaded, but I could not do it. I did not want to be there any longer.

"Katherine do not do this. Please, I can't. I will only hurt you again, I have to go."

She looked at me in shock, she was still on top of me and I didn't want to push her away from me. I was waiting for her to get off me, so I could leave. She got up and walked away from me. I did the same, only I was heading for the door.

I paused by the door, turned towards her and said. "Katherine, I am sorry. You were such a good host and this situation, this awkwardness is all on me, you've done nothing wrong. I'm sorry I can't make this work. Goodbye, Katherine!" she did not turn to face me, and I knew why: I turned her down again and she was embarrassed. I knew this was going to happen and I should have prevented it, but it's done now and we both knew now that we could never be in each other's lives again.

Chapter 14

I quickly got out of her house and into my car and drove back to my mum's. I had planned to go straight to bed, but my mum was waiting up for me.

"Robert, I didn't expect you back so soon. Tell me, how is Katherine?"

"What? How did you know where I went?" Then, I remembered Katherine mentioning her mother always getting updates about my life from my mother and I was not surprised anymore.

"Carol told me, you and Katherine ran into each other today."

"So?"

"Oh Rob, it's not a secret, she told her mum that you were coming around for dinner, why do you think I did not get annoyed when you left dinner early?" I rolled my eyes, was there nothing that was personal to these women? Or they just can't help it. I was happy I did not sleep with Katherine. Or that would have made the headlines for sure.

"Well, she is fine, I guess you already know that," I said sarcastically, but she ignored me.

"Hmm, so what is happening with the two of you? You know she's alright. That girl, she will make a good wife. She is a lawyer now, very respectful and from a very good family; you two could make a good couple if you put your heart into it. Carol says she's never stopped asking after you."

I got out a drink from the fridge and listened to my mum go on about how perfect Katherine was for me. I knew at that point I had to tell her to stop dreaming of a union that will never happen.

I just can't settle for less. I wanted to be with someone that kept my heart racing each time I saw her face or even thought about her. She had to be someone I never wanted to be without, someone I would not want to spend a day without. That was what love was and that was what it meant to me. I knew it may never happen the way I wanted it, but I'm not one to settle for low. Plus, I didn't get where I am in business by accepting mediocrity.

I should not have gone to Katherine's house in the first place; it was a stupid idea. I wanted to be distracted from my own thoughts and I ended up hurting her again. I was lost in my thoughts; I had not realized my mum was still talking.

"Seriously, Robert. Tell me, why are you so particular? I know I have asked you this same question time and time again. It is just that I still do not get it. What is it you are looking for in a woman? You cannot know if you do not even try them. If you don't give one person a chance to get to really know her, how would you know what it is you are after?"

I took a quick gulp of the drink. "Hmm, you've got a point, mum," I said, yawning. I agreed with her, so that I didn't have to listen to her lecture.

"Mum, I am very tired, I agree with everything you said. I will have a think about it, but I have to go to bed now. It's been such a long day and I have serious meetings tomorrow."

"Okay darling, just, you know, think about it, Robert." I nodded and kissed her on the cheek.

"I will. Goodnight, mum."

"Good night, darling."

A week flew by since I moved back to my mum's and each time, I was alone with my mother all our conversations had ended and started with Katherine. I was fed up and regretting the decision to stay at her house. She just would not give it a rest. In addition, Jane constantly reminded me of the date I was supposed to go on, the list was endless. I was living in my worst nightmare, but the irony was that their constant naggings kept me normal. I hardly thought of, you know who, but in a weird way, I missed not thinking of her and this imaginary world I had built up in my head where we both live in. However, it was fine to be finally back to normal. On occasion, when Jane and Mum's nagging became unbearable, I used my memories of her as an escape, which was very ironic that the very reason I moved in with my mum was now my only escape.

On Friday morning, while I was getting dressed for work, Jane was in my room to remind me of the date she had set up for me. Then, on my way to work, I got another reminder from her as though we had just not spoken about it. At noon, she sent me another text and another and then another, if she was not my sister and if we had not had a deal, I would have gladly missed the date. Nothing was worth this much hassle, but if I do not go, she will use it as an opportunity to keep bothering me with these strangers she brings into my life.

There was no escaping this date, and even through my business meetings, my phone kept vibrating with reminders. The date was for six in the evening, I had a late business meeting planned for that time, but I asked my secretary to cancel and reschedule. I hardly cancelled my meetings, but I also promised myself to be more sociable. So, for the very last time, I would indulge Jane, go and see if all the stress I had had from her since I moved in with them was worth it.

I parked my car in front of the restaurant, the time was six minutes to six and I was early. I never wanted to keep anyone waiting, I scanned round the room, not that I knew who I was supposed to be meeting. Everyone seemed very engaged with one thing or the other. I wondered how I was meant to know whom my date was, Jane never told me what to look for and I never asked. I went over to the bar and sat down.

The bar man came over. "Whiskey on the rocks, please," I said. I looked at my watch, it was now six o clock. The waiter placed my drink in front of me. I nodded in acknowledgment, lifted the glass to my mouth and took a sip. I thought about the comments my mother had been making since I moved in with her,

"If Katherine is not good for you and all these other ladies are not what you want, perhaps you are the problem. Robert, you need to have a serious think about what you want. Life is not as complicated as it may seem to you." My mother was right; there must be something wrong with my approach to this situation. I had always believed that I was created to love one person. What if I was wrong about that? And we aren't made for just one special person and all we need to do is make do and try our best to be happy. I took another swig from my drink. The issue I had was that I had actually not given anyone a chance and if I did not, how could I be sure of anything? I looked around and saw a beautiful woman walking into the restaurant. I took a deep breath, but she walked past me and into the arms of her date. I smiled. I checked my watch again; the time was fifteen pasts six. I decided I would leave after my drink.

"*Be patient,*" I heard myself say. I downed my drink and asked the waiter for another. I was not a big drinker, but for some reason, I was nervous about tonight's date. The waiter served me another round, I held the glass in my hand and twirled the content around the glass, and then I heard someone say my name.

Chapter 15

I looked up from my drink and for a moment, I was not sure if I was meant to recognize the person before me.

"Robert Parkman? Are you Robert Parkman?" the man asked again.

I cleared my throat, "Whose asking? I am sorry, do I know you?" He pulled a stool and sat next to me; I was still confused. I raced through my brain, I was trying to think of where I may have seen him before or even if I had seen him before today. I had met many people through business, but I could not place his face.

The man beckoned on the waiter, "I will have whatever he is having," he said. I looked at him through the corner of my eyes and saw that his eyes were on me. I quickly looked away.

Then he spoke. "Have you been waiting long?" he asked. I was confused; I looked at him, my eyes narrowed as I focused on him. I did not understand what was going on. Then a red headed woman walked in and strolled towards the bar, I heaved a sigh in relief.

Then he continued, "There was so much traffic and of course it takes time to dress up and look just right," he said.

"Sorry what?" I said, moving my eyes from the woman to him,

"Do I know you? I do not believe we have met before, but why are you telling me this. I am actually waiting for someone and I think she has arrived." He followed my eyes to the woman that was now talking with one of the waiters.

"Listen, allow me to introduce myself, I see you haven't been told anything about me."

"Sorry, excuse me," I said, completely confused. He was distracting me from the woman; I needed to know if she was the one, I had been waiting for. I noticed he was still looking at me.

"If this is about business, I am sorry, but we can't do this now. Make an appointment with my office," I said refocusing my attention on the redheaded woman. She was led to a table, I got up, brought out my wallet to pay and then I saw a man approach her table, shortly afterwards they embraced. I looked down and then at the man and then I understood what was happening. I did not want to believe, but his earlier conversations now made sense somehow.

"Are you…" I refused to believe that Jane would set me up with a man, this must be a joke. I laughed softly; he then got up and faced me.

"It's clear we've both been misunderstood, I was of the impression you were like me, I see now what you were expecting…" he looked from me to the woman now enjoying the company of her date. "Someone of a different gender."

"I am sorry you wasted your time; this is very awkward for me and I don't mean to be rude, but I have to go now. However, don't leave on my account, your drinks are on me," I said. I beckoned at the waiter and dropped the money on the bar. "Please get him whatever else he wants, that should cover it," I told him. The man smiled and sat back down. I was fuming inside; I could not wait to get home and have a word with Jane. Why would she do this? Was this all a joke, to think she messed with my day with her constant reminders? I had never given her a reason to believe I was attracted to men. What was she playing at, setting me up with a man, she had definitely gone too far now with this?

I pulled into the driveway and hurried inside; my mum was in the kitchen. "Hey, Rob, how was your date? You're back early, how did it go?"

"Did you know about it? Were you in on Jane's games?" Where is she?" I was still fuming,

"Jane, get down here now?"

"Calm down, Robert, what happened? Why are you so upset, what games are you referring to? Robert, look at me? Robert, wait, talk to me. Tell me what happened?" My mum was very concerned. I knew then that she did not know about it.

"Ask your daughter, she will tell you everything." I marched up the stairs to Jane's room. I had never been this upset with her before today; she crossed the line and I was going to put her in her place. Without knocking I opened her door, she was on the phone with someone; I had to calm down, I wanted to snatch the phone from her so I could have her attention. She hung up immediately when she saw me, I could see in her eyes, she knew what she had done didn't go down well with me, but I needed her to explain why she thought it was cool to embarrass me that way. I remained quiet; I wanted an explanation for what she did. Finally, she spoke. "I am guessing that I am in trouble?" she said timidly. I would have laughed it off, but I did not find it funny and I needed her to know it was not okay. My mum joined us, she walked past me and into Jane's room.

"What is happening with the two of you? Jane, what did you do? Why is Rob this upset with you?"

"He didn't like who I set him up with, I may have taken it too far, but I just thought you needed a little push, you know. I didn't do it to harm you."

"Are you for real?! Seriously, do you think that was okay?"

"What are you too arguing about, will someone fill me in properly?" I looked at Jane to explain to my mother what she did, but she was quiet.

"She set me up with a man, that date that she had been disturbing me to go to all week, was so I could meet with some random man ... I can't even begin to tell you how upset I am with you..."

"Jane, why did you do that to your brother, why did you do that?" my mother cut in.

"I don't know, I sincerely thought I was helping. I was just exploiting all avenues on your behalf and I thought if you didn't like women, perhaps you liked men and maybe if I pushed you into a situation like this one, you would then admit the truth to yourself."

It occurred to me that this was my fault, I had given her too much liberty to interfere and think that she had a say in my life. But that would not be tolerated anymore.

"That was wrong, you should never have done that. You crossed the line there and you need to apologize to your brother," mum said.

"I'm sorry, Rob, my intention was not to cause you any embarrassment," Jane said.

"I want you to stop, this time I mean it. No more meddling from you; I am an adult, if I want to be with anyone no matter what gender, I will do that myself, that goes for you too mum! I always knew I would regret coming back here and I was right. If you did say to me that you did it for a laugh, I would understand, but you actually believed it. Stop poking your nose where it doesn't belong, do you understand?" I said with a firm voice. Jane looked away and said nothing to me.

"I said, do you understand?"

"Yes, Robert. I understand. I am sorry, I did not mean to upset you," she started to look around her room, anywhere, but my face… it reminded me of when she was younger, and she got into trouble. I suddenly felt silly for yelling at her so much, maybe I was too harsh with her, but how else was she going to learn to stop meddling.

I was done with living with them, but I did not want to leave immediately. Deep down, I knew she meant well and even though I had originally wanted them as a distraction for the craziness that was going on with me before. I had come to accept and learn to deal with the crazy feelings I had for the girl I met at the airport. Living with that feeling felt a lot saner in comparison.

I packed up my bag after the Sunday dinner and Jane went on a date shortly after dinner. I wanted to be gone before she arrived; I did not want her to think I made the decision to leave because I was still upset with her and at the same time, I did not want her begging me to stay. Mum was not happy when I told her I was going back, but she always knew this had been a temporary arrangement.

"Robert, you know she's very sorry. It was a silly thing to do, but you have got to understand her reasons, she adores you and she was just looking out for you. You've only just come here; I mean, it's not even been two weeks and you are already leaving!"

"Mum, I told you this was going to be temporary. I never said how long that would be. I have enjoyed staying here with both of you, but it's time to go back. I will be coming around more now mum, that I can promise you."

"So, is this about what Jane did or is there another reason you are leaving now?"

"No, it's not about Jane, I am over that now …um…look mum, you've just had almost two weeks of me at a stretch. Even for you, that is a lot. I loved being back here, but you knew this was never permanent."

"Why did you come in the first place? You never got around to telling me why you came around so suddenly," Mum asked.

"Not today, not now, it's really nothing," I replied.

"It doesn't look like nothing to me, you have to tell me if you don't want me to worry. What's the story?"

"Mum, there is really nothing to tell, I just needed to clear my head and I am fine now. I have got to go now," I leaned over and kissed her forehead.

"Okay, Robert. Have it your way but know you can tell me anything. Even though you are all grown and successful, you are still my baby." I chuckled, she smiled as I unlocked my car and threw my bag on the passenger's seat, I saw mum, standing by the doorway through my rear-view mirror and I smiled. I knew I would miss her, but the constant meddling was now getting irritating. I started the car; she waved as I drove away. I thought about what I was going to do next on my way home. Somehow the twelve days away from my home helped get rid of my frustrations. I did not know how but thinking about the airport girl now had a calming effect on me.

Chapter 16

Just Chilling

Jane called my phone several times; she left messages on my house phone, with my secretary and, sent me a thousand texts. I was no longer annoyed with her, but I did not respond so she would never think it was all right to pull that kind of stunt with me again. Moreover, I did not have the energy to convince her that I did not leave because of her.

I finished work quite early; I sent my chef and housekeeper home early. I wanted the house to myself and I did not want any disturbance. I had food already prepared by the chef in the fridge; but I did not have appetite for anything fancy. I opened my freezer and found some pizza; I chucked it in the oven to cook. I took a cold beer from the fridge and switched the TV on while I waited for my pizza to cook.

I flipped from one channel to the other; there was nothing on that interested me. I went on the sport channels; there was a premiership football game on. I flipped past it, I was not a football fan. I loved tennis, I loved swimming and I loved playing golf. Any other sport was of little interest to me. I used to know what was going on around me, news about celebrities and what they got up to, but something changed in me after my father died ten years ago.

I became too serious and everything else that wasn't work and family was too frivolous for me to consider. I remembered when I used to love throwing parties and hanging out in clubs with friends. All that seemed a lifetime ago. I was only twenty-nine years old and already I had forgotten how to have fun.

I flipped past the music channels; there was a countdown of some sort going on. Rihanna was singing, I watched for a bit before finally deciding to listen to the news. The timer went off in the kitchen and I got up to get my pizza from the oven. Then my phone rang again. I looked at it, it was Jane, I contemplated picking it up, but I thought otherwise. She would keep me on the phone for way longer than I wanted to and I wanted to eat. I brought my pizza back with me to my living room. I had a bite, and it felt like heaven with my ice-cold beer. I loved being at home, it had been long since I had a day like this to myself and I was loving it. There was not a sound, no nagging, not even the girl from the airport infiltrated my thoughts. My mind was clear. I had another slice, switched off the TV and went to bed. I shut my eyes and tried to sleep, but I could not. I felt lonely again, I shut my eyes harder and tossed and turned until memories of the airport girl flooded my mind again and I felt at peace. As long as I could see her face in my mind, I wasn't lonely anymore and before I knew it, I fell into unconsciousness.

Chapter 17

Hasina Suri Fayed aka Anna Fey.

The dance audition was closer now; and my routine was starting to come together. I could have done better than what I currently had, if only I had a bigger space and I did not have to work so much. I had been working six days a week because I had no money left and the only day I had to rehearse, I sometimes sleep the whole day through as my body couldn't function due to tiredness. There had been times when I wondered why I was putting myself through this hardship and I reminded myself of the reasons I ran away from home. Money was not always happiness; I knew this very well because I grew up with money. I wished I could have it all, the career, the man of my dreams and the money; it definitely would make life much easier.

Now that my audition was only a couple of weeks away, I had stopped working the weekend to allow me time for rehearsals. It was not always easy to get off with not working at least one of the days in the weekend, but Jane put in a word for me with the manager. She wanted us to go out together after I was done rehearsing. I told her I would, but not until I had perfected my dance. The audition was more important to me than my job at the moment, but that didn't mean I was willing to lose my job because I needed it to fuel my existence.

After work, Jane was driving me home as usual; she was a lot of fun to be with and she was just easy to love. She loved to look after others, she couldn't help herself from doing that really. She told me how she got in trouble with her brother of recent and she had been trying to get hold of him to apologise again. Jane loves talking, if she was not talking about her relationship with Dave Porter, which was going fine, I'm happy to report, then the next topic would be her brother. I told her I understood why he was so upset. I hated it when people were set up to date each other; I was of the opinion that people should meet each other naturally on their own. If they were meant to be, they would gravitate towards each other eventually. My opinion on that was mainly based on my parents setting me up with a mate for life. I hated it, I hated for anyone to assume they knew what was right for me without allowing me to exploit that situation for myself and coming to a conclusion of my own.

Jane knew she messed up; even if her heart was in the right place, there were lines you could not cross in life when it came to other people's lives, no matter how much you loved them. However, I loved the way she loved, and I loved that she had siblings that she could lean on.

I was not sure I could still go out with Jane this weekend after my rehearsals, so I tried to get out of it. She's asked me to come to hers twice now and I felt terrible that I had to decline when she had been nothing but a good friend. I just couldn't justify having fun when I had the audition lingering over my head. I felt as though if I failed in this, then I would have let myself down and perhaps I was not as good a dancer as I thought I was to warrant fleeing from my home.

"You know that audition thing I told you I am preparing for?"

"Yeah, I still remember, it's still ages yet, isn't it?"

"Mm-hmm, it's getting closer now and my nerves have taken over. I don't feel prepared at all. And I know I promised that I will come over to yours afterward, but I don't think I should, you know. I feel like fun right now is out of the question for me. Please tell me you don't mind, I know my promises count for naught these days and I am not being a good friend, but I will give you all the time in the world after the auditions are over," I explained.

She rolled her eyes at me. "Anna, you are so funny. Why will I mind? I mean this is obviously very important to you. If you can't make it to mine, then you can't, and I definitely don't want to be a distraction to you. I want you to do well, but can I come and watch? Remember you said I could." Jane asked.

"I don't know; there is hardly enough space as it is, you know I love it when you're around, but I don't know yet." To be realistic, it would be nice if she came, so that I get used to someone watching while I dance as I was going to be judged by a group of people.

"Oh, pretty, please, I promise, hands on my heart, I won't distract you. You won't even know I was there." I wanted to protest, but I could not refuse her.

"Okay then. If it means that much to you, you may come. It's a good thing anyway, you might actually be of some help, who knows."

Jane grinned excitedly. "Gosh, this is fantastic. I am going to pop in at my brother's first thing in the morning and sort out the mess I created with him and then I will be at yours. Let's see, say around one o'clock, tomorrow afternoon?"

"One is fine. Listen, you can come anytime you want, as you know, my flat is really very small, so you have to stand out of the way, by my bathroom door all through, you don't move until I have finished." We both laughed; it sounded ridiculous, but it was also the truth. Jane was quiet, then suddenly looked like something had hit her.

"Anna! You know what, I have an idea. Let me pick you up early and you can rehearse in my brother's house. He has a very large house; and there is this room which I call the ballroom: he does not use it for anything. Look, I just solved your space problem. Say yes." She looked excited and I was too for a short second, but then I remembered that she and her brother had not even resolved their issues and I did not want her to get in more trouble because of me.

"Jane are you serious?" I asked, unsure of the idea.

"Yeah. You need a bigger place to dance."

"I know, but your brother has not even forgiven you for the last issue he had with you, and you want to take a stranger to his house? I don't think it's such a clever idea. Yes, I need the space. But I really don't want more trouble for you."

"Anna, trust me, he will not mind this. It's not like I am setting him up with you or anything. I'm done with all that. I swear, that brother of mine is going to die a bachelor, but you know that is his business, I am no longer getting involved. You know you need space, so after I get the apologies out of the way, I'll talk to him about you using the ballroom for your dance," Jane explained away.

I said nothing, I could not allow myself to get excited because I knew if he declined, my hopes will be dashed. She looked at me, expecting me to say something.

"Come on! Say something, Anna. It's a brilliant idea and you know it is," she tried to persuade me.

I looked at her, not sure if I should accept the fantastic genius offer of hers. "It's a fantastic idea, but I don't know; I just don't feel comfortable. What if he is expecting a guest or something, I don't want to intrude. I mean, I am kind of scared of what his reaction might be; he isn't talking to you at the moment, what if we go there and he yells at you again?" I asked.

She laughed. "Trust me, he is nothing like that; he hardly gets mad at me, which is why I have to see him and sort out whatever issue he still has with me. Nonetheless, he would welcome you as long as this is not a set up and it's not. You don't want to be set up, he is the same, the two of you are weird like that. Don't worry, it will be fine.

"Okay then, your brother's house it is. Jane, I don't say this enough, but you have been more than a friend to me. You are a star and you are God sent. Thank you for always being there, I just love you."

"Aww, do not get me started, I hate compliments. Listen, Anna, you deserve the world; you know it and I know it, so there. You have my back and I have yours always, right? I mean, what are friends for, eh?"

"Wait a minute, Jane. What if he is not home tomorrow and we have travelled all that distance only to be locked out? You need to call him so he knows that we are coming. Where does he live, again?" I asked.

"Somewhere in Surrey, but it does not matter. If he isn't home, even better, it means that he has gone on a business trip. Anna, stop worrying, I have a set of keys to his house; everything is taken care of, only if you just don't want to come."

"Oh, of course I want to come, I just worry about everything."

"Relax, Anna, its fine," she smiled, "Anyway, Dave asked me out again."

"It's a lie" I yelled excitedly, she nodded; they had both been on a few dates since that awkward day he asked for a drive. Each time they went out together, Jane pretended that she was not impressed with the things he put together for her. I did not understand why she still gave him a hard time when she clearly wanted him. "This will make it the fifth time you are going on a date with him."

"Yep, look who's counting!" she smiled.

"So, where is he taking you this time?" I asked eagerly.

"Told him I already had plans."

"Plans! What plans?" I asked disappointedly, she shrugged, "You blew him off to watch me dance?" I asked.

She laughed, "No, that's not why."

"Please do explain."

"You know, I don't want to come across easy, especially when I know he had eyes for you before, no offence." She looked at me, tilting her head to the side.

"You are joking right, are you for real. You know he's always been all about you, but you want a reason to justify your behaviour towards him. He's only had eyes for you. Why else do you think he is still interested in you after the way you've been treating him? There's only so much a guy can take. You need to stop this now."

"I don't know what is wrong with me; I don't want to treat him like that, but I've been so mean to him and I am kind of finding it hard to put down this wall and show him the real me."

"Just be you, stop overthinking things. You really like this person and he worships the ground you walk on. You do not know how lucky you are, call him back and tell him you have changed your mind."

"Anna, I don't want to rush into anything with him. You know I like him…"

"I hear a but coming?"

"No, no buts, that's not it. I think I am just nervous that I will ruin things if I allow myself to be the real me with him. I will fall in love so easily and I am scared that if he knows how I truly feel he won't be interested in me anymore. You know, what if, at the end of the day, he doesn't fall in love with me or what if he thinks I am too much and walks away?"

"Life is all about taking risks, you won't know the answers to these questions if you don't give yourself the chance to be happy with him and allow him to love the real you," I responded, she was quiet. I looked out the window. When it came to relationships, I did not have a clue what it took to make it work. I had never dated anyone, but I knew if I was in her shoes and this was the man I had fallen for as she had, although she was in denial, I would do absolutely everything to ensure it worked.

"So, you think I should just lay all my cards on the table?"

"Jane, I have never been in your shoes and by that, I mean being in love with someone that also wants me."

"But, if you were in my shoes what will you do?"

"Oh Jane, I don't know. I will probably go on that date. I mean, you are lucky, you like someone and he by some miracle seems to like you too and you people live in the same city and work in the same place, it is a blessing, you know. Look at me, I am daydreaming about some guy that does not even know I exist and on top of that, I feel I may be in love with this idea of a man, you know. How pathetic is that? So, if I were in your shoes, I think I will call him and tell him I made a mistake and I want to start afresh. No more games, just let things fall the way they may and you might get hurt or he may actually be the greatest love of your life. However, if you don't give him a chance, you will never know." She stopped the car in front of my flat and switched off the engine. We talked all through the drive, I did not even realize I was already home.

"I don't want to lose him and if I don't stop this nonsense, I know I will. You are right, Anna, I have been acting stupid, and I am going to call him. Thank you for knocking sense into me and you thought you were clueless about relationships," She said graciously. She held my hand; I smiled because at least one of us got to enjoy falling in love.

"What are friends for?" I said, she smiled and I got out of the car. She started the car and yelled, "See you tomorrow at eleven."

"Wait, I thought you said one earlier?" I asked. She did not hear. I stepped away from the car to allow her room to move and said, "Goodnight, Jane." I stood and watched her drive off until her car was out of sight before heading inside my flat.

I was tired; but I managed to sort out my outfit for tomorrow. I laid them on the door of my wardrobe. Back when I still lived at home; three choices of dresses were laid out for me each morning, so it had become a habit of some sort. I put my dance clothes in the bag and the CD of the song I had been dancing to. I ate the leftover chicken that I had in the fridge, laid on my sofa bed and rubbed my feet. They ached from being on my feet all day. As much as I loved proving to myself and everyone at work that I was a hard worker, it had been very hard to adjust from being pampered to now slaving at work to pay my bills.

I flipped on the TV, but I kept thinking of my discussion with Jane on the way home. I hoped that she would stop playing games; she didn't know how lucky she was. I switched off the TV, sleep was coming. I shut my eyes and thoughts of the airport man flooded my mind once again. I had become used to his face, it was a part of me and without his face on my mind, it would be difficult to sleep. I imagined that he held me in his arms while I gazed into his big greyish blue, beautiful eyes; I was lost in his world as I fell into a deep sleep.

Chapter 18

I must have been dreaming, just as I had done quite many times before. I felt his caressing hands on my face. He touched the top of my lip and slowly moved his fingers to the ridge of my nose. I could feel the warmth and the softness of his hands as he touched me. My heart was beating so fast that I could not move. I felt my body freeze at his presence, then he moved on top of me, his elbows at my sides. I looked on in amazement; I was mesmerized, the way he looked at me as if I was the most precious human alive. His lips moved closer to mine and mine parted in submission as my eyes shut in surrender and anticipation of what is to come next, then I heard a loud buzz in my head. I opened my eyes and he was gone; the buzz got louder. I reached for the alarm clock and threw it across the room in frustration. I was covered in a heap of sweat, it was not the first time, I had had this type of dream, but this was the first time I almost kissed him in my dream. I sat up on my bed and looked at the clock, it was three minutes past nine, and reluctantly, I got up and made my way to the bathroom. I ran myself a bath and while the bath filled, I began brushing my teeth. Then, I wrapped the towel around my hair and got in the bath. The water was very warm, just like I liked it

I shut my eyes and enjoyed the heat as it massaged my body. I rubbed my feet again and massaged them thoroughly with my footstone. When I was done with my feet, I lay in the water and shut my eyes; a part of me hoped to fall asleep again and miraculously continue with the dream I was so rudely awaken from by my alarm clock. However, I knew I had no time for such frivolities because I had to be ready before Jane arrived. I wondered how long I would sustain this behaviour for. I should break myself from this obsession, but I had come to depend on it almost like a drug. In a way, I felt ashamed that I had subjected my mind to this, but to break away from him was almost like not breathing.

For sanity's sake, my thoughts went to my mother. That was another issue that had been bothering me a lot. I wondered how she was now; it was almost five months since I disappeared. In the past, I had often used my thoughts of him to escape from the guilt and now I was using thoughts of my mother to help keep me sane.

Each time this guilty feeling flooded me, I tried to remind myself that what I was doing outweighed the tears my mother was shedding over me. My reasons for fleeing were still very valid to me. If I was given a choice by my parents, I still would have wanted to live in London on my own and pursue a dance career. However, my free will was in question here, what was I to do?

I shampooed my hair and gave it a quick rinse and got out of the bath, I was running out of time. I dried my hair and pulled it into a ponytail. I dressed myself in jean and red V-neck jumper; then slipped into my pumps. Checked my bag again to ensure I had all I needed with me. It was almost fifteen minutes to the time; I poured some milk into a glass and gulped it down. Then I applied a light makeup on my face.

My phone vibrated; it was a text from Jane, I looked through the window, her car was already packed outside. I picked up my bags from my bed and headed out to meet her. I was excited and nervous at the same time; it was the first time I was going anywhere that was not work related.

"Sorry I kept you waiting," I apologised to Jane as I sat in the car.

"It's alright, I just got here too," Jane responded as she started the car.

"I am so excited, you don't even know how much," I said, she giggled.

"Me too, I am excited for you. And I know you are going to be busy most of our time there, but at least I get to watch," she looked especially happy.

"You look like the cat that got the cream; this can't be because we are going to your brother's house?" I looked at her as she made a U-turn from my street.

"What are you talking about?" she cast a quick glance at me.

"I don't know, there is something different about you. Tell me, is it Dave Porter? Did you call him?" I asked.

"It's not Dave, I haven't gotten around to calling him yet."

"Then tell me, I am not good with suspense."

"Okay, I'll tell you. Listen, my brother called this morning; you know he's not been returning my calls," she started to explain.

"Mm-hmm…" I listened.

"Well, he wanted to let mum and I know that he was going on one of his business trips to Austria and he would be gone the whole weekend. So, you know what that means, right?"

"No, I don't, you have lost me. How is this good news and where are we driving to, if he is not home?"

"Anna, I can't believe you don't get it! We have the house to ourselves! I told you I have a set of keys to his house; we can sleep over if you want and make it a weekend retreat. Isn't it exciting, you don't have to be nervous anymore, we would be gone before he returns!"

"Really! We have the place to ourselves! And your brother doesn't even have to know we were ever there and I can rehearse all weekend? That's fantastic news, Jane. I get to have two days!"

"Two days, babe, you get the ballroom to yourself for two days. That should help, won't it?"

"Of course, it will, are you kidding? I do not know how to thank you, Jane. This is just too much, see I knew there was something different about you, immediately I saw you. You couldn't hide it."

"Anna, I was always going to tell you, but I wanted to surprise you when we get there. We are going to have so much fun, we should stop and buy a few things, just in case he has no food in the house."

"So, the house is definitely empty, right?" I asked.

"Yes, it should be," Jane replied.

"What do you mean by it should be? Is it empty or not?"

"Relax, Anna, my brother has a chef and a housekeeper, they are usually never around when he travels, so it would be empty."

"But, what if you are wrong and they are there?"

"No, there is no one there. I called his home before I came here and no one picked up," she said. She gave me her phone, "Call, see for yourself." I took the phone from her and dialled the last number: The phone rang continuously and no one picked up. My face began to spread into a grin.

"You see, I told you, Anna. You need to not worry so much," she smiled. We were both silent for a moment, then all of a sudden, she said, "I am thinking of setting my mum up with someone." She gave me a quick glance; I knew then she was addicted to interfering in other people's lives.

"What! You cannot be serious; surely, you must have learned your lesson by now, what, with your brother barely speaking to you. You know what, you are an addict and you cannot help yourself." I said, looking out the window.

"Seriously, do you really think that of me? It's not an obsession; I just want the people I love to have a fuller and more colourful life and if they won't help themselves at least they have me in their corner, fighting the good fight."

"Is that what you think." I half laughed, then added. "Jane, being addicted to something does not necessarily mean you are not being helpful, but if you ask me, I think you get too involved in other people's relationships, so you don't have to work on yours. I think you should ask your mother if she won't mind before doing anything. She is an adult and she knows what she wants, what if she never wants to date anyone again. You can't just decide on your own that she needs a man, find out first."

"I disagree; you don't know her like I do. You would soon find out first hand when you start coming around mine. My mother is lonely, it's been ten years since we lost our dad and she has been on her own. It's time she lets someone new in, Alex is in the states, Robert is never around and I will one day leave home. I don't want her all alone," she explained. It made sense what she said, but I needed to make her understand that people have to make their decisions on their own.

"I see your point, Jane, but you really have to understand that your mother knows all this, if she felt lonely then she would be with someone. You setting her up with someone may not be the best of ideas, Jane. If you gave your own relationship with Dave half the attention you pay everybody else's, I do not think you would even have time to worry about whether your mother or brother is lonely or not."

"I know, but I feel like I can't allow myself to be happy if they are not. But, I get what you mean, but it's just hard for me to let it be. I love to fix things, people. I'm a fixer. That's who I am, I can't help it." she smiled.

I chuckled. "You're right, it's who you are and you can't help it. You were put on this earth to help others, but you have to help yourself too. I am just so glad you have not done the same to me. When we get to your brother's, promise me you would call Dave or I will do it for you," I threatened.

"I will think about it, it makes me nervous, you know, being around him."

"That is because you are falling or have fallen in love with him. Just think, how would you feel if he decides to move on, if he finds himself another person and the person doesn't waste time as you have done?" She was quiet. "Would you be okay with him moving on?" I persisted.

"It would kill me; I will literally want to die…" She turned away from the road and looked at me. "Anna I can't lose him."

"Then put your priorities in order." I reasoned.

She was quiet; "Jane, look, I don't mean to pressurize you into anything you're not ready for."

"It's okay, you are right, it's just what I need. Dave actually texted me this morning." She now had a little twinkle in her eye.

Elizabeth Johnson

"He sent you a text and you kept that quiet?" I never took my eyes off her; she smiled and gave me a quick glance. "Mm-hmm? Go on, what did he say?" she looked at me again and shook her head.

"And I thought I was the nosy one," she said, raising her eyebrow, I laughed.

"Can you blame me; I learned from the best, so go on, spit it out."

"Anna, it is nothing really. I mean it is something, you know, he wants to meet up tonight. I really want to see him too, but I don't know."

"What does that mean, you just said if he moved on, it will kill you. That is your answer there, you are going to call him and tell him you will meet him."

"How about you? I can't just leave you alone; I already promised you I will watch you dance."

"Oh no, you don't, you are not going to use me to get out of this. You are going to call him and tell him you will meet him. Go please and be with the man you want, at least one of us gets to be happy."

"Really, you don't mind being on your own? If I go, I won't stay out too late, but I will worry about you," She said. She was looking for an excuse to get out of seeing him again and I was not going to allow it.

"Don't worry about me, I am a big girl. I'll be fine and stop with the ifs, you are going and that is final," I said.

"Okay, mum," Jane joked. We both laughed.

"I never asked! Do you have spare clothes since it looks like we would be staying the night? I only have my dance outfit, I wish you told me this when I was at home, but it doesn't matter. I will change into my dance clothes and wear that all day and save what I am wearing now for tomorrow."

"I could get you something on my way out, a spare jumper and toiletries, I doubt Robert has any feminine toiletries. No woman, has seen the insides of his house apart from his housekeeper. Count yourself lucky, girl. I am only joking," she laughed. I rolled my eyes.

Chapter 19

The meet

We had only been friends for about three months or so, but the way we were when we were together, anyone would think that we have known each other for a lifetime. We saw each other almost every day, even days when Jane was off work. She came around to have lunch or drove me home. I had come to depend on her friendship a lot. She spoke about her family a lot and I felt guilty because I did not like to talk about mine for obvious reasons. She asked me once when we lunched together, who in my family I took after; my answer was short and to the point. "My mother." The atmosphere felt awkward, because she was expecting me to say something more, but I did not want to talk about them. The way she spoke of her mother made me miss mine, so it was always hard to keep it together each time she went on about her family. I missed home, I missed my mother, but I didn't miss my father as much; because if not for his stubbornness, I wouldn't have had a need to run away. However, every cloud had its silver lining; if I did not run, I would not have met Jane and I would not have had that brief encounter with the stranger from my dream. "Your mother must be really beautiful."

"Yes, she is..." I answered.

She laughed awkwardly. "You know I say that because you are very beautiful, but you act like you don't know it. Your hair is always in a ponytail, you don't dress up to impress, not that it takes anything away from you. However, if I had half the beauty you have, perhaps I won't be so insecure."

"Don't put yourself down Jane; you are a very beautiful person inside and out. And you are just very easy to be with, no complications. What you see is what you get, with you." I said, reassuring her and bringing a smile to Jane's face.

"Thank you; I could say the same about you too." She had not asked me about my family since then; I did not know if it was on purpose or if she took her cue from my unwillingness to talk about them.

Jane drove into a country road and then we came by a gate. She got out of the car and typed a code into what seemed like an intercom. The gate opened, and we drove for about half a mile before approaching this very massive, beautiful house. "Is this your brother's house?" I asked in shock. I was not expecting it to be quite as big, not that I had not seen anything bigger; Jane never prepared me for this. Jane turned off the engine and we both sat back and admired the exterior of this beautiful house.

"Jane, you could have warned me. I don't know what I expected, but this wasn't it. And he lives here alone?"

Jane nodded. "I know; I get like this each time I come here. It's… it's kind of overwhelming, that is why I worry about him. I don't like that he is alone, but… okay, let us go inside." We got out of the car, and I waited for Jane to fondle her bag for the keys to this enormous house. If I compared this mansion to my family home, mine was almost three times its size but still this house had an appeal that mesmerized me. It felt like home, somewhere I could buy if I had the money.

Jane unlocked the door; we entered this huge hallway with very high ceilings and two grand stairs. From where I was standing, I could see three doors: one each on both sides of me and the third was somewhere beneath the stairs. Jane walked toward the one beneath the stairs and I followed. She pushed on the door a little and the double doors automatically opened to expose the beautiful kitchen. My eyes caught another door at the far end of the kitchen. Jane opened the fridge; I walked towards the door and saw it led to an indoor swimming pool area. I pushed on the door a little, but it did not bulge. Jane came over,

"Robert keeps it locked, come and let me show you round." I followed; we went back the way we came. We entered into one of the living rooms through one of the other two doors. It was beautifully decorated. Two neutral- coloured, buttoned armchairs facing a purple corner sofa. Another pair of winged armchairs faced a beautiful fireplace. There were exotic and beautiful lamps and lampstands everywhere I looked, there was a huge vase in one corner of the room, but there were no personal pictures. I looked around for pictures, but there was none of him. Above the fireplace, there was a picture of an older man. I asked Jane,

"Who is that?"

"That's our father," She replied solemnly. I stared at him for a while. Jane then broke the silence.

"Come let me show you the other rooms." We went through the door on our right into another living room, but this one was more formal. It had a grand piano facing an arched window. There was a fireplace dividing the room and on the other side of the fireplace was a very large dining area and two doors, one led to the kitchen and the other into the famous ballroom that Jane spoke about before.

"So, this is the place where you can dance your little heart out," she smiled, knowing I was loving the space.

"I can't ask for anything better really; this is just the perfect place." I hugged and squeezed Jane.

"Anna, let go of me!" she laughed. I released my hold on her and looked around again. Jane held me by the hand and pulled me away.

"Come let's go upstairs, so I can show you to your room." We half ran up the stairs; the landing was almost as big as the rooms downstairs. It was landing slash library; there were bookshelves on the wall that filled the whole breadth of the landing and the shelves were as high as the ceiling. They arched in shape and the shelves were filed with books. There were two passages, one on either side of the landing that led to the bedrooms. On our right was the one that led to Robert's room, we did not go there. Jane took me through the passage on the left, she opened the first room we came to,

"This is yours, and you can change and get started if you want. I am going to take the room next to this one." The room was as big as the one I had back home; it had an en-suite. The bed was big; there was a dresser with a large mirror above it. I threw my bag on the floor and threw myself on the bed. The sheet felt succulent against my skin and the bed moulded to my frame. I felt like sleeping, but I had to get on with the reason I came. Jane knocked on the door.

"Come in," I said.

"Are you settling in okay?" she checked on me with a can of coke.

"I just looked in the fridge and I need to go buy some food. If we are to survive today—not to talk of the weekend—the fridge is basically empty." I opened the can of coke she gave me and started to sip it. I had not realized I was thirsty until I started to drink, and before I knew it I had consumed it all.

"There is a convenient shop not far from here, but they close early. I am going to go there now so we have something to eat later. Do you need anything before I leave?" she asked.

I smiled. "Erm... a CD player will be good."

"Oh yeah, right. I will be back in a minute." She dashed out of the room; I changed into my dance outfit. Jane came back with what looked like an antique CD player. "This should work fine; I got it from my brother's room, he's had it for ages."

"Thanks, Jane. Um... don't be long, please."

"Don't worry. I'll be back very soon." I heard her steps and the click of the door as she went out of the house; I found some white towels rolled up in bundles in my bathroom, so I picked one and went down the stairs to the ballroom shortly afterwards. I began doing my stretches: first the hamstring, then the centre split stretch to warm up my body. I inserted the CD into the player and selected a Lady Antebellum song, "Need you now." The music filled the room. I turned the volume up and put it on repeat. It was much easy to be carried away here; there was so much space to dance around in and I did not have to worry about disturbing anyone. It was liberating a passion in me to dance around with no hindrance, my movements were more relaxed and fluid. I was able to do big extensions and execute my turns with precision. I loved it. I incorporated more moves to my routine; I added a mid-air split and a couple of tumbles, but I had not realized Jane had been gone for so long. I was sweating; I picked up the towel I brought with me and wiped off the sweats.

Then I continued dancing, starting from the beginning each time the song ended or when I made a mistake or fell. I was in my own world; everything was coming together fine. I kept wondering about Jane; she said she would not be long, but it looked as though she had been gone for over an hour. Nonetheless, I knew when she arrived, she would come find me. Even though I knew I should take a break, I wanted to do the routine again from the beginning; I was half way through my routine when I felt the hair on the back of my neck stand. I was no longer alone in the room and I knew it. I was certain in my mind that there was another pair of eyes watching me. I was scared, afraid to turn around. If eyes could burn, I would have a hole through me. I stopped dancing; the music was still playing. All sorts of thoughts jumped through my mind in that split moment, my heart nearly jumped out of my chest as I slowly turned to face the intruder. He had a look of shock in his eyes, and so did I. This could not be. This certainly could not be real. I was frozen and so was he, I just stared at him. His eyes were confused. He had his trench coat on and a suitcase that must have dropped when he saw me laid beside him. I did not know what to do, by the way he was dressed, he did not look like an intruder. I was clearly the one that was invading his space. However, I could not move and I could not open my mouth; those eyes; his greyish, beautiful, blue eyes questioned my presence here. This surely could not be the Robert Jane spoke about; this could not be the man that had invaded my mind and hunted my dreams these past months. The beatings of my heart were uncontrollable, I wanted to explain my presence here. He looked like he wanted me to, but I could not find the words. The music was still playing loudly, I might add. I suddenly felt this heat come over me; this was too much for me. I felt my knees give way and the shock of it all overwhelmed my body as it slumped and I hit the ground.

Chapter 20

Where do We go from here?

When I opened my eyes, everything felt fuzzy; I noticed someone brush my hair from my face. I was lying on something, a chase maybe. I tried to move, but a hand gently held me down. I could smell him; his face was close to mine and I smiled in contentment. I was having another dream, but it was okay as long as I got to be with him. I lifted my hands to his face and caressed it; my heart began to beat in succession. His eyes looked at me strangely; I wanted to drown in them. He did not flinch or recoil from my touch, he just stayed there and let me touch him; all the while, his eyes remained on mine. I could not tell if he was happy to be with me or not. He looked concerned and worry creased his forehead, but his beauty overwhelmed me. His face was not as I remembered or dreamt these past months. In fact; my past memories did him no justice at all.

My eyes wandered to his dark chestnut locks that graced his head; I wanted to reach out and touch them and bury my hand in them, but somewhere deep down my courage failed me. Even though I was dreaming, it felt so wrong to have him all to myself. I was still mesmerised by his closeness. I tried very hard to still my heart from exploding as it pounded against my rib. I could hear him breathing and he was not doing too well either. This was all too much. I wanted to say something, but my lips would not move. I tried to move again, but his body was too close to mine. He must have realized my intentions because he placed his hand on my back to support me as I tried to get up.

My head rang with a banging headache; I laid back down and moved my hands to my head in reaction to the ache. The worry on his face was more pronounced now; I could tell he was anxious although his body was very composed. I kept my eyes on his face, not wanting to blink in case I wake up and he disappeared again. I wanted this moment to last forever in my mind.

Then he opened his mouth and I heard him say, "Hello." His voice was faint, just more like a whisper, but smooth and calm and just as I remembered. Hearing him speak to me sent my heart racing again. "How are you feeling?". He was making conversations with me and I had lost my voice it seemed. I just stared back at him in disbelieve. He smiled as if to assure me I was safe. I did not know why he did that. It did not help me; I was in awe of him. "Listen, don't move, I am going to get you a glass of water. Alright?" He looked at me to see if I understood what he was saying. I did understand, but I started to panic inside as he was about to leave. I held his hand to pull him back; he looked from my hand to me and smiled.

"You don't want me to go." I smiled; he placed his hand on mine and sat down next to me. Suddenly, I remembered where I was, and why I had come, and then my mind replayed how and why I fell and, in that instant, I understood that I wasn't dreaming. I was in Jane's brother's house and the stranger I had fantasized about was her brother. I raised myself up; I could still feel the ache in my head, but we needed to discuss the situation we had both found ourselves. Even though he did not know me, he did not even look like he remembered me from that day. What was I going to say to him, how was I going to explain being in his house? This was the time when Jane's return would really have helped smooth out my presence here. I looked behind me towards the doors, his eyes followed my gaze.

"Do you want something? Do you need water?" I shook my head.

"Jane..." I murmured.

"Jane?" he repeated, "You know her?" I nodded. "Did she bring you here?" I nodded again. He took a deep breath and looked away for a minute. I knew I needed to explain better because his face looked perplexed.

"She is my friend, we met at work and she told me you won't be around, and we could, well I could use your house for my..." I didn't know why but I began to hesitate. He looked at me and as I explained, my heart stopped. I needed to do a better explanation than that; I wondered what he was thinking right now. I knew things were not good between him and his sister and now he had just returned to find a stranger in his house. Jane was only supposed to be gone for half an hour I thought and now I had to deal with this situation alone. He had been generous; I was surprised he had not called the police on me. As I was thinking that, my heart was also hoping that he remembered that he had seen me before today. However, he gave no indication of any previous knowledge of ever seeing me before now. I must admit, I did not feel good about that because it meant that I had been dreaming and lusting after someone that did not even know that I existed before now. After he throws me out of his house, as he might do once Jane returns, he would return to his life and I would be plagued with loving him. From what I had heard Jane say about him, I had no chance whatsoever with him. The thought of not being wanted by him thrusted deep in my heart and it hurt. I could feel a cloud of tears gathering over my eyes, but I tried my best to send it back.

I could feel his eyes on me, but I could not complete my sentence. I was going to choke, and I did not want him to see me like that.

"You were dancing when I came in?" I nodded and he smiled. I was relieved a little that he did not look mad. The way he looked at me made me nervous, as if he did not believe my explanation. I looked away. This was not how I thought it would be. I had envisioned meeting him again, bumping into him at a mall, on the street, anywhere, any scenario—but instead, it turned out this way and I did not know how to deal with this situation.

He laughed as if to himself, then he got up and walked a few steps away.

I did not know what he was going to do, but I would give anything right now for Jane to come and save me.

"I can't believe you are here," he said more to himself.

"I am sorry, I never…"

"No! No, please, don't get me wrong, I am not sorry you are here. It's just that I can't believe that you are here." I looked up at him; I was lost and my head still hurt a little. I placed my finger on the back of my head and rubbed it absentmindedly. He walked away. I looked down. As happy as I was inside to have finally met this person, I knew I was not going to do anything about it. He came back with a half-filled glass of water.

"Sorry, here, drink this; it should help you feel a little better. Do you need any painkillers or something?"

"No…. thanks," I said as I took the glass of water from him. I tried not to touch his hands, but our hands grazed each other and an electric feeling sprang through me. I looked away to try to disguise what just happened to me. I seriously hoped he did not notice my reaction to his touch.

I could still feel his eyes on me and the silence was beginning to feel uncomfortable. I did not know where to look or what to say. I wanted to thank him for the water, but I could not face looking at him or he would know I was dying inside.

Somebody had to say something and it was not going to be coming from me.

"Are you alright?" he finally asked.

"That… depends on what you mean?" I said nervously. He sighed and took a deliberate step towards me and then he sat next to me.

"I think…I have seen you somewhere before?" he said. I looked up in shock. He remembered. He remembered me, I wanted to shout aloud, but I had to keep my composure.

"I mean erm…your face…I cannot forget that face. Do you… erm… do you remember seeing me?" he asked, looking puzzled. I didn't know what to say, should I tell him the truth or should I pretend I don't remember seeing him? What if lying destroyed any chance of ever knowing him? I wanted to tell him that I remembered. I wanted to tell him how memories of him had driven me insane since that day I laid my eyes on him and that looking at him now had caused chaos in my heart. Where did I begin? I would tell him the truth, but I will try to present it coolly. His eyes looked like they were studying me, I could not even lie if I wanted to. Before I could speak, he spoke again.

"I have seen you before, haven't I? Your face, I remember it like it was yesterday." I felt his hands on my face as he gently lifted my head up to meet his gaze. I froze. My heart felt like it would jump out my chest and if he listened hard enough, he would hear it beating fervently against my rib.

This was unbelievable. *He remembered me, I remembered him.* Those words sang happily through my mind. Then I responded.

"You do?" I asked. He smiled in relief and my heart melted.

"How could anyone forget such a face?" he said and I could hear the sincerity in his voice as his eyes penetrated mine. My heart started to flutter again and the pounding in my heart increased.

"You're the girl I met at the airport. I never in my wildest dream thought I will see this face again."

"I never... forgot yours too," I blurted out. He looked a little shocked and then he smiled.

"May I?" he said as he gently tucked a strand of my hair behind my ears. Everything he did made me combust on the inside. I did not know how much of him my heart could take. The way he looked at me, as if I mattered to him, did not make any sense. I looked down and tried to change the subject to Jane.

"So, you are Jane's brother?" I asked. He watched me carefully before answering.

"Yes. I am."

"Erm... I am... sorry about all this. Like I was trying to explain earlier, Jane said that you were out of town for the weekend and I needed a place with space...um... to rehearse... I am sorry." I was nervous. It was unimaginable, the effect his presence had on me.

"It's alright; I believe you; I know what Jane is capable of..."

"Please don't be mad at her, she was just helping me out," I pleaded.

He half laughed, "I am not mad at her, for the first time, I am actually..." Then she walked in.

"Oh, Robert!" Jane gasped, "Don't get angry with me. Before you say anything, let me explain. I…"

"It's fine, Jane," he said to her without looking away from me.

"Please don't be mad, I didn't think you would be here, not that it made it okay.... erm..." she laughed nervously and continued, "You've met my friend, Anna... she needed a place to rehearse and I just wanted to help out..."

"Jane, I said it's fine," he reiterated, breaking his eyes from mine. He shot her a quick glance.

"You're not mad?" Jane asked, "I was so scared when I saw your car outside, but I wasn't sure if it was you and Anna, I am so sorry. I took a wrong turn and ended up on this diverted road, it was terrible. I am so upset I left you by yourself for so long."

"It's okay, Jane. I was fine." I cleared my throat as I tried to focus my attention on her. Robert got up from beside me and walked over to the window. I did not want him to leave; I did not want him out of my sight, but I needed to speak with Jane and he wanted to give us the space to do so.

"I got a lot done while you were gone." I was really trying to focus on

Chapter 21

What happens next?

I went back to the ballroom to try to continue with my rehearsals, but my heart was not in it, just knowing he was upstairs. I was more mindful; I did not feel as free as I did earlier before he arrived.

I turned the volume down and every turn and every extension was not with precision anymore as earlier, and it frustrated me. It felt like a mistake; staying here alone with him when I did not know what to do with myself. I could not go upstairs because he was there and I was not doing too well down here either.

I was distracted, but I cowardly hid away in the ballroom, afraid of what my heart wanted. It was quiet; I could not hear anything. Perhaps, he had gone to bed, or maybe left the house. The thought of him not caring to check on me almost broke my heart, but I knew I had no right to feel the way I was feeling.

I wiped myself down with the towel; I was sweating not only from the dance, but also from nerves. I decided to stop the charade now. There was no point dancing if I could not get the job done properly. I stopped for the day and headed upstairs; I was hungry now. I didn't eat the fish and chips Jane had given me earlier and now I felt famished, especially after all the energy I expelled dancing. Half way up the stairs, there he was heading downwards. I stopped and so did my heart. I held on to the rails for dear life. I did not know what to say to him, but I was glad he had not gone to bed and he was still in the house.

"Oh, there you are! I was just coming to find you," he said, stopping two stairs from me.

"Me! Why?" I said, thrilled on the inside. I was glad that he was coming to find me.

"I just wondered if you… if you don't mind joining me for dinner. You've been down there for a while now. You must be famished by now. I know I am and I haven't been doing what you've been doing." He smiled; his eyes remained on mine and for a minute, I did not know what to say. I just could not believe he just asked me to dine with him.

"I…I …I don't mind at all. And, you are right; I am starving." I smiled, he smiled back.

"But if you don't mind, I need a few moments to get cleaned up."

"Take all the time you need; I will be waiting for you downstairs." He took a couple stairs down towards me; we were now closer, our shoulders almost touching. I took in a deep breath as his scent consumed me. Then he asked,

"Where is Jane? I have looked and I find her car is gone. Don't tell me she's left you all by yourself again." My heart could barely take this closeness, but I tried to remain composed.

"She went out to meet with a friend. She came to find you, but you were… you were busy. She said to tell you not to wait up."

"A friend? Ah, I see." All this time, his eyes remained on me. I could not meet his, I looked down and it felt awkward. He must have noticed this as well. He took a step downward, leaving me still and frozen on the spot.

"I will wait for you; I hope you have a healthy appetite."

"That depends on what you're cooking," I joked. He half laughed.

"I don't intend to cook… Trust me, you don't want to eat anything I cook and I am a really terrible cook. I have already made reservations for us in a restaurant."

"A restaurant? I do not think I can."

"Why not?" he asked.

"Don't get me wrong, I… want to, but I don't have anything to wear."

"Hmm, ok then. How about we order in?" he said.

"Yeah, that would be nice," I replied.

"Do you have an appetite for anything in particular?"

"I don't know. I will leave that up to you. Anything would be nice," I said.

"Oh, okay then. I'll see to it. Sorry, I have taken so much of your time. See you downstairs, I will be waiting," he said. I smiled nervously; I was doing my best to keep myself from screaming out loud with joy. I liked that he was in control; I could not think straight, being so close to him. This could not be happening, not only has fate brought me to him. I got to dine with him as well. My heart was floating with joy; he continued downstairs, turning my head slightly. I watched as he went. I took a deep breath to steady myself; my head was spinning from the attention he paid me. I was not sure if he was doing it as a courtesy because I was a guest in his house or if he liked me a little.

I took off my dance clothes; I laid them carefully on the bed. I went into the en-suite and turned on the shower. I let the water spray me down; I loved the warmth of the water on my skin, but I knew he was waiting for me and I did not want to keep him waiting. I wanted to go to him, even if I was not hungry and he had asked me to dine with him, I would have gladly accepted. I turned off the shower and dried my skin and hair before blow-drying my hair. There were some toiletries on the counter. I sprayed myself with a gorgeous body spray and then I wore my jumper and my jeans. I yanked the brush through my hair and pulled it into a ponytail. I examined myself in the mirror and decided I wanted my hair down. I applied a lip-gloss to my lips, shaped my eyebrow with my fingertips and coloured the edges of my eyes with dark eyeliner. I knew I was doing it all for him and I was not ashamed of it. I heard the doorbell; I thought about Jane, but I knew she had her own keys. I examined myself once more before the mirror and then decided it was time I went down to meet him.

He was waiting for me by the door that led to the living room with the dinning space. He watched me as I walked down the stairs; I did not know what was going through his mind and my heart was raced up the closer I got to him. I tried to place one foot in front of the other as the distance between us became smaller. His eye remained on me until I was at his side, his hands were out as though he wanted to take my hands in his, but I was too scared to touch him. Our hands grazed earlier today, and it sent an electrifying spark down my whole body. I couldn't imagine what being held by him would do to me. I pretended I did not see his hands, so I walked in front of him and he gently led me towards the dining room. There was a platter of food waiting. There were at least four different cuisines. There was curry and rice, potatoes and steaks, pizza, Chinese cuisines with spring rolls, you name it. I stood there speechless at the amount of food he had ordered. Who was going to eat all this? I thought to myself. I was staring at the table aware of his eyes on me, refusing to meet his gaze as it always left me feeling vulnerable.

"You smell very fresh," he said to me. I pretended as if I did not hear him; I did not know how to react to compliments from him.

"May I?" I asked, gesturing to the table.

He smiled. "Yes please," he said.

I picked a spring roll and had a bite. "You ordered so much food! Are you expecting anyone else? I asked, knowing all too well what the answer to my question would be.

"Erm... no, I ...I wasn't sure what you would like, and I wanted to get it right, so I decided if I ordered all of these, there must be something here for you," he explained, moving closer to me, but he stopped a chair away from where I stood.

"That is... very kind of you. I feel silly now. I should have been more specific, instead of putting you through this trouble," I said and then he moved even closer towards me. I did not know why he was coming so close. My heart began pounding against my chest and I looked down. His scent overpowered me, he pulled out a chair for me and then he returned to the other side of the table and sat down opposite me. I filled my plate with little bits of food, picking a little from everything he ordered. I looked up and noticed he only dished himself a bit of curry and some rice. I felt silly; I wondered if he now thought I was a glutton. I felt embarrassed; he noticed my eyes on his plate.

"Would you feel better if I have more food on my plate?" he asked.

I laughed; it made me feel better that he was quick to understand what was going through my head. He then started to add more food to his plate until his plate looked like mine. He looked at me.

I giggled shyly.

Elizabeth Johnson

"It's my fault for getting carried away," he said.

I tried hard to concentrate on eating but found it very difficult. I needed to eat because I was hungry, but every now and then, I could feel his eyes on me; and it filled me with excitement. Butterflies filled my tummy, tumbling and jumping hoops.

There was silence between us to keep my eyes from him; I stuffed my stomach with food. He poured me some red wine, I sipped a little and it tasted beautiful, but the alcohol went through me and I felt a little tipsy. Nonetheless, I tried not to show it. Back home with my family, I never drank alcohol because I was not allowed to. However, Louise and I have had some alcohol on a few occasions when we were together. She brought a bottle of wine with her those days when we were planning my escape and we sat in the changing room and drank after our dance lessons. The wine I drank in the past was not as strong as this one sliding down my throat. Even though I only had a couple of sips, it felt like I had drunk the whole bottle.

I suddenly felt tired, even though I did not want to leave his presence. I yawned from exhaustion; I was disappointed in myself, but I was too tired to engage in any type of conversation.

"You look very exhausted; would you like to be excused?" he asked. I wanted to say no, but who was I kidding?

"Yes please, if you don't mind," I said, disappointed at myself.

"It's alright, you get to bed, and I'll see you tomorrow," he said. He came over to me; I stood up and he pulled my chair.

"Thank you, dinner was lovely. I think I over-did it," I said, and he smiled too,

"As long as you … liked it. Would you like me to see you off to your room or you think you'd do just fine on your own?"

"Oh yes, thanks, I will be fine. I will see you tomorrow then?"

"Yeah, see you… tomorrow." He moved out of the way for me to pass, I tried walking away carefully so our bodies didn't touch, although, I wanted nothing more, but I know I couldn't handle it if it did. This was so intense, these feelings coursing through me, I had never known anything like it, but I loved how he made me feel and he did not even know it.

In the room, I took off my clothes; I had my vest on and I lay it on the bed. I pulled the cover over me and closed my eyes. I never in my life thought this day would actually happen. I didn't know what tomorrow would bring and it filled me with excitement, but truth be told, I was exhausted, and I didn't think it was the dance that put me in this state. I was so tired out by this man. For the first time, I did not want to dream of anything again, there is only so much my heart could take. Jane, but Robert's presence in the room was distracting me. I looked in his direction, he was looking out the window. I looked away, not wanting Jane to see me staring at her brother.

"Oh…that is good, erm… you must be really hungry," Jane said.

"Um... yeah a little," I responded.

"Oh, good because I got us some fish and chips. Rob, I didn't know you will be here, but I can share mine with you if you like." Jane offered.

"Thanks, Jane. That will not be necessary, erm… I will be in my room if you need me." As he made his way out, he stopped by me.

"It was nice meeting you again... Anna... I hope to see more of you." He smiled as he walked away. I followed him with my eyes until he was completely out of my view. I wondered what he meant by seeing more of you. It made me happy that he thought about me in that way.

As soon as Robert was out of the room, Jane ran over to me. "What was that about?"

"Um... what do you mean?" I said, pretending that I didn't know what she was referring to.

"Anna, this is me you're talking to. Robert, just said "nice meeting you again" to you and when I came in here, I had a feeling I interrupted something."

"Oh, I don't know what you are talking about Jane." I did not know how to tell her that her brother was that person I told her of.

"Stop playing games with me, I saw how you were when you were around him and he could barely take his eyes off you. He wasn't even mad at me, that was weird. Do you two know each other?"

"I won't put it like that exactly."

"Are you going to tell me, or do I have to force it out of you?"

"Jane, I don't know what to tell you really. The thing is you...you already know."

"What are you talking about? What do I already know?" I did not know how she would react to me liking her brother.

"He's the one, the man I told you about. The man I met at the airport, the one I ..." I couldn't finish that sentence, I knew what was going to come out of my mouth and I wasn't sure I should say it out loud, especially with him under the same room. She stared at me for a while and then gasped;

"You mean Robert is that guy, the one you talked about!" I nodded.

"Wow! I cannot believe this. It... It is such a small world. Are you sure it's him?"

"Jane c'mon! It's him, alright. How could I not be sure when I couldn't stop myself from thinking about him," I said.

"I am in shock, all this time you've spent wondering about him and it's been my Robert."

"Yeah, I know. It's bizarre. It's been your brother all along... imagine my surprise when he walked in," I said. We were both quiet. I didn't know what she was thinking or how she felt about this now.

Then she spoke, "You know, I always thought about introducing the two of you, but I never thought you would go for it."

"You did? I won't put it past you," I said.

"Yeah, I wanted to, but your head wasn't in the right space. I didn't think you would want to and Robert would not want me to either, not after the last time. Well, it seems, you two did not need me at all, even if I was the one that brought you here and made it happen in a way. But like you always say, if two people are meant to be together, fate will always draw them to each other."

"So, you don't mind that I like your brother then. I mean, not that it matters because... I am... I am not sure if he likes me like that, I mean the fact that he remembers me doesn't necessarily mean he wants to be in my life. You've told me a lot about him, he is very picky, and what's so special about me, besides? He barely knows me. I barely know him..." she held my hands.

"Anna, you are wrong, he likes you too." She laughed happily. (I smiled.) "He must do because I have never seen him look at anyone the way he looked at you. He was not mad I brought you here, you two are just weird and how do you meet someone so briefly and not be able to forget him or her after all this time. I do not know what his story is about you, but I do know that he remembers you and he wants to see more of you, Anna that makes me happy. I am happy if being with Robert makes you happy, if it ever happens, you have my blessings, not that you need it. However, I will give it to you anyway."

171

Elizabeth Johnson

I wanted to burst into tears, but I knew I had to control myself. A lot was going on at the same time; I still wanted to keep things in perspective.

"Jane, I don't know what to say to you, I am just going to let it play out however it does, but thanks for being such a good friend."

She smiled, "Are you still doing any rehearsals today?" Jane asked.

I had forgotten what I came here for. My routine still needed a little twitching here and there, but I just could not bring myself to think about anything now, not with him this close to me.

"Come, let's go and eat. I am starving and you must be too," Jane proposed. I couldn't even think of food; how could I be hungry when I was filled with thoughts of him? But, I followed her to the kitchen. I sat on a chair next to the island and watched as Jane plated our food. He could walk in any moment now, what would I do? I thought to myself. There was a collection of musical instruments, a saxophone and guitars leaning on the wall in the kitchen.

"Is your brother into music or something?" I asked as I stared at the corner where the saxophone and guitar sat.

"Why do you ask?" Jane requested.

"It's nothing; I just saw those instruments and wondered. That's all," I said.

"Yes, he was. He is actually very good with most instruments, but I think the piano is his favourite. He used to play a while back. He was actually in a band once, but he stopped when …our dad passed."

"Oh, okay. Do you know why?" I asked.

"I don't know the exact reasons, but he says playing reminds him of a time he wants to forget about. It is a long story and I had better not get into it."

"Hmm, okay. So, what's happening with you and Dave. Are you guys... um... still meeting today?" I had to change the subject; I did not want to pry, and I did not want to spend all day talking about him, moreover, I needed to know that Jane and Dave were going to do fine.

"Oh, that reminds me, I called him and told him where I was, and he said he would come here, but now that Rob is here, I better call him and cancel."

"Don't cancel. Why don't you go and meet him instead? You need to do this."

"And I want to, I am just a little nervous, you know. Plus, I don't want to leave you here alone, I don't know how comfortable you will be staying here alone with my brother."

"Um, I know what you mean., but I think I will be fine, so, don't put this off on my account. I am a big girl I can take care of myself and I am sure your brother is a gentleman. We were fine a moment ago before you came in and interrupted," I joked. Truth be told, I was glad she came in when she did or I would have melted into him.

"Are you sure?" Jane asked.

"Of course, I'm sure, you need to do this..."

"I am talking about you. I don't know if I should leave you at the mercy of my brother. You don't look like you have any blood left in you. Are you sure you can handle spending time alone with him?" We both laughed. I looked towards the stairs and I wondered what was going through his mind right now. All of me wanted to stay, to get to see more of him while Jane was away. But if I did, what would happen? Was he as excited to see me as I was? I guess there was only one way to find out, even if it meant I would have to ask him.

"Yeah, I'll be fine. I am going to resume rehearsals anyway. You go and have some fun, you deserve it." She pushed a plate of fish and chips my way. I picked at it and Jane watched me and giggled.

"You don't have the appetite to eat, same here. I better get going." She got up and threw the rest of her food in the bin.

"I'll just let Rob know I am going out for a while. It seems like you two have unfinished business." She winked and went upstairs to find him and before I knew it, she was back.

"He's having a shower. I was not able to tell him, do me a favour and tell him. I will be back soon," she said and rushed upstairs to her room. I started to panic inside. The thoughts of being alone with him made me nervous. Jane came downstairs; I met her in the hallway.

"Jane! I don't know..."

"Don't worry, you will be fine. Rob will look after you… and erm … yeah, if I'm not back early, don't wait up for me." She came over and kissed me on the cheek before rushing out to her car.

Chapter 22

I was asleep when Jane finally arrived; she snuck into my room and lay next to me. I felt her next to me, I opened my eyes a little and smiled at her. She looked happy, but now was not the time for me to ask her about her date; the sleep had taken over my body like a heavy drug.

The next morning, I was still in bed sleeping when I heard her tiptoeing around me. I managed to open my sleepy eyes and saw she was all dressed up. I did not understand what was happening. I sat up on the bed and cleared my voice to get her attention. "Hey, what's happening? Are we leaving?" I asked, disappointed to be leaving so soon.

She came and sat down next to me on the bed. "Oh no. It's just me. Sorry I woke you, I wanted to leave you a note."

"A note, why? Where are you going?" I asked confused, because she was going to leave me all alone with him again. It was not that I did not like being around him, but the intensity of what I was feeling inside scared me.

Beaming, Jane said. "I am meeting with Dave again; we want to spend the whole day together. I am so sorry I came back late yesterday; I was going to tell you all about it, but you were asleep when I got back. Don't worry, I will tell you all about it when I get back today." I was confused, I did not know who this Jane was. She had certainly changed from being reluctant to an eager beaver; I had never seen her in such high spirits. I had never seen her so happy to be seeing Dave Porter.

"I take it yesterday went very well then?" I asked.

"Like you would not believe, he invited me to his church, so we are going to the early morning service. You know he is a good Christian. We were meant to meet later this afternoon, but he told me if he did not have to go church, he would want to spend the whole day with me. I felt the same way, so I asked if he did not mind taking me to his church. He asked if I was sure, I told him I wanted nothing more. Anna, you are right, I am done with pretending he does not mean the whole world to me. He loves me, he told me last night. We were both honest with each other, I summoned the courage to tell him that I was being mean to him because I thought he liked you and not me. He laughed, and you know what he said? He said he knew and that's why he kept coming back for more." We both laughed.

"Anna, if not for you, I wouldn't have spent the whole night in his arms. I love him, Anna; when he told me how much he loved me, I didn't say it back. I don't know why, but I am going to tell him today." Jane smiled happily. I was happy for her; this was all I ever wanted for her. She deserved to be happy, and I was relieved she had stopped pretending with him.

"Hmm, this is very good, what are you waiting for? Get out of here already." I encouraged.

"You're not mad that I am leaving you again?" she said, pulling a sad face.

"Well, I will live, I am still here, aren't I? Your brother took good care of me yesterday, stop worrying about me for a change and do the things you need to do. I am a big girl. I will be fine." The thought of being alone with him again made me tingle with joy.

"I have nothing to worry about then," Jane said as she put her shoes on, wriggling her fingers like a school teacher, she added, "And you two need to sort things out. It's a good thing I won't be here… wait before you say anything; I didn't plan this, but hey, you guys get to spend more time together and that's a good thing is it not?" she asked.

I kept mute.

"What happened yesterday, anyway? How did it go?" Jane asked.

"How did what go?"

"You know what I am talking about," she said, narrowing her eyes; she did that a lot when she wanted to get something out of me. I laughed.

"Nothing, nothing happened, he just got me dinner and I came to bed. That's it, nothing juicy like you and Dave Porter. Now, enough about me, shouldn't you be on your way?"

"Yeah, that's right, I should go. When I come back, you have to tell me everything. Erm… in case I forget, I bought a dress and a jumper as spares for you. I was not sure which you would prefer. I hung them in the wardrobe; I hope you like them. Also, could you do me a favour? Rob is probably asleep, could you help me out again and tell him that I'll be away all day? I will probably come back very late, but I will try for your sake to come back on time."

I wanted to thank her for the clothes she bought me, but when she informed me that I would be telling Robert about her being gone all day, the prospect of being alone with him all day scared me. As much as I wanted him to myself, I couldn't trust myself around him.

"Why don't you leave him a note then, like you were about to do for me?" I asked. I knew there was no way I could avoid him, not that I wanted to, but I did not like situations that deliberately put me in front of him.

"Yeah, but I am already late as it is, love. I have to go now, just tell him I will be late."

Before I could protest, she was off. I lay down on the bed; I was not sleepy anymore, thanks to Jane. I heard her footsteps on the stairs. I smiled. So much for being discrete, if I could hear her, then Robert probably could too if he was awake.

What do I do now, I thought? I was awake now, and I did not want to sleep anymore. I looked at the time, it was seven thirty in the morning. I got up and ran myself a hot bath. While the bath was running, I went to see the clothes Jane bought me. There was a red knee length, short sleeve wrap dress and a navy-blue jumper with hearts patterned studs on it. I could have worn the dress yesterday, I thought. I knew which I would be wearing. I picked the jumper and laid it on my bed. I did not know how the day would go; I would prefer to get my rehearsals out of the way, especially now that he was still resting, but I also knew it was too early to play music so loud, that would wake him if he wasn't already awake. Somehow, it did not feel right that I was here in his home because Jane had hardly been here with me. I laid down in the bath and enjoyed the hot water caress my skin. If I did not know beforehand that Jane had plans with Dave Porter, I would have thought she set up this weekend on purpose. As much as I loved being close to him, the way I had felt since I laid eyes on him again was much different to anything I had ever felt. It couldn't be right to feel like this for someone I barely knew, just as it was not right the way I yearned for him in the past. This was not healthy, and I did not think being around him would help me and, yet, I didn't have the strength to stay away.

I could always call a cab if the situation got too much for me to handle. I came here to rehearse, I told myself, but my mind couldn't get off him. I got out of the bath; and made up my mind to get on with the purpose of the day. I changed back into my dance cloths, tied my hair up and then I went downstairs to the kitchen for breakfast. The chef was back. Jane had mentioned they came around when he was home. I greeted him; I did not know he was going to be there. Before I could say anything, he had greeted.

"Morning ma'am, Mr. Parkman is waiting to have breakfast with you…" I was in shock; this was not what I had expected to happen, I thought he was still sleeping. I was clearly wrong. The housekeeper was back as well.

She was coming into the kitchen through the door that joined the kitchen to the dining room.

"Good morning," she said.

"Good morning," I responded. She held the door open for me,

"Mr. Parkman is waiting for you in the dining room," she notified. I nodded in acknowledgement and walked through the double doors. I saw him across the room, although I could not see his face because he was reading a newspaper. I stopped to look at him, and my heart began to race again. I was breathing so fast; I had not gotten over dinner with him and I was now going to have breakfast with him so soon. He must have noticed my presence, so he folded the paper he was reading and got up. He smiled, I tried to smile too, but it was impossible. I needed my heart to slow down.

He walked towards me. "Did you sleep well?" he asked. I nodded and he stopped about two feet from me. "You look very well…" he said, I did not say anything back. I always found my tongue glued to the back of my teeth each time he was so close to me.

Elizabeth Johnson

"Do you mind joining me for breakfast?" he asked. I looked from him to the dining table where we both sat yesterday. I was quiet, he looked a little worried.

"I am sorry, if you would rather eat by yourself by all means..."

"I don't mind," I said, cutting in before he changed his mind. I did not want him to think that I did not like his company. He smiled; I could tell he was relieved. I smiled too in relief that he cared about me enough to want to be in my company.

"Here," he pulled the dining chair adjacent to his. I sat down and he sat on his chair; the chef came in and started to serve. He poured me a hot coffee; I was glad he was here because he distracted me from being so close to this man that had taken over my senses. We were having a full English breakfast; the chef served me first, I declined the sausages and the bacon, and he smiled at me. Then the man left us. I looked down at my breakfast. I picked up my toast and buttered it; I then added marmalade on top, Robert did the same with his toast. I wondered if this was how he liked his toast or if he only did it to please me. Before I could finish my thoughts, he said,

"I know what you're thinking; I was thinking the same when you added the marmalade to your toast. It's how I like it." I laughed softly, we had something in common, I thought. We ate in silence, although I was mindful of every bite. I knew I needed to say something to him, but I could not think of what to say to him. Then I remembered Jane's message.

"Jane left early this morning," I said.

He looked at me, wiped his mouth with a napkin and said. "Yes, I know. I caught her sneaking out this morning; she must have thought I was still asleep." He chuckled.

I smiled.

"She left you alone again," he said.

I glanced at him quickly and returned my gaze to my food.

"How do you feel about that?" he asked.

"About Jane?" I asked, not sure of the question.

"About Jane leaving you here on your own with me?" he clarified, his eyes were on me. My heart started to pound louder; I could feel it on my palms. I dropped my fork because I had lost my grip from nerves.

"It's okay…" I said.

He looked on as though he expected more from me. So, I continued. "I should ask you that question, I am clearly the one invading your space and you've been nothing, but a gentleman. Let me use this opportunity to thank you for your hospitality. Yesterday's dinner was good. I am sorry I was too tired to chat. And breakfast is beautiful as well. So, thank you for letting me stay here."

"Don't mention it; it's my pleasure really. Do you have any plans for later?" he asked.

I wondered why he asked.

"No, nothing at all apart from my rehearsals."

"Oh, I see, you look ready," he said, referring to my dressings.

I smiled, I had finished my breakfast and so had he.

"I won't take any more of your time today then, I shall let you go about your day." he said. I smiled apprehensively. I did not want to hear that, I wanted him to tell me he had something planned for us, but he did not. I got up; he got up from his seat immediately and pulled my chair for me.

"Thank you so much, for breakfast; it was delicious," I expressed.

Elizabeth Johnson

"Again, my pleasure," he replied. I walked away nervously. I was supposed to walk through the doors in the dining room to the ballroom, but I found myself walking towards the lounge. I was half way through when I realized I was going in the wrong direction, but I did not want to turn around. I went through the doors to the hallway and stopped by the first set of stairwells facing me. A strong part of me wanted to run back inside the dining room and tell him that I wanted to spend the rest of the day with him. I wanted to tell him how I felt inside, how not knowing how he felt about me was killing me. I wanted him to know how his presence affected me, how my pulse raced, how my palms sweat and my heartbeats became uncontrollable when I'm near him. How could I dance with him here? I had lost all control of my senses and this insanity has to stop or I could not bear to be around him any longer.

Chapter 23

Confessions

"This is ridiculous," I said to myself.

"What is?" I heard him say from behind me. I spun round immediately to face him. I was so busy pondering what to do next that I had not even noticed he had come to find me and he was standing close to me.

"What?" I asked, unable to concentrate as I took in his scent.

"I was referring to what you just said," he said slowly, moving closer to me one-step at a time, it scared me. I had to take a step back the closer we got. I did not understand; the way he was looking at me as if I mattered to him confused me.

"Erm... what was that?" I asked, my mind was suddenly blank; it felt like all my blood had drained out of me. My heart rate was over the roof. He stopped, he must know the effect he had on me by now, it was better that way before I lost my mind. My breathing was hardly slowing down. "Never mind, I am sorry if I startled you. I didn't mean to do that."

"It's alright; it's... it's my fault, I ...I didn't hear you coming," I blurted out. He chuckled.

So I was glad one of us found this very amusing. Then there was silence.

I did not know what to say and so did he, he did not strike me as someone who would not know what to say in a situation like this because he seemed very articulate and intelligent. Nevertheless, I guessed nothing prepared anyone for circumstances like this, or perhaps it was not like that for him at all. Maybe I was alone in this state of affair, it felt awkward. I reluctantly decided to excuse myself and find my way to the ballroom. "I should go and..."

"Would you like..." we both spoke at the same time. He smiled, and I smiled nervously.

"You first," he said.

"It's nothing, I ... I was just going to go back that way to the ballroom. What were you going to say?"

"Yes, of course you must... practice, you said so earlier. I shouldn't take any more of your time... erm, did I mention that you dance very beautifully? From where I was standing yesterday, I couldn't take my eyes off you... you were beautiful to watch." I blushed with embarrassment. He must have been standing there for ages when he first saw me yesterday.

"Thank you," I wanted to compliment him on something as well.

"And you... you have a very beautiful house," I said.

"No... not when you are in it. In comparison to you, there is nothing beautiful about this house."

The drumming of my heart began to pound again. He liked me, I thought to myself. I could not move, my eyes stayed on his.

"Thank you, you're...you're very kind." He took a step closer to me, his eyes fixed on mine; I looked to the ground.

"I wasn't being kind; I was merely stating the fact. You are the most beautiful person I have ever come across; you don't look like you believe me." The pounding in my chest took another turn; I rubbed my palms down the sides of my legs. I looked up at him and wondered how he could say that when he was standing in the same room as me. I did not know what it was about him that made me run out of breath each time I looked at him. Everything about him mesmerized me, from his eyes to his smile, his smell, his height, his hair, the shape of his mouth when he spoke to me. Where did I begin to describe how beautiful he was and he thought I was the most beautiful person he had ever come across?

He took another step towards me, we were now very close. I was frozen, I could not move. I did not know what he wanted, but I was ready for anything. That was how much he consumed me.

"May I?" He tucked a strand of my hair behind my ear just as he had done yesterday. I wanted to faint.

Then he asked, I could hear the nerves in his voice as he spoke. "Earlier I... was wondering," he said slowly, checking to see if I would approve of what he was about to say.

"if... you wouldn't mind... joining me later, that is after you have finished your rehearsals. We could go out, for lunch and afterwards do something fun together."

I was quiet, he did not say anything else again. He was waiting for my response, but I was still flabbergasted with the realization that he actually did like spending time with me for whatever reason.

"It seems you like feeding me," I joked, he half smiled.

"We... don't have to eat. I realize, I have done that twice now. It does not have to be lunch; we could actually do anything you... want. And later, I could go feed you if you don't mind," he said.

"Like a date?" I asked, he took a deep breath, and I took two quick ones. I did not know if I did the right thing by calling it a date.

"Yes, like a date. I guess I am asking you out on a date. Would you like to be my date?" he asked.

Who was I kidding? If I could shout it from the rooftop, I would. "Yes, I would, and I don't mind being fed at some point as well," I said, he smiled, and I was relieved, but then we just stood there looking at each other for a moment too long, not that I minded, but if only he knew the damage he was doing to me by just looking at me.

"I should go now, I will see you at ...," I said, but could not finish because his expression changed as if he had something on his mind. Then he said,

"Look...I don't know how to say this or even if I can say it out without looking..." he paused, and then he continued. "erm... for some reason beyond me, I have been unable to... to." He stopped talking again, took one look at me and took a few steps away from me. I wanted him to continue, what was he about to say? He looked worried as if he regretted what he was going to say.

"You were saying?" I asked, trying to urge him to continue.

"Sorry about that. Please don't let me take up any more of your time, I will see you later," he said, his voice rougher now, and he started walking away and for one mad second it felt like he was walking away from my life. As if I was never going to know what he was about to say and I did not like that, I was a little angry he was walking away. I had to know what he was going to say, or better still tell him how I felt; the worst that could happen is that I embarrass myself and I could surely live with that, when it came to this particular man.

"Don't go... Please. Tell me what you wanted to say." He did not say a word, so I continued. "What were you going to say?" I persisted. I felt frustrated; why would he not just say it so I could know for once. I knew we've only just met again, but it seemed to me like I had known him for ages and I was annoyed because I felt like I had been carrying this load around in my heart and now I just wanted to unburden myself.

Whatever he would say would have put things in perspective for me, and I will know where I stood with him.

"I can't stop..." I said. He stopped. I continued anyway, I had nothing to lose; I could leave it and see how things played out, but at this moment now, I wanted him to know the truth. I wanted him to know that I never forgot him, that he left a mark in me and if that meant that he didn't want to see me anymore after this then it was a risk I was going to take, but he had to know.

"I can't get you out of my mind and am not just talking about now. This is not something that happened to me since yesterday."

He turned around to face me, his face looked confused and shocked, but I had started now, and I was not going to stop until I had told him how I felt.

"Since that day I saw you at the airport, I was only with you for about five minutes, but something very strange happened to me. You have been in my head and on my mind since then... I think about you all the time. Dreamed of meeting you again, it was like a curse. I know I sound weird, I'm sorry, but it's the truth I had to let you know." He was quiet, I felt foolish, everything was going well but I had to ruin things when I opened up my big mouth. Surely, he wouldn't want anything more to do with me, I was sure.

"Look, I get it I sound mad and it is fine if you want me to leave, if you told me what I have just said to you, I would have that same look you have now." I was scared, I did not know what possessed me into telling him. But, I had unburdened myself and, in a way, I was relieved that he knew what was going on up in my mind. I closed my eyes knowing I just blew my chance with him. My heart felt like it would explode, I felt my body shake for fear of rejection, but I had brought it upon myself. I laughed nervously, I was thinking of ways to make it better, but he said nothing, so I tried to convince him I was not as crazy as he now thought I was.

"I tried, you know. I tried to stop myself from seeing your face, from thinking about you, but... I could not because I...I ... loved it, but it was fine. It was fine because you did not exist, not really, I never thought I would meet you again. Then Jane invited me here, and I come here to this house, and it so happens that you are real after all and seeing you in person blew my mind. Believe me, I tried. I really tried so hard to forget you, but you are real and so close. You are here, and you have been so nice and generous to me, all this brings out these ... these feelings that I cannot explain. I have never felt them before, and I have no right feeling them. I don't...I don't know how to handle it or behave around you." I took two quick sharp breaths and continued, I opened my mouth, but my mind was now blank, there was nothing more to say. I had said it all, he just stood there and stared at me strangely. I always knew the odds of him feeling the same was zero to none, but the attention he paid me since yesterday led me to believe he liked me, or so I thought. I had put my foot in it now and I had destroyed whatever could have happened between us.

"You must think that I am mad; I am sorry I told you. I'll just go get my things and I will be out of your hair and you never have to see me again." With two quick steps, he was at my side almost immediately. He gathered me in his arms and pulled me towards him. I did not know if he just wanted to calm me down, or because he felt the same way.

I was confused, but content to be in his arms, however long it may last. I laid my head on his chest; he held me close to himself. I could hear the beats of his heart, his and mine were going in quick successions and I could feel his breath on my neck. He did not say a word, but I knew he was thinking, thinking about what I just said. I wish I knew what was going on in his head, but I was content for now.

Chapter 24

We must have been standing there for half an hour or a minute. I could not be sure; I had lost my sense of time. Nothing around me seemed to matter now that I was in his arms. I was so happy; it felt like heaven to me, to be locked in his arms, taking in his scent and feeling the warmth of his body. I shut my eyes and tightened my hold on him, pulling myself closer to his masculine chest. I felt his hold on me tighten and he started to stroke my back. Everything was quiet except for our breathing, and my ever-racing heart. He seems in control of himself, I thought. He must be used to silly girls like me throwing themselves at him. However, none of that mattered now; I just wanted this moment to last forever.

"I feel the same way about you," he said, and then he continued. "I have felt this way since I first laid eyes on you." I felt as if I was going to die from a heart attack, I could not breathe, nor could I believe what I just heard.

"You don't know the joy I felt when I walked into the house and saw you here… in my house." He pulled away from me so he could look at me. The way he looked at me made me feel so beautiful.

He smiled, I tried smiling, but I could not; I was still in shock. Gently, he moulded his hands on my face.

"You are so beautiful, and you take my breath away each time I look at you." My eyes clouded with tears, I tried blinking them back, but a stream of tears rolled down my face instead. He wiped it away with is finger.

"Please do not leave, don't go. I want you to stay. I may not have had the same courage as you, but I felt what you felt all those months ago. You do not know how I am feeling now that you tell me this. How is it possible that two strangers feel the same way about each other?" I half laughed; I wanted to return into his arms, he must have known because he pulled me into his arms once again. I looked up at him, his eyes met mine and my lips as if by some magnetic pull were heading towards his. I was yearning for his kiss. His lips were barely inches from mine and then he whispered. "I have missed you".

"So have I," I replied. Then our lips met. I had never had such a sensational feeling before; it burned right through my whole body, setting every nerve in me on fire. I held him closer, and he pulled me nearer to him until there was no more space between us. His kiss was so passionate I could feel his hunger burning through me as our lips moved in synchronization with each other and my hands held him closer to myself with every strength that I had. He didn't seem to mind and we were lost in each other for a moment. Then, he pulled away from me, his hands still on my face.

"You don't know how much I have longed to do that." He stroked one hand over my cheek caressingly and my whole body shivered down to my spine, my knees were weakening with every single stroke. I could not believe this was happening to me. "I can't believe this is really happening to me," I said, he pulled me towards him again and our lips found each other once more.

Dancing was the last thing on my mind; I just wanted to stay in his arms for as long as I could. I tried so hard to remove the thoughts that I would be going back home to my flat today. I resented the idea, but I knew I had to. We spent the rest of the day talking; he told me everything from how he battled with himself on the plane, and how he wanted to wait and talk to me when we landed to how ridiculous and crazy, he felt when he could not get my face out of his mind. I told him all about my escapades, right to how I met his sister Jane. I was never bored with him, even when we ran out of things to say, we just sat on the sofa in the living room and cuddled one another. The feeling was amazing, like nothing else mattered besides him.

We did not go out, as we had planned earlier before my confession. It felt like we were making up for all those times we spent apart. I wasn't hungry, his presence filled me; we must have been talking for hours when I realized it was getting dark; I became annoyed because I knew I had to go and I didn't want to leave. I couldn't bear being apart from him, it was horrible. Then, just as if he read my mind again, he asked.

"Do you plan on sleeping over tonight? It does not look like Jane is coming back anytime soon," he said. I had forgotten all about her, I mean how could I think of anything else with this man here.

"Hmm… that's true, she said she might come back late."

"You do know that you can stay over if you want to," he said. I considered it, but I knew they would have to pull me away from him if I stayed.

"Thanks, but I should go home," I said reluctantly.

"Anna?" he said, looking serious all of a sudden. I turned to face him.

"Yes?"

"Listen, I will never take advantage of you in that way," he said, and I could see the sincerity in his eyes. He did not know it was not him I was worried about. Every touch, every kiss, every smile, every gesture he made had created a hunger in me for him and if I stayed, I knew I could not control myself. My body felt strange, I had never known anything like it and that was what this man did to me.

"I know, that's not why I have to go, though. I am not worried about you in that way. Since I saw you again yesterday, I haven't done what I came here for and it's no fault of yours." He smiled, I laughed.

"Before you go, let's go have dinner, we haven't eaten anything since breakfast, you must be hungry, right?" he asked. I shrugged.

"Now that you mention it, I don't mind dinner."

"Do you want the chef to prepare something, or do you want us to go out?" he asked.

"I don't know, whatever you think is best," I said. He looked at me and shook his head.

"You keep leaving these things in my hands, but I'm afraid I will get it wrong. I will love to take you out, but you will probably tell me that you have nothing to wear."

"Oh, but you're wrong. Your sister brought me some clothes, so we can go out if you want."

"Let's go out then, I will call and make a reservation, how long do you need to be ready?"

"Half an hour."

"Half an hour it is then. Go and get ready, I will be waiting for you. He went to the phone; I rushed up the stairs like a little girl. I took my clothes off and rushed into the shower. I creamed my face and my arms and sprayed some of the gorgeous body spray on my body. I knew what I was going to wear, the red dress that Jane bought me. It was as if she knew that this would happen. I pulled my hair into a ponytail leaving a few strands to lay about on both sides of my cheek. I knew Robert would probably tuck them behind my ears and I did not mind him doing that. I applied some neutral lip-gloss and coloured the edges of my eyes slightly. I stepped into my red dress. I heard footsteps outside; I thought of him, he must have come up to change. It was almost thirty minutes. The dress fitted me like a glove, and it made me feel beautiful. I stared at myself through the mirror before starting to make my way downstairs. I was nervous because I knew he was waiting for me, but I felt like I was seeing him for the first time after a long time apart. I wondered what Robert would think of me in this dress. I found him waiting as he said he would. He had changed his shirt. He was now wearing a light blue shirt and a blazer. He looked so handsome, and his eyes were on me like he had never seen me before. I smiled nervously; I was not used to him looking at me like that. When I got to his side, he said,

"How do you do that?"

"Do what?" I asked.

"Make me see you differently each time; you look breath-taking in that dress," Robert said.

I smiled. "Thank you," I said. I was glad he loved the dress. I have Jane to thank for that, I thought.

"Shall we?" he asked. He led me out, putting his hands on the small of my back as we made our way out of his house

Chapter 25

"Do you mind if I gave you a ride home after dinner?" he asked as he drove. I looked at him and looked away. It would be nice to get to spend that extra time with him, I thought.

"But what about Jane?" I asked.

"It seems like she is enjoying herself with this new friend. I was just thinking she doesn't have to rush back if you don't mind me taking you home," he said, his eyes on the road.

"Thank you, I will really like that," I replied. He glanced at me quickly and smiled.

"You would love the food here," he said as he pulled into a parking space. He brought out his phone and typed on it. I waited with him in the car as he texted. He looked at me.

"Sorry, I am just sending Jane a message. To let her know I would be taking you home." He got out of the car and walked round to my side to open the door for me. As we walked into the restaurant, his phone beeped, but he ignored it. We were shown to our table as soon as we entered. The waiter referred to him as Mr. Parkman. It seemed like they knew him here. We took our seats; as always, he pulled mine for me before taking his. Then the waiter returned with a menu and read to us by heart the specials of the day and his recommendations of wine to go with each dish. Robert asked him to give us a moment to decide what we would like. When the waiter took his leave, he asked me what I fancied. I could not make up my mind. From what I recalled, I heard the waiter mention a lamb dish and another that had to do with crabs. He noticed I was struggling, he said.

"Take your time, there's no rush." I smiled and cleared my throat, I did not like the fact that I was keeping him waiting. I thought about the two dishes on my mind and I decided on the lamb dish, but I wanted to know which one he took a fancy to as well. "I can't seem to make up my mind at the moment. What are you looking to have?" I asked. He smiled.

"I am easy. I will have anything with lamb in it." I smiled raising my eyebrow.

"It is funny you should say that; I was leaning towards the lamb dish."

"Really?" he asked, I nodded. "It's settled then," he said.

"What about starters?" he then asked.

"No, I will pass." I said.

"Perhaps another time then." I nodded, the waiter returned; Robert gave him our orders, and the waiter asked about the drinks. Robert told him to bring the best wine to go with our lamb. He returned later with a bottle of red wine. He stood beside Robert and described the wine to him. While Robert gave him his attention, my eyes remained on Robert. I could not believe I now had the man of my dreams and he was better than I ever imagined. I did not know what it was we were, but I was content at this moment. He was beautiful, even more so tonight. I could not take my eyes off him and my stomach was filled with butterflies. The waiter poured our wine, I lifted my hands to stop him from giving me too much, I then requested for water. I intended to drink more of the water than the wine. I cannot let anything dilute what I was feeling at this moment and I did not want the alcohol to spoil things for me.

While we waited for our food, I told him, "You look very handsome, and I love that shirt on you."

He looked at me, sighed and said, "Thank you, I am glad you like it." Our food arrived and we both began to eat. He did not lie when he said I would like it here; the food was delicious. I loved it, and I told him so after my first mouthful.

He said, "I told you, you would like it."

We chatted some more as we ate, he didn't ask me anything serious, we just spoke about my love for dancing, and he told me how he had promised to work less and enjoy life a little bit more. He asked about my family, wanting to know if I had any siblings. I told him I was an only child. He wanted to know if I lived at home with my parents, so I told him I moved out of my parents' house recently, which was technically true. I felt the need to let him know I was a Muslim in case he had issues with that, but he said it did not matter to him what religion I was. I was even more overjoyed that he did not see my religion as a hindrance, although, I had not been practicing of late. Had a Muslim girl like me decide to marry a Christian, my children will automatically be Christians because of their father and that was why Muslim girls were not encouraged to marry outside the religion, whereas the men could. However, if a Muslim girl married outside her religion and her husband decided to convert to Islam, and truly practices it, then the union could be accepted. I was not thinking of marriage, but his acceptance of me without hesitation had me in awe and I knew I would do anything to be with this man. Then he asked about my plan for the week. I had nothing but work, next to him. I wanted to drop everything, but I knew I could not, I still needed my job to pay my bills.

"I have got to go to work," I said.

"Ah, work." He looked disappointed and so was I. Then he informed me that Jane had sent a message that she would see me at work tomorrow. We finished dinner; I cleaned my plate; the food was that delicious and he felt as much. I was not sure if he did that because of me, because I had noticed he would do something he would not necessarily do to please me, like the dinner situation last night.

I wanted to be sure, "I see your plate is empty too, did you enjoy it?" I asked.

"The lamb was beautifully cooked, I couldn't help it," he said. Someone came over and cleared the dirty dishes. We were then given another menu for dessert, but I was not going to have any. He picked up his menu, and then he noticed I was not having a look at mine.

"What's wrong?" he asked.

"I don't want any?" I said.

"Okay then, shall we take our leave?" he asked, I nodded. He called the waiter and asked for the bill, and then he gave his credit card. Moments later, the waiter returned with his card, and we left the restaurant to return to his car. As we settled in, he asked me. "Do you want me to take you home now?"

I missed him already, but I knew I could not stay. If I did, I would not be able to stay away from him. I did not know about him, but what I was feeling was too intense to be anywhere alone with him tonight.

"Yes please," I said reluctantly.

"Okay, tell me your address and postcode?" I gave it to him and he punched it into his car navigation system.

"What about my things?" I asked.

"That would be a reason for me to see you again; don't worry, I will bring them to you," he said. I was happy to know we were going to be seeing each other again. He started the car, and I silently prayed in my heart for there to be traffic, but there was none. We drove in silence, but it was not awkward or anything like it; I actually enjoyed it. The simple fact that we were together was enough for me. I kept stealing glances at him all the way while he concentrated on his driving, his eyes were on the road the whole time, as if he had something on his mind. I was guessing it's just a look he had when he didn't want to speak. I did not care, I just wanted to enjoy the little time I had with him before the journey ended. Before I knew it, we were on familiar territory, and then he turned into my street and finally, he stopped the car in front of my flat. I knew I should get out of the car, but I wondered if he might want to come in for a little while. I did not want to leave him; I had no idea when I would see him again. He sat back too, then he said.

"So, this is your place?"

"Um... yes. Do... do you want to come in for a while?" I asked him, hoping he would say yes. He did not answer straight away. He turned around and faced me and I could see through his eyes what he was about to say.

"Anna, I want to..."

"But?" I interjected.

"But not today, believe me, it is not that I don't want to, but I have a meeting very early tomorrow. I never knew I would meet you yesterday. I already had this planned. This weekend with you was beautiful," he said. "It was magical for me too," I cut in, he smiled.

"I am sad it's come to an end; I loved every moment I spent with you," he said. My face brightened with a happy smile; my eyes swelled up. I wanted to cry, but I knew I was being stupid and too emotional. Jane always said he was a workaholic. I knew it was selfish of me asking him in after we had spent the whole day together. He needed time to process things and I should too, but my heart was sad. It felt like I was not going to see him again.

"It's okay; I understand, I was stupid to ask anyway," I said, opening the door to get out; he reached across and stopped me just before I got out.

"Don't say that, you're not stupid, you are a very brave girl. I'll see you soon, alright, sooner than you think." Then he planted a kiss on my forehead; I nodded to affirm what he said, then he said. "Wait there." He got out of the car and opened the door for me as he has always done. I stepped out of the car, and he gathered me in his arms and kissed me on my neck. Then he looked at me, tucked a strand of my hair behind my ears, and said, "I will miss you." I did not say a word, but my heart definitely skipped a beat. He got in his car, glanced at me and waved and then he drove away, leaving me there as I watched his car disappear from my view and I felt as if he took my heart with him.

I could not sleep; I tossed and turned all through the night with dreams of him. I woke up and thoughts of him flooded my mind again. I went over the weekend right from the moment he came back and saw me in his house to the last words he said to me outside my flat. I lingered on every touch, every stolen glance and the magical kisses we shared. There was an undeniable passion for one another, and it was like nothing I had ever known. I did not know if it was the build up to seeing each other that made it so intense. All the craziness we both experienced before fate finally brought us back together. And the way he made me feel like I was the only girl in the world was amazing. We connected so easily and it was weird how two people from two different worlds found comfort in each other

Chapter 26

Getting to know him.

I got to work early, hoping I could get some time alone with Jane before the store opened for the day. I did not want to wait until lunchtime before speaking with her, but I did not see her. I had so much to tell her, she had said we would see each other today. I called her phone, but she sent me to her voicemail. I thought perhaps, she was starting at noon today. After my lunch break, I went in search of her; another colleague she called while I was on break told me that she had taken the day off. I went to look for Dave Porter, but no one had seen him either. I was a little disappointed, because she had not called me. I had so much to tell her and I needed to hear everything about her date with Dave Porter, but they have both skipped work. I smiled happily; even though I would have preferred to have her with me, I knew that she and Dave Porter were together, and it meant they were doing well together. I kept checking my phone through the day, I was expecting a call or a text of some kind from her, and it was not like her not to get in touch with me. I did not want to worry, but I was a little concerned. I had never been to Jane's house, so I would not know where to go to put my mind at rest. I also did not have Robert number neither; we never exchanged numbers. I did not know what I was thinking and I tried not to panic. He told me he would be busy, but I felt incomplete all day. I knew talking to Jane would help.

I tried very hard not to think about him; it was difficult, a part of me wondered if he had regrets about me already. What if my confession was too desperate? But then again, I tried to reassure myself that he actually liked me, especially because of the things he said to me. He said he felt it too, what I was feeling. I was overthinking things, I tried to push him out of my mind and focus on my work. I was glad when I finished work; the day was a long, boring struggle. I had never felt more alone; yesterday, I was feeling on top of the world and for some reason, the thought that I would never see him again over-took my mind all day. As I walked to the bus station, my phone started to ring; I searched through my bag quickly. I had waited all day to hear that sound, and now I was rummaging through my bag for my phone. I finally found it and pressed the receiver before the ringing stopped.

"Hello?" I voiced.

"Hello, Anna," Robert's voice filtered into my ears and my heart skipped a beat. I had not expected to hear from him again, not to talk of this soon. I stopped in my tracks; I could not move, my stomach dropped.

"Robert?" I asked. I was quivering with happiness.

"Were you expecting someone else?" he asked playfully.

"No, it's not that, it's just how… how did you get my number?"

"Oh, I rang Jane last night when I left you, she gave it to me. You don't mind, do you?"

"No, I don't mind, I am glad you called," I giggled.

"How are you today?" He asked, I was quiet; I didn't know if I should tell him the truth, that my mind was going crazy because I had thought I wouldn't hear from him again. I didn't know why my mind made a point of deceiving me because yesterday, he never gave me the impression that he didn't want me. I decided to tell him a shade of the truth.

"I was miserable…I missed you," I said, I did not know what he would make of it. He chuckled and then he said.

"I'm glad." A certain kind of calm came over me; I was all right again, but I was still worried about Jane.

"Have you heard from Jane today?" I asked.

"Funny you should say that, she called me this morning. Something about her going away with her new friend; she didn't speak long which I found strange, but she sounded happy. Did she not tell you?" he asked. I was not happy she did not call me to tell me; I was of the impression that I would be the first to know, but clearly, I was wrong.

"No, she didn't, but I am glad she is okay."

There was silence on both ends, I could hear his breathe on my receiver. I took a deep breath to still my heart.

Then, he spoke, "Do you have any plans for later?"

"No, I'm on my way home. I am actually just walking to the bus station."

"I can see that…" he said.

"Wait, what do you mean by that?" I asked.

"You look stunning by the way, even in work clothes."

"What! How can you tell what I look like Where are you?" I was happy, I looked around for him.

"If you turn around, you'll see." I turned around there was a car behind me, but he was not at the driver's seat. There was a chauffeur behind the wheels; then Robert stepped out of the car, and he looked so graceful. I was speechless. Thankful, but in shock. I never thought I would see him this soon, I remembered he said I was going to see him sooner than I thought, but I never thought it would be the next day.

I hurried towards him. He was smiling, I wanted to rush into his arms, but I stopped myself and stood a foot from where he was. Desperation was not an act I wanted him to see in me.

"Wow, I didn't think I was going to see you so soon!" He chuckled and said,

"I couldn't stay away; that is how much you got to me."

"But how did you know where to find me?"

"I can be very resourceful, especially...because you were on my mind all day." He reached his hand to my face and caressed it and I wanted to melt. Then he said,

"It wasn't hard to find you, you work with Jane, so I knew where to look." He smiled and pulled me into his arms. I summited myself and laid my head gently on his chest, taking in his beautiful scent. Then he pulled away a little to look at me, "Would you like to ride with me?" he asked. I nodded, he placed his hands on my shoulders and opened the car door for me, and then he got in with me. I was so happy and nervous; I did not know what to expect from him.

"So yesterday, because of me, you weren't able to rehearse and as much as I love staring at your beautiful face, I will not be happy if you don't get to do what you love. Your dance the other day was extraordinary, so I have a plan for you. Would you like to hear it?" he asked.

"Yes, go on. Let's hear it."

Elizabeth Johnson

"I would pick you up after work each day and drive you to my home so you can rehearse to your heart's content and I will also drive you home each night, what do you think?"

"It's fantastic, but I would be taking up a lot of your time. I can't believe you would do that for me? Thank you."

"Don't thank me; you forget I get to see you every day, that is a bonus."

"I love your plan; I am so happy, thank you so much. When do we start with this plan of yours?" I asked.

"As soon as possible, today if you are up to it. I promise not to get in your way. I was amazed, to think earlier, all sorts of negative thoughts ran through my mind. It all felt unreal, like a dream. Too much was happening too fast, but I did not want any of it to stop. In fact, I was afraid I would wake up and find out that it had all been a dream, or a wild imagination. He instructed the chauffeur to drive.

"You're too good to me; I don't know what to say."

"Say nothing, just let me be there for you." I smiled and looked away shyly. On the way, he told me about his day, what he did at work without going into details. I complained about my feet hurting because I had to stand all day; he placed my feet on him, took off my shoes and massaged my feet.

"There, better?" he asked, I nodded.

"Are you going to be able to dance, because if you would rather not today, it's fine?"

"I will be okay, thank you, but I don't know if I will be able to do anything with you around. You make me very self-conscious." I said, he looked puzzled.

"I do? I am sorry... erm, I don't know what to say. I erm..."

"It's not a bad thing, I am very conscious around you because I am still getting to know you." I explained. He smiled in relief, then he said,

"I know we only just really met, but I hope you like being in my company. If this is all too much for you or too fast, please let me know. My intentions are not to…" I did not know where he was taking this talk, but I had to let him know I loved every moment I spent with him.

"Robert, stop; I love being around you, I want nothing more and you make me self-conscious in a positive way. Don't worry about what I said, okay?"

"Okay, if you say so." The driver drove through the gate; as we approached his house, he said,

"Look, I asked my assistant to do a little shopping for you and have it delivered to the house. Just a few things you can use while you are here. I did not want you to have to worry about change of clothes and other essentials. If it is too forward, I will ask them to take it back and I apologize in advance."

"No, it's not, it's very thoughtful. Thank you, but how do you know my size?" I asked.

"I kind of… described you to her, does that sound terribly bad?" he asked.

"No, not at all thank you," I said, I didn't know what to make of him buying me clothes, not that I did not appreciate it, but I didn't want him to think that I just wanted to depend on him or that I wanted to be with him for the wrong reasons. The chauffeur parked the car and opened the passenger door for us. Robert thanked him and asked him to leave. He helped me out of the car. When got inside his home, he said to me,

"You can go upstairs and get changed if you want. I will try and stay out of your way, but when you finish, please come find me and we can have dinner together before I take you home. How does that sound?" He asked,

"It sounds like a plan to me."

"Okay, I'll leave you to it then," he said and walked into the kitchen. I stood where I was and watched as he walked away, then I heard him talk to someone. My guess was that he was talking with the chef. I went upstairs to the room; I slept in two nights before. It had been updated; there was a chest now, with a mirror above it, a chaise at the foot of the bed and a dressing table with an oval mirror on it. Also, the bed was beautifully made and my dance clothes that I left was laying perfectly on it. I dropped my bag on the bed, I walked over to the wardrobe and found the rest of my clothes and about a dozen more clothes, dresses, jeans, jumpers, tops and jackets all hanging beautifully in the wardrobe. I ran my hands through them; they still had their tags on. I looked at one of the tags and gasped at the amount it cost. I had worn and owned expensive designer clothes in the past, but I did not expect him to spend so much money on me. At the bottom of the wardrobe, there were shoes. They were all amazing and all too much. I did not know if I could accept it all. We were still in the early days, and if I accept it all, what if he thought I was just a gold digger after his money, but at the same time, I didn't want to sound rude or make it awkward for us if I turn down his presents.

I could not think now, I needed time. I changed from my work clothes into the dance attire on my bed; I packed my hair up, so it was out of the way as I usually did and headed downstairs. I walked through the lounge into the dining room; he was nowhere to be found. He meant it when he said he would keep out of my way. I walked into the ballroom; the CD player was still where I left it. I walked over and put it on. The song filled the room. I began my stretches; I wondered what he was up to right now. I tried to concentrate on what I was doing, but I kept thinking about the clothes and shoes upstairs. Now was not the time, I told myself. I got up and started my routine. Blocking everything out of my mind, I danced my heart out until I was too tired to move. As I walked back through the lounge to the hallway, I saw him walking up the stairs; he must have gone for a swim. His body was wet and he had a towel across his neck. I looked away; it did not feel right looking at him in his swim shorts. I hide until he was no longer in view before going up the stairs. Once I got in the room, I stood under the shower and washed off the sweat; he might be doing the same about now, I thought. I wondered about the clothes again, I did not know want to do. I got out of the shower and creamed my body. I opened the wardrobe and picked out my clothes that I left the last time I was here. I dressed up and stared at myself in the mirror. I did not feel happy with my decision to turn down his presents. I took off my top, and looked in the wardrobe for something amongst the clothes he bought me. I found a white top; I did not bother looking at the tag because I knew they were all very expensive. I took off the tag and slipped it on, I did not feel so bad anymore. I walked down the stairs; he did say that I should come find him, but I did not think that by that he meant for me to come to his room. I walked into the kitchen; the chef had just finished cooking, and the aroma of whatever he just prepared smelt delicious. I suddenly felt hungrier now. I greeted him, he smiled and nodded. I walked from the kitchen into the dining room to look for him, but he was not there. Then I saw him by the doors that led to the ballroom. I walked over, but he did not turn around. I did not know if he had heard me coming, but from where I was, he looked so beautiful. I put my hands around his waist and hugged him from behind. It was brazened of me, but at that moment, that was all I wanted to do. He let me hold him for a while, and then he turned around to face me and said,

"That felt good." I laughed softly.

"Come, you must be hungry, I know I am," he said. Together, we both took our seats; dinner was beefsteak, potatoes and asparagus. As we tucked into our dinner, he asked, "Do you like the things in your room? If they are not to your taste, I will have them replaced."

207

"No, they are fine," I said, he smiled. Then I knew I needed him to know that I was not comfortable with the idea if it would make him think I am with him for the wrong reasons.

"I just want to say that I do like that you want me to be comfortable when I am here, but you don't need to buy me things. They are nice and very expensive, but that is not why I like being with you," I said. He dropped his cutlery and looked at me, and then he placed his hand on mine.

"I know that, Anna; you didn't ask me to, I just wanted to do something nice for you. I apologize if you think I crossed the line. I am not very good at this, and we are still just getting to know each other, but I do not want you to lack a thing. There are things we would do together and while we are together, even when we are not, I want you taken care of. I want to look after you if you allow me." I always knew his intentions were genuine. I didn't know why I felt uncomfortable, perhaps, it was because I had been brought up with so much wealth and living on my own with very meagre funds as created this independence in me, but I didn't mind anymore as long as he now knew that money isn't what mattered most to me.

"I don't know what to say, thank you. I really appreciate everything you do for me. I am sorry I brought it up."

"It's okay, I like that you spoke your mind. Promise me you will tell me anytime I cross the line." I laughed,

"Don't worry; I'll let you know, not that I think you would.".

My mind went to Jane, I still had not heard from her and it worried me. I had to ask,

"Have you heard from Jane again."

"Yes, I did; she called from her friend's phone. She said I should apologize to you on her behalf, she said her phone died and she didn't know your number by heart," he explained. I was relieved to hear that.

"I feel better now," I said, he smiled.

"Do you know this new friend she is so happy to be with?" he asked. I smiled,

"His name is Dave Porter, he is such a good guy, and he adores your sister," I tried to assure him.

"Hmm, he does? How do you know that?"

"I just do; I work with the two of them and I see how he looks at her when he doesn't think anyone is watching. And believe me, Jane puts him through a lot, but I am happy they are giving what they have a go."

"Okay, I will take your word for it, it's not like her to just go away. That worries me, our mother is worried and you clearly were a moment ago, but she says she is fine. I guess I have to take her word for it." I laughed softly and then I said,

"You should be happy that she now has a life of her own. She told me about all the dates she set you on, especially the last one." He shook his head.

"She told you all that? What can I say, my sister is a nightmare, but I love her to bits."

Dinner was done. We moved to the living room, I sat close to him and placed my head on his shoulders, and we spoke about all sorts of things. We discussed my love for dance at length; I loved that he encouraged my passion. He told me about his music background, but he never spoke in detail, and then he suddenly got up and told me to get ready.

"Get ready for what?" I asked.

"To go home," he said. "You have work tomorrow, I will pick you up at the end of the day." He was right. I did not want to leave, I never wanted to leave him, but I knew I had to go. I did not bother changing; I went upstairs for my bag and work clothes and came back down the stairs. He was waiting by the car outside.

"I will drive you home, I sent the chauffeur home." He opened the car door for me and then he got inside, and we began the journey to my flat. It never felt good leaving him, but I now knew I would see him at the end of day each day and that felt good. As we approached my house, my stomach dropped; I was missing him, even though I was still with him. He stopped the car in front of my flat; the journey felt even quicker than yesterday. He got out and opened the passenger's door. I stepped out of the car; he could tell I wasn't too happy.

"What's wrong?" he asked. I smiled and shrugged my shoulders,

"It's nothing, I just miss you already," I said, he smiled. He pulled me into his arms and buried his hands in my hair.

"I miss you too," he said. Then, he pulled away so our heads would meet and planted a delicate kiss on my lips. I responded, moving my lips sensuously against his and once again all these funny feelings started to build up in me the more we kissed. It was as though we were kissing for the first time. I had wanted to kiss him all day, but never had the courage to initiate it. I loved the feel of his masculine body next to mine, as I shamelessly pressed my body closer to his. I did not want him to stop, but just then he pulled back from me. His breathing was rough, so was mine. His hands were on the back of my head, locking our heads together. I felt my body tremble, the feelings in me raged like fire all over my body. Then he kissed me on the forehead and pulled away completely from me. "You better go inside," he said, trying to compose himself. I nodded and without hesitations, I dragged my reluctant feet away from him and stood outside my door. He got in his car and waited until I was inside my flat before driving away.

Chapter 27

While I was undressing and changing into my nightshirts, my mind kept wondering over the kiss, and I admired him for not taking advantage of the situation. We were both burning
with desire; he could feel mine; I could feel his, and I was glad he walked away because I did not have the strength. Although I had never been with a man before, I knew that my feelings for him were too strong and if I was not careful, I will start craving him more than I should.

He did promise me yesterday he would never take advantage of me; I guess he is true to his word, which made me find him all the more irresistible. I couldn't even believe that I was acting this way, it was only just the second day, and all I could think about was submitting my body to him.

Two weeks passed, and he continued to pick me up from work as promised, and just excused himself when we got to his place, giving me room to practice. As much as I appreciated him not wanting to be a distraction, it felt like he stopped paying me attention. It made me feel insecure like he was no longer interested in me. I wanted to spend more time with him, I didn't enjoy dancing anymore, because I clearly couldn't concentrate on what I was doing. My mind went to him and the closeness we shared before. Even though I was under his roof, I was missing him.

Him? And if I did summon the courage to ask him to spend more time with me, would he not think me too clingy and that could drive him even further away. I didn't think I had the right to raise it with him. What were we? Who was I to him? It annoyed me that I needed him like the very air I was breathing. It annoyed me that he didn't make excuses to want to be with me. If being in his house was his way of keeping me close to him, I wanted more effort from him.

I just finished another round of undevoted practice for the day when he walked in.

"Are you calling it a day already?" I heard him say from behind me.

"Yes. Since I am allowed back tomorrow, I thought I would do a bit each day, or I will run out of reasons to be here." He chuckled and walked towards me, and my heart started again.

"So, where were you?" I asked, trying to distract myself from his closeness and not let my annoyance towards him show.

"I was in the garden, out back; I didn't want to distract you, but I caught the very end of it and you continue to amaze me with your moves; its spectacular!" I began to blush at his compliment; he must have noticed it, because he gently brushed my cheek with his fingers.

"Thank you, you flatter me so much." He put one arm around my waist and led me out to the living room where he had a glass of water waiting for me.

"You should give yourself more credit." He handed me the water; I downed it all gratefully.

"Now sit down." He said as he gently pulled me onto the sofa, knelt in front of me and lifted my feet up and began to massage it.

"You've been on your feet all day; this is the least I can do." He said. His touch was magical; it did things to me in places I don't care to describe. I shook like a leaf inside but tried to compose myself, so he doesn't see what his touch did to me.

I smiled, "You are so thoughtful and caring." All the annoyance that had built up in me earlier disappeared. My mother always said that when men cared for you, it was usually because they wanted something in return, but it was not the same with Robert.

Robert was different from all other men; I did not need eternity with him to know that. If my mother were here, I was sure she would say it was too early to tell. In any case, in the world I came from, I would never had met a person like Robert had I not escaped.

How could anyone else say with certainty what was good for another, or what you may or may not feel for someone else. My parents were so sure I would fall in love with Ashraf, how could anyone be so sure? What I felt now in my heart for Robert I do not think I could give to another. It consumed me, and I'm scared that if Robert knew how strongly I felt in my heart for him, he would run.

"I should take you home now," he said, brushing strands of my hair away from my face. He seemed to love doing that, I noticed.

"Absolutely," I said, disappointed to be leaving, but I knew it was the right thing to do. For about two weeks, he had not kissed me, nor had he pulled me into his arms as he did when we met again, and I missed that. Although I saw him every day, it was not the same any more, I felt like he had gone off me and if that was the case, I was in trouble because my heart had fallen completely for him.

"Let me get my things from the room," I replied, as I tried to hide my disappointment.

"Okay. I will be waiting outside," he said as I took the stairs two steps at a time.

He was already in the car when I got outside; I got in the car and we began the journey back to mine. It always took about forty-five minutes to an hour to get to mine. I looked at my watch; it was almost nine o'clock. I figured I will possibly get home at ten and then he would have to drive another hour back and get back to his place at eleven. He wanted to do this every day for the next few weeks, which I found crazy.

"What are you thinking about?" he asked.

"What makes you think I am thinking about anything," I replied.

He smiled and said, "You have that nervous look, the one I saw on your face at the airport." I smiled; I tried not to think about that day. A moment passed as I deliberated whether to tell him what had been upsetting me.

"I was just thinking about you," I blurted out, he turned his head to look at me,

"Why would you be thinking about me when I am right here?"

"You have been avoiding me for some time now, since we started this plan and I know you are doing all this for me but somehow in my head I think I agreed to this, so I can get closer to you and it seems all this has done is the complete opposite. So perhaps I have read all the signs wrong, and you're not that into me as I thought you were. Jane told me you can't commit, and I fear that's going to happen with us. That is if you haven't already decided that I'm not what you need." He was quiet for a while before answering me.

"Have you finished?" he said, not taking his eyes off the road.

"No, I still have a lot to say actually, but go on and tell me it's not true." He pulled the car on to a side road and switched off the engine. We sat still for a moment before he spoke.

"Isn't it obvious…?" he said without looking at me.

"Isn't what obvious," He took in a deep breath before turning towards me.

"Anna. That I love you." My heart drummed hard, I had not expected him to say that at all. He half laughed, then continued. "I'm no good with words but I'll try to explain how I feel. For me with you it's different. I don't know, yes people will say it's too fast to know for sure, but I know what I know. You've held my heart since that day I saw you. I love being around you, but you're right I stayed away because being close to you make me feel things that I have never felt for anyone, you make me weak, I may not show it the way you want me to but it's true, I have fallen for you. You are what I had waited all my life for, you are what I need. I don't know if this is what you want to hear, but there it is. And now, I've laid all my cards on your table." he said.

And I just stared at him. Happy tears brimming on my eyes, my head screaming he loves you too as relief washed through me and my poor heart swelled with joy at the same time, I could hear the rhythm of the beats rising and falling and I feared all the excitement would make my heart explode.

I wanted to say something, but I did not know what I could say that could top what he just said to me, and he must have known by now that I loved him too, but then I could not hold back the tears.

"Anna, you are crying? I am sorry, I … I didn't mean to make you cry," he looked confused.

"I am… I am alright, I … just don't know what to say after that; I feel foolish now, saying what I said."

"Ah, I told you I was no good with words," he said, leaning closer to me.

"I don't want you to cry, Anna, that's not what I was aiming for."

"Believe me, these are tears of joy. I was scared; I thought you didn't want to be with me anymore."

"Why would you think that?" he asked.

"I don't know, but you've changed, and you know you have. You kept your distance and I just missed you even though I've seen you every day." "I am sorry, if I made you think I didn't want you..."

"It's okay, I know better now. Did I ever tell you how emotional I get over the littlest things?" I half smiled. He reached out his hands and touched my cheek, wiping away tears from my face. He put his arms around me to comfort me and brushed his lips against mine.

"Don't worry, we've only just began. I will learn every little thing about you, you only have to promise me one thing?"

"Anything, name it."

"That you won't cry every time I tell you something nice, because you're going to get a lot of that from me," he said.

I laughed, "I'll try." I said

"Please do." He said, then he started the engine.

As we continued the journey to my home, I did not say a word; I laid my head on the headrest looking at him as he drove. My mind hung on every word he told me. I shut my eyes. I did not want to think anymore; it always makes me paranoid.

My mind went to Jane, and the discussion we had earlier at work. She said Dave would be leaving work and moving to Cambridge where Dave had enrolled to do his masters. And she had gone with him to see where he would be living the days, I couldn't get hold of her. She also told me she would be applying for a transfer to be closer to him. I couldn't tell her not to, I had my Robert now and I didn't want a day apart from him so, who was I to tell her not to go and be with Dave. However, this was not good news for her mother. Jane said her mother thought it was all too fast and wanted Jane to take things slowly. I wasn't sure what Robert's take was on Jane moving to Cambridge to be with Dave, I did not know if he already knew, but I knew it was not my place to tell him.

We arrived at mine; and as expected I didn't want to be separated from him. We sat quietly for a moment, I looked through the window to my flat, and then at him and sighed. He leaned towards me and drew me closer to him; he gently pulled my face to his and planted a kiss on my lips.

"I know how you feel; I'll see you tomorrow, Love." I nodded; and got out of the car before he could take off his seat belt, so he didn't have to open the car door for me, and quickly walked towards my front door. My heart was strained; I did not understand why I felt that I needed him with me always. If he could control himself, why couldn't I? I turned around to wave him bye, he waited until I was inside my flat before spinning his car around.

***

Six months had passed now since I ran away from my family. I promised Louisa that I will write to her, but I hadn't done that since I arrived in England. So, I wrote her a long-deserved letter. I wanted her to know I was happy now, that I was doing alright and that I had found the man of my dreams because of her. If she had not helped me, I would not have met my Robert. I told her everything in detail, how my heart pines for him, how we had met at the airport and how fate brought me back to him through his sister who was now my best friend. I wanted Louise and Jane to be friends too and hoped that one day the three of us could meet. I asked her to reply with news of her own new experiences and news of my parents, especially my mother. Although I had escaped, I still loved my mother very much. So, I begged Louise to go see my mother and reassure her that wherever I was, God would take care of me. I put the letter I wrote, all five pages, into an envelope. I addressed and stamped it to be posted on my way to work.

Chapter 28

Hearts entwined (Four months Later.)

We had a routine now, he and I. I go to work and he picks me up from work and feeds me, a couple of kisses in between before he took me home. We had been together for almost five months, but it felt like we had known each other all our lives. Sometimes, I slept over at his and he slept at mine. It was not easy when we did sleep overs. He told me he would not touch me until he knew I would be his wife. I found it ridiculous; he knew my heart belonged to him, not that he had proposed to me. When I slept at his, it was easier because I had my own space, but when I forced him to stay at mine, it was difficult for the two of us. He asked me once, "Why do you keep insisting I stay here with you? You know what you are doing, you know I can't escape you. You torment me, but I am not going to give in." I laughed.

Dave Porter and Jane finally left work two months ago and moved into a little apartment in Cambridge. Robert offered to buy them a house of their own, but Jane declined; she did not want Dave to feel indebted to her family. Robert invited them over last weekend and we all had a beautiful time together. It was so much fun. Robert did a lot of scrutinizing when it came to Dave Porter as all big brothers do, but Dave, as usual, was a very lovely person, so Robert had no choice but to fall for his charms like Jane and I had, Jane more so than I, though, as expected. This was the life, I told myself, nothing can go wrong now. Jane and Robert talked a lot about Alex their brother and they are excited that I should meet him. He was to be visiting with his fiancée, April, this Christmas. We had another three months before it was Christmas, which Robert and Jane had insisted I would spend at their family home. But, I was apprehensive because Robert had not introduced me to his mum yet even though we had been seeing each other for five months. I really would love to have met with his mother before then. I had asked him once or twice why he had not taken me to meet his mother, but he always found a way to change the subject.

Apart from that, my life was the happiest it had ever been. Robert worked less, but at times he stressed about work, about deals that weren't going right. When he stressed, I just listened and traced the lines on his face with my fingers; it seemed to relax him. And for me, it was another way to enjoy his beautiful face. He had not travelled for business since we met, I don't know if he cancelled deliberately or if it was just coincidence. There were also no late business meetings anymore, which was great for me, he was never late to pick me up from work. Although he could always send the chauffeur if he had meetings to attend, but Robert wanted to be there every day when I finished work which suited me just fine. We had talked about me quitting my work; he insisted on paying my rent, which I declined so many times. Jane spoke to me about it; she did not understand why I was being stubborn about it. I did not enjoy work as much now because she had left but giving up work felt like giving up my independence. After my talk with Jane, I told him he could pay my rent, but I still had to keep working. I thought it was a good compromise and he accepted. I no longer lived in fear of mounting bills because Robert took care of everything for me. He opened an account for me and put a lot of money in it. I had not touched the money because he bought me everything, I needed so that I never wanted for anything. He spoilt me rotten, he tended to every need I had. He was incredibly attentive to anything I had to say, and he had the patience of a saint.

My dance auditions passed, and I did not attend. I didn't feel ready but luckily there was another which I registered for and now preparing for. The routine was always going to be the same, but I needed to nail three different routines for three different songs. When Robert has time to spare, he sits and watches me rehearse, each time, he claps and compliments my skills, I smile.

"If I were terrible, would you tell me?" I asked once. He laughed softly. "You could never be terrible at anything," he said, "Moreover, you were born to dance. You've got it, babe, you have nothing to worry about." Though I knew I was good enough, his encouragements went a long way.

One evening, after I had finished rehearsing, and we were having dinner, Robert asked. "So, would you love to meet my mum this weekend?" he said, I raised my brow, I had thought he was never going to ask, I couldn't think of a reason why not. He loves me, his sister adores me, I was optimistic his mum and I would get on as well.

"Sure," I said after a long pause. "I thought you would never ask." I said, although I must admit, my heart feared the possibility of his mother not liking me.

"Okay," He said, and not a word more. That night he was weird, he didn't speak much. We kissed, and he went to bed. I couldn't sleep, my mind wondered why he had not introduced me earlier, I wondered what would happen to our relationship if she hated me.

As the weekend drew closer, I became very nervous, but I didn't mention my worries to him. If he knew I was worried about meeting her, he would not take me to her and I needed to meet his mother. Robert meant everything to me, and my future even though we had not discussed it was going to be with him. So, meeting his mother was a good thing.

The day came, we had breakfast, watched TV together and then at one we set out for Robert's family home. I was quiet, I didn't know what to expect.

"Are you okay, darling?" Robert asked on our way.

"Yes, I'm fine. My tummy feels strange." I said, he smiled and held my hand with his free hand.

"You are nervous, you'll be fine. It's mum. She's great, you'll see." He said.

I heaved a heavy sigh. "Okay." I managed to say, I noticed my throat was patched, and my hands were sweaty. I had to try calming myself, we were only visiting his mother.

"Does she know we are coming?" I asked as Robert pulled into their drive.

"Yes, darling. She knows."

Robert rang the bell, but no one opened the door, then he used his keys to let us in.

"Are you sure you told her we were coming?" I questioned again. Robert nodded.

"She probably went shopping, make yourself comfortable." Robert said as he gestured to a seat.

We sat around for almost two hours before his mother finally came home. Robert had wanted us to leave earlier, but I insisted we waited for her. When she entered the living room, I got up to say hello, but she ignored me as though I was not present in the room. She hugged her son. I waited until they had finished greeting each other before trying again, but, she refused to acknowledge me, I could tell from the look on Robert's face he was angered. I held his hand; I didn't want him to get in an argument with his mother over me. His mum left for the kitchen and he turned to me and said, "Wait here, I got this." Just then, his mother asked,

"Rob, what would you like to drink?"

"Mum, Anna greeted you, you didn't respond. Did you not hear, or can you not see her?" he asked.

"Oh, I heard all right," she replied.

"So, why are you being rude to her?"

"Son, don't tell me how to act in my home. You don't tell me what to do," she defended herself. This was more than awkward for me, I wished I had not insisted we stayed. I wanted to be anywhere but where I was, I knew this was going to test our relationship.

"Do you care to explain why you have decided to embarrass me this way?" Robert asked as he left to go meet his mum in the kitchen.

"Because I told you not to bring her to me." She said without a care if my feelings were hurt. I wanted to run out, I didn't want to be there in her house anymore.

"I don't get it, you don't know her, how can you hate her this much." Robert shot back.

"I don't need to know her, I warned you before now, so don't act surprised or don't think that just because you brought her here, I won't tell you exactly how I feel."

"Well, I guess this is my fault. I thought you were better than this." Robert said, I wanted the ground to open and hide me. I wondered what it was that I had done to make her hate me this much.

"As you can see, I'm not, and I'm never going to change my mind. So don't waste your time thinking I will accept her. You can choose now son, your mother or that woman out there?" There was a deafening silence.

Then Robert spoke, "Mum, it's a shame you are so narrow-minded. Anna makes me happy, I love her, she is important to my life. She has not wronged you, but you have judged her unfairly so. As long as you decide not to see her, you might as well say goodbye to me."

He walked out of the kitchen, looked at me, his eyes were pained. He wanted to apologize for what I just heard, then his mum came into view. I felt my whole-body shake, tears pushed through my eyes.

"That's your decision, Robert? You have only one mother, girls go, and they come. And you choose this one? I know it has not been easy for you to find someone you like, but for goodness sake, Robert, is this what you want? You know I would never accept it. So, I suggest you end this madness now or you will break this family. If you stay with her, never come back." That was hurtful to hear, she hated me unjustifiably with a passion. I couldn't believe this was happening to me, it felt like a dream. I always knew everything was going too smoothly, and now we're here.

What now? I was sure we were over. No matter what happened as long as his mother refuses me, I couldn't see us lasting and it killed me. I didn't want the resentment he will feel later if he chose me over his mother.

Robert was fuming, he held my hand, as we made our way out, then at the door he stopped and turned on his heels.

"Well I guess it's goodbye, Mum." He said sadly. "This is not what I wanted. You've made something that has nothing to do with Anna her fault. If you ever change your mind, you know where to find me—if you change your mind."

"Don't count on it, son; you know now where I stand on this. Since you want to pretend that what happened never took place, carry on with your life, but leave me out." She looked me over and walked away.

What took place that I'm supposed to be guilty of? I wondered, what they referred to, the way she looked at me just then made me feel unworthy of Robert's love. And my heart broke all over again.

Roberts's eyes were red; he was so hurt; I could tell he regretted bringing me to her. Now I understood why he changed the subject so much when I had asked him in the past.

"Let's get out of here, Anna!" he uttered, I followed him immediately. I did not want to be anywhere near her, neither did I ever want to come back to this house ever again. While we sat in the car, tears poured freely down my chin. I knew it was not his fault, but in my head somewhere I blamed him. If he knew she did not want to meet me, why bring me to her at all? I thought to myself.

"I am so very sorry Anna, I never… I never thought she would…. I never thought she would do that to you. I thought that if … if she met you, she would change her mind." He tried to apologize, but I could not even look at him. I knew he chose me over his mother. But what took place at his family home made me feel dirty somehow and he should have told me what problems his mother could have had with me before bringing me to her. I wanted to ask him, but I was too angry, I didn't want to talk. As he drove, he turned towards me, but I could not bring myself to look at him. "Say something please, Anna," he said.

"I just want to go home," I said.

"We are almost home," he said.

"No, I don't want to go back to yours. I want to be alone; I want to be in my own house alone. Please take me now."

"Don't do that, Anna. I know you are angry and you have every right to be but let me make it up to you." I did not want him around me now; I had never felt such shame. All that kept going through my mind were the words his mother spoke.

I could not let it go; she may have said those words, but he put me in that situation and I did not want to be around him. I felt like I was suffocating,

ou need to stop the car and let me out," I said.

He was quiet and then, "Anna, you are not thinking straight right now. Please just let me take you home, I will explain everything to you."

"It's too late, Robert, I don't want to hear it. I just want to be alone; I don't want to be around you. Please stop the car and let me out," I said, doing everything to stop myself from screaming at him.

"Anna..."

"I said, stop the car!" I yelled. He drove to the side of the road and I quickly got out, I needed to breathe. He came after me, but I just ran until my legs could not run anymore. He must have stopped chasing me because I could not see him anymore. I walked to a filling station and asked the man at the reception for a number to a cab office. He called me a cab. I sat outside the filling station until the cab arrived and he took me home. When I got home, I sent him a text saying I did not want to see him later; I did not want him to come and pick me up from work. I just needed him to stay away from me for now.

It finally hit me, that we had both been deceiving ourselves. I knew my parents would never accept him and, now, I know his mother would never accept me. So, how can we move on with the way things are, except we decide that our families matter not. The honeymoon period was over, and it was now time to look at this situation with my eyes wide opened.

Chapter 29

Love sick.

A week passed, and my anger subsided; I had not heard from him in all that time. He stayed away as I asked him to, but I was missing him. It was hard not to when we had always been together every day since we met at his house. I stared at my phone each night wishing he would call, but he did not. I found it hard to sleep, my heart was in trouble, and it throbbed for him. I would hear a car outside my door, and rush to see if it was him and the disappointment was overwhelming when I realized he was not going to call or come because I told him to stay away. I was now even angered that he was not fighting for me. I knew I told him to stay away, but did he not miss me? Had he just moved on, had he finally realized that he should never had chosen me over his mother? I wept to sleep each night. There was an unbearable pain inside me, and I could not bear to be around anyone. I called in sick at work. I was annoyed with myself, for being angry at him when he had chosen me over his mother. Not that I had wanted that outcome, when I still don't know what I have done wrong. However, my anger towards him built the more space he gave me. Yes, I told him to stay away but did he have to listen so well?

Two weeks passed, and still no word from him; I was now truly sick, I wasn't eating, or sleeping very well. I missed him so much. Jane called; it had been a while we spoke last. I was glad she was checking up on me but then she asked if I had heard from Robert, she couldn't reach him. I did not know what to say to her, I did not want her knowing we were no longer together. That thought alone tore me apart more. I tried to pretend everything was alright, but Jane sussed me out. So, I told her what happened at their mum's. Jane apologised for her mother's behaviour. Then she told me that I needed to call Robert, but I argued that he should be the one calling. She explained that Robert would not call because I had told him to stay away and that he probably thought if he called before I was ready for him, he would make it worse. Still I was annoyed, but I understood her point. I had to swallow my pride and make the first move if I still wanted him in my life, and so I did. That night, at nine, I sent him a text saying, 'Robert, can we talk? Call me please.' He did not reply, I waited an hour and still there was no response. Two hours passed and still, he ignored my message. A fresh surge of pain hit my heart; I found it hard to breath, my mind ran to a sudden conclusion. Robert did not want me anymore, my greatest fear had now happened, I had to fix things before it became final. I needed to see him, if he did not want me anymore, he had to say it to my face. It was late, almost midnight, but I had to see him. I called a cab to take me to his home. I sobbed all the way to his house; I couldn't control the tears. "*Get it together.*" I told myself. But there was no controlling my broken heart. The cabman worried, he asked me what was wrong, but I could not even speak, I was so broken. He dropped me outside Robert's gate; when I paid him, he asked if I wanted him to wait for me, but I told him to leave.

I was not thinking clearly; Robert could throw me out and I would be stranded, but I was ready to take that risk. I punched in the code, and the gate opened. I was glad he had not changed the code. I started walking to the house, it was a long walk, I was so cold and, in a hurry, to get to Robert, I had not thought to wear a jacket.

Strong cold wind blew as I approached the house, the heavens opened, and it began to rain. I was so cold; everywhere around me was dark and it did not feel like anyone was home. I got to the front of the house and pressed the bell twice or three times, but there was no response. He was not at home; it finally hit me. I walked forward a little and sat down on the ground and wept some more. I didn't have a key to his home, because we were always together. I felt lost. I looked for my phone in my pocket to call a cab as the rain beat down on me. When I found my phone, it was wet, water had gotten into it through my soaked clothes. I was now truly stranded. Just then a loud thunder struck, I held my ears to block out the noise. I didn't hear the door open behind me. The air at the back of my head stood up as I felt someone approach me. Afraid, I turned my body to see who it was, I could not see clearly; my eyes were swollen from tears and the rain blocked my view. Then my vision became clearer, I could not mistake him for anyone else, I wanted to smile with relief, but my body shivered with cold.

He looked shocked to see me, he had on his pyjama-bottoms, rain water trickled down his muscular chest. "Anna?" He called, I didn't respond, I just watched him as he walked closer. "What are you doing here so late?" he said,

"I… I…" I tried to explain but I could not form any words, instead a fresh stream of tears clouded my eyes. He put his arms around me and lifted me up. "You're freezing, Anna, what were you thinking?" He sounded angry, as he carried me in his arms like a baby and he took me inside, through the stairs and into his room. He placed me on his bed and covered me with his duvet. Then he went into his bathroom and ran me a bath. While the water was running, he returned to me. We did not speak. He could see I had been crying, he looked unhappy, but my vision was blurry, but I felt safe, and I just wanted to sleep now.

"Your bath is ready, Anna, come," he said. I shook my head in protest.

"No Anna, you have to, your body is too cold, you need heat." He said, I nodded, he was right, I knew that much. He picked me up again and carried me into the bathroom. "Do you need help?" he asked. I shook my head, and tried to unbutton my top, but my hands were shaking. "May I?" he asked, I looked at him and nodded. He helped with my buttons and then he excused himself. I took off my clothes and let myself in the bath. The heat from the water consumed my body. I laid in the bath, my knees to my chest, I was tired. I couldn't stop my eyes from closing and I must have slept off in the bath.

I woke up and found myself dressed in a nightdress, tucked into his bed. I did not remember leaving the bath. I looked around for him, but I could not find him. My eyes were still heavy with sleep. I lay back on the bed and slept. As I slept, I could hear him talking to someone, but I could not get up. He came into the room, so I tried opening my eyes, but they felt swollen and heavy. Still, I squinted so I could see him. He sat at the end of the bed and observed me, I felt like an invalid, I tried siting up; he came closer and told me not to get up. He looked concerned, and I did not understand why he was fussing over me. We needed to talk, that was why I came. I remember what happened yesterday right up to when I went in the bath. "Don't get up, Anna, you had a fever, you were burning up all night. I had to get a doctor to come see you, and he says you need rest." I wanted to speak but my throat felt dry.

"Wa-water!" I said. He brought me a glass and some pills,

"The Doctor prescribed some pain relief for you." He said. I didn't like taking pills, I shook my head and pushed the pills away.

"Anna, look at me, you are not well. You're burning up and I need you to get better, please take this pill darling" I could see the worry on his face, so I nodded and took the pill from him downing it with a little water. Heaviness soon filled my eyes and I fell into unconsciousness once again.

When I finally came to, another day had passed, Robert was asleep on a chair beside my bed. "Robert! Robert!" I called. He opened his eyes immediately.

"Oh, Anna, thank God you're awake. I was so worried, darling." He said as he reached for my hand.

"I'm fine, I just needed to sleep." I said, he placed his hand on my forehead and smiled with relief.

"You're no longer burning up." He said,

"I don't understand." I said

"The pills the Doctor prescribed for your fever, worked." he said.

I did not understand what he was talking about, I did not remember seeing a doctor or taking any pill. "I took a pill?"

"Yes, love, and it worked. It brought your temperature down. Do you want some water?" he asked., Until then, I did not realize I was thirsty. I nodded. He got up to get me some water and I watched as he went. When he was out of the room, I got up and walked weakly in front of the mirror, my eyes looked very swollen and sunken. My legs felt very weak and my head was light. I held on to the bed frame for dear life. I looked like I had not eaten in days, I did not like the image that I saw in the mirror. I heard him coming; I walked back to the bed and lay down before he came back to the room.

"Here, drink a little," he offered, as I tried to sit up. He supported my back with his arms and I had a couple of sips.

"Thank you," I said.

He smiled at me, but I could tell he was not happy. I had so many questions to ask him, but now did not seem the right time to start all that talking. "You need to take another pill, but you need to eat first. Are you hungry? Should I ask the chef to make you some soup?" he asked.

Elizabeth Johnson

"No, I am fine, I am not hungry, thank you," I said. He looked worried.

"Anna, you do not feel hungry because you lack appetite, but you must eat, so you can take your pill, or the fever will be back. Please, darling, for me." He said, I sighed.

"Why are you so worried?" I asked, he was quiet and looked away from me. I reached my hands to his, and he looked at me.

"You scared me, Anna, it's been a nightmare, the thought that I could lose you was unbearable. Please, darling, eat a little for me." I could see that whatever happened with me really terrified him; I moved my hands over his to comfort him.

"I am okay now, tell the chef, I'll have some soup." I said to him. He tried to smile, and I could see it, but he did not.

"Okay, thank you!" He said as he rushed to get the message to the chef.

I tried staying awake while I waited for the soup, but sleep soon found my eyes.

A moment later, Robert woke me up.

"Here, Anna," he said as he sat opposite me with a tray of food. Soup and bread.

Robert fed me some soup, and I ate some bread, then he gave me another dose of pills, which I swallowed quickly, so he didn't worry too much about me.

He looked happier now, and I was glad, I wanted to sit and talk, but I was too tired to do anything.

"You need to rest now, go back to sleep," he said, but I needed to know what exactly happened to me. "Tell me, what happened! Why am I so sick?"

"Sleep, Anna, let's talk about it later," he said, but I was not having it. I wanted to know what got him so worried.

"No, tell me, I want to know everything." He looked at me hesitantly, then he began to speak.

"It's my fault, I shouldn't have left you in the bath by yourself. When I came back to check on you, you had slept off, but when I tried to carry you, your body was very hot. At first, I thought it was because of the heat from the water, but it wasn't. Your temperature increased. I placed a cold towel on you to get the temperature down and that was when it started, you became somewhat delirious. You were saying I abandoned you, that I should leave you alone, you said something about your parents; you said it's their fault you left home. You had me very worried; I had to call my doctor to come see you. He gave you an injection, it calmed you and allowed you to sleep. Your blood glucose was very low, you had not been eating, Anna, why? I'm just glad you're better now, please rest we'll talk later. Okay?" He got up to go and I held his hand. He placed his free hand on my cheek and caressed it for a moment, and then he said. "I am not leaving you by yourself; I will be sitting over there. I moved my head to look at the wing chair in his room. "Is that okay?" he asked, I nodded. I let go of him and he leaned over and planted a kiss on my forehead. "Sleep now, my love," he said. I turned on my side so I could see him as he sat. I smiled and then shut my eyes again. Before I came over to his house, I knew I was not well, and the rain and the cold, plus my continuous crying, must have made me worse. Sleep soon reclaimed my body, this time I felt at peace, my heart was no longer in pain. I don't know how long I had slept before I heard him call my name.

"Anna, wake up, you need to eat again, so you can take your medicine," he said. I opened my eyes slightly; I was still very drowsy. I nodded slightly. "I ran a bath for you. Would you like to have a bath?" he asked. I felt weak, but I understood, I had been in bed too long.

"What's the time?" I asked.

"It's seven in the evening," he said. I was shocked; I had slept for almost two days as it is. I tried getting up. "Wait, let me help you up. I swung my feet to the side of the bed; he came to my side at once. I placed my foot on the floor and pulled myself up to stand. He held me, and I felt light-headed again. I tried to find my balance, and when I was sure I could walk by myself without his help, I told him to let go, but he was not having it. He held me close to him until I was in the bathroom. "Would you like me to stay?" he asked. I looked from the water in the bath to him.

"No, I will be fine, I promise. Don't worry so much, Robert," I said, trying to smile. He left reluctantly. I walked to the mirror to look at my face, my swollen eye had decreased significantly. There was a spare toothbrush on his counter, so I pressed some toothpaste onto the brush and gave my mouth a good clean before I took off my nightdress and stepped into the bath. What he said to me earlier played on my mind, especially the bit about my family. I wish I knew exactly what I had said. I did not stay too long in the bath; I stepped into the robe he placed on the Louis chair in his bathroom. When I re-entered the room, he was sitting on the floor with his back to the wall of the bathroom; he got up as soon as he saw me.

"How do you feel now?" he asked.

I looked at him cautiously before answering. I felt fine now; I did not want the fuss. "I am fine now. You have to stop worrying. It makes it seem worse than it actually is. Look, I am fine," I said.

He sighed. "I have asked the chef to have your dinner brought up," he said,

"No, absolutely not. I want to come down for dinner,"

I said. He looked at me for a second and then he asked, "Are you absolutely sure because it's not a problem. I will stay here with you and we could dine together," he said.

"I am sure, Robert. I want to have dinner downstairs with you; if you keep me up here, I will feel like an invalid and I don't like that feeling," I responded.

"Okay then, I brought you some clothes from your room, they are in my dressing room. I will excuse you, take your time and there is no rush," he said and excused himself.

I went into his dressing room and picked out the first dress I saw as now was not a time to be choosy. It was a black dress: the sleeves were see-through lace. I put it on and let my hair fall freely to my back. I had no time for make-up, but my lips felt dry. I applied a lip-gloss to moisten them. Then I went out of the room. He was waiting at the top of the stairs, I thought he would be in the dining room.

"What are you doing here?" I asked. He laughed.

"I can't let you go down the stairs on your own," He replied. I smiled, he held me close to him and together we walked down the stairs and into the dining room. We sat down, and the chef served us; I was not hungry, but I knew if I did not eat, he would worry, so I tried to eat half the contents on my plate. He then brought out a couple of pills and asked that I take them. I downed them with water and I saw he was not so worried anymore. As soon as he realized that I did not want to eat anymore, he left his meal and took me with him to the lounge. He put on the radio and music filtered through the room and then he sat down and placed my head on his lap. We did not speak; it was just nice to be back together as we used to be. Now was not the time to discuss what had caused us to be apart; I wanted to enjoy this moment and tomorrow we could talk about it. After about an hour, I was tired. I looked up at him with sleepy eyes. He knew, I had to get to bed.

I got up, but he picked me up. "Shush," he said as I tried to protest. He took me up the flight of stairs and into his room and laid me back on his bed.

"Where would you sleep?" I asked.

"Don't worry about me, there are many rooms in this house," he reassured me. I smiled and then I coiled back into the arms of sleep

I slept through the night and when I woke up, I looked at the time on the wall: it was a few minutes past six in the morning. I looked across the room and found him. He did not sleep in another room as he suggested; he was asleep on the chair. I got up and picked up the blanket at the end of the bed and covered him, he moved a little then resumed sleeping. I stared at him as he slept, he looked so beautiful. I moved away; I didn't want to wake him up. I was feeling better now; I did not want him worrying about me, and I went into the bathroom to get ready for the day. I must have been in there for fifteen minutes, when I heard a knock. "Anna, are you in there?" Robert asked.

"Yes," I replied.

"Are you okay? he asked.

"Yes, I am fine; I will be out soon, Robert," I said.

"If you need anything, let me know," he said.

"Okay, thank you, but I am really fine now," I said. He stood at the door for a bit before he left.

Chapter 30

When I re-entered the room, he was nowhere to be found. The blanket I covered him with earlier was now neatly folded on the bed. I looked through the rails in his dressing room for something casual to wear; I found blue jeans and a white jumper. He seemed to have moved half of my clothes to his room. That made me smile, it meant he still cared. I had not had time to think, but his behaviour confused me. If he still cared about me as he had been showing, why did he not come find me? Why did he leave me alone? Why did he not respond to my text? I went down the stairs to find him. I met with the housekeeper on the way; we exchanged pleasantries, she seemed happy I was feeling better. My eyes were no longer swollen and I was hungry, my appetite was back. I went to the kitchen; I greeted the chef, calling him by his name, "Jeff". Jane always made a joke about him; she called him Jeff the chef. He looked happy to see me looking all better. I sat by the island.

"Has he come down yet?" I asked Jeff

"No mam," he said. He placed a teacup in front of me and poured me some tea. He knew how I liked my tea; I thanked him and took a sip. I sat there on my own while Jeff got the breakfast ready. Robert came in search of me,

"Ah, there you are." He planted a kiss on my cheek and sat next to me. "You look better. Do you feel better?" he asked.

"I feel great! I am better now!" I said, he smiled. Jeff started to plate our breakfast; he poured coffee for Robert.

As we ate, Robert looked at me and said, "Your audition is in two weeks." I didn't say anything. I didn't like the fact that he had refused to address what happened to us. He seemed to just want to pretend that everything was fine now.

"What's wrong? Did I say something wrong?" he asked. I took a deep breath,

"No, I just don't think my audition is what we need to discuss," I said. He looked at me, and our eyes stayed on each other for a bit. Jeff left the room.

"I am sorry, Anna, I do not know what to say. It was not what I wanted, but you did not want to see me. I didn't like what happened; I could not bear not seeing you. And you asked me to stay away to give you the space you wanted. I went away. I had a business trip I had postponed earlier. I asked my secretary to set it up and I went. Listen, Anna, it was difficult for me. It was hard, Anna, I kept my phone by me all through, but you never called. Then I decided I would come find you; I came back the night you appeared in front of the house. I wanted to call you, but apparently, I left my phone on the plane. I had planned to come to you in the morning hoping to catch you before you left for work, but you beat me to it. When I saw you outside in the rain, it broke my heart. I'm so sorry I can't begin to tell you how much I regretted going away, it wasn't the wisest decision. You were so ill, and it is… it is all my fault. All of it. I knew that my mum was not a fan of ours, still I took you to her. Please can you forgive me, for putting you through so much? I love you so much, you don't know how much, but I know that you are my life, you mean absolutely everything to me, Anna."

As I listened to his explanation, I was no longer annoyed. My eyes began to water again, and a fresh pool of tears rolled freely down my face. He wiped my tears with his hands, but I could not control my emotions I had feared the worse and now relief washed through me after he apologised.

"Please don't cry anymore, Anna," he said, pulling me closer to him and placing my head on his chest.

"I don't want to, but I can't help it, Robert," I sobbed into his chest, "I thought you didn't care anymore, I thought you didn't want me any longer, you stayed away too long. I couldn't breathe, I missed you so much, I thought you didn't love me anymore. I did not know how I would survive losing you because I love you. Robert. I love you so much and I am sorry I told you to stay away. I was angry with the way your mother treated me and I took it out on you, but I never meant what I said. How can I? When I can't live, I can't survive without you?" I said through tears.

"It's okay, my love, we are together now and nothing else matters." He pulled my face up so he could see my face. "Listen, not my mother, no one comes before you. I love you; I want you in my life for as long as I live. This situation just proved what I already knew, you are my life Anna." he said., I laughed happily. "Anna, next time you come over, look under the flower pots, I always leave a key there." He said, I nodded. "Look, I have decided to take the week off. Let me take you somewhere to make up for what happened please," he said.

But I had work and I had not been to work for almost two weeks. How could I take more days off? "What about work?" I asked.

"Anna, you don't need to go back; I know you insist it gives you independence, but if you think about it carefully, it takes away time you can use to prepare for your dance. You can do anything you want in all that time, so why do you insist on slaving away there? It tires you out each day. Please do not go back," he pleaded. His argument made sense, but what would I do with all the time I would have on my hands? It would be like when I was back home with my parents. I wanted to please him, but I needed a bit more convincing.

"If I don't go back, what would I do after I have danced to my heart content and you're not here? I'm not going to dance all day!" I argued back.

"You could use that time to discover things you are passionate about. I mean apart from dancing; you are better than working in a stockroom. You could even have your own dance studio. I will support anything you decide to do, but please don't go back there," he said. He had a point; I never thought about opening my own dance studio, it was a very good idea.

"Okay," I said.

"Okay what?" he asked.

"Okay, I won't go back," I said happily.

"Really?" he looked like he did not believe me.

"Really, I am not going back." He got up, picked me up and swung me around. I laughed hysterically as he did. "Put me down, Robert!" I screamed amidst my laughter. He finally stopped and planted big kisses all over my face. It warmed my heart to be so loved by him.

"Go pack your bags, love. I am taking you anywhere you want to go." "Anywhere?" I asked.
"Yes, anywhere in the world you want to go, just name it. We will take the jet and fly there. I will call my flight crew to ready themselves," he said.

"Really? Anywhere?" I could not believe we were just going to leave.

"Just name a place darling, hurry up. Where do you want us to go?" he asked. I could not think of a place off the top of my head. I said, "Mexico!"

"Mexico it is then, darling. Come on, pack a bag," he said.

"Now?!" I asked, unsure.

"Yes now, love; go pack a bag, we are going to Mexico," he said.

I ran towards the stairs.

"Anna," he called out.

"Yes, Robert?" I replied, spinning round.

"Be careful, love; you only just got better," he said, smiling; I laughed and continued racing upstairs. I could not believe we were really going to Mexico. Half an hour later, I had hauled everything I could fit into my travel bag into it. I stopped to think of what I may have forgotten, but then I remembered my passport was not with me, it was at my flat. I ran out the door and into Robert's arms; he was coming to find me.

"Are you ready?" he asked.

"Oh Robert, I don't have my passport with me," I said.

"Then we would go and pick it up. Don't worry about it. Are you packed?" he asked, I nodded. "Okay, I will bring your bags down for you. Go downstairs to the car; the chauffeur is here already." I walked away to go down the stairs, but he pulled me back into his arms, and held my face.

"You are so beautiful, Anna; you just leave me breathless when I look at you. I am truly lucky you are mine," he said, and then he kissed me slowly at first and then intensely and I responded with the same passion. When we broke off the kiss, I could barely stand. My head was spinning. I could not think. His breathing was heavy,

Elizabeth Johnson

"I will see you in the car," I whispered.

"Okay, I will be right behind you." I went down the stairs to wait in the car, as he asked, the chauffeur was waiting. He opened the door for me and I thanked him. Five minutes later, Robert came with our bags, he placed our bags in the truck and got in the car sitting next to me. He instructed the chauffeur to take us to my flat. He told me we were going to a private beach that belonged to a friend. He held me in the car all the way to mine; we shared a few more kisses along the way. The passion was too intense, and I started to think about being together in Mexico by ourselves in a romantic scenery might tempt us to take things further. The chauffeur arrived at mine, Robert wanted to come inside with me, but I needed a few minutes away from him to cool this hunger burning inside me for him.

"No, stay here," I said.

"Are you sure?" he asked, I nodded. I ran inside my flat and went straight to the bathroom. I opened the tap and splashed cool water on my face; I didn't know if it would help cool me down, but I needed something cool right now to stop me from feeling the way I was. I wiped the water off my face with a towel, and then I sat down for a while before going to get my passport.

Chapter 31

Tough times ahead.

When I came out of my flat, Robert was standing by the car, he was on his phone; I could not hear the conversation, but he did not look happy. As soon as I stood next to him, he ended the call and helped me back into the car. Whatever he was discussing must had been serious, he wasn't himself, "What is wrong?" I asked. "Don't worry about it, it's nothing," he said. I wasn't buying it, I needed to know who called and got him in that state. *Perhaps it had to do with business,* I thought, he always stressed when something wasn't going his way.

"It doesn't look like nothing to me, is it business?" I asked, he shook his head.

"Anna, don't worry about it, something came up, a little hiccup, I'm sure it's nothing." He said, but I wasn't prepared to leave it be.

"Tell me please," I insisted. He was quiet, he looked away from me.

"Please, Robert, tell me, you look disturbed," I persisted. He took a deep breath.

"It's my mother; I was just on the phone to Jane and she said…" he choked up. I did not push and I held his hands. "Jane told me she is at the hospital; she collapsed earlier in the morning. The postman found her and called the ambulance. Jane says she was revived, but she is being monitored."

"What! That's not a little hiccup, that's your mother! Why are we not going to her this instant? Tell the chauffeur to turn the car around; you should go see her now," I said. He held my hands,

"What about you, darling?" he asked.

"What about me? Is that even a question? I will be fine. I am not the one hospitalized. Your mother needs you now and you need to go to her," I told him. He looked sorry.

"I will make it up to you, love; I am sorry about Mexico," he said.

"It's not your fault, we don't need to be in Mexico, but you need to be with your mother," I reassured him; he put his arms around me and hugged me. He told the driver to turn the car around and we started towards the hospital, he told me Jane was on her way. I felt a little guilty that he was torn between going to his mother and staying with me. He loved his mother, I knew this and I felt bad because she was the reason, we were not together these past weeks, but I would not stand between him and his mother.

Seeing him so cut up about his mother's health brought mine to mind. I missed my mother so terribly, all these incredible feelings and experiences I was having, I wished I could have been able to share it with her. I knew I had to tell Robert the truth about my family eventually; he had to know that I ran away from home. But for some reason, I don't know how or when to tell him that my parents would never bless our union.

The chauffeur parked the car outside the hospital, "Go on, I will wait here for you," I encouraged, he nodded and went inside to see his mother. Jane called a few minutes later that she was about ten minutes away. Robert came back out; he had been gone for twenty minutes. I was waiting outside the car and gave him a hug; he didn't look so upset.

"She will pull through; the doctor said she had a heart attack. I could not

speak with her because she is sleeping. Come let me take you back to mine, I will come back and check on her," he said.

"Jane said she was ten minutes away; shouldn't we wait for her?" I asked.

"It's alright, let's go. I don't want you stressed, Anna, you only just got better yourself," he said.

"Why don't I go, the driver could drop me at yours and you stay and wait for Jane, so together you can both be with her when she wakes up," I said. He put his arms around me,

"What would I do without you?" he said and then kissed me on the temple, he pulled me into his arms and buried his head in my hair for a moment.

I could tell that he would blame himself if anything happened to his mother. The timing was too untimely for his decision of choosing me over his mother.

"I'll see you soon, love," he said. I nodded, and got into the car, then he instructed the chauffeur to take me home and come back later for him.

****

Getting back to his with nothing to do, I went to dance to take my mind off things. When I finished rehearsing, he still had not come back; it was late in the afternoon now. Jeff asked if I wanted something to eat, but I could not eat, I had not heard from him and that bothered me. I prayed his mother had not taken a turn for the worse. That would destroy him. Sleep must have claimed me, while I waited in his living room. When I opened my eyes, he was carrying me up to the room.

"You are back." I whispered sleepily. He did not say anything. "Is she okay?" I asked.

"Yes, love, she is a fighter," he said.

"What happened?" I asked. He took me into his room; I wanted to tell him I could sleep in mine now, but I did not want to upset him than he already was.

"She had a cardiac arrest, the doctors said she had an aneurysm, a first heart attack, so they had to do an emergency operation…".

"Oh, I'm so sorry, love. You must have been scared."

"Yes, I was. I was scared. Especially because of how things are now between us, I didn't want that to happen… I thought, we lost her, but she… she is a fighter. Jane is staying with her. Sorry I didn't call; my head wasn't thinking right." he said.

"I know, it's okay, I just wish I didn't leave you there," I said, "Like you said, she's a fighter, she will pull through." I tried to comfort him, he looked resigned.

"I hope she does," He tried to smile but I could see the sadness in his eyes. He had been worried about my health a day ago and now, he is worried about his mother's. He needed to rest, he needed to be taken care of too. "Jeff told me you didn't eat, he left some food for you. Would you like me to get it for you?" he asked.

"Only if you eat too," I said.

"I am not hungry, honey; I just need to lay somewhere and sleep." he said.

"If you don't eat, then I won't either" I insisted, I wasn't trying to add to his burden, but I knew he needed to eat as well. He looked at me, and he saw there was no point arguing with me.

"Okay, I am too tired to argue, I'll go get it," he said.

"No, Robert, I'll go get it. It's about time I became more useful around here," I said.

"No, love, sit down please; I don't want you doing that, I will get it okay, so lie down and I will be back." He went out and returned fifteen minutes later with a tray of food, bottled water and two glasses of wine. Dinner was rice and curry and we both shared a plate. When we were done, he placed the plate outside the room and returned to tuck me in,

"Sleep here with me," I said. He stopped to look at me,

"No, I don't think that is a very good idea, Anna."

"Please, I don't want to be alone. I will behave, I promise."

"Anna, I don't want to, you know how you make me feel. The temptation would be too much for me," he protested. I held him back.

"Robert, I trust you, but if it happens, then it has happened. I just want to hold you through the night." I could see he was trying to fight it, but then he gave in. He lay next to me and held me. I tried to sleep, but I could not; this was what I wanted; I wanted him to kiss me. I turned around to face him, he gazed into my eyes. I took his hands and kissed it, I then moved closer to him, he didn't move. I kissed his chin, then I moved my lips to his neck, his eyes, his forehead, his ears and then I found my way back to his lips. He tried to resist me, but he couldn't, he pulled me closer and we began to kiss. My hands moved over his chest and then I moved on top of him and we kissed. I could feel his hands on my thighs, and my body was electrified, I was on fire. His hands moved to my back, and he moved me beneath him, I gasped for air. In my mind,

247

I knew this was it, the moment had come when I would submit myself to this man that I loved more than life itself. He was breathing so hard and fast as he pulled me towards him, our eyes met and then he stopped, and said. "I want you so bad, it hurts, but please, love, let us wait; this is not what I want, not tonight." I closed my eyes in frustration, but he was right. He was not ready and if I insisted, I knew he would, but he would not be happy and that would make me unhappy as well. I didn't know why I wanted this tonight. I thought somewhere deep inside, I was afraid that my parents would find me eventually and take me away from him and we would never be able to be together like this, like I wanted. If he took me tonight, then I would be soiled, and I would not be worthy in Ashraf's eyes to be his wife and I could be with Robert and spend the rest of my life with him. I wanted to tell him, but I knew he would not understand and tonight was not the night. He kissed me on the forehead and left the room. I tried to calm my body down; I went into the shower to wash myself. I deliberately thought about the situation with my family and how I would break it to Robert. My heart was troubled all night until I fell asleep.

Robert was gone by the time I was awake and Jane was here. My mind went to what almost happened between us; I felt a little ashamed for pushing it when I knew he wanted to wait. I sat up on the bed and my eyes caught a note he left for me. I took a deep breath before picking it up. It read,

"My love,

I tried to put to words each day to explain how you make me feel, but I don't think the words I come up with can actually justify and describe what you mean to me. I am sorry about last night. I came back in to apologise for leaving you but you had slept, so, I sat and watched you sleep. I thought about waking you up and telling you this, but you looked perfect as you slept and I could not dare to. Each moment I get to spend with you is a rare treasure and I am still not sure what I did to deserve you. Anna, do not let what happened or did not happen make you feel that I do not want you.

I do, I do so much that it takes an exceptional grace to stop myself. I want to wait because I want us to do it right. Ours is no ordinary love and for now, my love, I beg you to wait, so when that day comes when you truly become mine and I yours, we would be together and we would celebrate the unification of our love as one, submitting completely to each other. I dream of that day always, when every inch of your body becomes mine and mine yours as we melt into one another. In my mind, I am hoping that that day is very near. Until then, please accept this letter as an apology for each day you would have to wait, and humour me by not speaking about it.

Yours eternally,
Robert.

I smiled as I read the letter repeatedly. Something in that letter made me think, he could ask me to marry him soon, meaning I had to tell him who I really was. and I wonder if it would bother him that in a way not saying anything to him about something so important was the same as lying? Would he still want me if he found out that my parents had betrothed me to another man?

Jane came into Robert's room to find me; I thought about telling her the truth about my family, but I immediately decided against it. They had a little too much on their plates now. She walked towards me,

"Robert said you were home, so I went to your room to find you and saw your bed hadn't been slept in, I did not know you two now sleep together," she quizzed. She sat on the bed and then purposely jumped out of it, "Eww," she joked, I laughed softly.

"How is your mum?" I asked.

"She will be fine, she gave us a scare, but she is doing better; the doctors say it's early days yet, but they don't think there would be any complications."

"Have you called Dave?" I asked.

"Yes, we spoke earlier this morning, he wants to come, but he has exams so I told him to stay and read, but he feels bad," she explained.

"I am sorry, Jane," I said, trying my best to console her. "If there is anything you want me to do, tell me and I will see to it," I offered.

"Don't worry about it, look, I didn't come here to talk about hospitals, my head is spinning I need a distraction. Please come, let us go for a swim," she said.

"Okay. I will join you."

We swam together and after showering, we ate lunch and discussed anything but her mother. Then Jane left. Alone by myself, I went to do some more dancing. I danced until it was late; when Robert arrived, he came to find me. He looked exhausted, I went and gave him a hug. I wanted to thank him for the letter, but he had asked that we do not talk about it and I needed to respect that. I held him a little longer than I normally did, just to let him know I appreciated every little thing he did for me. I knew it will be hard being around each other and wanting him so much like I did, but if he could endure, then so could I. Ten days later, his mother was no longer critical, that was a relief for everyone.

My audition was now just a couple of days away. I was nervous now more than ever. Robert was not always home, his work had suffered too, he spent his time at the hospital in those ten days. Jane had to return to Cambridge, she had work commitments. Although Robert wasn't always home, he left me cute little notes that lets me know he misses me and I was always on his mind. It was always good to find these notes. I moved back to my room to not further complicate things; I wanted him to have his room back, he did not want me to leave his room, but I insisted. I had not been back at my flat since I went to get my passport. It felt like I had moved in with Robert completely and as much as I wanted to hold on to my apartment, I always knew my place was by his side.

Chapter 32

❧❧❧❧

Auditions

On the morning of the auditions, I laid in bed worrying over my decision to open a dance studio. Yes, I knew I was a good dancer but was I good enough to teach others? I wondered.

I had worked so hard to prepare for the auditions to join a dance company, but that would mean travelling a lot if successful as noted by the dance company. I had not told Robert this part of the situation, and I wasn't willing to be torn away from him either if I was chosen. A part of me wanted to go and be auditioned, just so I could get feedbacks from professionals and another part of me feared what they would say to me.

Robert slipped a good luck card through my door. I picked it up and smiled, when I opened the door, Robert was standing right outside.

"Hey, morning." I said as I leaned over to plant a kiss on his lips.

"Morning, darling."

He looked me over, "What's happening, you're not ready. You're going to be late!" he said.

"I know, I'm just not sure… if this is what I should do." I said

"What do you mean? You've prepared for this since forever, you are a great dancer, there's nothing to worry about, Anna." Robert reassured.

"I know but, you will always tell me I'm great, you love me, but out there, whatever they tell me could, you know, make or break me." I said panicky.

"No, I disagree. Yes, I do love you very much but, I'm not blind, you are a great dancer, and you work very hard. So, go out there and wow them, because I know you will but even if they say no, their opinions don't count at all."

"Hmm, you're sweet. But no, I can't do it. I think I will just go back to bed and sleep, and before I know it, this day will pass and the pressure would have passed and everything will go back to normal." I said as I turned my heel towards my room. Robert grabbed my hand.

"Anna, tell me. What's wrong, why are you giving up?"

"I'm not giving up, I just… I just don't think I need to prove myself to anyone. I mean you said it yourself, I'm a great dancer." I said, he chuckled.

"That you are. But tell me the real reason you don't want to be auditioned anymore."

I was quiet, then he tilted his head to the side slightly in a bid to urge me to speak.

"Okay, you know how much I wanted this, but I didn't really think it through, I think. Successful candidates will have to go on a six months tour. I can't do that… I don't want to be apart from you. I know I may not get it and that would be fine but if I do go and I get it, I don't want to have that choice."

I said,

"Oh, now I get your reluctance, but still…"

"No, there's no *but* Robert. I can't do it."

"So, what are you going to do, I mean all those hours you put into getting your routines right, just wasted?"

"No, not wasted, I think before opening my own dance school, I should teach somewhere first."

"Oh, I see. That's not a bad idea, you get to learn the ropes and see what to do to make your dance studio a success." Robert said.

"Exactly. And I can use the routines, I learned to land a job, you know and if I'm successful, I won't need to be away from you at all."

Robert pulled me to his chest.

"Well, I like that very much. The thought of you not being around would have driven me crazy."

"I know, me too." I said before kissing his lips.

"Okay, so what are you going to do today, I was going to cancel my morning meeting so I could take you to your auditions before."

"Well now, you don't need to do that. Go about your day, and I will browse the internet for a dance teacher's job." "Well, I do love a girl with a plan." Robert said

I laughed and planted another kiss on his lips.

"Now get out of here already, before I'm tempted to ask you to stay home with me."

"Well, all you need do is ask, I will drop anything for you, darling, you know that already."

I chuckled, "Really, if I ask you to just stay home with me today, you will really blow off work and stay?"

"In a heartbeat."

"But I don't want you to do that, work is important too."

"I know that love, but you come before everything."

"Well, then. Why don't we do this, I've never seen you work, why don't I come to work with you instead, watch you do your magic." I suggested.

"That sounds like a brilliant idea, I will wait for you downstairs." Robert said as he made to leave, I grabbed him and slowly planted an intense kiss on his lips.

When we were done, he smiled, "Wow! Remind me to always agree to take you to my work." He said,

"No, that was for your understanding and not forcing me to go for the auditions."

"Force you! darling. I will never dream of it. You know that's not me. I'm supportive and loving, not a tyrant."

We both shared a laugh. "I know, and that's why I love you." I said, "Now, let me go and fix myself up, I won't be long." I said as I rushed inside to shower.

It was almost noon when we left home, Robert cancelled the meeting because he said he would not have time for me if he was held up all day. Although it defeated the purpose for which I came, I wanted to see him be the boss at work, however, I still loved the fact that he dropped everything for me.

His office was a very large, executive-looking space, a big conference room table at the end of the room, with an automatic see through door dividing his office from the boardroom. He went behind his desk, brought out a key and picked up something. Then he said we should go.

"We're leaving? I thought, I'll get to see you at work."

He smiled. "Anna, I've been so busy these days, I've not spent enough time with you. Work can wait, today is all about you." He said as he led me out of his office.

Back in the car, he looked at me and said, "Okay, since the auditions is cancelled, and I'm not in the mood for work. What will you like to do?" Robert asked. "I don't know! I have no plans. My number one plan was to browse the net for a job and the second plan, which now seems to have to pause, was to watch you at work." I said, he smiled and then sighed.

"Okay, I guess I messed that up." He said

"You kinda did, I have to agree with you."

"Well, what now? Shall we go back home to mine?" It was my turn to sigh,

"No, let's go to mine. I've not been to my flat in a while. I mean I've practically moved in with you." I said jokingly but then it really occurred to me that we're leaving together like two married couple without the advantage of proper intimate contact. I noted then that I had to discuss it further with him. I had never been with a man before, he was and is my only boyfriend and somewhere at the back of my mind, it just seems like although I wanted to respect his wishes, I felt like I was running out of time.

"Oh, ok. Let's go to yours then. We don't have to hurry, we could sleep at yours today if you want." he said, I smiled. His voice broke my thought, he held my hands and my heart warmed towards him, in that moment, I knew I had to tell him everything about me. We were at that stage where I knew I definitely couldn't live without him and I couldn't keep anything from him any longer.

As I stepped out of the car, I noticed a car with tinted windows parked outside, and just across the road from my flat. I stopped and stared at the car in shock; I could feel my heart drop in fear, blood drained from my face, something did not feel right. Robert noticed my attention was elsewhere, he followed my eyes to the car and looked at me, but before I could say something, we saw a man in a suit approach the car, got inside and drove away. I did not recognize the man and he did not even look in our direction. I took a deep breath in relief, I was beginning to get paranoid about my parents finding me and I knew I mustn't delay, I had to tell Robert the truth. Then he pulled me into his arms, as I stood shaking like a leaf. Robert looked into my eyes to comfort me; concern was etched on his face.

"What is wrong?" he asked. I looked at him and smiled, I wanted to tell him, I knew I should then for a mad second that seemed like an eternity, I thought what if he gets so annoyed that I had kept this from him for so long.

"It's nothing, I was just spooked by something, it's silly, there's nothing to worry about," I lied to reassure him.

"Are you sure? What spooked you?" Robert asked, he did not look like he bought what I had just said,

"Yeah, I was just being silly, I thought I saw something that wasn't there. Crazy, right? Let's go inside." We entered; I collapsed on my sofa bed, my heart was still beating fast and I was doing my best to hide it from Robert. He joined me on the sofa; I turned my head towards him and wondered if I decide to tell him now, if he wouldn't get angry. My mouth opened to speak, but then, cowardly, I said, "It's nice having you here." I couldn't do it, not now but I would later.

"It's nice being with you, full stop. It doesn't matter to me where.".

Then he placed one hand on my face and said.

"You know you can tell me anything right?" I nodded; I knew that was my cue to tell him the truth but I couldn't get my mouth to open. His eyes remained on me, but my mind was elsewhere. I could see in his eyes that he did not believe me, but out of respect for me, he said nothing and for a while, my mind churned and turned over telling Robert who I really was.

"What's on your mind?" he finally asked. I squinted and acted surprised

"Why do you assume I'm thinking and not just admiring your beauty?" I responded, deflecting from talking about what I was thinking.

He smiled and then he said, "Stop, Anna, I know something worries you and for some reason, you are not ready to share, but when you are ready, just know that I would always be on your side, you should already know that by now." he said. I smiled sadly, I knew he was right, he would be okay with it. But still, I could not bring myself to tell him the truth. Then he said, "When you call someone a beauty, do they really deserve to be called that word? You said you were admiring my beauty;" I smiled and nodded, "Well I think, you're using it inappropriately I don't deserve that word when I am flawed next to you."

"Well, it's subjective. You are beautiful to me in every way." I defended.

"You cannot say that word to me, Anna, when I bask in your beauty. The word 'beautiful' was intended for you and anyone that remotely looks like you do. Your beauty is beyond words and I just love the way you are both inside and out, I love your confidence, your smile, I mean, it lights me up, and your silky beautiful hair, they were the first thing about you that pulled me to you when I saw you at the airport... and then we touched, I lost my heart to you in that moment. So, for the rest of my life, I want to tell you how beautiful you are because you are truly one of God's gift to earth, His gift to me. This is not how I planned to do this, but now feels right, Anna. I …"

"Shush, don't say it," I said. I knew what he was about to say, and as much as it filled me with joy; this was not the time for it. Not when I had been keeping secrets from him. I wanted to tell him the truth so much, but how could I spoil the moment for us after all he just said? He looked confused.

"Wait for the right time, now may seem right to you, but it isn't for me and I have quite a bit to tell you first," I said. His eyes questioned me, so I continued,

"You shower me with unwanted compliments and I don't begrudge you because it's your truth, but you can't ask me not to speak mine. I have eyes too and I see you clearly, and I also know my own reflection, but I do not need you to tell me every day. Not now at least, perhaps I will demand it from you one day when we have been together for so long than humanly possible and I look in the mirror, and don't recognise who's staring back at me. And I'm feeling weak, and unattractive, but I look at you and even in old age, somehow age had not taken your beauty away and my stomach drops and my heart skips a beat because you smiled at me. That is when I will ask that you tell me; I will demand that you tell me that I am beautiful even though in your heart you will know then that all that beauty you saw when we were younger has faded. That's the only time I would know you're lying but I would know it's because you love me." Robert shook his head in disagreement.

"Nonsense, that will never happen. Even when this outer beauty fades, which I doubt very much. Your inner beauty which is what I love most about you will never fade. Let me compliment you darling, this is not a competition" He said, and smiled.

"No, it's not. I'm just telling you my truth. Robert, when I said you are beautiful, I don't mean just your physically appearance. I mean in every way, I see the way you care for those around you, you

Elizabeth Johnson

respect your workers, you care for your family. Sometimes, I feel unworthy and undeserving of you, I wonder how I got so lucky."

"Okay enough now, or I'm going to start blushing." He joked

"Well, now you know how it feels."

"So, are you saying you don't want me to compliment you?"

"I do, but don't make a sermon out of it."

"Ouch, that hurts." He said. I laughed.

A moment passed and then I said,

"I want to talk about the letter you wrote."

"I wondered how long it would take for you to bring it up." He said,

"I didn't bring it up because you said you didn't want to discuss it."

He sighed, "Okay, what do you want to know."

"Well it is clear how we feel towards each other, I just wanted you to know that, when I kiss you, or touch you, even as we lie here together, feeling you next to me, it stirs something strong in me and sometimes I want to explore those feelings further."

"Darling, I feel exactly the same way, if not more but I don't see you like other relationships I've been in, perhaps you see this differently from your past relationships as well. You mean a lot to me and soon, we would be able to explore further. I ..."

"But I've never been in any relationship before, I've never been with anyone or kissed anyone before you." I cut in.

"What are you saying?" He asked confused.

"I'm saying what it means, I've never been with a man in that way. I was raised to save myself for marriage."

"Oh! I didn't... I didn't know. You surprise me every day, Anna. So, if you've waited this long, what's a few more months? And we can do a lot of exploring together then." he said. I blushed.

"Okay, a few more months." I said with excitement.

"Shall I order something in?" He asked I nodded, then he said "I guess we would be sleeping here tonight then." He added.

I smiled, "Yes, please, let's just chill here tonight." He planted a quick kiss on my lips and got up to order some food, I shut my eyes and waited for him to return but then sleep claimed me.

Chapter 33

I woke up and Robert was gone; he left me a note, he had to go to work very early, but he would be back to take me out for dinner. I looked at the time, it was ten in the morning. I knew I should get up, but my eyes were still sleepy and I had nothing planned for the day. Except waiting for Robert to come back from work. I missed having something to do; I placed my head back on the pillow and tried very hard to allow sleep reclaim my body when the phone rang. I picked it up; Jane was at the other end, she sounded excited. I sat up in my bed to keep up with her excitement.

"I am getting married!" she screamed.

"What?!" I responded, happy, but in shock.

"I am getting married!" she yelled again.

"I heard you the first time," I said.

"Well, say something," she demanded.

"Oh sorry, I am sorry. Congrats! I mean I am really thrilled for you, but I am also in shock here," I said.

"I know. I can't believe it either. This is actually real! I mean, I love him so much, Anna, and I said yes to him yesterday, I mean I know that I cannot imagine my life without him, but do you think I am doing the right thing getting married this soon? We've barely been together for six months. I need you to talk some sense into me, Anna." She spoke so fast. I didn't know how to respond or what to say to her. Yes, it was quick but how can I tell her that when I would do the same in a heartbeat when Robert ask me to marry him?

"I don't know what to say Jane. He makes you happy, you have to go for it if you believe you are ready to be with him for the rest of your life."

"I do, Anna, I don't see how anyone else can make me this happy. I'm in love, Dave is it for me. But, look at Alex, he has been engaged for almost a year and he is not rushing to get married and I don't know why, because he loves April and when you love someone more than life itself, you marry them, right, Anna? That is why I said yes. Do you think we're moving too fast?"

Jane was panicking and I knew I had to calm her down.

"Jane, listen to me, you are doing the right thing. Don't panic, you love him more than life itself, you just said so yourself and I'm sure he feels the same way about you otherwise he wouldn't have asked you. You both deserve your happiness, you've said yes. Why are you worrying so much, you are now engaged to be married? Can you imagine that? I'm so happy for the two of you. You and Dave Porter are engaged! You remember when I used to try and get you to be nice to him and now you are going to be his wife and he is going to be your husband?" I laughed softly, she responded with a joyous laugh.

"Hearing you say those words makes me happy, but then why am I panicking?" she asked.

"There is nothing wrong with that either, it's alright to panic, it's alright to be scared a little. Marriage is not a joke, but at least you have both agreed that this is what you want. You're both making a big commitment to be in each other's lives, so, it's okay to panic a little, I probably would too if I were in your shoes. but don't panic too much, this man loves you so much and you love him just the same so, he's worth all the risk, is he not?" I was doing my best to be there for her.

"Thanks, Anna, this is exactly what I needed to hear. I have not told anyone, so please don't tell Robert, I want him to hear it from me. However, I have a favour to ask you,".

"Anything, name it, it's yours," I said.

"Would you be my maid of honours?" Jane asked.

"Of course, Jane, it will be my honour. We are sisters now, remember? I am so excited. I can't believe we have ourselves a wedding to plan!" I said, screaming down the phone, Jane was screaming on the other end of the phone as well.

"Wait, have you met his family?" I asked.

"Yes, he took me to see them a few months ago, they are a very nice bunch, I've been to see them a few more times. I love his mum, everyone is just so nice, I have no compliant just happiness. Anna. I keep looking for something to go wrong, but everything is just fantastic; Dave is amazing, I am just a lucky girl, I guess. I know he is still studying, but I don't mind, we have money saved up and we don't want to wait or waste any time before starting our lives together. I mean, like you and Rob, I can see you two getting hitched very soon," Jane said, I chuckled embarrassingly.

"I… I … don't know, I mean maybe … we don't know that, but enough, this isn't about Robert and I, we need to start planning your wedding. Have you both decided on a date?" I said, diverting the conversation back to her.

"Yes, we are thinking in four months' time. Mum would have recovered properly…" Jane was saying and then her voice faded, it felt like she started talking to someone else, I could not hear what she was saying. Then she said.

"Anna, I really have to go now, I will call you later and we can discuss more. Love you."

"Love you more," I responded and the phone died.

I could not sleep any longer, not after the news about Jane's engagement. The conversation took my mind to my mum; I could see her face when she thought I had finally agreed to marry Ashraf. She was so excited; she was overjoyed you would think she was the one getting married. There was something going on, I thought. I did not like all these situations that were pointing at the obvious. This was a sign; I could not lie to Robert any longer. I made up my mind to tell him today when he came to pick me up for dinner. I looked around my flat, it was not filthy, but it was not tidy either. Because I stay at Robert's house more these days, my flat had suffered a little. I decided since I had nothing to do, I would use the time waiting to do some spring-cleaning.

I cleaned until everywhere was sparkling, cleaning helped a little as my mind went off the subject of marriage for a little. But then, I was reminded of the one I ran away from home to avoid and was scared that the one I ran away from will catch up with me before I had the chance to say I do to Robert.

It was five in the evening when I finished cleaning; I looked around and everywhere looked good. I could now start preparing for my dinner with Robert. Normally, I would be very excited, but because I had made up my mind to tell him my secrets, I felt drained. I had my wash, painted my nails, and straightened my hair and dressed up for dinner. By the time I was through, it was almost six thirty. I knew Robert would soon be here. I started re-evaluating my decision to tell him who I really was. I was scared, I wondered how he would react when he realized my name wasn't even Anna but Hasina. I could see him getting very annoyed in my head and the thoughts of that made me realize I could not tell him. Not today, a couple more days and I would be able to tell him, I told myself.

Not long after, I looked outside and his car was parked. I rushed to the door just as he got to the door. Seeing his face and the way he looked at me, as if he had not seen me in months made me sure I was doing the right thing not telling him.

"You look… I mean… you look mesmerizing, you are just breath-taking," he said, I smiled. He complimented me always, I wondered if there was anything, I wore that he did not think was beautiful.

"Thank you," I said.

"Shall we?" he asked, I nodded. He took me in his arms back to the car and off we went to have a great dinner. We laughed so much, I could not really eat and Robert kept distracting me, pointing out people in the restaurants and making faces and pretending he knew what they were discussing and what they sounded like while also trying to remain undetected by whomever he focused on. He even tried to get me to make faces at people, he asked that I pick a person whom I thought appeared hard and rude and when they were not looking in our direction, I make a face at them. I gave in since I laughed when he did his. So, I tried to impress him with a frog face. He busted into laughs, I had never seen him laugh without so much care, everything about the dinner was special to me, I guess I was still learning, I never knew he could be so goofy when he wanted to be. So much to learn about him, I thought as I admired him. If he was not well respected at the restaurant, we might have been asked to leave. I forgot all about my worries, I just wanted to be in the present with Robert. He asked that we went back home to his, but I wanted to stay in my flat, especially after all the cleaning I just did today. I needed to enjoy the fruits of my hard labour. He wanted to leave, he said he had to be somewhere very early, but when he saw that I was not happy that he was leaving, he changed his mind and stayed.

I felt a little guilt, but he was a grown man and he was in control of his own mind. We lay on the bed together, exhausted. As I lay next to him, all I could think of were the number of times Jane told me about her brother that didn't want to be in a relationship with anyone. And here I was in the arms of this incredibly gorgeous man to think he had saved all the dating and all his love for only me made me feel so wonderful. He looked sleepy, but I had to ask him the 'why me?' question.

I could not help myself, I had to know what he saw in me that he did not see in others, my insecurities never let down no matter how many times he reassured me. "Can I ask you a question?

"Anything," he replied sleepily.

"Why me? What do you see in me?" I asked. He sighed and opened his eyes surprised.

"You know the answers already, Anna," he said.

"No, I don't," I said, urging him to tell me.

"Okay, how about because I love you," he said.

"No, I want a better explanation than that," I persisted.

"I can tell you, but I don't know where to start, Anna. It will probably take me all day," he said, trying to discourage me

"I've got time."

"Hmm, okay. How do I put this, pardon me if I sound lame?"

"Consider yourself pardoned." I said excitedly.

He smiled and touched my face lovingly, then he said "The moment I saw you, something in me flicked open, like a dark cloud lifted. At first, I didn't understand it because I thought right before

267

I met you I had just visited my brother and his fiancée, so I felt perhaps that was why I was longing for someone of my own but I was wrong. You came into my life for a brief moment and you disappeared and became a figment of my imagination that I could not get over. I did not know that wanting someone could be that painful. I never thought in a million years I would see you again. But, I wanted you to be real so badly, because you got hold on my heart so easily, so quickly and I didn't even know you. Then as though by some miracle, I walked into my house and there you were dancing your heart out. I knew it then, that day that I was never going to lose you again. I wasn't going to let you out of my life as long as you want me in yours. Before you breezed into my life, I felt, empty, numb, I had no spark when a girl said they loved me, I didn't understand what they meant because I didn't feel like they did. And I've heard people talk about love, sing and write about it and I wondered what drove them to write such beautiful heart wrenching songs. For a while there, I actually started to believe at the time that I was incapable of falling in love with anyone. But you, you did something to me, to my heart and just like that, you switched me on, you set my heart racing for you a thousand miles an hour. When I kiss you, or touch you, even as we lie here now, the feeling that courses through me is indescribable. And I have to always control myself, because I feel so strongly about you. And it's everything about you that I love, your smile, the way you walk, your eyes when you look at me, it's as if you can see my soul. They pull me... closer to you- so yes, if all these does not answer the question, then perhaps it's because some people on some levels were created just for each other and I believe I was created just for you. And that's why you are the one." he was quiet for a while. My eyes were clouded with tears, I tried to blink it away, but the tears rolled down my face instead.

"Shh, you promised me you wouldn't cry; that's the last thing I wanted to do to you."

"But I want to because I am so happy, I am truly the luckiest girl in the world. I love you," I said, he laughed.

"I love you too," he said.

Robert looked like he was about to sleep, he closed his eyes and then out of nowhere, he said, "Can I ask you something?" I did not know what he wanted to know, but I was not expecting what he asked next.

"Why were you running at the airport, was someone after you?" I did not know where to begin; I knew I should tell him the truth now. I should have told him a long time ago. And now that he has asked, I couldn't lie to him. He deserved the truth.

"My… my mother… I was running away from my mother." He opened his eyes at once; he looked shocked although he did not move from where he laid. He was calm. I was gauging his reaction to help me determine if I should continue. He was quiet, he did not say anything. I knew his mind was full of questions, but he left it to me to decide if I wanted to tell him everything.

"I was meant to be shopping for my wedding, that was why we were in America…" I stopped to check his reaction gain, but he still stayed calm. I expected him to say something or even flinch after I mentioned a wedding, but he said nothing so I continued.

"My parents were going to marry me off to some guy, everything had been arranged. I tried to make them understand I wasn't ready for marriage. I didn't want them to make that choice for me. But, they wouldn't listen. They wanted our two families to become one, this union they wanted it so badly and so did the man I was meant to marry. It was the lowest point of my life, I couldn't get out of it no matter what I tried, at one point, they arranged for us to meet, but I refused to see him. My mother sent me an album with his pictures, I told her I didn't want to see it. She won't take the hint. I didn't want to be married to someone I didn't know. My mind always longed for more, like something out in the universe was calling me, I just knew I had to run away. They were relentless, they disturbed and suffocated me constantly with the idea of this man and how he would make a wonderful husband and all that nonsense. They were not going to be happy until I had said yes to being married off to a stranger." I paused for air and gathered my thoughts. "It is tradition that your husband is picked for you where I come from, they don't force you, you will have to accept the man before the marriage can commence. However, my parents were sure they found the right person for me. They made it quite clear that no one else will do, but they made it sound like it was my choice, which we all knew was a lie. I started putting a plan together and for that plan to work, I had to accept I would marry this man. Once I accepted, they let their guards down and I played along. This was my life and I didn't care how wealthy this man's family was, something in me just rebelled the whole idea. I was supposed to count myself blessed to be wanted as a bride from such a family of good standing, so mother says. I do not know why because money has never been a problem where I come from. My father is very wealthy and I'm his only child, I didn't want to break their hearts but I would not let this part of my life be dictated. I never understood why children from wealthy families have to marry into each other's family. Then there was my dancing, you know how much I love to dance, I wanted to pursue it further but my parents won't hear of it. It all became too much; my voice was not heard but they claimed to love me. I don't know sometimes, I think that maybe if I thought that they actually listened to me and considered my feelings, I might not have run off, I might have stayed and married Ashraf to please them." I paused a little to think about what I had just said to Robert and our eyes met. He looked down, I knew the things I was saying affected him, but he needed to know the truth, so I wasn't going to stop until I had told him everything.

"So, I sold my mother the idea of us going to America in a kind of last hurray before I get married and to do some shopping and bond as mother and daughter before the wedding. However, my friend Louise, had my new document waiting for me at the airport to start a new life and when I saw a chance to leave my mother, I took it and ran. That's why I was running like a mad woman at the airport, but it led me to you."

I could see he was still processing everything I just said to him, but he didn't make it about him, he pulled me into his arms and held me close. Then he buried his face in my hair. "I am glad you told me, you have been dealing with this on your own when you could have shared it with me. "

"I know, I wanted to tell you, I should have told you."

"It's okay now, we will figure it all out together."

"Robert?" I called

"Yes, love?" he responded.

"There is one more thing I have to tell you," he looked like he wanted to sleep, but I had to tell him now that it was all in the open.

"Go for it, Anna."

"My name is not Anna; my real name is Hasina Suri Fayed. I had to change my name so it won't be easy for my parents to find me." He was quiet for a while, and then he said.

"Hmm, Hasina Suri Fayed. Sounds more like you," I could not believe my ears; why was he not angry I held the truth from him for so long? I could have told him the truth before now, but I did not and he was just lying there without a flicker of anger.

"What? Aren't you even going to ask me why I kept such a thing from you," I said getting up?

"Don't worry about it, darling. I am tired, you can fight about it tomorrow if you like."

"So, you are not annoyed with me? Tell me you are honestly not thinking I could have trusted you with my name at least?" he sat up to face me.

"Your right, Anna, I mean Hasina. I should be livid right now, but I am not; I should be storming out of here cursing or something because you did not trust me enough to tell me your real name. You had the chance to do so every day; we have been together for eight months now. However, I am not; because I know you must have had your reason and I know it must have been eating at you all this time you not telling me these things. You want to know why I am not angry with you? It is because you have gone through enough already. It is my job to make you happy and make you feel safe, not fight with you over little things like your name. Now do you want to continue fighting or would you rather lie here with me." I raised my brow at him, I was going to say something when he drew me back into his arms and I forgot what I was going to say. I kissed him on the forehead, to think I had been so afraid to tell him and now I did and he did not get upset that I kept it from him for eight months.

Chapter 34

Robert had left for work by the time I woke up, but he sent me his chauffeur to take me back to his. I had nothing to do in my flat anyway, so when the chauffeur arrived, I left with him. The chauffeur asked me if I wanted to do any shopping before heading home, but I declined. Although my birthday was around the corner, I would be 23 in a matter of days. I had not reminded Robert, and didn't think it necessary, he spoilt me enough and everyday as it is felt like a celebration and I couldn't justify spending more money unnecessarily. More so, becoming a year older meant it was almost a year I ran from home. I put the thoughts away I didn't want to spend money on things I didn't need. What I needed was a dance job, so in a way, being alone gave me time to search the net. I tried to focus on that, but every time, a little warning in my head took my mind to the man in the suit outside my flat. Although I knew it was nothing, the fear of being caught by my parents worried me. Especially now, that I had told Robert the truth, I was very happy and I wouldn't want anything to bring that happiness to an abrupt halt. To take my mind off, I let my thinking wonder to Jane. Robert had not mentioned anything about Jane getting married, so I couldn't show my excitement for Jane in front of him but it was killing me to stay quiet about it. Jane had mentioned that she wanted me to come along to shop for dresses and I was excited about that although I never asked if she would be bringing her mother along. Wedding dress shopping should be enjoyed by mothers and their daughters and as much as I wanted to be part of the process, I didn't want to get in between Jane's relationship with her mother.

For Robert, this had become a touchy subject, Robert never talks about her to me and I never ask, not because I don't care but because I want her to like me and she's made it clear she didn't want to get to know me. Another conversation, that I knew I had to have with Robert to better understand his mother's distaste of me.

I applied for two jobs, one of them wasn't far from Robert's house and the other was in London. I would have applied for more positions but everything else that came up were in places too far for me to consider.

I looked at the clock and it was a quarter to four, so I decided to nap a little. On getting to my room, I saw a file of listings on my bed, I didn't understand. Robert must have had them put there for a reason, I thought. There were pictures of office spaces, all within a mile or two of his office building. I wondered if he was looking to get another office space for himself.

Moving them, aside, I shut my eyes and slept. And then I felt a tap on my shoulder, I struggled to open my eyes, squinting just a little, my eyes took on the vision before me. It was Robert, "You're back early," I said,

"No darling, it's seven o' clock."

"What! I just literally shut my eyes." I argued; Robert chuckled.

"Come, let's go have dinner." he said,

"Okay, give me a minute, let me freshen up." I responded.

"Okay," he said,

"Oh wait," I said remembering he forgot the office listings in my room.

"You forgot these." I said, "Are you getting another place for work?" I questioned absentmindedly as I walked into my bathroom.

"No, those are for you." He replied.

I poked my head out, "For me? Why?"

"I was just thinking that, even though you want to teach, there's no reason why you can't own the studio and teach at the same time. You can hire other teachers, and someone to manage it, while you learn the ropes but essentially, the business would be yours." He explained.

"Wow! How did I get so lucky, you are so thoughtful, I would never have thought of that? In fact, I spent the whole afternoon looking for jobs."

"It's the least I can do, I asked you to quit your job and you did, I don't expect you to mope around waiting for me to come home every day, I want you to live your dreams."

"Thank you, thank you so much. I can't believe it; you are just incredible. No, scrap that, you are more than the best human in the world, you are just my incredible superman!" I said, splashing water on my face, and then towelling, I applied a little cream and gentle massaged it on.

"Although, I have a bone to pick with you." He said,

"Mm, what have I done now?" I wondered moving towards him.

He pulled me towards him and placed me back on the bed next to him.

"What is it?" I asked, unsure of what he was about to say.

"You knew about Jane's engagement and you didn't tell me?" he said firmly.

"Jane asked me not to; she wanted to tell you in person," I explained. He looked at me questionably.

"But, Anna, I mean Hasina, this is me we are talking about, and you could have told me and asked me to pretend like you didn't tell me," he said.

"Robert, I love you, I think we've established that, but I love your sister also, she is my best friend and she said I should keep it quiet."

"So, you chose my sister over me?" he questioned. I did not know where or what he was getting at with it and I was getting irritated.

"Don't be daft, it wasn't my news to share even if it meant you," I said. He noticed my anger and he smiled.

"It's okay, I was only joking with you, but notwithstanding, it would have been nice to know from you."

"What brought this on? Jane told you already, so what is the problem."

"No, Jane didn't tell me; my mum called me and gave me an earache. She was not happy, apparently. Jane told another friend that told someone that knew mum and mum is furious her daughter is engaged and she knows nothing about it."

"Oh, I get it now, Jane is coming next weekend and I am sure she will tell you two then. At least your mum approved of Jane's choice of a partner, so there is nothing to fear there," I said. Robert was quiet. Then he pulled me to him.

"Don't worry about my mum, I love her, but she has no say in who I love," Robert reassured me. I always knew this, but I really did not understand her hatred for me. Jane would not tell me, neither would Robert.

"Are you ever going to tell me why she hates me this much, I know you tell me not to worry, but if I know why, then I can understand where she is coming from,"

"Darling, let's not talk about this now, it's not necessary," he said; the word necessary infuriated me.

"What do you mean by not necessary; you don't get to decide what is necessary or unnecessary for me to hear when it concerns me. If you know and you don't tell me, then this can't work, we can't go the distance if I don't know why. I need the truth and I need it from you today." I said firmly.

"Okay if you put it like that, I would tell you…"

"Go on, I am listening," I pushed.

"My father died on the … nine eleven plane from Boston; my mother blames Muslims for his death. She can't believe that I fell for a Muslim girl. Now you know the truth, are you happy that I told you?"

"Oh." I said, I wasn't expecting that for a reason.

"Yes, it's nothing to do with you and she knows it; she can't just tar every one with the same brush. But mum feels robbed of her husband and she thinks that me, dating you is spitting on my father's grave. But she's wrong, I know my father, all that mattered to him was his children's happiness. Love knows no colour or religion. It's sad that we lost him to a terrorism but what my mother needs to realise is that it was not your fault he died; she can't blame every Muslim. Matter of fact if she's looking for someone to blame, then she should blame me. You did not put him on that plane, I did."

"Why blame yourself? How can it be your fault Robert, you didn't crash the plane," I said.

"You don't understand! it was my fault he was on that plane. He wouldn't have been if I wasn't so stubborn." I knew I should not ask, but I wanted to know why he was blaming himself for his father's death.

"What did you do?" I asked. He was quiet for a while, his fist clenched; I could see he was uncomfortable, but I needed to understand why he blamed himself, so I could help him lay it to rest.

"He wanted me to join the family business; you know work alongside him and learn the ropes. I was not interested; I was living life the way I wanted. I wanted to be a musician, I loved playing the piano and I was very good at it. However, my father would not have it, I told him to give the business to Alex, but Alex was a playboy; he knew how to spend and spend, but not how to make any money. I was the first child, so naturally the burden was on me, but I did not want it. My dad just kept pressing me to join the business; he would not leave it alone, every opportunity he got, he made me feel bad… so I decided to leave the country. I had a friend that moved to Boston; he asked me to come join his band, so I packed up and flew to Boston. I kept receiving phone calls from Dad asking me to come back home. When I could not take the pressure anymore, I stopped talking to him. So, he … decided to come to Boston to see me; he had a meeting in New York the next day, but he wanted to meet with me first. We met at his Hotel lobby. He begged me to come back home, but he said he finally understood my passion for music and was okay with it if that was what I wanted to do, so I told him my band and I were in the middle of a tour that I would return home after we had completed our dates. I met with him again that morning at the airport. That was the last time I saw him, I did not get a second chance to put things right. That is why I blame myself and that is why my mother should blame me. If he did not come looking for me, he would not have been on that plane. I caused his death and they all know it. To right things a little, I took over the business, that is all he asked from me and I built it from where he left it and turned it to a massive success. The most annoying thing is that I am really good at it and enjoy doing it, and he will never know he was right all along. So now you know why it is my fault." He got up and walked away, I did not follow him; I knew he wanted to be on his own. I wished now I did not push to know, but it was not also right that he blamed himself for his father's death.

I waited a while before heading downstairs to meet him; he was not in the dining room, so I went back upstairs to his room. I saw him inside his dressing room rummaging through something. I stood by the entrance of the door. He turned to look at me and then resumed what he was doing.

"Robert, I hope you know what happened to your dad is not your fault. Your father was in Boston because he loved you, he wanted to see his son, he did not know that some monsters were plotting evil. You did not know that too. Who can explain why things happen the way they do, but it has happened and look at you, you have made him proud; you have taken care of all your family. You have made more money than your father could ever have thought you capable of and you have not lost yourself. Lay it to rest now, darling; I do not know him, but I do not think he would be happy wherever he is knowing you blame yourself for something that has nothing to do with you. I am sorry he died, but you said so yourself, just because I am Muslim, I should not be penalized and you should be kinder to yourself. It's time to let it go. If you can't then in a way your mother is right to feel the way that she does." He looked up at me, he looked lost for once.

"What are you talking about, Hasina?"

"Don't you get it? If you can't forgive yourself maybe you shouldn't preach to your mother about blaming all Muslims. If it's not right for her to think all Muslims are at fault perhaps it's not right for you to think you are at fault either. If you can't let it go, I don't see how we can work."

The way he looked at me, I had never seen a face so sad in my life; it was as if I had just squashed his heart with what I said. I did not even know what I was doing any more.

"Ann, sorry Hasina, what are you implying"

"That, I am a Muslim, Robert, to have anything to do with me will only be a constant reminder of your loss... and a slap on your mother's face. Can you honestly tell me what I am saying is not true?" He kept quiet.

"Well there goes your answer. I don't think we should see each other anymore. With what you just told me, there's no way what we have can work. Is love really enough, your father was killed by Muslims, I don't blame your mother for not wanting to have anything to do with me. I may not have caused it but I will constantly be a reminder of what she lost." He walked over to me and placed a finger over my lips; I was a pack of nerves, I just ended it. I just cut myself away from his life and now I was going to just go and die a slow but painful death if he agreed with me. I immediately wished I could take it all back. He did not say anything. His face was confused. I suddenly felt light headed, I walked away, but he grabbed my arms to stop me.

"Wait," he said. I looked at him cautiously. "Hasina, what are you saying?" he asked. I could not breathe, but I could not bring myself to repeat what I said earlier.

"You heard me," I replied. He let go of my arms and I walked away. I did not really know where I was going. I was hoping he would stop me again, but he did not, I was in a lot of pain and this was my fault.

Chapter 35

I went into my room and sat on my bed, I waited for the doors to open and he enter, but he did not. I began sobbing quietly, I was losing it and I could not control the pain that hit my heart. I found myself crying uncontrollably; I had just ended what we had and I had no one to blame but me. I wish he had told me this information long before now, long before my life became so tangled up in his. I must have cried myself to sleep. When I woke up, the room was dark; I tried to push myself up to flick on the light, when I saw his image before me and my heart jumped, he was sitting on the chase in my room.

"Robert? Is that you." I asked.

"I heard you crying," he said.

"Yes, I was…I don't know what came over me." I said.

"Do you feel better now?" he asked.

"I don't know, can… can you switch the light on, I want to see your face."

"Of course." He said and got up to flick the light on, I frowned my face into a squint as the stream of light hit my face.

Elizabeth Johnson

"I wanted to come in earlier, when I heard you crying but I thought you might not want me near you then. I'm sorry I'm here now." He said.

"Don't be sorry, I'm glad you came."

There was a moment of silence in the room. I didn't know what to say or if he believed it was that easy for me to break away from him. He ran one hand through his hair and said, "May I," Pointing to the chase.

"Yes, of course Robert. This is your house, sit down if you want to." I said avoiding his eyes, I was scared he had come to say that he agreed with what I had said

"What you said earlier about us not belonging together, is not true. It does not matter to me where you come from or what anyone has to say about it. The only opinion that matters to me is yours. Now that you have had time to sleep on it, do you still think we can't work? And before you answer, I want you to know that, saying we can't work, is a load of nonsense, maybe you are scared to commit fully or maybe you have another reason but don't use your religion as a reason to end things with me. I can tell you this, I will be committed to you for life, as long as I know that you want to be with me. I have to accept I didn't kill my father, I have always known this but I am human and sometimes, we like to apportion blame, just like my mum has done with you, I did with myself. I think to myself, what if I had gone back home a week before, or all those numerous times he called asking me to come home, then he wouldn't have found himself on that plane. The point is I cannot change what has happened, but you, you stormed into my life and I do not know how to be the way I was before I met you. I do not know how I would cope if you decide or truly believe we should not be in each other's life. Hasina, you are my world and I would do absolutely anything for you, but if you don't believe we should be together then…" He paused and came over to where I sat and pulled me up to him. "I know I have told you this before, but I will continue to tell you if that's what it takes to make you understand what you mean to me. I am in love with you, Hasina; I am at peace when I am with you. Do not say such silly things, darling except you truly mean it. You, own my heart." He then placed my palm on his heart; I could feel the thud of his heart against my palm. As tears of joy poured from my eyes and my heart raced in close distance to his.

"I have never felt for anyone what I feel for you, I belong with you, Hasina, do you understand me?" he said, I nodded vigorously, smiling and crying at the same time. I needed him to know that I made a mistake earlier and that there was no possible way I wanted what we had to end. I did not know how my attempt to console him turned out into this big break up drama.

"Are we okay?" he asked.

"I must be the luckiest girl in the world to be so loved by you. I keep doing and saying the stupidest things and you never give up on me." I placed his palm on my chest as he did his. "My heart is yours; it will always be yours, Robert, that is just the way it is. I don't know any other way. I am sorry; I don't know what came over me. I can't live a day without you, I love you so much it hurts to think I almost lost you." He chuckled happily and I was over the moon.

"Come here, don't ever do that to me again." He pulled my face closer and kissed me slowly, we broke it off and he held me in his arms.

"Now, come downstairs with me. Jeff has gone home but he made us a super pasta sauce for dinner."

"Dinner, now that you say that. What time is it again?"

"I think it's almost midnight."

"Wow! I slept too long. My tummy is rumbling for food."

He laughed. "Yeah, I guessed as much. I will make us pasta. You just sit down and watch me do my magic."

"Magic! You're only boiling pasta."

"And it takes some trick to cook it perfectly, it has to be just right."
"Okay, I don't care how it's made, just as long as it's eatable."

****

Two weeks passed, and my birthday came and went, Christmas was around the corner, and Robert was happy that Alex and April would be visiting. I celebrated my birthday quietly and felt guilty I didn't tell Robert about it. But I didn't want a party, I had no one else but Robert and Jane and Jane lived in Cambridge. Things returned to normal. Robert and I had been to see two of the office spaces for the dance studio. I loved the two spaces, they were equally big, one had potential for more development. Struggling to make an economic decision and since it was going to be Robert paying, I decided to let him make the decision on which space to get. Jane was to arrive at the weekend and I was excited at the prospect of helping to plan her wedding.

Before Jane arrived, on the morning of Friday, Robert called from work and asked me to prepare, he was taking me to dinner.

"What's the occasion?" I asked.

"Do I need an occasion to dine with you." Was his reply.

"Just dress nicely, I'm taking us to a special place." He said,

"Okay, I love a surprise." I said, immediately looking through my wardrobe, and found that I had worn most of the dresses I had, I wanted to wear something Robert had not seen on me before, so I decided I was going to shop for another dress. When I got downstairs, I found the chauffer had taken the housekeeper out to do some food shopping. So, I decided to get a cab to town, on my way, I remembered I had another dress that would be perfect for the occasion in my flat, so, I decided to head there instead. The plan was to get the dress, do a little shopping and get back to Robert's house before he even knew it. On my way to my flat, my phone rang, it was Robert.

"Darling, where are you?" I giggled; I loved the way he called me darling.

"I'm making a quick dash to my flat, I just need to grab a dress."

"Oh, I thought you were going to buy one. That's what Jeff said."

"Yes, I was but I have a perfectly good dress in my flat. I won't be long, I promise."

"Well, don't be, because there's a slight change of plans."

"Yeah, what's that?"

"When you get back home, I want you to pack for Paris."

"Paris, for the night?"

"No, for the weekend."

"Oh, but Jane is coming this weekend."

"Yeah, I know, but she will be at my mums, we would be back on Sunday, and the two of you can spend the rest of the week together. I just thought she might want to do some wedding stuff with mum first and then you two can be together after that."

"Oh! Okay, you're always very thoughtful. I can't wait to go to Paris."

"Okay darling, see you soon, please be back home by five."

"Okay, I will try." I said

"I love you."

"I love you too."

I smiled from ear to ear, as I hung up the phone. I was living the dream; my life couldn't be happier I thought. I looked out the window as the cab man came to a halt at the front of my flat. I paid for my fare and entered my flat. I quickly went in search of the dress that brought me to my place, with hopes to fit in a few more shopping before heading back to Robert's house.

PART B

Chapter 36

Tears of sadness.

I found the dress I came to hunt and then I placed it on my bed and went to the bathroom. I found the note Robert wrote to me on my bathroom floor, the one he left me at his home. I must have read it a million times; I picked it up and tucked it into my pocket so I did not forget it again. Then I heard the front door click open; I wondered who it could be. I rushed through the door to see who it was. "Who is there…?" I started to say on my way out when two men grabbed me, I did not have time to speak as one of them put a tape over my mouth. I tried to fight, but they were too strong for me and before I knew it, they carried me out and bundled me into the back of a van. I could not see, they put a dark cloth over my face and I was terrified. I had been expecting this to happen, but I never thought it would be like this.

There was silence all through the bumpy ride, no one spoke to me. My mind was thinking a thousand things. What if this had nothing to do with my father, there was no way my father would let anyone treat me like this, not in a million years. That realization made me more afraid of what was happening, no one would know where I was. My thoughts went to Robert, he was going to worry, and we were meant to travel this evening. It occurred to me that I might never see him again. I threw myself at the side of the moving van; I had to do something, anything to help myself out of this horrid situation. There was a man there with me, until then I did not know someone else was in the back of the van with me.

He said, "You are going to hurt yourself for nothing. No one can hear you; no one will come save you." He took my hands and tied them behind my back. The fear that overtook me spiralled; I was shaking with fear. I couldn't control myself. My body was covered with sweat, especially because I could not see around me. I did not know where I was, or where they were taking me. I could not think, only two things became clear, the fact that I would never see Robert again and the possibility that they were going to kill me. But why? I thought.

After about two hours or more, I heard the engine of the van stop. The man with me at the back of the van came to me and took off the cloth over my head. My eyes were covered with tears, I could not see clearly.

he said, "Listen, I am going to take the tapes off now but you must not scream. If you do, you wouldn't like what I would do to you. Nod once if you understand me." He gave me that look that said I shouldn't dare him, I nodded to let him know I would be abiding by his rules. He took off the tape, spun me around and untied my hands. Then he opened the van, the other man was waiting outside the van. He put his arms around me to help me out of the van and together, they both led me into a house. Before we went inside, I tried to look around, but there was no one, no houses in view. I was taken up the stairs, they opened a room with a single bed and pushed me in and then they locked the door from outside. There was no need fighting, no one would hear me. I sank into the floor and wept as I had never done before. My life as I knew it was over, this morning I was with Robert, I should be with him now on the way to Paris and now I was here and he may never know what happened to me or even where to look.

289

The room looked a mess as if no one had lived in it for some time; the bed was horrid-looking, someone must have slept in it. The sheets were filthy. There was a chair in the room. I sat on it and looked about me, the ceiling was covered in webs and I could see a few spiders crawling around and just then I suddenly felt the urge to scream. Once I started to scream, I couldn't stop; I couldn't bring myself to accept what was happening to me. I was in hysterics, I banged on the door and yelled repeatedly until my arms hurt too much. It all felt like a nightmare and I needed to wake up, this could not be my reality. There was no sound, no one came. I placed my ear to the door. I did not hear anything, no movement. I sat down on the floor and curled myself into a ball. I was freezing and I was hungry. I looked up through the window, the sky was dark. I had no idea how long I had been in the room. The window was too high to get to, even with the chair, but it did not matter. Even if I could get to it, I would have to jump, which would be suicidal. Then I heard footsteps and then the door opened; there was food and water on a tray. The man pushed it towards me and then shut the door again. I did not see him again until the next day; he brought me food and water once a day for three days and let me out to use the bathroom on occasions. Then on the fourth day, the door opened and instead of food and water, he threw some clothes on the bed and said.

"Change into this now!" When he left, I inspected the clothes, it was a long blue dress and a matching scarf. I took off my jeans and my jumper and wore the dress. I then remembered the letter Robert left me that I tucked into my jeans. I went to look for it and cried in relief when I found it; at least now I had a part of him with me. I tucked the letter into my bra, I did not want to lose it and I did not want whoever was holding me here against my will to find it.

The door opened again and the man appeared, he looked me over and said,

"Tie your scarf over your head, I don't want to see your hair." I complied immediately. He waited as I tied the scarf, then he held me by my arms and led me down the stairs and into a car. His partner was already behind the wheels; he sat next to me at the back of the car.

"Look at me," he said, "No funny business and you would be fine, do you understand?" I nodded a response. The car started; I had no idea where they were taking me. We drove through the back roads, we were in the countryside, and there were houses, but a few at a time. After about thirty minutes, the car stopped in front of a gated mansion, and two men came out from behind the gate. They looked like guards and they spoke to the men in the car. I was not paying attention to what they were saying, I was trying to look around me to know where we were.

The door opened and the car started again and we drove for another minute past the mansion and then finally stopped in front of a little building in the compound. The man got out and let me out. A woman came out of the house, she did not look at me and she spoke to the men,

"Everything is ready," she said. I wondered what was ready. The man held me by the arm and led me into the house. We walked past a small living room and a kitchen and straight into a room. He looked at me,

"Go inside," he said. That was the last I saw of him, he shut the door. I heard him talking to someone and subsequently, they said their goodbyes. I waited until they were gone before turning to examine my environment. I looked at the room; it was tidy, the sheets were white, the windows were not high and they were clean. They were normal. There was even a rug in the middle of the room. There was a dressing table with an oval mirror; there was chair and a chest of draws. I did not understand any of it. I had been taken against my will, first into squalor and was treated badly and now, I had been brought here and into a place that looked like it was meant for a human to inhabit. I did not understand what they wanted from me; I did not know if they expected thanks because they gave me a decent bed. There was a door not far from the chest, I walked towards it and turned the handle, and it opened and I walked into a bathroom. I had not had a bath in days. I went to the sink and turned on the water; I took off my scarf and splashed water on my face. There were fresh towels on the cabinet. I picked up a towel and wiped my face. I needed a bath, but I could not allow myself to have one. I stank, but I was okay with it, they just had to deal with me the way I was. I was not going to allow myself enjoy whatever they gave me, I did not ask for any of it. I was still in the bathroom when the door opened, it gave me a flashback.

I remembered how I was taken, it was just like this, I was in the bathroom in my flat when the door to my flat opened and those men grabbed me. I remained where I stood; I was scared. I did not know who it was or what they wanted. I heard the footsteps stop outside the door to the bathroom. My heart pounded with fear as the door knob pressed down and the gap in the door enlarged.

Chapter 37

I looked down afraid to see who ever it was, then I heard this familiar voice call my name; I could not believe my ears, I could not believe whose voice I was hearing. In a moment, my fear switched into hope, it had been a long time since I heard that voice. Tears of joy clouded my eyes; until that moment, I had not realised how much I had missed him until I saw him standing before my eyes. I rushed into his arms; he did not pull away from me, I broke down and wept like a child into his chest. I held him so tight, I never wanted to let go. I had never felt so safe in my life, I was so relieved to see him. I had thought I would never get out of here or see them again.

"Father…" I said as he pulled me away from him, but he took one look at me and slapped me across the face. I found myself on the floor, holding onto my burning cheek with my two hands. He had never hit me before, but I knew I deserved this. After all, I must have put them through hell, but if I had to do it again, I would, meeting Robert is definitely worth a million slaps from my father.

The way he looked at me, I knew whatever was coming after that slap was not going to be good. He started to pace the room. I remained where I was; when he paced like that, it was usually not a good thing, especially with my mother not around to talk him out of whatever decision he was making.

I tried not to look at him, my brain started to work. I now knew he was behind my kidnap, which meant, there was no way I would see Robert again. Then the last thing I said to my mother came to mind. 'You have my passport remember, and I thought this trip was meant to be fun for the two of us. I'm just going to the ladies' mother…". Father was not saying anything, he did not have to; I always knew he would find me and that he would not give up until I was found, however, I never thought he would do it like this. I never thought he would allow anyone treat me, his only child the way I had been treated. I never thought he would put me in a position where I feared for my life. I guessed I did not know him as well as I thought I did. Seeing his reaction now made me realize that what I had done would not be forgiven easily. Even so, I have lived on my own and now know what I wanted from life and I would not go down without a fight. They have to understand that I was happy now, and that was all that mattered to me and should matter to them. They wanted me to be married, they wanted me to be happy and my happiness was only with Robert I just have to help them realize this truth. What I was hoping for may never happen, but I would do my best to make my father understand. He was still pacing, since he refused to speak, I decided to take my chance.

"Father…" I said and he stopped, "I am sorry for what I did. I know I must have put you and Mother through…"

"Be quiet," he interrupted sternly and then he sat on the chair. He groaned as he looked at me and I looked away.

"Look at you…! I can barely look at you. You have disrespected not only me and your mother, but yourself as well, you have no respect whatsoever for your religion…! No respect for your family. We have done nothing, but provide for you, taken care of you and protect you all your life and how do you repay us…? How do you repay us?" he shouted.

"You heartless, spiteful child, didn't you think of your poor mother and what your selfishness would do to her; you have no regard for nobody…! No regard for your God! How could you? Did we not teach you enough about the ways of Allah, did we not love you enough? You were the envy of most girls your age, you had everything given to you literarily on a platter of gold and yet you betrayed us, you brought shame upon us. Did you think because you are my only child that I could not disinherit you, or better still disown you? I am only here because of your mother. I can barely recognize her now, your callous behaviour have brought her so much pain. While you were busy whoring yourself like a dog, she suffered. She had become the shadow of herself, she does not sleep and she hardly eats, mourning the loss of her only child. How could you do that to your mother?"

I started to sob uncontrollable; father was right, what I did was selfish and heartless. I always knew, but I wasn't faced with the consequences, I couldn't see the pain I had caused. I knew she would suffer, but I put my happiness before hers. I accepted it, it was cruel of me to run, but if it meant spending a day with Robert, I would do it all again. I knew seeing my mother like that would have killed my father, not that he did not care for me, but I had always known that his love for my mother came before his love for me. I supposed I had tried very hard not to think about what I was doing to them, but as guilty, as I was for all the pain I had caused, I wished that they could realize that it was their selfishness that led to this.

I tried to look at my father through my teary eye, his face was like thunder, he was saying something, but I was trying to build up the courage to tell him that I was sorry, that I met an amazing person and if they just took the chance to know him they would see what I saw in him. My heart was beating so fast; he was going to do something or make a decision, but before he did, I needed him to hear me out.

"Father…" I said, interrupting him. I waited for him to shut me down, but he was quiet, so I continued. "I am sorry for the pain I caused you and mother… I am sorry that I did this and made it necessary for you to have to kidnap me. I wish I did not have to put you through that, but I wanted a different life for myself than the one you and mother planned for me. I wanted to make my own choices, to do the things … that mattered to me, I wasn't happy at home; I knew if I told you I wanted to live on my own you wouldn't approve, so I hid things from you, like who I really was and how I felt inside. If I thought you would understand, I would have come to you, I would never have thought about running. You wanted to marry me off to a man I hardly knew, I felt like a prisoner, you are meant to love me, that means my happiness should matter to you, but I don't think it matters to you how I felt. But now, I'm happy, I found someone that loves me and I love him…"

"Enough of this nonsense, you think this is a good life that you are living? Selling yourself cheaply? Living with a man that is not your husband? You have shamed me; I can barely look at you." He got up and walked towards the door. I did not want him to go, I just had to let him understand that I was still as I was when I left home, I had not done anything to bring him shame. Perhaps, if he understood that, he will see that Robert was a good person and his intentions were good.

"Father, I am happy here… I am not going back with you, I love this man you are talking about and he loves me so, oh father if you would just let me explain it to you, you would understand. He is a good man and he wants to marry me and that's all the happiness I want," I pleaded with him. He turned around stoned faced.

"Who told you, that you have a say in this, you ungrateful child. I cannot bear to think about the things you've been up to. We raised you up a good Muslim and you decide to ruin yourself, did you lose your senses, did we not teach you right from wrong, you call yourself my daughter and you sleep and uncover yourself in the presence of a man that is not your husband? You have shamed us greatly. What do you really think this man of yours was after? Men are just after one thing or in your case two things, your body and money. Or are you too stupid to realize that? Do not worry, he shall be dealt with appropriately. And for your own sake, I hope you have not lost your innocence. You will not bring that shame to my house; from now on, you are no longer my problem, but another man's. Ashraf is here with me...! He never gave up; he went through hell when you decided to go missing. I do not know what it is with him, but he never gave up, he still wants you after all of this, after all the shame you caused and you will make this right. You will marry him; you will show him gratitude for taking you back. I am done with you, but you will remain with him as his wife, a little ceremony would be conducted at the request of Ashraf to make it official, but there would be no celebration as you have made it clear you do not want one. Goodbye, Hasina." He turned towards the door to leave, I felt like the ground had just opened and buried me. I needed to beg him; I needed to ask his forgiveness so he did not leave me here.

"No! No father," I cried and grabbed his legs. "Please don't do this to me, please, father, I am your daughter, your only child, don't do this to me. I am sorry, father I don't love, Ashraf, I can't marry him. Father please, punish me with something else. I know I hurt you; I understand, but please do not leave me here with him. I cannot be his wife; I will not be his wife while I am in love with someone else. I do not mind if you disinherit me, I do not want anything, just let me go and be happy. Please father, if you leave me here, then you have killed me, please, show mercy I am your daughter, your only child, forgive me and let me go and live my life." He shrugged me off him as if I was some dirt on the back of his shoes. And I landed on my side.

With snorts and reddish blurry eyes, I shouted. "Do you hate me this much, father?"

"No, Hasina, I am being kind to you, although you don't see that now. If I hated you, I wouldn't be here at all. If that brain in your head were working, you would realize that I am actually doing you a favour. I am looking out for your future, for your own sake, I hope you realize that soon enough." He opened the door to leave.

"Wait father, what about mother? Don't I get to see my mother at all?" I asked, hoping that when she comes, I could talk her into talking to my father and perhaps she would understand that I am in love and that Robert is a good man, I just couldn't bear the thought of being married off to Ashraf and never seeing Robert again.

"Of course, you would, once I get back, I would tell her that we found you and you are now with Ashraf where you belong. She would come and visit you and your husband... Goodbye now." He walked out the door; I threw myself at the door. I heard the key turn. He spoke to someone briefly and then he walked away. I could not believe this was happening to me, it did not feel real, it felt like an out of body situation. I felt dizzy; I sat down in a pile and wept until my eyes were sore. My heart was in excruciating pain, everything felt hollow, I felt lost and alone in the world. If only I could see Robert, I would be better again, I tried to remember him, his voice, his smell, his laughter and the last time I spoke to him, he said he loved me. That was my escape but thinking of him and realizing I may never see him again brought a different kind of pain. I felt empty, all my dreams have been taken away by the very man that was meant to protect them, and he's left me with no hopes, no dreams, no love and no future. He left me a broken person. I wanted to die, if only there was a way to kill myself, I thought, no! I can't kill myself; suicide is for the weak, and I am not weak. There must be a way out of this mess, I began to think. I looked around, and reality soon hit again, there was no getting out of this, the marriage to Ashraf would soon be formalized and I would be condemned to an unhappy life. Just then, I felt my mouth open as a bitter scream escaped repeatedly from my lungs.

"No" I screamed, until I completely lost my voice. I became too weak to even move, I did not get up from where I was, there was no reason to. I do not know how long I was sat there for; the only thing I remembered was looking through the window and noticing that the sky was darker than it was when I first arrived. I stared at the sky from where I sat, a little breeze blew in, and I envied its freedom.

I heard the door crack open; I did not bother to look up, I did not want to see anyone, nothing matters now. I felt like a slave, I felt powerless.

Then I heard these footsteps walking towards me, but I paid no attention to them it felt like something in a distance. I was not interested in anything or anyone around me; my mind went blank and emptiness consumed me. No one can wake me from this nightmare, my heart was wrenching away at full speed, I wanted to die, now I was sure there was no point living if Robert was not a part of my life.

Chapter 38

A Whole new era

All I remember was sitting there on the ground, my knees to my chest; I must have blacked out, because when I came round and took consciousness of my environment, I found myself on this huge bed. I tried lifting my head, the light got in my eye, the room was so bright, the curtains were opened. I found it difficult to see, my eyes hurt, I couldn't open them. Then I felt this blinding headache. I realized I wasn't alone in the room when someone came close to where I was, I squinted my eyes as I tried to see who it was, I remember her face, it was the woman from the other day when I arrived. She was in a maid's uniform, she looked worried, it seemed like she was inspecting me. I covered my face with my arms to avoid her probing eyes.

She rushed out of the room, I did not know why, but I was not interested, I wished I could sleep again. I did not want to be aware of anything. Waking up and still finding myself here was a nightmare. I needed it to end. I do not want to remember what happened to me or speak to anyone, I just wanted it all to stop. My heart felt heavy, at the same time I felt like a sledge hammer was forcefully drilling nails of pain in me.

I remembered who's to blame for this pain—my father. I pray never to see him again. He does not deserve to be a father, he may think he is justified to do what he has done, but I would never forgive him for this.

Thoughts of my situation brought fresh tears to my eyes, but I could not bring myself to cry anymore, my eyes were hurting so bad. My heart yearned for Robert; but then, I worried for him too. I wondered what my father meant when he said he would be dealt with. I wish there was a way to warn him about my father. I pulled out the letter Robert wrote to me ages ago from where I had hidden it, I clutched it to my chest. At least I had this I thought, it would remind me of a time I found a love so great it cannot be compared with anything. Another surge of pain erupted in my heart; I curled up and held my chest tight the pain was scorching burning my whole being. I felt crushed, I couldn't breathe, I screamed in pain, I wanted the feeling to stop. My whole body felt flushed with heat, and covered in sweats, it was killing me and I was helpless to do anything about it.

The maid rushed back in with three other people, I quickly hid the letter from view. I couldn't make out the faces of the people in the room with me. They tried to hold me down, but it just made me more uncomfortable, every unsolicited touch. Someone placed their hands on my fore head, another sat next to me and held my hands by my bed and the third person stood by the end of the bed with the maid. It was all too much; I did not want this people around me invading my privacy. They started to talk; I tried to listen to what they were saying amidst the pain that consumed me.

Someone said, "She's been like this for three days, drifting in and out of consciousness, her temperature was stable before, but it's beginning to rise again. I cannot continue to treat her if she does not eat; you have to talk to her. The other choice would be to feed her intravenously, and we may have to admit her in my clinic to do that, as for now there is nothing, I can do to help her. Talk to her, see if you can get through to her or we may lose her." The man said.

"Thank you, Doctor Hassan." That was when I heard my mother's voice, it was nice to hear her voice, I tried to look for her and found that she was the one sitting next to me holding my hands. I felt a little calm knowing she was here with me. I could really do with a hug from her, but I did not have the strength to pull myself up.

"Please can I have a moment with my daughter" I could hear them all leave. As much as I was happy, she was here, my hopes were not up. I knew she would be on my father's side of things. Which made me angrier; she had never really stood up for me, not when it counts like now. She is just the better of two devils.

I waited for her to speak; I was too tired to initiate anything.

"Hasina, it's me your mother!" she said with shaky voice, I could hear from her tone, she was trying to be strong, but I was not moved by her emotions, she was not the prisoner, I was. She placed her hands on my hair and brushed my hair lovingly. It felt nice—the affection she gave—I smiled a little to show approval.

"Mother" I whispered. She moved in front of me so I could see her, and my heart broke, she looked withered and unhappy, like she had not eaten properly for a long time. She smiled, and my heart sank deeper because I knew I did this to her. "Mother, I am very…. sorry" I said, if I hadn't been too tired, I would have explained better, but I could not. I did not have the strength.

"Hush… don't talk baby, I know, it's all right, I am here now and I'm just so happy to see you, we have to get you better." I could hear the strain in her voice; she wanted to cry, but she held on to the tears for my sake. It pained me even more the situation we were both in, my eyes started to water and I had to do all I could to stop myself from crying because the tears have turned into torture.

"Hasina, you have to eat something so you can get better, it worries me that you haven't eaten anything for three days. Everyone is worried about you. I am worried darling, you are everything to me, you are my life and I cannot watch you do this to yourself. Please eat, do it for me."

"I …can't …I'm not … hungry mother"

"Hasina … please listen to me, you are very sick, you've been feverish for days and your body is burning up again, but the doctor can't treat you if you don't eat. Please Hasina, I beg you, I beg you darling eat. I will ask the maid to bring some food, let's start with some soups. Anyone you like." I kept quiet; she will never understand that food is not the cure for my disease, Robert is.

"How long… how long have I been here?" I asked.

"Three days darling, I got here yesterday, I came as soon as your father told me he found you. Baby, listen to mummy. You need to eat, baby, I can't lose you again, I only just found you…" she was still trying not to cry, but I could see the tears clouding her eyes. I felt terrible, she suffered so much and I was still making her suffer. I reached my hands gently and touched her face. No wonder my father hates me so much. Look at what I had done to the woman he loves.

"It's okay mother… for you I will drink a little soup." I said, she smiled in relief and the tears flowed freely down her cheek. It was okay, because I knew it was because she was happy and I was responsible for that smile. I wondered if she had anything to smile about since I left her at the airport.

"Thank you, my darling," She kissed my hands and rubbed them lovingly. Her words— '*my darling*'—only did more to remind me of

Robert. I closed my eyes and I could hear him calling me. I tried to hold off the pain I was feeling for my mother's sake.

"I will be back, let me tell someone to bring the soup." She went out the door; I knew I had been selfish; I was guilty of the very thing I accused my parents of. I had not thought very deeply about the consequences of my actions and as justified as I was in my feelings. Seeing my mother, a shadow of her former self made me realise, for now, I had to do better by her. I closed my eyes to sleep. I figured it would take a while for them to prepare the food. She walked back in with a tray of soup a moment later; and climbed into bed with me, sat me up and rested my head on the pillow she probed up.

"Here, drink some water first. You must be thirsty" I had a sip, and then she started to feed me soup. I had no taste for anything, I could not tell what was inside the soup, but I wanted mother to be happy, I did not want her to worry about me, I had caused her a lifetime of worry already.

After a few mouths full, I could not eat anymore. It took too much effort to swallow she did not force it. She was just happy I had eaten something. I wanted to sleep, she helped me to lie down and then she lay next to me and held me for what seemed like eternity until sleep reclaimed my body.

It had been almost a week since my mother and I have been together, I am not sure of the actual length of time, and I do not care. It was just great to have someone that truly cares for me close. She had not yet told me, when she would be leaving me and I seriously do not want to have that discussion any time soon, thinking of it will mean I will be left here alone with that stranger; I just cannot bear to think on it.

When I woke up late at night, mother was by my bed, even though she was doing her best to hide her worry, I could tell she was still so worried. Her eyes gave it away.

"How are you feeling?" she asked, as I tried to get up.

I wanted to use the loo, my head felt light. She held me and helped me as I walked, if she had not offered to help, I knew I could have fallen flat on my face, I was that weak. When we returned., I didn't want to sleep anymore, I wanted to talk to her about helping me escape, I knew the possibility of her doing that was very slim but still I had to try. I was dying inside, anyone with eyes could see.

"Should I ask them to get you something to eat?" Mother asked,

I shook my head. I was not hungry for food even though my senses told me that I needed to eat. I felt lost without Robert and I knew by now, he would have gone mad with worry. I regretted leaving his house to go to my flat, if I had not perhaps things will be different now.

"Hasina, you need to eat, if you don't you will leave me no choice but to agree to the doctor feeding you intravenously." Mother pleaded.

A cloud of tear rolled down my cheek, "I want to go back mother, I need him."

I said, my mother looked away.

"You must not speak of that here, Hasina." she said,

"Well then, that's all I need, that's who can make me better." I pushed through teary eyes.

"Please Hasina, your father can't allow that. Now stop this please, or I will have to leave."

"No! Please don't leave me here." I begged.

"If you promise not to talk that way again, I will stay but you must eat, Hasina, if your father doesn't think my presence here is not helpful to you then he will ask that I come back and leave you to your husband." Mother argued.

"He's not my husband yet."

"Yet, but he will be soon. Please, Hasina, this doesn't have to be a tug of war, Ashraf loves you. Get to know him, that's all I ask."

I knew at this stage it was pointless arguing, I would try another time, I decided.

"Good girl, now eat something little and then rest so you can get better." She said, I nodded.

"Okay." I said. It was clear that as long as I was eating and taking my medication, she would remain with me. So, I remained on my best behaviour, I did everything they required of me. I let them wash my hair and run baths for me. I let them change my clothes and brush my hair. It made mother happy and my thinking was that as long as she was happy, she would not leave. I was dying inside, but I tried to hide my pain for her sake, I knew she would not stay forever, but she was here now and it made my irrelevant life bearable. Each time, mum or some other person spoke to me about their nonsense marriage; I pictured Robert's face, I see him telling me it is okay and that there was no way this nightmare would last forever. Picturing him gets me through the day, on tougher days, I run into the bathroom and read his letter and it gives me hope and strengthens me knowing that even though I may never see him again.

I have known a love like no other and the memories are mine alone to cherish and keep.

And with as much passion as I love Robert, I hated and detested my father, who had decided that it was his God-given right to drag me down from what seemed like heaven and inflicted me with this indescribably painful existence. What use was all the money and power he has, if he could subject and suppress his only child to this misery?

A month and half passed slowly, I think, as I wasn't counting days. Mother had been pestering me to go out and exercise my legs as I had refused to step outside of the house, I was held in. I didn't want to go out and make it okay for them to think I was adjusting to captivity or to encounter my captor Ashraf.

"Hasina, you are looking more like yourself again," mother said as I was dressed for the day, the maid brushed my hair and placed the brush on the dresser as mother entered the room.

"You may take your leave." Mother said to the maid.

I nodded at the woman to thank her for brushing my hair as she left the room.

"Darling, come let me take a look at you." She said, I got up and she smiled. "You are beautiful, it's good to see my daughter back in good health and I'm hoping to help liven your spirit too."

"How are you going to manage that?

"Well, I think a good walk will do you good. You cannot stay cocooned up in here it's not healthy. You need the sun; you need your daily vitamin D. Come, let's talk about the future, while I am here. You know I can't stay with you forever."

I sighed, the dreaded conversation I was avoiding.

"Mother, must we do this? I don't want to go out." I said defiantly.

"Oh Hasina, but you must. This protest or whatever you are doing, how long do you think it will work for? You have to stop fighting this, we have prepared for you a great future, if only you can see it. One day you will be a mother and you will understand that as a parent you do your best to give your child the world."

"And I thank you, but what about happiness, does that not count?" I asked.

"Oh Hasina, Ashraf, will make you happy, you haven't given him a chance. Trust me on this, and you will thank me later. Do you not think that I care about you? If I didn't why do you think I nearly died when you went away? I was so worried about you I forgot how to sleep; my mind imagined all sorts. I just thank Allah that he brought you back in one piece."

"He could try to make me happy but I don't think I have it in my heart to love anyone else, is that fair to him? What you and Father have is mutual, you love each other, I don't think I will ever have that in my life if you put me through this." I protested.

"Why? Who told you that? Marriage is about faith; you go in with a positive mind and work hard at your own happiness. If you want to be happy, that will be your own doing. You make your husband happy and he will make you happy."

I sighed heavily, this discussion was not going how I wanted it, I felt permanently trapped, I didn't know how to appeal to her to help me, her mind was set on Ashraf.

I kept quiet, frustrated with everything. I sat on the edge of my bed, mother sat next to me and placed her hand on mine.

"You know you could have written to me baby, just to let me know you were well, that would have been enough for me." I could feel my eye rolling in my socket, whom was she kidding, if I had written to her, then they would have even found me sooner and subjected me to this, it was always going to be the same outcome.

"I thought we were close, you and I. Hasina, when you were young you told me everything that bothered you and we found a way around it, didn't we?" I smiled, I almost busted into laughter, is she saying she was not aware I never wanted this marriage from the beginning, or that I loved to dance?

"Mother, if we must talk about this, don't pretend that you care about what I want?" I said as I felt a sudden burst of anger growing in me towards her.

"Hasina, I know this is very hard for you… these things you say you want, they are not right for you, the way you feel right now... it will pass with time." I kept quiet there was no point replying, I knew what would come out of my mouth next would be rude.

"You need to try and forget about that man;" she continued, "please you must forget him and start afresh. I know your father will come to his senses eventually. No matter what you make of him now, he loves you dearly, but he is hurt by your actions. You just have to show him you've changed and he will forgive you I promise." I cannot believe how ridiculous she was beginning to sound; she was worried about my father being hurt. I wanted to scream what about me? I am hurting, I am hurting so bad I do not think I will ever recover and she is only concerned about how I hurt my father. What about what they are doing to me now? How selfish can this people get that they only see what they want? There was no point talking to her, she will never see reason, she is too far-gone. If I had any sense, I should have stopped myself from falling in love with Robert. I should not have let myself get that sucked in with him. I mean, who was I kidding? There was no way I could have the life I truly wanted, not with the type of family I have.

"Say something, baby." My mother spewed in frustration. "You know if it were within my powers, I will give you anything you want... nothing would be beyond your reach." I turned away from her; I could not bear to listen to her. If I could, I would run away again just so I do not have to hear her tell me words that carry no meaning.

My eyes clouded up again, and I turned towards her, "Mother, can't you see what you are doing to me? You say that you love me, but you go along with father and treat me like a prisoner, you take my free will from me yet you preach about loving me. The two of you behave as though I am your property, but I am not, I am your child, a human being with her own God given free will. Do you really know what love is? Right now, I will prefer to die than to be married to that man, but I decided to eat for your sake because I saw that I did made you suffer. I did not have to, but because I love you, even though I know you are one of my kidnappers, I ate to make you happy. When I was away, fate brought me to Robert, he is an incredible man, I love him, and he loves me. He would never do what you and father have done to me because unlike you, he does not treat me like his property. I love him more than life itself. I cannot be with anyone else; I am not capable of loving anyone other than him mother. My heart belongs to Robert, I was created for him and he was made for me. You see when you say I should forget him, do you think that ever being possible because without him, I am nothing, I am lost. So, know this, you may drag me into hell with this unwanted marriage to Ashraf but he would never, ever have my heart; I will never be his… how can I?"

"You must never spit such vile words again, like I have told you a thousand times before, you feel this way now, but with time it will be different I promise. Love does not always bring happiness; happiness is what you make of life, the journey, the struggle, to build a life of substance together, you will get that with Ashraf and you would appreciate him for it. He will make you laugh and add colour to your life. And maybe even one day, you will surprise yourself when you realise you have fallen madly in love with this man you fought so hard not to be with. Even perhaps love him more than you've ever loved anyone. That is the beauty in this, love creeps on you. It is a beautiful journey you are going on; and if I did not think he was good for you, I would fight for you to be with this man you said you found You will see. You must now forget about that man and keep an open mind with Ashraf, you are still young and with time, things will fall into place naturally."

Just then, I realized I wasn't sorry I ran away anymore. I wasn't sorry she looked the ghost of her formal self, in fact I wished she had suffered more than she did, just so she could feel a portion of the pain she was subjecting me to. She and father deserved every bit of hurt life could throw at them for this wickedness towards me. She never fought my battles not really; she would not accept that I am my own person with my own brains, if anyone could get my father to reason with me, it is she, but she never tried. Her voice continued to drown my thoughts and I hated it.

She continued talking, brushing my hair with one hand as she spoke.

"Give Ashraf a chance please, this is the life for you, the right path for you to follow Hasina. And it will please your father. Do this for your mother."

I was fuming at what she was saying, how dare she say I should do this for her? Can she not tell that I am broken beyond repair? I had to cut her off, I wanted rid of her, I couldn't bear to be in this same room let alone breathe the same air as her. I jumped up from the bed and stood a distance from her before hitting her with my words.

"To think that with all that money you both have and the civilization your wealth has afforded you, you will realize that times have changed, and we live in a different world. A world where a girl like me at the age of twenty-three is old enough to decide what she wants in life. I will never be happy with Ashraf no matter how much you will it to be. I have chosen for myself what I want in life, and although you make me a prisoner for someone else's pleasure it will never change what I feel for Robert." I told her through gritted teeth and continued.

"You would never understand mother; you only see things your way. Let this be the last time you tell me you are doing this for me, and do not patronize me with your love either, I find it very hard

311

to believe you ever loved me. Love is selfless, but yours is tainted, flawed and selfish. All you care about is wealth, power and control. You suffocate me with your presence, pretending to care when all you really wanted from me was to agree to your will. The moment, I marry Ashraf, is the moment that by your hands you killed whatever was left of me. When you go back to your husband and lie in bed at night, know that you have done this to me. At least with father, I always knew where I stood, but you, you are worse than he is; you are a snake in green grass you pretend you care but you are relentless in the venom that you spout. Your work here is done you can go now. Go and be with your husband.

She started to cry, normally I would stop, but not this time.

"You can leave now mother,"

"Hasina, that is no way to talk to your mother. I am your mother and I demand your respect."

"You lost my respect when you sold me into this marriage, now leave and let me get on with the rest of my miserable life!"

"How dare you, speak to me like that?" Mother said crying, but my anger towards her just rose to another height. Mother got up and walked closer to me, I saw no reason to curb my annoyance at her and she had to feel the strength of my pain.

"I will speak to you anyhow I want, cry all you like, it will not change how I feel about you. You are useless, worthless and not fit to be my mother." I lashed out and she whacked me hard on my face. I sighed and looked at her with a clenched jaw, I said. "And now, you're dead to me."

"You, ungrateful child, you will never speak of me like that. You may not like my decision but it's my decision to make as your mother." I laughed out loud.

"If you were truly my mother, you would fight for me. You will seek my happiness at all cost."

"Stop it, Hasina, stop it, you know that is not true. You're clearly not thinking right,"

"I cannot bear to look at you any longer, please leave now and never come back. If you do, I will never see you."

"Hasina, no, please darling you have to stop this nonsense now, you mean the world to me, you must know that by now."

I scoffed at her plea. "You really think so? Think again. You of all people should know not to treat anyone like this or do I need to remind you?" "What are you talking about?"

"Please do not play ignorant, mother, it does not look good on you. Your mother was not a Muslim; it didn't stop your father from marrying her even when everyone else was against their union."

"Hasina, how can you say such things to me… this is different, you know very well if I support what you want that our family will turn their backs on us, you will shame us, what you're asking me to do, Hasina, I cannot." She tried to touch me, but I recoiled from her, I felt sick at her presence.

"Well then, I think we are done here. Please show yourself out."

"Hasina!" My mother called.

"No, I don't want to hear no more. leave now and don't come back." for the first time I hated my own mother, I turned my back to her until she was out the door.

I remained in the room for the remainder of the day, I was told that Ashraf came in to check on me, but I refused to see him or anyone. He of all people is the last person I want to see. I expected a bit of a fight from him, but surprisingly he let me be. I went to the safest place I know, I read Roberts letter repeatedly and envisioned him with me. Just lying next to me, I did not want to cry; crying had not done me any good. I just wanted it all to stop. The memories of Robert were unbearable, the pain unstoppable and the loneliness killed me. I wanted to press reset in my heart, if only it were easy but for now a pause will do.

Chapter 39

Robert Philip Parkman.

It had been over a month since Hasina vanished. I went to the police to declare her missing; but they have not been of any help.

Because I was not married to her and not a blood relation, there is little they can do. They said she probably left me and they could not take the case seriously if her family has not reported her missing, plus, there is no one in the country apart from me looking for her. It has been very frustrating, how could she just disappear into thin air, we were very happy and the last time I spoke to her, she was excited about going to Paris. Although, I cannot prove it, but I suspect that Hasina's disappearance may have something to do with her family. If only I knew where to look, I have no clue where they could have taken her and it kills me now that I didn't ask all the relevant questions about her family when she told me who she was. Now that she needs me the most, I feel useless. Her flat has been cleared out; there is no trace that she ever lived there, all her belongings are gone. I spoke to the landlord, he said he found the place had been emptied and an anonymous envelop full

Elizabeth Johnson

of cash left in the flat for him, I persuaded him to come with me to the police, but he said he didn't want to get involved.

Not having Hasina with me, has been difficult, it feels like hell to lose her. I miss her so much that it kills me; the agony I feel is indescribable. I feel so useless, I worry about her safety, is she alive? Has she been hurt or forced to marry the stranger she ran from? My work has suffered, I find myself lashing out on others, yelling at them unnecessarily, I was finding it hard to function. Jane is the only person that truly understood what Hasina meant to me, but with her planning her own wedding bringing up Hasina's disappearance felt like injecting a dark cloud over her excitement. I was dying without Hasina, the feeling of lost and emptiness was second to nothing and it drowned me each day. I wanted to cry so much and scream, as the pain of her loss ate through me. To make matters worse, sleep evaded me, I coil on her bed just so I can smell her. I had instructed the maid not to touch her room, that was all I had left to remind me of her. Her scents on her cloths, her dark hair on the brush, her cream, and soaps. Everything just placed the way she had left them. Even though, being in her room helped remind me of her, it also pushes me farther into the empty hole my life had become without her. Looking at all her things the way she had left them, one would know she meant to come back.

The Paris trip wasn't just going to be an ordinary weekend getaway; I had planned to celebrate her birthday and to ask her hand in marriage. I placed the yellow diamond ring on Hasina's dressing table, with the rest the of her jewelleries. I couldn't bear to look at it anymore, it only brought regrets. Why did I not marry her sooner? I ask myself, I knew that I loved her above every other person in my life, so why did I wait? If we were already married, perhaps they would have left her well alone. Being in her room became too much for me. I requested that the house maid lock the room so I didn't go back in there. There was no point moping about it, if I wanted her in my life then I knew I had to put in the work to find her as I knew she would be counting on me to do so.

I hired a private detective, to help me locate her, according to the private eye, an eyewitness, saw a van parked in front of Hasina's flat on the day she went missing, but no one saw what happened next. There were no outside street cameras around the flat that she lived but even so, it doesn't take a genius to conclude, that her father was behind it all. Hasina mentioned briefly that her family were wealthy, so naturally, I suspected that her father would do and spend whatever it took to get his daughter back.

What she failed to tell me, which my detective has filled me in on, was the influence and power her father's wealth affords him. My private eye advised me to forget her. He told me he heard a rumour she had been married off, but I would only believe it when Hasina tells me so herself. The fear that she may now be another man's wife consumes me. The thought of never seeing her again is unacceptable. I told the detective to keep digging. I wanted him to find out where they took her. But he refused to look into it farther, he said it was too dangerous he has been threatened to stop investigating if he wanted his family in one piece. With a little more persuasion, my private eye introduced me to another colleague of his who has now taken up the job after I doubled his fee.

In the end, I regretfully had to tell Jane about Hasina's disappearance. I had hoped that Jane would know something relevant that could lead me to finding Hasina. But Jane knew nothing, instead, all I achieved was disrupting her wedding plans and made her worry about Hasina. It angered me, that Hasina claimed to love me, even her friend Jane and still she kept vital information that could save her now from us then. How could she be so close to us, and knowing her family's expectations of her and not tell us anything that could have helped us now in case we found ourselves in a situation like this? I knew I should not be mad at her; it was the circumstances, the helplessness, emptiness and loneliness that was killing me. I had shared my life with her, loved her with every fibre of my being shared absolutely everything with her and it seemed I did not know her very well at all.

Jane suggested postponing her wedding, but I would not have it. There was no point in her suffering because of me. Jane now comes around to my house a lot, she sleeps over most weekends, I have told her to stop, explaining to her that it is highly unlikely that I would kill myself. My intentions are to find her not end my own life.

Chapter 40

Six months flew by and still I had no news of her whereabouts. My private eyes travelled to the east, to dig up more information, he usually checked in once every week, but for the past month, I haven't heard from him and that worried me as well. At this point, I was beyond feeling useless. I can only assume the worse at this point, nothing was in my control. I decided to arrange another meeting with another investigator, to find out what happened to the first one that travelled to the east. On my way back home from the meeting with the new private eye, my chauffeur pulled up in front of the gate. Another car, a black Rolls Royce was parked in front of my gate, I noticed a man walk up to my car and knocked on my window. I rolled down the glass, he said. "Your attention is needed," he gestured to the other parked car. I didn't understand, what he meant by that statement, but then I wondered if this had to do with Hasina's disappearance. My chauffeur tried to get out of the car to keep the man away from me, but another man appeared out of nowhere really, as it seemed, and pushed him back in the car.

"Hey, what do you think you are doing?" I complained, as I got out of the car to investigate who these strangers were. The first man pulled me by my shirt, I pushed him away, "Get your hands off me." I said firmly. The other guy walked towards me with a determination on his face, the type that said I was about to get my ass kicked. I quickly took off my suit and rolled my sleeves. I didn't know what this was, but if they thought they were going to come beat me up in my house, they had another thing coming. I was ready for anything, even though I didn't regard myself as an aggressive person. The two men flanked me on both sides as they forced me to walk towards the Rolls Royce. The car door opened, I stood still with my eyes darting from the opened door to the mean-looking men that surrounded me.

"What do you want?" I asked. But somehow, at the back of my mind, I knew what this was all about. If my suspicions about Hasina's family were true, then I wouldn't put this craziness pass them. Her father has come for his pound of flesh.

"Get in the car." One of the men said.

"No, if you need to say anything to me, you will say it to me right here." I said standing my ground.

Then one of the men put his hand on me to push me in, I swung my free fist in his face, hitting him hard and breaking his nose. Just then I felt a cold metal, at the back of my head.

"Make any more moves and it will be your last." The other man said. Breathing hard, I placed my two hands in the air in surrender as I watched the man I just broke his nose scampering to his feet with the look of death on his face.

"Get inside the car now." He commanded.

"No." I said firmly.

Then a man stepped out of the car, "Leave him be. It's okay." he said. He walked towards me; I didn't need the introduction, I could see the resemblance in his eyes, I was staring at Hasina's father. Before she went missing, I had often thought about meeting her family but this wasn't the exact scenario that I had played in my head. I was not holding out any hope, this wasn't a nice to-meet you situation. He had come to warn me to stay away, that could only mean Hasina is not going along with their plans for her. That made me happy a little, but what I needed more than anything was information that she was okay.

As he got closer, the man with the broken nose, held both my hands firmly behind me. From the corner of my eyes, I could see my chauffer was worried, he wanted to come out of the car and I didn't want him getting hurt on account of me.

"Stay in the car, Paul. I just need to talk to these gentlemen." I instructed.

"Good advice." Hasina's father said and scoffed.

"Hello young man" he said patronizingly,

"Who are you and what do you want?" I asked pretending I did not know who he was."

"Ah! Funny you should ask," He looked at me and looked in the direction of my house as if he was weighing me up.

"I am going to make this very quick; I have other places to be."

"I ask you again, what do you want?" I asked as I fought to get out of the man's hold even with a gun held to my temple.

"Patience is a virtue, have you never heard of that saying? Anyway, I will get to the point. You don't know me, but you took something that belonged to me, you took what I treasured and you destroyed it. Now here lies my dilemma, how do I handle this situation? Do I blame you, or her? Mostly her, I think, because I raised her better and you didn't know whose she was, but still, however I dice it, I can't forgive you for your part in all this mess. Now, what you say at this moment in your defence might change that?" He said.

I narrowed my eyes, "Don't talk in riddles; I am direct in all my dealings. I take it you are Hasina's father?" he nodded. "So, from what you just said, it is pretty safe to assume you have her with you?"

"Yes, you assume rightly. She's is back where she belongs." He said.

I sighed in relief, at least now I knew where she was, I now only had to correct his mistaken assumption that I had done something bad to his daughter which is not the case.

"You are wrong about me, I did not treat her badly, I love her, I respected her. Have you asked her? Ask her, she would tell you I never took advantage of her she means more to me than you would ever know. I love your daughter, and she loves me too. Please you have to let her go, I promise you, I will care for her, she is my world. You cannot force her to be with someone she does not want. She wants me, she belongs to me and I will make her happy. Is that not all that matters? Is that not what should matter to you— your daughter's happiness?" I said. And he whacked me across the face, before I could look up, the two men held me down against his car, Paul, my driver came charging out of the car. I shouted at him to get back inside, he did not listen, but I did not want him involved.

"Get back now; this has nothing to do with you." I watched him re-enter the car. That was a damn hot smack. My nose began to bleed, I knew there was no reasoning with this man, he wanted blood, but he would not get mine.

"You see young man; I didn't come to do that, but let's get something straight do not ever presume you can lecture me on what I should want for my child. She is my only child, she is my world, you could never love her as much as I do. You think you love her, because you filled her head with that nonsense you call love? You are very mistaken, I have protected her and loved her since her mother carried her in the womb. My daughter, stayed in this house with you, and shamed herself messing with the likes of you. You think that you are worthy of my child? Because you own a house and a business? You and the little money you have acquired, will never be worthy of her hand in marriage. She is the apple of my eye, very precious to me, but I know she doesn't believe how much I care, still it doesn't make it any less true. Now listen to me carefully, son, I want you to stop looking for her. And like I told you, she is now home where she belongs, where she should have been all along, with her husband. She is happy, even happier than I expected of her, she has realized the errors of her ways, and is now making her husband happy. Move on with your life, do not look for her anymore, what you had is over. Listening to you talk about her, I forgive you of the role you played in all that mess. But I won't pardon you a second time. Find somebody of your own culture, marry and be happy."

I knew he was lying, there was no way I would believe that Hasina was now happy with someone else. If that was true, then why go through the trouble of warning me off her? I was going to fight for her even if her father thinks that his thuggish behaviour was enough to scare me away. I chuckled sadly, and with a stern face, I said, "I didn't ask for your forgiveness, I did nothing wrong and I will continue to look for Hasina until she tells me herself that she doesn't want to be with me. If she is truly as happy as you say, then why don't you let her come and tell me so herself or better still, tell me where she is, let me ask her, let me see for myself that she has found happiness greater than what we shared and I will walk away and never look back." I said.

He laughed softly, "I don't owe you any favours, you are nothing to me." He said.

I laughed, "I thought you might say that. You know why? Because you are a liar and a bully. You call what you are doing love, you don't know the half of it, you are forcing your daughter into a loveless marriage. All for what? The money you have, you couldn't spend it all in five lifetimes, you have power, you are a household name in your country. Yet, you treat your only child that you claim to love like a prisoner. She doesn't need your forgiveness, you need hers, but now that I know the type of man that you are, I'm not surprised at your behaviour." He looked down for a second and then looked up at me.

"Tell me then," he said, "What type of man do you think I am?" he asked.

"You are a stubborn old man that is too set in his ways and all that money you have did not buy you enlightenment. In layman's terms, you are a fool." I saw in his eyes glints of anger, I had hit a chord, he did his best to control his temper. His two thugs held me tighter waiting for instruction to beat me up, I was ready for it, whatever he had to dish out, I was ready to take it. There was no amount of beating that could equal the pain of not being with Hasina.

"You think I am lying? I didn't want to do this to you, but you asked for it." He smiled, and then beckoned to someone in the car to bring him something. The man came with a large envelope in hand. Hasina's father collected the envelop from his man, took one look at me and then at the envelop and smiled.

Then he said, "Take, knock yourself out. You will see that whatever you shared with her was only short-lived. You had your fun and now it is over. Go on living your life; I will not give you another chance if I hear that you are still sending people to find her. I will not tolerate any type of disturbance in her marriage, if you do not listen to my warnings you will only have yourself to blame, you wouldn't want to do that to your poor mother's heart now, would you?"

"Is that a threat?" I asked.

"Take it as you will." He responded and threw the envelop at my feet and then looked at his two thugs holding me down and gestured to them to let me go. He got in his car with his goons and I stood there and watched as they drove off. I did not know what was in the envelope, I could not bring myself to open it, it would all be one fabricated lie I told myself. I straightened my shirt and entered into my car. The gate opened and the chauffer pulled into the compound. Before getting out of the car, Paul asked.

"Are you alright, sir?" I paused before responding, I didn't know how to respond, I was clearly not, but I didn't want to discuss what happened any further.

"Yes, I am, Paul, thanks for asking, but Paul, I need to rely on your discretion. I don't want a word out of what took place out there. Do you understand?"

"Understood, sir." Paul replied.

"Thank you, Paul." I said and got out of the car; I took the envelope inside the living room with me and poured myself a drink. I downed it at once; and poured myself another. I stared at the envelope; I did not have enough courage to open it. Her father sounded very sure of himself; as if he knew what I would find would help me make up my mind. I downed the drink and poured myself another and downed that immediately as well. If any of the things her father said was true, I didn't want to be sober for any of it. In that envelope was probably the evidence that I had lost her, I sighed heavily as I braced my heart for my worst nightmare. I tore open the envelope. And there she was, smiling, her eyes full of joy, I could not take my eyes off her. Then I noticed she was looking at someone, I quickly got another picture out, this time I could see him clearly, he looked happy, his eyes were on her, and I could tell he adored her. Whoever this man was, he clearly loved my Hasina. Hasina leaned against him in another picture. There were lots of them like that with her and him, holding hands, she looked content and happy, she looked like she loved being around him. This wasn't what I wanted to find; my heart broke with each evidence of her happiness. Then I saw another picture: she sat across him with a little wood burning fire between them. Her eyes glistened from laughter, her head was thrown back and her dark hair dangled in the air. She must have laughed at what he said and it made me jealous. She used to laugh that way with me. How could she forget me so soon? Was what we had a lie? and there were time stamps on the pictures even as recent as the day before. Her father did not lie when he said she had moved on.

My heart sank. It was terrible—the pain you feel when someone you love more than life itself betrays you. I still cannot believe she moved on so fast, it was hard to ignore the evidence staring at me, according to these pictures it didn't look like she was being held against her will. She probably played with me. What was I? Her last hurray before marriage? How could I ever believe anything she ever said to me after seeing this? Come to think of it, I knew her as Anna fey, her fake name for more than half our relationship. I was indeed the fool, and she the punishment for all the women I had wronged in my life. She has chosen her path and I must accept it. I poured myself another drink; I did not want to think, she had just killed whatever hope of happiness I had left in me and I wanted to drink myself into oblivion, until I could no longer remember her name.

Chapter 41

Hasina—Life with Ashraf Mohammed

Three months passed since my sudden kidnap; I had spent the best part of these dark days in bed not wanting to interact with anyone. Mother left two weeks ago at my behest. Still, I felt as dreadful as I felt since that day, I was forcefully brought here to be Ashraf's wife. I had not seen that man, since my unfortunate kidnapping. He had come calling, but each time he came knocking, I refused to see him. I don't know how else to let him know that I am not interested. I know mother said with time, I would feel better. Well, that has not been the case. This emptiness in me, and the horrible pain it drilled into my heart has not going away and I do not know how to feel any better. There were days when I felt dying was better, if only I had the courage to do it.

A flicker of hope springs to mind always and reminds me that I might get to see Robert one day and that has been my reason for living. However, I knew I could not avoid Ashraf forever. The marriage was to take place soon; the only reason I was not married to him yet was because he had graciously requested that the date be moved until I was in better health.

When I was told that he worries about my decision to stay in bed, the picture of a very kind man had been painted to me. But there was no way I could see him in that light when he and my father colluded to hold me like a prisoner. The thought of him claiming me as his wife and touching me has haunted me ever since my father announced I had no choice in the matter.

Since my mother left, Ashraf had come every evening to request my audience which I refused each day. I cannot bear to face the monster. For the life of mine, I do not understand his insistence on marrying me. I did not treat him well before my great escape and I have not acknowledged his presence since my imprisonment.

I do not know what he looks like as I have never set my eyes on his face. I have wondered about my decision not to see him, and at the back of my mind is the fear that I may actually like what I see. That thought alone felt like a huge betrayal to Robert, but perhaps, throwing in the towel will make my life much easier to bear. Hearing everyone around me tell me how great Ashraf is, has not helped either, even though I am in pain. I have sometimes questioned my decision to go against my parents' wishes. In the end, I guess we both have questions that need answering. He must be wondering why I gave my consent and then ran, as I wonder why he wouldn't just walk away.

The compound was guarded by a little army. From my bedroom window, I watched the guards daily patrolling the compound. Although none of them carried guns that I could see, I knew there was no getting out of this situation unless Ashraf requests my release. And if I wanted out, I needed to play him and stop acting childish. After coming to that decision, I woke up early and decided it was time I faced the world gain. I got up and stood in front of the mirror, I did not recognize the person looking back at me, my bones where sticking out in every direction. It made me sad. I looked like my life had been drained. I picked up the brush from the table and began to brush my hair, as I did, I knew that I wouldn't want to return to Robert looking this wasted. I don't think Robert would even recognize me; not in the state am in. If I am to be married to that monster, Ashraf, at least I wanted a chance to prove to him that he made the wrong choice choosing me as a wife. When he realizes that there can be no future for us, he would tell my parents he does not want me and they would have no choice, but to let me go and live my life.

When the maid arrived, I was ready for the day, I had had my wash, dressed, with my hair brushed, lip-gloss applied, eyes lined. She looked shocked to see me. She was bringing me my morning tea, normally I would still be in bed, I never even bothered to ask her name. However, today was different, it was the beginning of my fight for freedom, I was done with being the victim and I have to make everyone around me believe that I was now okay with the arrangement to marry Ashraf.

"You are up… already?" She said, I smiled, as I tried on the jewelleries on my dressing table.

"I brought you your tea; shall I pour you a cup?"

"Yes, please…! Erm, what's your name?" I asked, she has been serving me for about three months or so and I do not have any idea who she was.

"Fa…tima" she said nervously as she poured my tea, I smiled to try to relax her. I do not know why she was nervous; she had served me since I was imprisoned here. And today, I decide to do things differently and she seemed all nervous.

"Fatima thank you for the tea, and thank you for looking after me since I got here. I haven't made it easy for you, but I am fine now." I said placing my hand on hers to reassure her. She smiled nervously.

"I am happy for you, everyone would be so excited. Do you want anything else?" She asked.

"No nothing, I am alright for now." I watched as she hurried out the door, I wondered who she was taking the news to.

Twenty minutes later, she came with a tray of food.

"Your breakfast madam." She said.

"Please take it back; I will have breakfast at the dining table. Where my husband-to-be eats. Please, ask him if it is okay to join him." I said to her, she looked at me in shock, as though I had said something no one's ever heard before. She nodded and headed out with the food.

Fifteen minutes later, she came, "He said he would be delighted if you joined him for breakfast."

I smiled. Only I knew the game I was playing. And as long as they believed me, then I had a chance of escaping. Although, I was aware that my parents would have told him, how I pretended I wanted this marriage in the past and their gullibility ended with my great escape. I intend to do the same again, but this time, my target is Ashraf and my aim is to have him count me unworthy.

"Great! I am ready; can you please take me to him?" I asked.

She nodded eagerly. We walked out of my room into a hallway and then through a kitchen and a living room space and out the door. It was my first time stepping outside in months, the light affected my eyes, I stopped for a moment to adjust to my surrounding. I loved the fresh breeze that greeted me wrapping round me like a long-lost lover. I looked down, away from the sun, and followed Fatima into the big house. A mansion—a house befitting of a king. You could see the wealth and self-indulgence as soon as your eyes greeted the building. I remember seeing the front of the house as those men drove me down here two months ago. As expected, the interior was tastefully decorated, it oozed with money, huge gold wall paintings and mirrors hung on the high walls, with beautiful and expensive chandeliers crowning the ceilings. The green and gold drapes from ceiling to wall welcomes you into the opulent lavishly decorated room. Huge luxurious Persian rugs that glorified the floor, and the walls were painted in gold, red and hues of green, it had a Moroccan feel to it. Everything in the house, from vases to little ornaments, were the best money can buy. It was indeed beautiful, and it reminded me of my home. Strangely, I loved it. But I could not allow myself to like it, as beautiful as it was, it wasn't my home; it wasn't owned by Robert.

It was a long walk to the dining area; I tried not to let the shiny things distract me. I have other things on my mind now— convincing Ashraf I was ready to make things work between us, but on my terms. As we walked into the dining room, there he was sat at the table already, I looked down, it had become a force of habit avoiding him, but I knew that had to stop now if I wanted him to believe me. He got up immediately I approached the table and then sat down back after I had taken my seat.

Then I looked up consciously wanting to see what he really looked like and I immediately tore my eyes from his. I didn't like the way he looked at me with concern. I knew I didn't look the best these days; but couldn't he had pretended for my sake? However, what stayed with me, was how handsome he looked, he didn't look anything like the monster I had painted him to be all this while. I was disappointed. I cannot bring myself to think of him in any way that will make him look good. But now I see what all that talk was about, why girls my age thought I was crazy not to want this marriage. There was something there, he has a lot going for him, good looking and rich. Every girl's dream, but not for me. It would have been better if he had given it to a girl that actually wanted to be in his life and was capable of loving him as he deserved.

I concentrated on eating my breakfast. All the while, I was aware he was looking at me, burning a hole in my face, but I refused to look up. Finally, he spoke.

"I am glad you are feeling better now." I looked up slowly,

"Thank you. I thought some fresh air will do me good, I plan to take a walk around later, I need the exercise…"

"Oh, that's good… that's very good indeed." he added, I continued to eat,

"Would you mind if I …if I accompany you?" he asked, I should say yes, but if I agreed, I knew he would suspect my motives so I declined.

"Erm… I am sorry, but I just want to enjoy the surroundings on my own for now, just for today if you don't mind, I mean off course I will have Fatima with me to show me round.".

"Yes, yes off course, I totally understand." he said,

"Thank you." I said with a half-smile.

He nodded contently, and I could see that he appreciated the smile. His eyes were happy, then out of curiosity, I stole a few glances when he was not looking. It seemed that the concern he had on his face for me earlier had subsided and replaced with something that resembled hope. Whether that was hope he felt I was doing better, or hope that we would be happy together in the future, I wasn't sure. When breakfast was done, I excused myself and retraced my steps the way Fatima had brought me. On my way I noticed a huge painting of myself hung up by the fire place in one of the many sitting rooms this house had. I stopped for a minute to look, everything was set up as though I had decorated it. A few pieces of house accessories I had remembered picking out for my mother when she asked my opinion in the past were carefully placed around the house. I sighed, this meant that my mother had been working with Ashraf to decorate, and she wanted it to be with the things I liked. I didn't know what to make of it all. I found Fatima, she was chatting away with two other maids. When they saw me, they straightened up, greeted me with warm smiles and went about their chores quickly. Fatima followed me, once we were outside the house, heading for the annex where I am imprisoned, I told Fatima I wanted to take a walk around the compound.

she came with me and we walked across the fields.

The view was amazing, there were rolling hills looking over the house. We finally stopped by a little quiet stream that ran across the land. There was a weeping lily tree by the stream. The atmosphere it created felt peaceful, I closed my eyes and listened to the water flow and my mind wandered to Robert. But I didn't want that, thinking of him brought me constant pain. There was no way I can plan another great escape if I was constantly in pain. Opening my eyes, I sat down on the ground and rested my back on the tree truck. Fatima stood some distance away, we didn't speak, I had nothing to say to her, I just wanted to gather my thoughts and think through everything that I needed to do now. After a while, I decided it was time, we went back. On the way back to my little annex, Fatima decided to break the silence.

"This place is beautiful." She remarked.

I nodded, "Yeah, that it is." I said.

"I've been told the land is about two hundred acres." She added.

"I see, it's vast." I said. Then I decided to do my own enquiry especially after seeing the portrait of myself earlier.

"So how long have you lived here?" I asked.

"Um, it's coming to six months now." she said,

"Oh, I see." I said,

"Your mother, she employed me. I and the other maids were given the jobs about a year ago."

"A year ago!" I repeated,

"Yes, we were meant to have started work then, then we were told that your wedding was on hold, and we couldn't start work."

"Oh, I see." I looked away, knowing she must know that I ran away the first time and now I have been forced back again.

"May I say something, please, madam?"

I looked at her and wondered what this would be all about. I stopped walking, and nodded in approval.

"I don't mean to speak out of turn, I just wanted to say that I understand why you ran away. But your betrothed, he is one of the best men in the world. And if you allow yourself to see him for who he is, I am so sure you will be happy in this marriage." She said.

I half smiled. "Hmm, thank you Fatima." I said and continued walking. When we got to the front of my room, Fatima waited until I was inside before excusing herself.

I laid on my bed and thought about everything. I wondered what Fatima really thought of me. She must like her boss and they must all think I have been treating him unfairly. She wanted me to like the place, perhaps if I did, I would want to stay and that spiral effect might affect my relationship with him. If I am honest, I liked the place even though I did not want to, and I expected Ashraf to be a monster, but, so far, all I have seen from him is kindness, if I can call it that. After all, I'm just still his prisoner. That should make me really hate him, but now that I have seen him, I didn't want to and not hating him felt like a betrayal to Robert

Chapter 42

I began to have both breakfast and dinner with him, the change was good for me, as I was tired of fighting the inevitable, in a way. But I could also see how happy Ashraf was that I was willing to spend time with him. I am merely keeping up appearances, I told myself. He asked questions in the bid to engage me in conversations and I answered. But for times I reminded myself that I was still his prisoner, I didn't talk when he engaged me. But then again, he would say something funny, and try as I might, I'd find myself giggling at it here and there. I knew it wasn't right to encourage him that way, but he was easy to be around. I started to question my resolve: why I ran; why I never gave him a chance; from the little I had seen so far, he seemed to be a very nice man, the kind of man I should be proud to call my husband. On top of it all, he was very handsome—I loved stealing glances when he wasn't looking. Once he caught me looking at him and he asked if he had food on his mouth; I lied and said he did, and laughed as he did his best to flick away the invisible crumb from the corner of his mouth. Being with Ashraf made sense now, and it would make my family happy; but then memories of Robert come crashing through me and I feel ashamed of any thought that welcomed the idea of Ashraf as my husband.

It was all my fault, I drew Robert into my world, and now each time I looked forward to being in Ashraf's presence, I felt like I was breaking Roberts heart.

Two months passed since my decision to integrate with him more, making it five months since I was forcefully brought to Ashraf. I still live in the annex, and he, in the big house. I don't know when the marriage ceremony would take place as he had not mentioned it, even though we've been getting along. My thought is that he didn't want to seem pushy and I loved that about him.

"Good morning!" I said as I sat down for breakfast.

Ashraf responded with a nod.

"Are you okay?" I inquired with concern.

"Why do you ask?" he re-joined.

"You're quiet." I said pouring myself some tea.

"I was just thinking," he said.

"About what?" I pressed.

There was a moment's silence. then, he asked

"I don't know, I… I was thinking if maybe you might let me join you for one of your walks tonight? I think we've gotten along well, but I don't know if you are ready for that yet." he explained.

I was quiet, I did not know if I was ready to have him that close to me. During meals, we were surrounded by other people—the chefs, the maids, and the butler—but in this case, it would be just he and I alone. However, I knew if I still wanted to escape, then I had to let him feel like he had a chance. The problem was that I was starting to lose sight of my plans, in truth, I enjoyed his company and I wanted to be with him more. There were questions that I needed to ask him. I wanted to know why he would not give up on me even after father must have told him I had been living with another man.

"Oh, it's okay, I will look forward to it." I said and watched his face carefully, a smile played on his lips. I started on my breakfast with intent on not speaking to him again until our walk this evening, but I could still feel his eyes burning a hole through my face. I looked up from my plate slowly, and he was still looking at me, and then.

"Hasina." He said slowly,

"Yes?"

"I was thinking that although we are not officially married yet, I want you closer to me. I think we are getting on well at the moment and I can only hope that we will do better as time gets on. So, I have prepared a wing for you in here in the main house, I don't want you in the annex any longer. I have never wanted you there to begin with."

"Erm… I…" I stuttered, finding my tongue.

"Please, Hasina, say yes." He interrupted. "And don't worry, you would have your privacy. I will be on the other side far away from you until we are married. Everything has been prepared for you, I saw to it myself. And I just hope that you like it." I could tell from the way he looked at me, that he feared that I might say no.

"Thank you, I appreciate it." I said, easing his tensed mind.

"Does that mean a yes?" he asked eagerly.

I nodded, "Yes. That means yes." I confirmed.

I saw as he sighed with relief. "Thank you for honouring me." he expressed some gratitude.

I nodded and began to eat.

Moments passed and we were almost done with breakfast, he said. "When we are done here, if you don't mind, I could give you a tour of the house personally. I have been told you haven't yet seen the house to its fullness or if you would like someone else to show you around." he offered, half overjoyed, half unsure what I wanted.

We still had the walk in the evening, I didn't want too much of him at one go even though I wanted to be with him. For some reason I couldn't yet understand why my heart was betraying my head. Which was one more reason to avoid being alone with him.

"Thank you, but I am sure you have more pressing matters. If you don't mind, we can do that tomorrow. I'm sure it's no problem." I politely declined.

He smiled, and my heart disgracefully fluttered at it. I looked down quickly ashamed he could tell something was happening to me.

"Very well then, as you wish, we'll take the tour tomorrow." He said, I got up to go and then he got up too.

"See you at dinner; I look forward to that walk." He added and then he excused himself. I could not tell if he was annoyed that I had pushed the tour until the next day.

I waited until he was gone before venturing out of the dining room. On my way I walked into one of the spacious rooms. My mind was churning over things, like why I wanted to be around Ashraf so much. This wasn't the plan, I didn't think that I would fall for him nor develop any kind of feelings for him, like the type that made me weak at the knees when I see him or catch him looking at me. The plan was to pretend to fall for him and now it seemed I was losing control of things, another part of me fought with my resolve to run away again. Why wouldn't I allow myself to fall for him, and marry him? So far, everyone has been right about Ashraf, he is a great guy, so why was I fighting it again? I knew the answer was because of my love for Robert, and I couldn't just pretend that Robert no longer existed. The drapes in the room were pulled apart. Light poured in and from where I stood, I could see the rolling hills and hear birds chirping. My mind went to that stream; where I now spend most of my afternoons. I needed to go there again for peace sake, my head was a constant battle field. As I stood looking out the window and gazing into the fields admiring the rolling hills, contemplating what to do next, I heard a familiar voice. But this time not from within my head. It came from within the room, right behind me.

"I know where you can enjoy that view better."

I did not bother to turn around, I could tell it was him by the sound of his deep, soulful voice.

"Where?" I asked, as my heart beat raised the closer he got to me. He stood by myside and I inhaled his presence.

"Come with me!" He ordered, walking towards the door.

I hesitated at first. But then I felt my legs moving towards him of their own volition and against the restraints of my heart. We went back through the dining room and went out through a double door. We were outside on a balcony, but there was a set of stairs that led to an even bigger curved balcony and there you could see it all, the beauty of the surroundings in all its glory. The wind caressed my skin; the air was fresh and cool.

I smiled; he looked ahead into the open field and said, "What do you think?"

"It's extraordinarily breath-taking." I remarked, as the wind brushed my hair away from my face. He looked at me and smiled.

"I knew you would like it." He said, I pretended as if I did not hear him. There was silence, and then he moved closer to me, his stare boring holes into my heart, as he ogled me. For a moment, I couldn't breathe. I stood still afraid he could tell that he affected me in such manner.

"Hasina," he called, locking his gaze into mine, "you had had me worried for a while, but I'm glad you are better now, and…it makes me happy." Then the wind blew hard again, and he reached out, as his eyes remained on mine, and tucked my hair behind my ear. My heart almost jumped out of my chest, I feared he could hear my heart beating. I tried to look away but I couldn't move. It was as though he had frozen me with his touch.

Then he looked away. I was glad he did. Yet I was sure he felt what happened between us. If I didn't know better, I could pretend that I didn't understand that my heart was foolishly falling for him.

He sighed and said, "Please excuse me." He began to walk away by the stairs. He added, "I will ask Fatima to come to you, in case you need anything."

I watched him leave, and I was glad he left, for sanity's sake. Something crazy was happening to me, he was beginning to feel like a drug and I wanted more. But I was ashamed to ask for more. Each time my heart did something stupid, like beat so fast when I hear his voice or watch him smile. I blame myself for the mess. I hate to admit that my parents were right: he is not that monster I hated ever since I was told his name. I should have given him the chance like everyone advised, but my strong will to be in control of my own life brought me to this situation. I had been sure this was going to be easy—plan the perfect escape and run back to Robert's arms. But I had fooled myself instead and, now, I don't know what the right thing to do is any longer.

I was staring at the fields when Fatima came to meet me.

"Ma'am! I was told to take you to your wing. All your things have been moved." She said.

I nodded and followed her. We walked past the dining room into the hallway and then through into an open beautiful courtyard. It is something of an art It had palm trees planted around golden pillars to shed the sun and there was a gorgeous fountain at the edge of a water pond beautifully decorated with blooming flowers. I wondered what this stately beauty looked like in the night. As we walked through the courtyard, I could see the kitchen, through the sliding glass doors. The chefs, were prepping for lunch and dinner, few other people were cleaning the floors and walls, everything was in order and everyone worked like clockwork. As I passed, they all stopped what they were doing to greet me. I nodded and continued to follow Fatima. I wondered how many staff he had in this house. Opposite the kitchen was another glass wall room. From where we were, I could see the indoor swimming pool, it looked huge about a hundred foot in length. We then walked through a set of double doors into what he referred to as *my wing*. There was a sitting area, a dining area, whose Moroccan theme can be viewed right from here. My room, was beautifully decorated in gold and lime green. Words cannot describe how beautiful it looked. From the golden drapes to the silky luxurious sheets and to every single furniture, no expense was spared. There were beautiful vases, with the biggest bunch of fresh flowers I have ever seen displayed in every room. There was a huge bathroom with a gold-plated standalone bath, a huge dressing room, with clothes, shoes and bags of every sorts and colour hanging off its walls. There was an island in the middle placed on a gorgeous dark red Persian rug. On the round island, was all sort of accessories, sunglasses, scarfs, hats, jewelleries, you just name it, neatly arranged. I knew my mother would have had a hand in picking everything, because he knew such as I would love it; every single piece was as though I had bought them myself. It was an extremely immersive sight and an elegant display indeed. But as much as he had put in such effort into it all, at the back of my mind was still the fact that I had been kidnapped, perhaps if I had come to him on my own all of this would have made me happy.

Fatima excused herself and left me to myself, I sat on the bed cautiously and then I curled myself up into a ball. I was tired of feeling guilty for liking him; I was tired of feeling remorseful that I ran away; I was tired of having resentments that I was kidnapped;

341

I just wanted it all to stop. I did not want to feel or think about anyone, not even Robert. Thinking of Robert, was a punishment, and since I couldn't do anything about it, I just wanted to push the reset button. Soon sleep came and claimed my body. It was dark when I woke up. I looked at the table clock beside me it was about six in the evening. I knew dinner would soon be ready, so I wanted to have my wash before going to meet Ashraf in the dining room. No one came to disturb me while I slept; it was nice to be alone. I ran myself a bath, when I finished, I looked for a pair of jeans and a white jumper. I wanted to be comfortable. I was tired of wearing long dresses. I pulled my hair back, applied a light make up and then made my way out; Fatima and another girl were waiting on me in the sitting area. They followed me as I found my way to the dining area. I did not want an entourage each time I made a move, but it was the way things were done in my father's house and it is the same tradition Ashraf had here.

When I got to the dining area, Ashraf was there, he was standing by the doors that led to the balcony. He was staring out, he turned around when he saw me, and he smiled, and my heart shamelessly did a double jump as he looked me over. This would be the first time he gets to see me in a jean and top.

"You look beautiful as always." He remarked.

I nodded. "Thank you!" I had thought he would complain about my choice of dress. "I didn't think you would approve." I confessed attempting to test the waters.

"Why not?" He asked.

I shrugged; I did not know what to say.

Then he said, "You are your own person, are you not? How you want to dress is entirely up to you." He expressed.

"So, you wouldn't mind if I strut around the house in skimpy clothes, I mean like you have said it's entirely up to me?" I said trying to push his buttons. I wondered why I was looking for a fight.

He smiled. "What do you want me to say? I trust your judgement, I won't respect you any less if that is what you are getting at, but I will like to think that you are a respectable woman raised in a respectable home and you know what is right from what is wrong. You don't need me to point that out." I looked at him.

He smiled softly.

I lowered my eyes not knowing what to say to that.

There was silence as the chefs began to bring in the food.

When they were gone and our food had been plated, he said, "I asked after you this afternoon, and I was told you were resting. Did you like your place?"

"Yeah, it's… liveable!" I stated. (He said nothing.) I played it down because my feelings about him were getting out of control. I did not know how I could easily fall for him when I didn't want to feel anything for him. And also, there are questions burning in my mind that I needed answers to before I can really let my guard down.

We ate in silence. Not a word was mentioned while we had our meal. Just as soon as we were done, my heart was gladdened when he finally broke the silence.

"Do you care to join me in the living room for coffee or tea before going for our walk?" he suggested. He sounded as calm as he could. But that did little to efface the underlying excitement in his voice.

I raised my eyes to meet his and affirmed my agreement. To be truthful somewhere deep down in me, I was also excited he was coming with me. But no way was I going to let it show. He got up from his seat, came over, and helped me to my feet. With my hands in his, and his scents bombarding my senses, I for one thought I would faint as my heart raced tirelessly within me. I felt so nervous to be standing so close to him. As soon as I came upright, he let go of my hands and led me through the hallway into the siting room.

There was a sitting area on the floor. He waved me to my seat. I obeyed and he sat himself down opposite me, leaving as much space between us, enough to make me feel comfortable. There was silence across the room, a man came in and poured us tea, another came in with a flute and started to play. I looked from the man to Ashraf; I wanted us to be alone, but I framed a smile despite the agonizing music. When he was done, Ashraf nodded his thanks at the flutter for his music. Then he smiled and waved, giving the man permission to go. Quiet returned once again.

"Do you like it better like this?" He asked.

"What?" I blurted even before I could have a thought.

He chuckled like I said something amusing to him. "The silence, I meant to say" He explained.

I shrugged. "I'd have it this quiet instead of that noise he called music." He laughed! It was the first time I saw him truly laugh. I must admit, he looked so very handsome. I looked away for too much excitement. This man was stealing my heart one day at a time with everything he did and I was helpless at it. It was quiet again, and I contemplated about asking him the questions on my mind.

But he spoke before me. "What would it take to get you to laugh? I mean what do I have to do?" He asked.

I looked up at him somewhat irked. The question irritated me. I'm sure he saw through that. But I decided to bite my tongue and not say anything.

"Hasina?" he called at me.

I looked towards him.

"I know that being here… your being here is not exactly what you want, but, I promise you that I will do my best to please you; and I hope I am already."

I kept quiet; I did not know what to say. I mean, what does he expect me to say to him?

"If there is anything at all that I can do to make you happier or more comfortable, please let me know." He said

I thought an answer to myself, letting me go of course, and telling my father you are not interested in me any longer would be a good place to start… But then again, do I really want that now? I inquired of my heart. So, I just looked at him and nodded once again. Finally, I asked him quietly. "Would you like to take that walk… now? The weather feels right!"

He nodded and added,

"Yes, I believe I would."

He got up quickly. I could see he was coming my way, so I made it to my feet before he could reach me. I did not want his help again. I didn't want for a repeat of that moment we had in the dining room—at least, for the sake of not beginning our awaited walk in such mood.

He began leading the way and I followed further behind him at first. We each walked through the main door out into the garden and then towards the stream. Then, two of the men standing by fell into pace quickly behind us forming a little procession. By now, I was walking at his far-right side, keeping an enormous distance between us. He complied by keeping to his own side of the walk, and not trying to force himself into my space. That I loved, and respected, about him.

As we approached the tree by the stream, he said, "I see you love coming here a lot. Is it peaceful for you here?" he inquired.

I nodded,

"I love to hear the sound of the water as it moves; and I could use the clarity my mind breathes in from here." I answered. "Plus, the view is to die for."

"I couldn't agree more," he said delightfully. He paused momentarily. And then he continued. "I bought this land, because of that view. I could not resist the beauty it eludes. It was originally owned by a farmer, he lived in that annex you stayed in. There used to be some sheds along and a few other buildings that had to be knocked down out of the way. I didn't want anything to take from that beautiful view, so no matter where you are in the house, you can enjoy God's work to its fullest."

"Well this was a good find for you, I love it." I remarked.

"I love it too, but what I love most is that you love it."

I looked at him for a moment and then swiftly looked away.

We walked past the tree and walked along the stream, then I suddenly summoned the courage to ask him the question that had been on my mind since my imprisonment here. "May I ask you a question?"

"Oh, yes, please! Anything!"

I stopped walking—he paused too, and the two bodyguards were a few feet away. I sighted at them to ensure they weren't within hearing range. I quickly returned my gaze at him. "We... I mean you and I are not married yet," I began letting out, "though the ceremony will be performed soon. And I am guessing you know when. But I'm not ready to be your wife."

He looked away. His eyes revealed the sadness of his soul.

So, I felt a need to quickly explain myself. "I mean "yet". And it's because I don't know you enough. I like that I am getting to know you, but if we marry now, I am not completely sure you are the

346

person I want to share my life with. I'm just not sure if this is what I want. and I would like to think that you want us to be happy, and I should want the same as well. But how can I do that now if I'm not sure?"

He was quiet, his lips pressed together; I wondered what was going through his mind. He started to walk and I immediately followed. "Your father…your father wanted us to do the ceremony as soon as he told me he found you, but…" he paused.

"But what?" I probed.

He looked at me, "I said no! Off course I said no! I would not have you marry me unless your heart truly chose to."

I was confused. He really thinks that by keeping me under lock and key he can make me like him enough to choose to marry him? I wanted to laugh, but I stopped myself. What an idiot! I thought.

"So? … What's your plan?" I asked doing my best to hide my infuriation but I could tell he knew I was angered the way I spoke

"There is no plan; I told your father when he informed me that he found you that I would love for us to have a chance to at least get to know each other. I know our religion does not allow dating. But do not get me wrong. I am aware that this situation is not ideal. Believe me, it's not what I want for us… I just thought after all that has happened… I thought if you got to know me, you might see that maybe marrying me wasn't as terrible as you thought."

I could not keep my anger concealed any longer, it was written all over me by now. I am sure he could see it.

"Why? Why me? You don't get it, do you? Can you not see I ran away to get away as far as possible from you? Do you really think all this is going to help see you as my husband? Keeping me under locks and keys? Whatever I feel for you, if I ever do, can't be pure to begin with. How could it be? When you've taken my choice away? And even if you blame it all on my father, you have a part in

347

it. You could have walked away and married another willing girl, or if you must have me, why didn't you come look for me yourself in London? Pursue me on your own and see if my heart follows? Then you would know for sure if I'm meant to be your wife. But now, how can I trust anything I feel for you, when I am only your prisoner?" I fired at him.

He stared at me wordless.

This is not going the way I planned it, as I could see he was hurt by what I just said. The pain in his eyes looked intensified. And I was immediately sorry I caused him pain, but it was nothing compared to what I had been going through.

"I have upset you; I can see that now and I am sorry. Please enjoy the rest of the evening, I … I must let you be, goodnight." He said and left me where I stood. I did not even hear his footsteps; it was as if he disappeared into the darkness.

I stood there rooted to the ground motionless, angry with myself for letting my emotions get the better of me. He is not going to trust me now, not after my behaviour, he will probably increase the security around me, knowing I will bolt the moment I get the chance. Every single progress I made with him, I just destroyed in a single outburst. I sat there on the floor, thinking about today's events; eventually I got up and journey to my room. I felt very emotional; I was angry with myself for the things I said to him. Even if he deserved to hear them, I felt bad for the way I lashed out at him. Then there was the thought of Robert, I was missing him and I knew that after tonight I might never get to see him again. I threw myself on my bed and cried my eyes out until sleep reclaimed me.

Chapter 43

The next morning, I did not bother to go for breakfast, neither was I present for lunch and dinner, I had everything brought to me in my wing. I sat by the window and admired the lovely view, at least one thing was quite clear, he is never going to force me to be his wife and I should thank him for that, because if it were up to my father, he would have had it over and done with.

I spent the next week in the company of myself, but I knew I could never resolve the situation we were both in if I stayed away from him. He has been nothing, but a gentleman to me, I decided I would apologize for my outburst the next time I saw him at breakfast.

So, I went to meet him for breakfast, but he was not there, neither did he show for lunch and dinner. When I went for my walks, I looked around for him with no success. I tried to be subtle about it; I did not want anyone knowing I was curious about his whereabouts for one week I came to dine with him, but ended up dinning alone. I felt ashamed, because everyone knew I came because of him and they all probably know where he went, but no one would tell me and I felt too proud to ask. Perhaps he had decided to leave me, but it would be nice if he told me so himself. And if he was no longer interested because of my behaviour, then

I'm sure by now, my father would be arranging for the next suitor to take his place. As long as

they were rich and powerful and of the same belief, they would pass his test.

I did not understand my need to see Ashraf again. Thoughts of him occupied my mind, I wanted to know where he was, I wanted to see him so I could apologise for my juvenile behaviour. If all my choices were to be taken away from me as my father had so done in this case, I would rather be married to Ashraf than another stranger father may give me to. As they say, better the devil you know than the angel you do not know. Not that Ashraf was any devil in my heart and mind, though.

Two weeks passed and we had yet to cross paths. I knew now—*figured* is more like it—that he went to see my father to tell him he was letting me go. It is all I had prayed for and wanted in the past, though, but yet, a part of me was not happy he gave up so easily.

After dinner, I took a walk alone. I felt lonely because he wasn't around. Fatima asked to walk with me, but I declined. Somehow, as I have now noticed, I'm trusted to get around the house on my own, especially since he disappeared. I do not know if he left instructions to let me be, but I am not being watched as I was when I first arrived here. I leaned against the tree by the river, it felt peaceful and the breeze was cool. Everywhere was quiet; I did not hear anyone coming, so I was surprised when I heard that familiar tone again when I least expected.

"When I first saw you, many years ago, I wanted you. I wanted you to be my wife and I wanted to make you the happiest woman that ever lived."

I spun round at the hearing of his voice. I almost quaked for joy, looking at him made me realise how much I had missed him. I did not think it was possible for me to feel the way I did as I looked at his face, and yet be terrified by it. I forced my bottom to the ground not saying anything, so he carried on.

"I was young, so were you, you did not notice me. I was twenty-one and you just turned sixteen. I was so sure I knew what I wanted from life until the day I saw you, and everything I had planned for myself from that moment included you. I saw you, Hasina, and you claimed my heart. I don't know how you did this to me, or how I did it to myself, but I knew I wanted only you and I fell for you and I did not look or want any other girl since then. So, I waited a few more years, when you were old enough, then I thought I better ask your father and tell him my intentions to have you as my wife. When I was told that you had given your consent to marry me, I wanted to give you the world. I was over the moon with joy. The news made me so happy. I came to England with a friend, we went to visit his relative an hour drive from here. As we drove, I saw this place and I knew you would like it here, the first time I saw it… I had you in mind; I thought this would be my gift to you." He recollected.

"What…? What are you saying? How could you… you had not even met me. I mean not properly." I cut in with my argument.

He chuckled slightly in his right lip, then he came closer and walked towards the stream.

"Don't get me wrong, I was not entirely sure. I had this idea about you but it was strong enough to make me not give up, I wanted to get to know you before the first arrangements were made. I know our ways, though I studied in the west. I lived in England for years before returning home to ask to marry you, but you wouldn't even look at me, yet I had hope. But I kid you not, there were times when I had wished I had not ever seen you or that you had not stolen my heart the way you did without even knowing me."

He chuckled.

I said nothing. I only moved closer to him so I could hear him better. Or so I thought. But the closer I got, the more my heart pounded after his.

He continued. "We started building. And as we built, I thought about you and how happy I hoped you would be here once we were married. Before long, I was told that you had disappeared. At first, I had feared you had been kidnapped. But then it became clear with time that you ran off." He turned around to face me.

"How did you know that I ran?" I asked.

"Your parents did all they could, you know your father would never give up on you. They found a letter you wrote to a friend. It became clear you had fooled us all. And that angered your father. He had been worried you were kidnapped, but when he found out you had run off to escape being married, it made him very upset. Then your mother let it known that you had discussions with her, something to do with dancing and you wanting to make a career out of it."

"Would you have approved?" I asked.

"Approved of what?"

"Would you have allowed me to make a career out of dancing if I had married you then?" I asked.

"Hasina, I would have let you do whatever it was that made you happy; you never gave me the chance. I am not your father; I just wanted to make you happy, I still do." He moved closer so that we were within touching distance, I wanted to close my eyes and bury myself in his embrace, but I willed myself to stop and focus on what he was telling me. His eyes bored holes in me, as a fresh breeze whooped at us ruffling my hair as it passed. Ashraf, moved his hands to tuck my hair behind my ears.

And then he spoke on. "My love, I know you hate me right now and you don't understand why I will want to marry you. However, we do not get to choose who we love. And I love you. I have for a very long time. And I do not know how not to love you. I cannot give up on you unless you instruct me to. I know you don't feel the same way, but all I ask is that you give me a chance to fight for us and show you that we can be great together and after wards if you don't feel the same way you don't have to marry me. Your loss will be my burden, but good thing is you will go and live your life as you will."

I did not know what to say. But in my heart, and at the tip of my tongue were the words, *I feel the same way now*. But I couldn't bring myself to voice it.

Instead, I heard myself say, "I am sorry I ran. I'm sorry I never gave you a chance. I judged you without knowing you. It was unfair. I saw all men like my father, strict and rigid in their ways. I did not know better. I do not know what to say to make it all better." I apologized.

"You don't have to say anything."

"Oh, but I do, at least to you. A lot happened to me when I was away. I met someone else. He made a big difference in me. But don't worry, I'm not tainted, not in that way. He is a gentleman, if I had not run off, I may never have met him. Now, I don't know what is right to do and what is wrong. But, for your sake, and how you have treated me so far, I am willing to try, I am willing to give us a chance." I said.

"What!" he exclaimed bemused.

"I am willing to give you the chance to show me if we could ever be good together, but on the condition that you would let me go if after we try I find that I cannot love you as I am meant to do." He smiled.

"Sounds fair enough, I won't have it any other way." I smiled, he chuckled and for the first time, he pulled me into his embrace and as he did, a terrifying spark ran through my whole body. I knew then that he had me completely. And even if I wanted to leave, I would not only be punishing him, but myself as well. I felt his heart beating as my head leaned on his chest.

"Thank you!" He said as he released me from his embrace. I couldn't wait around any longer, he made me weak to my knees.

"You must excuse me; I have to return to the house." I said, he nodded in response, but then out of curiosity, I wanted to know where he went for the past two weeks. I turned around on my heels and asked, "If you don't mind my asking, where did you go?"

He smiled and approached me. I stepped back spontaneously, for sanities sake.

"Did you… miss me?" he asked teasingly, I did not know if I was ready for this kind of situation between us.

"Miss you? of course not! Goodnight." I lied.

He laughed softly.

I was sure even he could tell I was lying.

"Sweet Dreams!" He relayed.

I smiled and quickly ran off.

Chapter 44

As I found earlier Ashraf's company comforted me, so I didn't need to try hard to be with him. The walls that I had put up in the early days tumbled over so easily with every little gesture he made. I was so drawn to him. I looked forward to every moment of the day that I spent in his presence and thought about him when I wasn't around him. He began to occupy my thoughts in ways I had not expected. I would dream of things we will do together once we were married, I would think of places I wanted to go with him on holidays and even names of every child we would have. It felt nice, but just as these thoughts flooded my mind, memories of Roberts stormed in as well and then the guilt that it seemed that I had moved on without him ate at me. Robert was very special to me, he was my first love and still is, but Ashraf surprised me in ways I had not expected and my love for him was not sudden as it had been with Robert. His grew with every day I spend with him. It intrigued me that I loved him for reasons that are very different from how I feel about Robert. I loved the way Ashraf's eyes lit up each time he saw me, how patiently he explained things to me, when I didn't understand, and how when he didn't think I was looking he'd look at me as though I was the only woman in the world. So, even though I didn't want to admit it, I had fallen very much in love with him, just as I did and still do with Robert.

Before I knew it, my birthday came around, I turned 24, Ashraf wanted to do a big celebration but I asked him not to, we were not yet married. I only wanted to celebrate our union, but since I had not yet told him I wanted to be his wife, we couldn't pick a date. Yes, I loved him, and wouldn't mind becoming his wife, however, I was still very much in love with Robert as well. How this could possibly be baffled me. I knew I couldn't have them both and my decision to marry Ashraf would mean, I had to be done with Robert, but, yet, I couldn't bring myself to forget Robert. And if I couldn't forget, I didn't think I could give Ashraf my whole heart, which he deserved.

Since, I didn't want any celebration, Ashraf took me to the stables to show me a beautiful white stallion. I loved horses, and he knew, especially now since we've been talking more, I told him about the horse I had when I was home. And how my father had gotten rid of it after I had fallen off the horse on my eighteenth birthday. Excited, I began to stroke the horse's mane.

"Wow! Aren't you gorgeous?" I said to the horse, "So, do you have a name?" I asked, looking at Ashraf. He smiled and walked closer to me.

"I see you love him," He said, as he held my hand in his.

"Of course, I do, he is so beautiful." I responded "So what's his name?" I asked gain.

"Well, I should ask you."

"Me?"

"Mm. Mm-hmm, he is yours after all. Happy birthday, my love." Ashraf said.

"Really! you mean he's mine? This gorgeous creation is all mine?" He nodded, "Oh, I don't know what to say, thank you so much." He smiled, I was genuinely happy and I wanted him to know so much that I wanted to give him a hug, but I restrained myself, it wouldn't be fair on both of us, as my mind wasn't yet made up. Instead, I took my hand from his hold and placed my arms around the horse as a deflection.

"He is so gorgeous. What shall we call you then?" I said to the horse.

"Shall we call you snowfalls?" I said and the horse neighed, Ashraf and I both shared a laugh. "I think we all can agree that you love that name. So, snowfalls it is." I said. "I can't believe you got him for me. When did you bring him in? I didn't see any of it." I said turning my attention to Ashraf.

"You weren't meant to see, otherwise it would have defeated the element of surprise." He took a deep breath and took a step closer to me, and touched the horses' face with his hands. "He was delivered yesterday, I planned it such that at the time you went in to rest after dinner, they brought snowfalls in." He said calling the horse by the name I just gave him.

"You, you do these things, you just give me everything. He is beautiful! Thank you, but you shouldn't keep buying me things. I don't need anything more. You've given me enough already." I said. He was quiet; he turned towards me and lifted my hands to his face.

"For you, Hasina, I will do anything." He said as our eyes locked and my heart raced within me, he then planted a kiss on my hand before letting go. "Would you like to ride?" He asked.

"I don't know; I don't think I am ready. It's been a while." I said.

"No pressure! He is all yours! And when you are ready, he would be here." He said patting the horse by his neck. "Come with me," He invited.

I followed, but not before giving Snowfalls one more loving stroke. Putting my arm in his, we walked silently for a moment or two.

And then he said, "Tell me, I have been curious, when you decided to leave me high and dry, why run to England, of all the places in the world? You came to the country with more cameras than they know what to do with." He said.

I laughed. "I don't know," I shrugged.

But his eyes questioned me further.

"I think I had all along fancied living here really. I always looked forward to the long summer holidays we spent here. I loved the way of life; It just felt like home to me. So, when I decided I was going to leave you *high and dry*—your words not mine."

He smiled.

"This was the first place that came to mind." I continued.

"I get it now. Come to think of it, I was here already when you came. I was building this place for us and you were hiding in the same country." He said.

I laughed. "So, if I hadn't run off, we would never have lived in our country?" I was being curious.

"We would own homes there naturally, because our families and roots are there. But we would live anywhere in the world that pleases us, *as* I hope we begin to do as soon as we marry." He said. And there it was, the word *marry*. I was wasting time, I needed to give him my answer now. But I still needed to be sure that I loved him above Robert, as I couldn't be married if I wasn't sure.

I held my breath as I waited for him to ask me if I had made up my mind about marrying him. But instead, he spoke to me of his life while he lived in America. And about Harvard, where he had studied.

And I had to ask, "And all the time you spent at university, you didn't find someone you fancied?" I asked.

"Oh, there were lots of girls, but none of them was you." He said.

I smiled. Seeing how devoted he was to me, even through the times when he meant nothing to me was quite impressive.

Later that night, after dinner, Ashraf built a camp fire, and put up a tent next to the stream by the spot that had become mine, and we both pretended we were stranded in a jungle. He told me stories of his youth and all the silly things he got up to with his cousins. I loved listening to him, he made me laugh so much that my ribs hurt and he will just sit there and watch me while I laughed my heart out. He was too good to me, and it'd be unfair to keep him waiting. But how do I tell him that I loved him and yet I loved another man too?

I must have fallen asleep in the tent, when I woke up, he was nowhere to be found, I couldn't tell the time, I poked my head out of the tent and squinted as I saw him sitting by the stream and throwing stones into the water. Rubbing my eyes, I came out of the tent and stretched my arms, before going to sit next to him.

He smiled to acknowledge my presence, "You slept like a log." He remarked.

"Yeah, I did, you should have woken me up." I said.

"No, and spoil my plan to leave you to the wolves? I don't think so!" He joked.

I half laughed, still a little tired.

Shaking my head, I said, "What am I going to do with you?"

"Marry me!" He said, unforced, as he turned to look at me.

I was quiet, I had heard what he said but I pretended not to hear.

He reached his hands towards me, and gently stroked my cheek lightly. We gazed at each other for a moment and then I lowered my eye, I could see through his eyes, how strongly his emotions were. He took my hands and placed it on his chest, so I could feel his heart beating.

Tears clouded my eyes, as my heart raced within me, I wasn't sure in that moment if it was because I loved him or because I knew I had to tell him about my love for Robert.

"Marry me Hasina," he reiterated, "and make me the happiest man in the world."

My eyes met his again, I tried to say something, but nothing came out.

"I know this has all been difficult for you, but I will make up for all the hurt I have caused you. I will devote my life to making you happy, I will cherish you along with every child God gives us forever. I love and respect you. I will listen when you talk. I will never take you for granted neither would I allow anything or anyone to hurt you. When you laugh, you light up my world. When I see you, my heart is pleased. Each time I hear your voice, I pray to God that in your heart, you see me as I see you. Please, Hasina, say you will be my wife. Please marry me."

He was quiet, waiting for me to respond, but I did not know what to say. How could I, when my heart was torn? Saying yes meant that I had finally let go of Robert and I could not. I didn't understand any of it, but I didn't want to lose him either. I understood one thing, however, I couldn't have them both and I couldn't choose one without hurting the other. My head was a mess, I looked away. It was uncomfortably awkward now. He buried his head in his hands and got up. I turned to look at him.

He smiled. "If only you could feel the pain of loving you." He said, and then added, "I am sorry, but I have to go. The guards are here. They'd will escort you home." He said, I didn't want him to leave this way, he had done all he could to make me happy and all I had done was throw it back in his face.

"Please, don't go." I said selfishly.

"I can't stay, I need to clear my head and I think you need to do the same as well. I do not know what I was thinking, but I have undoubtedly spoilt our evening. Enjoy the rest of your day." He said and left me with my thoughts.

The night was difficult for me, I wept, I hated that he suffered, but, for some reasons, I could not let go of Robert. I thought love was meant to be easy not full of pain, yet, I was in pain. I had caused others pain in the name of love. I wished that I had told him that I loved him, he needed to know that he was more than just a friend to me. I replayed the hurt in his eyes, and wished to take it away. But it was important to start our lives on the notes of honesty. To do so, I needed to have a closure on Robert, if I am to marry Ashraf.

The next morning, I was petrified he would not show up for breakfast, but he was there; and somehow, he had pulled himself back together again. He spoke with me like yesterday never happened and I was glad he did not put me under any pressure to say something back to him. Selfishly, I was quite happy to carry on where we had left off before he had asked me to marry him.

Chapter 45

Three weeks flew by since that day he asked me to marry him; he had not mentioned it again. Something had changed about him, even though he smiled on. I could tell that it was no longer effortless. He was putting on a show for me. He was sad, and he did his best around me to pretend he was okay. I knew the only thing that would make him happy was if I told him I would marry him, nothing else will do for now. He didn't stay up late with me as before. He didn't stay home as much as he did in the past. And although when he came home, he spent the rest of his free time with me, and when he left, I missed him terribly.

But how could I decide, when I was still in a way his prisoner?

One night as we stood on the balcony after dinner, I asked, "So why did you finish it, I mean this house even right after I left?"

He said nothing to me. He moved closer to me and took my hands. His eyes relayed to me all I needed to know. But still I wanted him to tell me with his own words.

"I had to finish it. I already started it. I don't know... I just couldn't give up... you won't understand."

"Try me!" I said.

"What do you want me to say? I don't know. I just couldn't abandon it. I guess I still had hopes… like I do even now… that you would choose to be with me one day. I had called it yours the moment I saw this place. I could not and did not leave it uncompleted. Moreover, it was something to engage in, as it kept me from worrying about your safety. If you did not run, we would have lived here as I have told you before. I wanted it to be a surprise really. But when you were found and your father said he wanted to take you back to Saudi, I told him not to, since you loved England and I had built us a home here. It just felt like the right place for you to be at the time. You've seen it now, and it's yours, it's always going to be yours if you want it." He said looking at me.

"I guess I should say thank you, for not letting father take me back to Saudi."

"No need to thank me, your father was wrong. He shouldn't force his will on you. I know you think; I am doing the same, holding you as my prisoner, but, Hasina, you are free to leave. At the time you were brought here, I knew if you don't stay with me, another suitor would be found for you. I didn't want that for you."

"So, you kept me here for yourself?" I cut in.

"I know how it looks. In a perfect world, you would want to be with me as much as I want to be with you, but I don't want you here if you don't want me. I just wanted a chance to prove to you I'm not as bad as you've thought. And if after all of this you don't want to be with me, then you may go."

I looked away, it was a lot to think about, especially now that he said I could leave if I wanted to, it meant I could go back to Robert if I had so chosen.

"And if I leave, what would you do? Marry another as soon as I'm gone?" I asked.

He smiled.

"Not so soon, as you've taken my heart. I guess it will not be easy to love another like this. But eventually, I will have to move on." I looked away, at the tip of my tongue was the answer he wanted. The bare thought of him with another girl made me so jealous.

"Hasina, look at me." He said.

I turned to face him.

"I know your heart is somewhere else. It is difficult for me to say this because I know it's the truth. You love another as I want you to love me. I hear you sometimes at night, you weep for him and it breaks my heart, that I am causing you, whom I love so dearly, such great pain." He added as he gently caressed my cheek, tears gathered to my eyes as I saw the sadness in his eyes. "I will fight for your love, unless you think we have no fighting chance. Tell me now if you want to go, so I can begin to find a way to move on, I will instruct the driver to drop you anywhere you want to go. I will tell your father that I am no longer interested in marrying you. Believe me it will be the hardest thing for me to say, but I will do it for you, to see that you are happy, but if you feel anything at all for me, my love, tell me that also, so my heart can sleep happy tonight." The tears rolled freely down my eyes now, as my heart thumped and ached heavily in my chest. I was overwhelmed, it felt so bitter and so sweet to hear him say I could go, but, I wanted to stay as much as I wanted to go.

Using his thumb, he wiped my tears.

I smiled through teary eyes.

"Thank you!" I said.

He managed a smile.

"So, I guess, I have your answer then." He said

"About what?

"You thanked me, because you want to go to him. If that's what you want, then you must leave" He uttered firmly.

"I thanked you because I finally understand who you are; also, because, 'I'm no longer a prisoner." I said. He looked away.

I knew I should tell him that I loved him too, just as much as I loved Robert that would have made him happy a bit, but I couldn't tell him that now, until I had seen Robert again and sorted through my feelings, so I know in my heart and head, who I couldn't live without in actuality.

Then he placed his hand gently on mine briefly. He looked at me for a while, and then he took his leave. I watched him go until he disappeared from my view. I did not know what to make of what just happened. I needed to think I needed time away from the two of them to decide what was good for me. Common sense told me Ashraf, but I couldn't just bin my love for Robert. Why couldn't I just listen to common sense. I had originally planned to gain his trust and my freedom and it seemed to have worked, but I was not feeling victorious.

I could not move; my heart was heavy. It was selfish to feel that way about two men, but I could not help it. What would I tell him, now that he said I could go and yet I still find myself unable to leave him?

As hard as I tried not to think about it, my mind kept going through the different things I love about them both, and why I wanted to be in both their lives. It was going to be a very impossible decision to make. My mother was right about one thing; love does have a way of creeping up on you when you least expect it to. The more I thought about it, the more it became clearer to me who I should be with.

The next morning at breakfast, he was absent, and I knew the reason why. I asked about his whereabouts from the maid, but no one had any idea where he had gone. Come lunch he was still missing, and by dinner when he was no show, I had concluded, that he already guessed what I would do and left before I had the chance to break his heart all over again. I did not blame him; I wanted to do right by him so much now that I have come to love him.

And his absence made my heart miss him more, I knew I had to find him and let him know now before I change my mind. To do this was to consciously forget Robert, to bury all thoughts and memories I have of him and think of the time I knew Robert as nothing, but an illusion.

Chapter 46

The next day, I hurried to the dining room hoping to see him, as he did not show the day before. I was so sure I would see him. I could not wait to break the news to him and watch his face glow with joy. It is amazing how one's thoughts and feelings changes when there are no restrictions placed on one's freedom. I had to find him at once and let him know that I'd choose him for all the right reasons.

However, to my disappointment, he did not come to breakfast again as I expected he would. I went around looking for him in places, I had found him in the past, but he was nowhere to be found. It angered me that he left without waiting for my answer. Dinner came and still he did not come, it annoyed me that he presumed to know what I wanted. How could he just disappear? I did not want to eat, I couldn't if I tried. His absence upset me very much. Instead, I walked to my spot by the stream and sat under the tree.

I must have been sitting there for about half an hour thinking things through when I heard his voice.

"Hasina." He said, I jumped up. My heart raced with happiness at the sight of him.

"You scared me." I said, glad at last that he came to look for me.

"I am sorry; I didn't mean to startle you; I didn't know you will be here." He apologized.

"Where were you? You were gone yesterday, and gone all day today. I looked for you everywhere" I attacked.

"I'm sorry, I should have left you a note, I thought … I thought you would have left at the first opportunity, and I didn't want to watch you leave." I looked down, I knew in my heart that was why he left and I didn't blame him. I had never made it clear how I felt about him, but now I needed to let him know that I loved him. And I choose him.

"Why are you still here?" he asked.

I smiled and took a few steps closer to him.

"You said before that you loved me long before now. Somehow, you knew from the first time you laid eyes on me that you wanted to spend the rest of your life with me, and even now you still feel the same way. I'm not surprised that one can fall in love helplessly at first sight. I know because it happened to me too."

He looked at me, his eyes narrowed. Confusion etched on his face as he looked at me. He moved a step closer to me, so that we were within touching distance. I waited for him to say something, but he did not, so, I continued speaking before I lost my line of thoughts.

"What you said yesterday got me thinking. I… had detested you for so long without knowing the real you. I think you became a victim of my will to do what I wanted when I want, plus, my parents forcing you on me didn't help either." I smiled.

He shrugged and half laughed. "If we had met on our own, maybe we could have avoided all these heart bleed. But now, I got to know you, and you are lovely, you are kind, you are patient, very patient, you make me laugh until my ribs want to crack. And, above all, you are my best friend. and I regret what I did to us, I regret how I treated you in the past, because I know now you would make for a good husband."

"What are you saying, Hasina?" He asked, his voice was low, but serious.

"I am saying that when you told me I could go, I realized that… that I didn't want to, because I was already home." I said placing my palm on his chest and I could feel his heart beating hard against my palm and so was mine. "And also, because you creeped up on me in ways I could not fathom, my heart is mesmerized by you. Each time I see you or hear your voice, or smell you, my heart races in me. I have fallen so much in love with you, I have come to love you in ways that I never expected I could, but I couldn't tell you because, as you know, I love another as well. How could I be sure of my feelings when I was, then, your prisoner?"

"Hasina!" he whispered; his face shocked; with every word that came out of my mouth. He took a step closer, and placed his hand on my face, our foreheads almost touched.

"I have waited for so long to hear you say these words to me." He started out; I could feel his body shaking as he spoke. "But as much joy as it gives me, I cannot be with you if you still love another." He said and moved back; my heart felt like he stabbed me in it. "I am giving you all of my heart; I want you to give me all of your heart or nothing at all." He declared.

This time my body shook with fear of losing him. I knew he was right I would demand the same, if in his position.

"I'm sorry, but you had to know the truth." I said.

He sighed. "Thank you for letting me know your heart, but, knowing that you love another punishes my heart just as much. Why did you have to tell me that also? Was it to punish me for keeping you here? I told you that you could go to him, but you had to stay and rub salt on my wound?"

"You get me wrong. It is not my intention to see you suffer. It is quite the opposite for me. And I would be a liar if I did not tell you how I still felt about him. I also thought you deserved to know how important you are to me."

"So, what do you want me to do? Celebrate? What is this? You build my hope up just to dash it. I cannot be with you if half of your heart belongs to someone else." He uttered in annoyance.

"Please don't be angry," I said.

"It's clear you need time to decide who you want to be with." He said.

I was quiet. "But I can forget him. I'll try."

"I don't want you to try to be with me, I don't want to wonder, when I see you thinking, if it's about him."

"I love you. I may love two men, but it does not cancel out my love for you. Some of those times, when you heard me cry, the tears were for you. My feelings for you are strong. I did not think that I could like you at first, let alone fall in love with you."

He forced a smile, and pushed his hair back with his hands in frustration. Then he came to me and pulled me into his arms. His scent and his manly frame consumed me and I closed my eyes as I relished his embrace.

"I love that you love me, I do." He said in a low voice, "And I am grateful to God for that. I love you so much, Hasina, I want you in my life forever, I want to marry you and love you with everything, Hasina... but I cannot marry you now, until you have seen him again. Go to him, and if your heart choses him, stay with him and live a great life. But if then you decide it's me you want, come back to me, my love, and we shall then wed."

He took a few steps backwards.

"Are you sure this is what you want?" I asked in shaky voice.

"No. It's not what I want. It's what must happen. I wish I never knew of him but I do, and I cannot settle for second best. This is your dilemma, you have to know for sure, so must I. Hence, you must go, but if you do come back; let it be because you cannot live without me. Goodnight, Hasina." He said excusing himself and walking away briskly.

I wanted to run after him, but he was right in all that he said, things had to be settled in my mind and I had to be fair to both him and Robert. I wished I wasn't so complicated? Whatever decision I make, someone is bound to be hurt and I could not celebrate either way, because I love them both.

Chapter 47

I went back to my room and found it hard to sleep. Ashraf had made his position clear and it was only right. I should be happy that I could go to Robert, and in a way, I was because I longed to see him again. My head and heart ached and I was scared that seeing Robert again would put me in the exact position I am now with Ashraf. He too would demand all of my heart. A year ago, he had all of my heart and now my story is different. I closed my eyes and prayed that sleep would claim me and soon it came and I crashed out in exhaustion. When morning came, Fatima, as instructed by Ashraf, came and started arranging for me to leave. I had breakfast brought to me; I did not think it was right to dine with him after our talk. It would be too awkward. As he had promised, a driver was assigned to me, who was ready to take me anywhere I wanted to go. Before entering into the car, I looked up to see if I could sight Ashraf anywhere. Fatima could tell I was looking for him.

She whispered, "He's not home, he went away, early this morning."

I nodded. "Thank you, Fatima."

She smiled, though, but you could see the tears clouding her eyes. I looked away afraid that I would cry too.

"Here, ma'am! He instructed that this should be given to you as well." She handed me a small brown envelope. I wondered what she thought of me—*the heartless woman that has brought her master nothing but pain*—as I took the envelope from her.

"Well, I don't know what to say," I said, not sure if I should give Fatima a hug, because I didn't know if this was the final goodbye or if I would come running back. Smiling sadly at Fatima and waving at the rest of the maids that gathered outside the house, I entered into the car.

Breathing very hard, and fighting to keep the tears away, I gave the driver Roberts address. As the driver pulled out of the compound into the main road, I closed my eyes and relaxed, clutching the envelope in my hands. I didn't know what it contained and didn't want to find out yet. He had said all he needed to say what more could the envelop contain. Looking out to the country side, we drove for almost two hours before entering into the city. My stomach dropped the closer we got to Robert. I was afraid of what might turn out. I didn't know if after all these time Robert will still want me, or if he had moved on. I tried to picture his face again, and I was filled with excitement at the prospect of seeing him. My heart began to race again. How could this happen to me, my heart racing unashamedly for two men? I didn't want this; I didn't ask for this. I wanted to love just one and, instead, life threw me two great men. Feeling my heart beat for Robert felt like a betrayal to Ashraf and vice versa.

Thirty minutes later, we finally pulled up in front of the gate. I never thought I would see this gate again. I got out of the car, leaving the unopened envelope on the back seat and walked towards the gate. I placed my hands on the gate just to feel it. It felt good coming back, it felt like home. I punched in the code to open the gate praying that Robert had not changed it. I was happy when the light turned green and the gates started to open up. I looked at the driver; he wanted me to get back in the car so he could drive all the way to the house. However, I didn't want that,

I wanted to walk the distance it took to get me to the front of the house. The driver got out of the car, and looked at me. I lifted my hands to stop him from walking towards me. Ashraf's instructions were for him to take me anywhere I wanted to go, not for him to follow me.

"I will go alone please; you can wait here. When I come back, I will let you know what I want to do."

He nodded obediently.

And I began walking towards the house, the excitement overwhelmed me, my walk turned into a jog, which eventually broke into a sprint. I could not wait until I was with him, as I ran; the sudden change of environment brought back memories of Robert and I walking this road together. It was as if an explosion of memories that I had suppressed in my head all came at once. I was out of breath when I eventually got to the front door, I pressed the bell, so many times, but there was no response. I had not looked to see if he was at home, Even the housekeeper and the chef were not around; that usually meant he was not in the country. I went around the house and looked through the window of his garage and saw that all the cars were there. My heart dropped, I could not believe this was happening, I eventually found my freedom and I could not reach him. I looked under the flowerpot for the spare key and let myself into the house. I went straight to the landline, and dialled his mobile. The phone took me straight to the voice mail, but I could not leave a message because his mailbox was full. I tried Jane's number and it said the number was no longer in use. Frustrated, I did not have any other way to contact him. Jane must be married now, and I had no idea where she lives.

I had a quick look round the house; it was messy, there were empty beer and wine bottles and pizza boxes littered around. There was a stale stench in the air, I wondered about that, Robert never liked mess. Which made me wonder about how long the house had been empty. No chef, no house keeper, no Robert. Where could he be?

I always knew my disappearance was going to hurt him just like I had suffered in the earlier months I was away from him. He suffers my absence still. We were not equal in our suffering, as I had enjoyed spending time with Ashraf and that guilt consumed me.

I wanted to see him to be sure he was okay, I wanted to be close to him, as though my life depended on it. I ran upstairs to his room; there I could smell him. His scent filled me, I picked up a shirt from his bed and lifted it to my nose, closing my eyes so that I was consumed by his scent. I sat on his bed, and wrapped his duvet around me; it made me feel closer to him. My heart was engorged within me, I knew I loved him, but coming back here made it that much clearer. Now that I was here, I did not want to be without him. Suddenly I burst into tears, and I cried uncontrollably it was all too much for me. I did not want to hurt anyone. But Ashraf was right, I couldn't decide until I had seen Robert again.

I laid on Robert's bed; I didn't know where to go. I had been in the house for a while now and I knew the driver was still waiting outside the gate. Sweat formed around my headline, as I wrapped the duvet tighter around me, I wiped the tears flowing freely down my cheek with the back of my hands. I wished he would just walk in now so I could explain everything that happened to him. Still it wouldn't make my decision any easier. Yet he had to know the truth, he had to also know that I had fallen for Ashraf.

I dragged myself away from his room and went into mine, as I swung the door open, I noticed the room was as I had left it. I walked in and stood in front of the mirror, my hairbrush was in my view, I placed my hand on it. I remember using it that morning before I left for my flat. My shoes, bags, jewelleries, make up, towels, everything was as I had left it.

This wasn't helping me to think clearly, the only other place to go look for him now was at his family home. I knew what awaited me there—his mother. but if I have to go through her to see him, then that is what I must do.

With no plan on what I would say to her once I got there, I went down the stairs, took one more look around the house before shutting the front door behind me.

As I approached the gate, I found the driver, his face stamped with worry. He looked relieved to see me; I gave him the address to Robert's family house and asked him to take me there. I could see he wasn't happy we weren't heading back to Ashraf's, I sat back in the car, with an unsettled mind as he began driving towards Robert's family house.

An hour later, he pulled into the driveway. The driver told me he was going to have lunch, and he would come back for me later. I had forgotten about food. Who could think of food when it came to matters of the heart? With my heart beating against my chest, and nerves having taken over my body, I stepped out of the car.

I rang the bell once and waited anxiously, the door opened and Robert's mother appeared. My heart was beating so fast; you could tell from the way she looked at me that I was the last person she expected to see standing here. She left the door opened and walked back into the house. I followed her inside immediately.

Before I could open my mouth, she uttered, "What are you doing here? You shouldn't be here." She did not waste any time before tearing into me. Notwithstanding, what she thought of me was the least of my concern. I needed to know where Robert was.

"Listen, I wouldn't be here if I had a choice. I know I am the last person you want to see, but I need to see him. I need to see Robert."

"Why? Don't you belong elsewhere with someone else?" She said,

"I don't understand. What do you mean?"

"Just what I said, you shouldn't be here, you and your family made it clear that you have moved on and I must admit I was over the moon when that news reached me. So, what are you doing here looking for my son? I take it you have gone to his house and you think I will help point you in his direction? If that is what you had in mind then I must disappoint you, even if I knew exactly where he is at this moment you will be the last person on earth, I will give that information to."

"I am sorry if I have upset you, but you have to tell me where he is please, I have to find him so that I can explain everything to him. Think about it, if I have moved on, I wouldn't be here now, would I?" I tried reasoning with her.

"Listen, don't waste your breathe. You are not good for this family; you are not good for my son. Since you stormed into his life, you have almost

torn my family in two. If you love him as much as you claim, then you must let him be. Let him find his happiness elsewhere. Go and marry whom your people chose for you. You've been gone for a year, he just managed to get himself together, now you're here again with your toxic love. I will not tell you where my son is, and I think we are done now, you may go."

I knew nothing I had to say would change her mind, but I still had to beg her.

"Please, I am pleading. I know he would want to see me, even if he believes I have moved on. Let me tell him what happened to his face. Give me a chance to explain things to him, I beg of you. He must have been worried about me. If nothing, let him and I have closure, or let's see if we are meant to be." I pleaded with her.

"What part of all I have said did you not understand? You are not the girl for my son; you are trouble. Call it a mother's intuition! If he starts again with you, I know trouble will come to him later and I am not going to gamble with my son's life for your sake. Go now, we do not want your kind of trouble. Please leave." She said proudly.

"I am sorry you feel that way about me, but I am not going anywhere until you tell me where to find him. Robert deserves to know that I came back to find him." I insisted.

"What will you do? Tie yourself to my kitchen door in protest...?" She laughed and then continued. "Listen Robert does not want you; he now knows what you are. And I will tell you what you are to your face. You are filth, you left him to be with another man, and you betrayed his trust and stamped on his heart. Your father brought pictures of you with another man. With all the love you claimed to have for him, it didn't take you long to move on. Then my sensible son almost became a drunk to forget you. He suffered, and no one could help him, he chased everyone away, he stopped going to work. What you did to him nearly drove him mad. Yet you have the audacity to come back here looking for him. Have you not done enough? Thankfully, what you did to him brought back his senses. Katherine, came back into his life and helped nurse him better. You have heard of Katherine, right? They were childhood sweethearts; I always knew they would end up together. You want to know where he is, listen closely, I will say it once; do not count on me repeating it. She has taken him somewhere far from here, far from anything that would remind him of you. So, you see, you are too late. Go back to your husband, and leave my son out of your drama. With any luck, he will marry her and live out the rest of his life in peace."

I stood speechless; this was all my father's doing.

The decision was now clearly beyond me, if what his mother said was to be believed. If he thinks I was married, then I could understand how he must have felt betrayed. I should leave, but I needed to let her know that I didn't move on, not really.

"But I am not married! My father must have lied to him; I am not married. I was taken against my will. I couldn't reach him because I had no access to phone. Surely even you can understand my predicament. I don't believe you to be that heartless. Please I beg of you, if it's not too late, do tell him everything I have said."

She looked like she enjoyed seeing me grovel; her eyes said it all…

"And then what?" She spat out, "Watch him drown in sorrow again, when next you are taken? I have never seen him deplete into such a low state, when he found out you had moved on. I hated the fact that I was right about you, but I was. And that's what mothers do; they take care of their own. You are his weakness, he loved you too much; he left no room for no one else, not even for himself. He gave everything to you, he made you his world, his life, and he didn't think to hold something back in case you left, just like you did. Are you so selfish you cannot see the hurt you carry around? Or do you think your beauty puts you above everything? What of your betrothed? Is he not also waiting for you? Or do you not care who you hurt? If I have one advise for you, find your happiness where it would cause less pain. Leave now, please, before I call the police on you." She scowled.

"I will leave, but promise that you will tell him I came back, and tell him that I did not go of my own will; my father took me. And if you can, please tell him that I love him still even if we are not to be together anymore, that I will always love him."

"No! I cannot promise you anything! I look at you now, and you look well to me. Your skin is glowing, someone is looking out for you, go back there and be happy. In time Robert will forget everything, as you will too, we don't always get what we want, and that is life. So, go now; run along, nobody wants you here. My children have moved on and so must you. You may see yourself out."

This time, she left me where I stood and went upstairs. There was nothing left to say. It did not seem fair, what has happened to the two of us. In a way, it made my dilemma easier. I could go back to Ashraf now, but this was not what Ashraf asked of me. He wanted me to see Robert again and be sure of whom I wanted to spend the rest of my life with. Going back to him with unresolved feelings was not the deal. But if I do go back, then, I must forget everything I had to do with Robert and give all my love to Ashraf. I slowly found the use of my feet and walked out of her house.

Thankfully, the driver was back, I didn't know how much time I spent in the house. I was exhausted, and hungry. And it was getting late. "Can you please take me to the nearest Hotel." I said to the driver,

"We can still make it back in time." He argued.

"No, take me to the Hotel, you may go back if you want. Come back for me in three days." I said.

He nodded and began to drive.

Thirty minutes later, we were in front of the hotel. Just then it occurred to me that I didn't have any money on me. But then I remembered Robert placed a large sum in my account before. Then my eyes fell on the brown envelope. I opened it, and inside was a black American express card with a note from Ashraf that read:

Hasina,

Please accept this as a token, you may need it to find your feet again. Understand that this is not meant to buy your love, but as you said, we are friends too after all.

Ashraf.

Ashraf took care of everything to the minutest details; he knew I may not want to come back and he still took care of my expenses. I checked myself into the Hotel, I couldn't go back to him now, nothing was resolved, and I didn't deserve him. If I could go far away from all of this and begin again, I would do so, but I knew running from matters of the heart solved nothing. The next day, I took a cab to Robert's house, and left him a letter, I had made up my mind to forget him but I wanted to apologise for the heartache

I caused him and to let him know that it was not an easy decision. He also meant the world to me, as Ashraf does. The letter reads:

My dearest Robert,

"I came back to you as I always knew I would, but you were gone. I do not know what you have heard, but whatever it was, it made you suffer and I am sorry that, because of me, you hurt.
Believe me, for the longest time after I was taken, I thought I was going to die because they had taken me away from you. I cannot put to words how I have missed you. To ensure my return to you, I had to get along so I could win the war. My father lied to you. I AM NOT MARRIED. But in my bid to escape, my heart began to betray you in ways I had hoped it would not. For that, I ask that you forgive me.

I love Ashraf, just as much as I love you. He is a kind, humble and the gentlest of men. It's only fair that you should know this, just as he does know that I love you too. Your mother told me that you are now being comforted in the arms of Katherine. I hope that you will grow to love her as I have grown to love Ashraf. I will go back now and be with Ashraf as I should have always been. I pray happiness for you and that you do not hold your mother or anyone responsible for anything.

We met, we loved greatly and that's all that mattered. Now, I will do my best to forget you, but I know it is impossible to do so. But however hard, I will try daily so I can make my husband to be the happiest man in the world, because I know he deserves all my love. If you wish to write back, only to tell me you forgive me, you may reach me at the address on the back of this letter.

Take care now my darling, and be happy, if not for you, then for me.

Your Hasina!

While, I was at his home, I tidied up the place as best as I could and aired the rooms so the stale smell could escape. While cleaning, I reasoned with everything his mother said to me, and it made my feelings clearer. Robert and I happened by chance only because I ran off, and I should never have. Thus, we were not meant to be. And if at all we were, it shouldn't be this hard then. After about three hours of cleaning, I found that I no longer hurt to be away from him. I had not seen him, but I had come to accept that it was for the best. I turned the key, as I closed the door and left my past behind with it.

Back in my Hotel room, I let my thoughts go back to Ashraf, I belonged with Ashraf and I loved him just as much. It was easy and it hurt less people, and I would be greedy and selfish to want anything more than what we already have.

Our love can only grow and the excitement of what's to come filled me up. I slept, and I was at peace at last. The next day, I went out to do some shopping, then I visited a saloon and had my hair washed and my nails painted.

It felt good, I felt alive again.

When I returned to the Hotel, I had dinner sent up to my room, I watched a movie, and then slept.

It was the third day; the driver would come back for me. As I laid in the bath, it occurred to me that I had no thought about Robert, since I left his home and now that I thought of him, it didn't hurt like it had done in the past. That made me happy.

I wanted to see Ashraf again. I dressed and put all my belongings in a bag. My phone rang, the driver was waiting downstairs in the lobby.

He smiled and took my bags from me, as soon as I sat in the back of the car, he asked, "Where would you like to go?"

I replied, "Take me home please."

He smiled.

And I felt joy at the prospect of seeing everyone again, especially my Ashraf.

Chapter 48

Wedding Preparations.

I went back into the surprisingly eager arms of Ashraf. The joy in his eyes when he saw me was unmeasurable. He did not question me and I was happy for that. He drew me into his arms and I let
him, it felt great to be with him again.

"I never thought I would see you again, my love." He whispered into my ears.

"I'm sorry I kept you waiting." I responded.

"You are worth the wait." He said as he lifted me off the ground and spun me around.

Everyone laughed as I screamed, "Put me down."

"Sorry, I got carried away." He said as he gently placed me back on the ground.

He held my hand as we walked towards the house.

"So, what's next?" I asked.

"Now, you pick a date! It could be tomorrow, if you so wish. But don't make me wait too long to marry you." He said.

I laughed. I could feel all the eyes on us, so I looked away shyly.

"Perhaps I will pick a date that will suit you, if you send everyone away." I said.

"Oh, you want them all out of the house?" He asked,

"No, not out of the house, I just don't want the attention on me right now." I said.

"Oh, in that case, everyone, she's here now, you can all rest easy. Back to your stations at once." He announced, there was a roar of laughter as all the staff returned to the house, leaving us to ourselves.

He turned to me and held my face, "I love you, Hasina."

"I love you too, Ashraf." and, now, I knew I meant every word.

His lips reached for mine, and the beatings of my heart increased as he planted a gentle kiss on my lips. I felt sparks of feelings run through me as we kissed openly, the kiss was short, but with every lock of our lips, I felt our love for each other. He took a sharp breath, and wrapped me in his arms.

"Thank you for coming back." He expressed his fulfilment.

I didn't need to say anything else, as he could feel my love by the way I held him.

He walked me down to my wing, and just before I went inside, he pulled me to him again and kissed me. This time, it was slower and deeper, I couldn't wait to marry him already.

Fatima, walked in on us, and shyly excused herself.

"Okay, enough now," I said panting.

"No, not enough, you don't know how long I had longed to do that." He said. I giggled.

"I know, but you will get all the tongues wagging, should we continue at this rate." I said.

"I don't care, this is our house and you are my wife, oh sorry, you are going to be my wife."

I laughed as he corrected himself. I had never seen him this happy, it made my heart swell, that I could erase the pain I had once caused him.

"You don't have any regrets, do you?" He asked.

This was when I should have told him that I never actually got to see Robert, but there was no need for that to be said. We were both happy and I had chosen him over Robert.

"No, I don't. I'm happy to be here and I want to be yours so desperately." I said.

He laughed. "Woman, you can't be as desperate as I am," He said, "I claim that one. I won first class in the act of desperation when it comes to you." I laughed so hard seeing he was that funny.

"Okay, you can have that one," I said and added, "It will please me greatly to be your wife."

He wanted to lift me up but I stopped him by raising my hand.

"Wait!"

"Wait for what?"

"You have to ask me again, so I can say yes, properly."

He smiled. "Okay, but I don't have the ring with me?" He opted.

"Improvise." I said.

He looked around and found a bunch of flowers, rolling the stems into a ring quickly, while I waited, he got on one knee. I giggled as I looked down at him.

"Hasina, you already know what you mean to me. You are the beatings of my heart, and the light of my soul. You are the reason I smile and the reason I cry. For you I will fight wars, and conquer many nations just to get to you. Nothing will ever be too hard to do for you, ask for the moon and, if it's in my powers, I will give it to you as long as you promise to always be mine. Will you marry me, my love, and make me the happiest man in the world?"

I could not stand there looking at him as he declared his love and proposed to me. I got down on my knees and held his hand and placed the ring on my finger.

"My heart is yours, Ashraf, all of it. It must have always been yours all this while. I ran, as I didn't understand that my happiness was with you. But you caught up with me, and when you did, it was easy to love you. Even when I tried to fight it, my walls crumbled around you. You made it easy to see the future, and I realized that, what I all along wanted was within my reach with you. I love you with everything and it will be a great pleasure to be your wife."

I didn't know if he wanted to cry or laugh. He just picked me up, and planted kisses on my face. "I better leave now," He said.

"Yes, you should." I giggled with happiness.

"Okay, my love, do you want dinner with me or have I overwhelmed you?"

"You could never overwhelm me, but I need to rest, I will have dinner in my room. Tomorrow I'm all yours and we can begin the plans for our wedding.

"Okay, my love, I'll see you tomorrow then." He said.

I blew him a kiss from my hands.

He shook his hands at me and wanted to come back and kiss me, but I ran inside my room quickly.

He laughed. I could hear the roar of his laughter as he retreated.

There was a change in the atmosphere, everyone in the household was happy. It was great to see what love could do. Love was in the air; we didn't want to wait any longer. He called my parents and they agreed we should marry in a month from now.

A month was too long for us, I wanted to be in his arms always. So, we would hide where no one would see us and we would share long deep kisses. Ashraf spoilt me rotten. He was on top of the world; he showered me with love, attention, devotion and gifts. Everyday a different set of gifts. The flowers, chocolates, jewelleries, dresses, bags, spas… you name it. We hardly eat at home, we dined at the finest restaurants most nights, and then went to see the latest shows in London—concerts, theatres, cinemas, talk shows, comedy shows… you name it. He always had time for me. Each time I entered the room, no matter who he was talking to, he gave his attention to me, and he let the world know that I was his universe. As the wedding day drew closer, the house got crowded. Designers from all over the world, caterers, decorators, makeup artist, hair stylist; the best of the best were flown from all over the world. Each person was given a room in our huge house. Even with all the crowd around us, Ashraf would look for me, and when his eyes met with mine, a warm loving feeling coursed through me that made me feel like I was the only woman in the world.

Ashraf begged me to forgive my parents, and for him I would do anything, they may have forced their will on me, but it was my will that chose him as my husband. If anything, I should thank them for sending this miracle of a man into my life.

I welcomed my mother back into my life, I had grown these past months she had been away, I had become my own woman and queen of my home and Ashraf's heart. For peace sake, I let my mother, once she arrived, continue with the wedding preparations. This was all she lived for, I could see the pride in her, when she saw me and Ashraf together. She did want to say I told you so, and so much more. But she bit her tongue and smiled instead.

Only a week to go now, and I will proudly be Hasina Suri Ashraf Mohammed. The ceremony had begun, my father arrived three days to the day.

The house was full; all sorts of people were arriving from all over the world. A huge marque had been set up in the garden, which was getting beautifully decorated as the day drew closer. Music and sounds of celebration filled the air, and I had never been truly happier. Mother brought some women to prepare me for a three days cleansing with traditional oils, perfumes and Henna designs.

One day to go, and the realization of it all hit me, I panicked for the first time since I came back. Why was I panicking? That I didn't understand. I was truly happy, but all the people around and the nonstop celebration, with every aunty telling me I was the luckiest woman alive, could be the reason why I got overwhelmed.

To help me calm, as I did not want Ashraf to see me panicking, I walked to the stream. I wished we were married already; I didn't like that my head was starting to question my heart. I needed to hear myself think or not think at all. I must have been sitting under the tree for about an hour when Fatima came to disturb my peace and announced that I had a visitor. My heart skipped a beat, I was suddenly afraid of whom it might be. The letter I had written to Robert came to mind; I gave him the address so he could write back, but he did not write. I wondered if it was Robert that had come to find me. Ashraf didn't deserve this, I hoped that it was not him. Getting to my feet at once, I followed Fatima back to the house.

As I approached my wing, a familiar face caught my eye. It was Jane, I sighed with relief. I rushed inside to see her and she ran towards me. We embraced. I never imagined that I would see her again. I was so happy that she came, she was first my friend before anything concrete began with Robert. I could see people looking to see who she was, I swiftly led her away from probing eyes and took her to my wing where we could have some privacy to ourselves.

Once we were alone, I just threw myself into her arms again, seeing her and holding her again felt so good that I began to cry. She joined me; it had been so long since we saw each other. We hugged again, giggled and wiped each other's tears away.

"I can't believe you're here." I said at last.

"I had to come." She replied.

"I take it to be that you found my letter." I guessed.

She only smiled sadly and then she dried the tears trickling down my face with her palm.

"I would have been here, if I had found the letter earlier. You know, just to see you. You look well." she said.

I nodded.

"I am well," I responded. I wanted to ask about Robert, but I didn't have the courage to, and I didn't think it was right to ask especially since I would be married the next day.

"Are all these people here because of you? Are you getting married?"

I nodded

"Are you happy?"

I nodded.

"I didn't think I could be happier." I said.

She smiled sadly.

"You know, he thought you were already married, he was really hurt, Anna, you should have seen him." More tears began to flow down my eyes, I tried to stop myself but seeing Jane after such a long time and hearing her talk to me about Robert aroused all the feeling I had locked away for Robert.

"I don't know what my father told him, but I'm now just getting married tomorrow."

"He went to the states to stay with Alex; Dave and I had to go with him. He was in such a bad shape. I couldn't leave him. I have never seen him like that, you wouldn't have recognized him."

"Didn't Katherine go with you to the states?" I asked

"Katherine! What Katherine?"

"Your mother said, he was now with Katherine."

Jane shook her head, "No, that never happened. We've not seen Katherine for ages."

"Your mum told me different. I had called your phone, but it seemed like you had changed your number. And your mother refused to tell me where I could reach any of you. I'm sorry I caused him that much pain."

"I cannot begin to imagine what happened to you, but Robert wanted to come back to England so we came back three weeks ago. Mum never mentioned that you came to look for him. You know, if she did, Robert would have kicked down walls until he found you." She explained.

I smiled.

Elizabeth Johnson

"I know." I said. This was not good! I thought, I didn't want the confusion over whom I loved to come back again, I couldn't disappoint Ashraf again. But with Jane right here talking about him, I wanted to see Robert again.

"So, how did you know where to come?" I asked.

"I went to mum's last Sunday for dinner. She asked me to fetch something from her room; I knocked over her bag and your letter fell out. I was mad at her for taking it. She must have gone to Robert's house to find the letter, when she learnt we were coming back, just to keep it hid from him. I showed the letter to Robert, but I didn't tell him mum hid it, because, I did not want them fighting over you again. You should have seen his face, when I told him you had come back for him. He knows you are going to be married, in fact we thought you already were. But he wanted to see you again, and so did I." She said.

"So why is he not here?"

"He is waiting outside in the car." My heart skipped a million beat to think my Robert was outside the walls of this house. This was not good; my head was mashed.

"You're not serious?" I said.

"I am. I know it's too late, but he really deserves some bit of closure. The letter is not enough. You both need to meet, so you can help him to move on, please." She urged.

"I don't know, Jane. Even if I was to do this for him. I would hurt Ashraf, if he finds out. My parents are here too; all these people, what will they think of me? I can't do this again; I can't run from my destiny. This is where I'm meant to be. That is not to say that I don't or never loved Robert. I did, and I still do. Talking about him and knowing he's outside this wall is not fair on Ashraf." I said.

"I know, and I understand. I'm not here to stop your happiness, all I ask for old times' sake is that you do me this one last favour. So, Robert can know from you that there is not going to be anything between you two anymore. So, he can move on. I beg you as my friend."

"Okay, but first I need to talk to Ashraf. He told me when I went away to look for Robert not to come back until I had seen him. And I was sure I wanted him over Robert. When I couldn't find Robert, I came back and I lied to him, I suppressed my love for Robert, because Ashraf deserved to have all my love. And so, does Robert. But in Robert's absence, I chose Ashraf. He doesn't deserve this, I can't bring myself to embarrass him again. But I need to tell him the truth today."

"This is not good; I wish I had not come here today. I don't want to spoil your happiness."

"I know but, your presence here, will help me decide and I will know for sure if I made the right decision."

"Robert gave me a letter for you; see if it helps." I looked at her, and for a second, I was tempted to read the letter. But I couldn't. I didn't want the war that wagged over whom I loved anymore.

"I can't, Jane, I'm sorry. I will go to Ashraf now and tell him about Robert. I will tell him the truth. I love your brother; he was my first love. But Ashraf is now my forever. But I promised Ashraf, that I would see Robert again and so I must."

"You don't need to, if it will affect you, I should never have asked this of you." Jane said,

"No, but I have to. When I marry, I need for Ashraf to know he is my universe as he has already made me his." Tears clouded Jane's eyes. "I'm sorry! Maybe if I had seen him when I came, things could have been different." I added.

"Wait here for me, I'll be back." I whispered.

Chapter 49

I took a minute to compose myself before setting out to find Ashraf. I looked everywhere in the house; he was nowhere to be found so I decided to walk the garden, maybe I will find him there. I had not seen him in two days. We were not meant to see each other until the ceremony was over, but I couldn't stay away, and I couldn't lie to him any longer. I asked Fatima to go find him and to tell him to come meet me by the stream.

Fifteen minutes later, he strode in, with a beautiful smile on his face.

"What is this? You know we are not meant to see each other until the day of the ceremony."

"Really, you don't miss me?"

"When you put it that way, I can't resist this secret meet. So, what is it? Were you missing me?" he asked.

I felt so guilty seeing him so happy to see me; I did not know how to tell him that Robert was waiting to see me outside the walls. I looked down and then up at him, he knew now that something was wrong. His face looked alarmed although he tried to control it, his eyes narrowed as mine met his. I looked away again, I could not meet his eyes, I thought about lying again. I hated the fact that I would have to see the hurt in his face once I told him why I had called him out here. Then he smiled,

"Don't tell me you're having cold feet already." he tried to joke.

That gave me a base to start. I found the courage to look at him and then I spoke. "Ashraf, I lied to you about Robert." He looked confused and rightly so.

"What are you talking about?"

"When you asked me to go to him, I never saw him... I am so sorry; I never got a chance to resolve my feeling for him to his face."

"Okay, so, when you came back, how did you become sure you wanted me over him?" He asked.

"I wasn't a hundred percent sure, but I don't need the percentages to know that I want to be with you. You are good for me and everyone can see we are good together." I said.

"Okay, if you believe so, why ask me out here now?" I was quiet.

"Hasina, speak to me."

"It's about Robert, I want a chance to meet with him one last time, so, I could give him the closure he deserves. This way, I will know that I made the right decision to be with you."

"Stop talking! You are insufferable! Must you embarrass me again? You want me to let you into the arms of another man a day before we wed?" he yelled out in anger. His eyes clouded with pain, he turned away from me, and I could hear him breathing hard as he tried to compose himself. I was grounded to the spot. He turned to look at me, and he seemed calmer than he had been just moments ago.

"I am sorry; I didn't mean to yell." He said as he tried to keep it together.

"Ashraf, I do love you, and I will marry you tomorrow, I just wanted your permission to see him again."

"To what end? Tell me, would it make him happy? Would it make me happy? Or would it make you happy? I told you not to come back unless you were sure. If you had been so sure, you wouldn't want to see him again. Tell me, why now? Why today?"

"I didn't ask for this, it just happened. And if it upsets you this much, I will not see him. My love, I have upset you and I am sorry. Please forgive me, I am truly sorry." I apologized.

"You didn't answer my question, I asked you earlier, why now? You know I am not stupid; I know about your visitor. I was informed about her, I could have denied her entrance, but I allowed her in because I was giving you the benefit of a doubt. How did she know where to find you?"

"I don't know what to say, please let's forget I ever asked."

"No, we can't forget it, I can't go ahead with tomorrow if you think that you still love him."

"Oh, but my love, I do love him,"

"So, what are you doing here with me?" His eyes were red; I could see the pain. So, I didn't repeat what I said to not cause him pain.

"I'm here because I want to be with you."

"Out of pity, is that it? Would you rather be with him? Would you rather marry him instead?"

"He was good to me, he was my first love, and he did well by me, yes, if I hadn't met you, I would have married him above all men. But I did meet you and you stole the heart that was always yours back. My heart beats right next to yours. My love for you supersedes all others. You are my forever. You taught me to love you in ways I couldn't imagine. I don't need to see him to decide if I want to be with you. I know in my heart you are my destiny, I wanted to see him to help him move on. You can understand that, can't you?"

He was quiet, he came closer to me.

"I promised to give everything to you, please, Hasina don't destroy us, don't break my heart again." He paused. "Go to him, if it's what you want. See that it is finished and if you find that it's not when you have set eyes on him, go with him, my dear... and never return." He added and walked away.

Chapter 50

The Final showdown

I waited a while until he was no longer in view before leaving for my wing, where Jane was waiting for me. I walked quick as I didn't want my parents to catch the wind of what was going on. Although, if Ashraf already knew Jane was here, I wouldn't be surprised if my father knew as well.

As I walked to my wing, I saw my mother, there was concern written all over her face like she already knew something was wrong.

"Hasina!" she called.

But I ignored her and made haste. From the corner of my eyes, I could see that my mother was coming after me. I hurried into my room and found an anxious Jane.

"Something is wrong, come with me." I said to her quickly.

"How did it go?" She asked.

I placed my hand on my lips to shush her as my mother finally caught up with me.

"Who is this?" She asked as she looked Jane over,

"She's my friend, Jane." I said placing my body in front of Janes.

My mother was quiet, she looked at Jane and said,

"Please wait outside, I need to talk with my daughter."

"No mother, I have to go now, whatever you have to say. Sit on it until I see you again." I took Jane by the hand and we began to walk fast.

"Stop her." I heard my mother shout.

"I looked and saw a few staff coming towards Jane and I.

"What is this mother?" I shouted,

"I am stopping you from ruining your life." She answered. I looked at
Jane and mouthed "*Let's run!*"

We started to run bumping into people along the way. A scene was created as we got out of the door. I closed the door behind me to buy us time.

"What is happening?" Jane asked.

"I don't know what is happening." I said alarmed.

"You spoke to your betrothed, what did he say?" Jane questioned.

"I can't speak now, but I think my mother knows something. Where did you park the car?

"Just outside the gate."

"Okay, let's hurry." I said breathlessly.

"As we got to the gate, I saw a dozen men with arms pointing outwards.

Colour drained from my body, I knew what this was. Whatever was happening had something to do with Robert being outside.

"No!" I screamed as I ran out of the gate.

My father was outside the gate, with the men of arms, two men held Robert as the other pointed their guns at him.

"What is this father? What are you doing?" I asked.

"Hold her he shouted at some of the men, before they could reach me, I wriggled away and ran with Jane straight into one of the men pointing guns at Robert. Knocking him down, his gun fell and I Immediately picked it up.

"Hasina! Get back in here." My father commanded.

"No! I can't. Tell these men to drop their weapons or…"

"Or what… What will you do? Shoot these men because of your heathen friends?

"No, it doesn't have to be this way! Why do you always have to make a scene father?"

"I already spoke to Ashraf; he gave me his permission. Why do you have to make it about yourself?"

"You insolent, ungrateful child, get over here this minute, I warned that boy. I told him next time I see him; he would answer to me. This is a private land; he is an intruder. Now get over here, Hasina."

"I won't, until you tell these men to drop their weapons."

"Or what?"

"Or…" I looked from Jane to Robert, tears rolled freely down my cheek.

This wasn't meant to happen. *Not like this*, I thought. Closing my eyes, I turned the gun on myself.

"No, Hasina!" Robert shouted.

"Don't do this," He begged.

"I don't have a choice," I sobbed. "My father will kill you, he won't let you leave here alive."

"No, I won't let that happen." Just then I heard Ashraf's voice, he must have just heard about the commotion.

"My love, what are you doing." He asked in a low voice.

"I'm sorry. I didn't want this. I didn't want this scene."

"Please put the gun down," He pleaded,
"You know; I would never want this." He
added.
I nodded, as tears blocked my vision.

"Tell him," I gestured at my father, "to tell these men to let Robert go."

"Let him go." Ashraf commanded.

"No, he must not leave." My father roared.

"Don't be stubborn. I don't want to lose her. I beg of you, let him go." Ashraf shouted.

I pushed the gun closer to my head, I was tired of all the heartache, if my father killed Robert, there was no way I could ever be happy again. It would taint whatever future I would have with Ashraf.

"Hasina, what are you doing?" My mother screamed. She finally arrived, I couldn't see clearly, tears covered my eyes and I couldn't wipe it, I had one hand on Jane and the other had the gun to my head.

I turned towards Jane, and whispered, "Get in your car."

As Jane made to leave, the men corked their guns.

"NO! NO!" My mother shouted.

"I don't want this, I don't want any blood spilled, let them go."

I could see the fear in my mother's eyes and the disappointment in Ashraf's, as almost all our visitors were outside the gate by now, watching the showdown.

Whispers were being made as people tried to connect what was happening. "Who is he?" I heard, as they looked from Robert to myself. Aunties and Uncles shook their heads at me. Ashraf looked away, I had done it again—embarrassed him. I didn't plan it but it's happened anyway.

"Just let them go, father, father please and everything will be fine again, I promise."

"If you want to die with him, then so be it." My father said.

"No! No! No!" Ashraf shouted and he ran in front of the men.

"No one is dying, she asked my permission to speak with him." Ashraf shouted. He didn't have to say that, but I had put him in that position. But what was I to do, allow my father hurt Robert?

I looked at Robert, I could tell he regretted coming,

"You are not going to kill my bride to be; you will not kill anyone. I am getting married tomorrow. So, please stop this madness now. *Let go of him.*" He said to the two men holding Robert.

They looked at my father for approval.

"I said let go of him now!" Ashraf shouted "This nonsense stops now." Ashraf declared.

My father looking defeated signalled to the men to put their hands down. But I still had the gun to my head.

I knew it wasn't over, until Robert and Jane were safely away, I couldn't trust my father.

"Hasina, put the gun down." Robert said, his eyes looked sorry.

"Please, listen to him." Ashraf said, moving towards me, I was tired of all the fighting, pulling the trigger would mean rest for me, but it would be a selfish thing to do to these men that loved me, and whom I adored. How could I do that?

I looked at Ashraf and smiled,

"I will go with him, so he is safe." I said, I could tell he didn't understand what I meant but there was no time to explain.

Jane started the car as the men moved away. Before Ashraf could say anything,

Jane shouted, "Robert get in the car." And as he did, I threw the gun on the ground and got in the back seat of the car with Robert.

I saw Ashraf, close his eyes, as Jane reversed the car in high speed.

"Hasina!" My mum shouted.

My heart raced within me, as Jane sped away

"Get in the car and go after her." I heard my father's voice and then nothing.

Afraid my father's men will catch up to us, we sped along. No one said anything, we were all hell shocked.

After about an hour's drive. Jane slowed down and pulled up in a car park.

I felt like I was experiencing someone else's life, never in a million years did I think these would happen to any of us. My heart went to Ashraf, he must have thought I had chosen Robert over him.

I had destroyed everything and knocked him down again.

"How is everyone coping?" Jane checked.

I didn't say anything.

Robert looked at me. "I'm sorry I came." He said.

I smiled slowly.

"It's okay, you wouldn't have known that all of these would happen."

We were all quiet again.

Then he said, "You love him?"

With tears clouding my eyes, I nodded. "Yes, I do. Very much."

"I had to know for sure."

"I'm glad you came; off course I wish things were different."

Jane got out of the car to give us space to talk.

He held my hands, "I guess I came too late." He said.

I was quiet.

"If I had asked you to marry me then, when we were together, would you have said yes?"

I smiled, "Yes, I would have. You had all my heart then. You were my world. And I hated Ashraf. I didn't know him then. But now things are different as I have come to know him already. He is not like my father. I love him for different reasons from why I had loved you."

"I can tell that he loves you, I saw it in his eyes. Even though I hate to admit it, I hate that you now belong to him. But you are happy and that's all I ever wanted for you." He said.

I smiled, as tears fell freely down my eyes.

"What about you? I need you to find happiness."

"My happiness started when I met you, I don't know if I will ever find that again. But for you, I will try. Each time I think of you, I want to know in my heart that you are happy. Only that will give me the strength to move on."

He pulled me into his arms and we both wept for what we had lost.

"I'm sorry, I did this to you." I whispered

"It's alright, my darling. You were the best of the good times." He said.

I smiled.

"Okay, we need to take you back to him now, you have a wedding to attend." He said.

I half laughed.

"Jane!" he called,

"You're not seriously going to go back there?" I said alarmed.

He laughed, "No, I am heart broken, but I don't have a death wish. We will take you far enough so you can safely walk back." He said.

"Thank you for saving our lives." He said, "You weren't seriously considering using the gun, were you?" His tone more serious now.

I was quiet, because for a moment, I had thought about ending it all, I was causing the two men I adored so much heartache. But it had all been a moment of madness.

"No, I wasn't, I just needed to show my father, if he hurt you, he would lose me." I lied.

"Please don't do that again." He said,

"Noted."

Jane got into the car, "So, where now?" she asked.

"We're taking her back." Robert said.

"Seriously?"

"Yes, seriously." Robert responded.

"Anna, are you sure you want to go back to that chaos?" She questioned looking directly at me.

"Yes, I'm going back for Ashraf. I have to." I replied.

She was quiet, then she looked at the two us, "I wish you had proposed to her and married her ages ago. We wouldn't be losing her now." She said sadly.

"Hey, come on, you are not losing me, Jane, we would still be friends.

You'll see." She laughed.

"Just don't invite me to any of your celebrations and we will be fine." She joked.

"Okay, noted." I said.

Jane began to drive.

I turned my head toward the window to avoid Roberts eyes. I could feel his eyes on me. He was hurting, but for me, he put on a brave face.

When Jane was close enough but far from any view, she stopped the car. A fresh set of tears clouded my eyes as I knew, for Robert, this was goodbye. I turned to face him fighting the tears storming my eyes.

He reached his hands and touched my hair, pulling his head close to mine, he drew in a sharp breath. We remained that way for a moment, then he looked up and said. "In another life, you will be mine."

"In another life." I repeated.

He smiled sadly.

"Go on, go have a great life, my darling." He said,

I could hear Jane sobbing, I didn't know what to say, there was nothing I could say at that moment that would take theirs and my pain away.

I looked at him and nodded, placing my hand on his for the last time, I planted a delicate kiss on his forehead. I heard him draw a heavy sigh, I pulled away, and with my spare hand, I found Jane's cheek. I lovingly caressed and wiped her tear with the back of my hand. Jane began to sob out loudly. I was overwhelmed by sadness. Without another word I opened the door and began to walk, I didn't look back.

Robert was my past; Ashraf is my present and my future. After a while, I heard the car start and they drove away.

This was good, I told myself, straightening up, I wiped my tear and composed myself. After walking for ten minutes, I was in view of the house, there were a few people outside the gate, I couldn't tell who they were, but my heart raced as I feared rejection from Ashraf. I knew there would be gossip, but none of that mattered as long as Ashraf was okay and still wanted me.

Then I heard my mother's voice. "Hasina, is that you?" I didn't say a word,

"It's Hasina." I heard another person say.

My mother ran towards me. She wrapped her arms around me and kissed me. Her face was wet with tears; I had given her another heart ache. I reached my hands to her face, and said. "I'm sorry I worried you."

"It's okay. You're here now, to think that I had I thought that I wouldn't see you again." She said.

"I'm sorry." I apologised again.

"It's alright, you are back that is all that matters"

"Where is Ashraf?" I asked,

"Oh, he and your father got into it, he was furious your father played with your life. I am annoyed with your father as well." My mother said, Fatima brought a blanket and wrapped it around me, we walked inside the gate, "I agree with Ashraf on this one, your father took it too far. We could have lost you because of his foolish pride. Come let me take you to him." My mother said.

"He's out in the gardens, he went for a walk." Fatima quickly added.

"Okay, I will walk with you until we find him." My mother offered.

"No, I will find him myself." I declined.

My mother smiled, "Okay darling, I'll be waiting in your room."

I smiled. Taking the blanket off me, I gave it back to Fatima.

****

As I approached my spot, which is fast becoming both our spot, I found him facing the stream.

I walked close, and stood behind him.

"You're back!" He said,

"I'm back." I responded.

Then he turned to face me, I could tell he'd been through the ringers,

He smiled, "What am I to do with you?"

I walked close enough so that we were within touching distance.

"Marry me tomorrow." I said.

"Why?" he asked.

"Because I love you more than you actually know, and I want to be your wife."

He inhaled sharply.

"Then I say, the wedding is back on."

"Was it ever off?"

"Not for me."

"Not for me either."

He drew me to him, my heart raced in me as our eyes locked on each other's.

"You've been crying." He said.

"Yes, I embarrassed you again. I didn't mean for that to happen."

"You're here now, that's all that matters." He said.

I smiled.

"Kiss me." I said,

He smiled, and pulled me even closer, his lips found mine and a passionate fire spread all over me as our lips touched. The kiss was slow and building with intensity as every twist and turns told of our love for each other. My body shook in submission. As he pulled away, I collapsed into his embrace.

"My love, my love. What am I to do with thee?" He whispered; his breath rough from the kiss.

I smiled and said, "Just love me the way you do."

He placed his hand at the small of my back, and turned me around. As we began to walk back to the house, he said, "that's easy! Loving you is as easy as breathing."

"Surely, I'm the most blessed woman in the world." I said.

He laughed. "No, I am. After all that has happened, you still chose to be with me." He said.

"Well, when you put it like that, I can't argue." I said, and we both shared a laugh.

He held my hands until we got to my wing, I didn't want him to leave, I wished we could talk all night. "You need your beauty sleep." He said,

"You need it more than I do." I responded. He was quiet, his eyes looked longingly at me, then he lovingly caressed my cheek.

"You are beautiful, my love, you are God's wonder indeed. Goodnight!

You need to rest; we have a big day ahead of us."

"I know, and thank you." I said.

"Why do you thank me?" he asked.

"For everything: for still wanting me, and loving me even after all I had put you through." I said.

He smiled. "Alright, if you say so." He said.

"Alright. Goodnight." I responded.

As he turned to leave, he suddenly turned back and said

"From tomorrow, you will sleep here no more, my bed will be your bed." He said.

I laughed. "See you tomorrow," I said,

"I can't wait." He whispered and then he walked away. I stood and watched as he went, my heart heaved a sigh in relief and I couldn't wait for the ceremony to be over the next day, so I could call him my husband.

****

The wedding and all the jubilation passed like a breeze. All through, my heart and my eyes had been unanimously tunnelled at my husband as his were on mine. It was as though we were the only two people left in the world and everything else and everyone else were just noise. I had found my true love; to think I had run away from him just to end up with him. My heart was blessed, and so were we.

We blessed our marriage in a heat of indescribable passion. The night was magical; it was all I ever dreamed it would be, and more. I had never felt such passion from Ashraf; it was as if he wanted me to see his soul. We melted into one another repeatedly, he was gentle with me, but I could feel all that he felt inside. I wondered how he could have held all of that intensity back for so long. It was pure and beautiful how our souls and spirits came together. I looked into his eyes, he kissed me gently, and I was happy that I was where I belonged. I had never been to heaven, but in his arms, I found my heaven. Ashraf showed me he loved me every day. Each time we melted into each other, he took me to paradise and I couldn't wait to do it again and again until forever.

The End.